SWEET
TEMPTATION

SWEET TEMPTATION

WENDY HIGGINS

An Imprint of HarperCollinsPublishers

HarperTeen is an imprint of HarperCollins Publishers.

Library of Congress Cataloging-in-Publication Data
Higgins, Wendy.
    Sweet temptation / Wendy Higgins. — First edition.
        pages   cm. — (Sweet evil)
    Summary: When Kaidan Rowe, Nephilim and the son of a malicious demon
Duke, meets Anna Whitt, daughter of a guardian angel and a fallen one, she has
a certain power over him, one that makes him wish for more than he could ever
deserve.
    ISBN 978-0-06-238142-2 (paperback)
    [1. Angels—Fiction. 2. Demonology—Fiction. 3. Good and evil—
Fiction. 4. Love—Fiction.] I. Title.
PZ7.H534966Swt 2015   2014047810
[Fic]—dc23   CIP
                                                                      AC

Typography by Michelle Gengaro-Kokmen
15 16 17 18 19 PC/RRDH 10 9 8 7 6 5 4 3 2 1
❖
First Edition

If you sigh for Kai, this book is for you.
With special love to two of my best friends,
and Kaidan's original fangirls,
Courtney Fetchko and Kelley Vitollo (Nyrae Dawn).

CONTENTS

AUTHOR'S NOTE

This is a companion novel to the Sweet Evil trilogy—it is parts of the story told from Kaidan Rowe's point of view. It's not meant to be a stand-alone novel; however, I've tried to incorporate as much as possible from the original books.

For those of you who read the first three, I should warn you that being in Kaidan's head is far different from being in Anna's. His thoughts are darker and rougher and, well . . . naughtier. Keep in mind, when the story begins, Anna has just turned sixteen and Kaidan is seventeen. By the last third of the story, Anna is eighteen and Kai is nineteen, so the crossover from young adult to adult was the natural progression of their story.

Happy reading, sweeties. Kai awaits.

PROLOGUE

*"I wanna hate every part of you in me . . .
You say that I'm privileged but my gift is my curse."
—"Bite My Tongue" by You Me At Six*

"Sit down, son."

Young Kaidan did as his father asked, obediently sitting in the oversized leather chair beside him in the sitting room of their London home. Kai's stomach buzzed with nervousness. He rarely had his father's full attention, so he felt heavy and exposed under his intense stare. Kaidan savored Pharzuph's eyes on him, and for a moment let himself pretend this meeting was something more than business—he let himself imagine his father's smile was born of concern for him, rather than the glee of malice. He wanted to tap out a beat on his leg to soothe himself, but his father couldn't stand fidgeting of any kind so he remained still.

Pharzuph looked over his young son, whose hair was

1

longer than the other boys' at school, and had unruly curls at the edges. Kai wore the same white shirt and navy trousers as his peers, but he still managed to stand out through his musical talents and the way he carried himself. The way he talked with blasé confidence and walked in an unhurried stride—all of this had been practiced and orchestrated by the handsome man sitting before him.

"You're eleven now. Time to begin your training."

Kaidan nodded. He'd known this day was coming. He'd watched last year as his friends, the twins Marna and Ginger, faced their training. He'd been frightened by the bitterness that overtook Ginger, and the sadness that seemed to drape Marna. They were no longer his mates in the carefree way of children. Even their eyes were different: calculating and searching.

"You know you're the son of Lust."

"Yes, Father." Kai had been made to watch his father at work for some time now. He'd been given magazines and films to peruse long before he understood any of it.

"Now, tell me the sins we deal with as Dukes and Nephilim."

Kaidan pushed the hair from his eyes and rattled off the seven deadly sins in a shaking voice. "Lust, greed, sloth and gluttony, murder, pride, wrath, and envy. The other sins we promote are hatred, substance abuse, lies, theft, and adultery." He placed his hands in his lap.

"Don't sit like that," his father snapped. "You look too proper. Put your hands on the arms of the chair like you own the place."

Kaidan quickly moved his hands to the arms of the chair.

"Why do you suppose the sins are called 'deadly'? Aside from the obvious. Murder."

Kaidan swallowed hard. He didn't know how to answer, and he was afraid of being whacked across the head, just as he had been when his favorite nanny was sacked and his father caught him crying.

Pharzuph leaned forward, placing his elbows on his knees and twining his fingers. "Listen well, Kaidan. Because this is the most important lesson of all. This is our purpose—the purpose of all demons and Nephilim. The sins are called deadly because they slowly kill one's spirit." His blue eyes began to glisten with fervent zeal as he went on. "Over time, something as simple as casual sex or nicking items from a shop can soon become obsessions. Humans need more. They are stupid beings, Kaidan. They never have enough. More thrills, more attention. They are selfish creatures. Never satisfied. It is our job to help them on their journey to ruin. Do you understand?"

Kaidan nodded. Disdain for humans had been ingrained in him from the beginning.

"They were chosen by the Maker to live lives of freedom here on earth while angels such as myself were banished for wanting a simple bit more." His father's eyes flashed red. "He chose *them*—this ungrateful race—to flaunt His blessings on, while we were left to rot in hell. But we've found a way to punish Him. . . ." Pharzuph smiled wickedly. "Every day we turn His beloved earthlings against Him. We cause them to focus on their bodies and their urges, their wants and desires. We give them something tangible to hold on to, but just for a moment. Because the sins are fleeting satisfactions."

Kaidan nodded, shocked that the humans could be so easily fooled. So blind. "They deserve it if they're that stupid," Kai said, and his father gave a laugh of pride.

"Indeed, son. They deserve every moment of pain they get. The Maker tells them to be careful—he dangles a bit of fun in their faces, but tells them they cannot have it. But we are here to tell humans to take what they want. And when they have the nerve to cry over the consequences—to pout and curse the world—we laugh. Because the Maker is hurting."

"Why?" Kaidan breathed. "If they're all so horrible, why does it hurt Him?"

Pharzuph's eyes narrowed into a sneer. "Because He *loves* them. Because He's promised them free will, which means he will not interfere in their idiotic choices. It's pathetic." Now Pharzuph chuckled. "He's backed himself into a corner and can only watch as His creation destroys itself . . . with our help. And never forget—as much as He loves them, he loathes our kind. Never. Forget. His unworthy humans are all born with a chance at reaching the heavenly realm. *You* were not born with that chance."

Kaidan pressed his hands hard against the chair arms to keep from trembling. He hated when his father spoke of hell— that place of dimness where joy could not be had—the place he was destined to go when he died.

At a knock on the house door, Pharzuph smiled. "Now you understand the why of our job. It's time to learn the how. Our helpers have arrived. Are you ready, Kaidan?"

The young Neph could not speak. He could only nod. He'd spent the last year mentally preparing himself for this and wanted to make his father proud.

"Very well," said his father. "You're going to love your job, son. I daresay it's the best of the lot." He leaned forward and grinned at Kaidan. "You've got all the makings of a superb Neph. You will be a powerful force. You will bring people to their knees with the desire they feel for you, and they will spend the rest of their lives wishing for another touch, searching for another man like you. But there is only one Kaidan Rowe, and you will be like smoke. Make-believe. They cannot hold you, because there is no one like you who exists in their world."

Kaidan's heart pounded in the wake of his father's words. Then he heard several sets of footsteps coming down the hall toward their sitting room—toward *him*. He gripped the chair's arms tighter and set his face in a bored expression to hide the fear and excitement exploding through him like indecipherable lyrics. It was time to set himself apart from the other boys. There was no room in his life for guilt or humanistic morals. He was born for this. He was determined to embrace it and finally earn his father's approval, despite the sourness rising up in his throat.

Pharzuph leaned back in his chair, lifting an ankle across his knee, staring darkly at Kaidan. A knock sounded on the sitting room door and his father's lips rose in a wicked grin. "And now, son, the fun begins."

PART ONE

Sweet Evil

"Break Me" by Kaidan Rowe

I can see you, see you, see you, seeking me out.
You can sense me, sense me, and it's freaking you out.
I make you thirsty, hungry, but you can't stay away.
Your eyes are on my body 'cause you want it my way.

Your mind and soul are screaming,
Saying RUN from the danger.
You know that something ain't right
But you're a bee to my nectar.
Your mind and soul are screaming,
Warning, "He's gonna break us,"
But your body is begging me
To feed your emptiness. . . .

CHORUS:

I want those eyes to push me
And those hands to pull me,
Need those hips to break me,
Baby, break me, break me.
It's gonna hurt tomorrow
When you're sayonara,

But for now, for now, baby, break me,
Break me.

You ignored all the signs
From your heart and your mind
Now your body is spent,
Baby, broken, broken.
You had a taste of the good life,
Sweet and salt from the high dive.

Now your tongue is left craving.
Baby, craving, craving.
You and me, we were doomed.
Now you're licking your wounds.
And I'm gone, baby, gone
On the winds of the dawn.

CHORUS

CHAPTER ONE

BEFORE

*"Like a big bad wolf I'm born to be bad and bad to the bone.
If you fall for me I'm only gonna tear you apart."*
—*"Break Your Heart" by Taio Cruz*

*"I'm never gonna fall, but I'm never hard to catch . . .
My heart will never break, I'm just here to break a sweat."*
—*"Casual Sex" by My Darkest Days*

I'm the last of the band to walk into the party after our gig. I feel the eyes on me before I see them—the energy of auras blasting orange and red—excited whispers of *"Oh my God, it's Kaidan Rowe"* carried along sublime waves of music at high wattage. Guardian angels float above their charges, wary when they see me.

I take my time entering the room behind our lead singer, Michael, who makes a grand entrance of throwing his arms up in the air as if to say, "These are my people!" Everyone cheers. Nobody seems to mind that he's a cheeky bastard.

I've been in America less than a year this March and not much has changed from when I lived in London. My life is still a blur of drums, sex, and food—the Kaifecta—the only things worth living for in this fucked-up world.

My fingers are in the pockets of my black denim jeans and the front of my hair covers one of my eyes, but I can still see through the strands of brown. In one quick moment I scan the room and find three girls from the gig with red-hot auras, eyes glued to me. In half a minute I'm able to gather all I need from their auras, their body language, and the whispered conversations they're having, which I hear clearly with my Nephilim senses.

"I am all over that. . . ."

". . . heard he's amazing . . ."

". . . probably a jerk. He's way too hot. . . ."

That last one is far more innocent than the others, and she is the one I choose. A cute brunette. I send her a nod. When she stares and slowly blushes, I look away. Then I turn and follow my mates into the kitchen for a drink.

The first seed has been planted. She will pursue.

In the kitchen a girl with short blond hair laughs at something some bloke is saying. He's the nice guy, comedian type, wearing an oversized T-shirt. The moment I walk in, her attention wavers to me and her happy yellow aura turns to a fog of surprise, a flame of orange excitement, and then an uprising of red. The bloke tries to get her attention back, but I've friend-zoned him. Poor guy. I do feel bad for the ones who have to try so hard. If only they'd act like the sexual beings they are.

Any bloke who seems not to think about sex all day and night is a right liar. Or he's attempting to train his mind for sainthood, which is idiotic.

Trust me on this.

When the blond chick turns to grab her drink, sending a fluttery-eyed glance my direction, the seemingly nice guy ogles her arse, as he should, and his aura goes thick as red mud. When she turns to him again, he quickly retrains his face into the quirky smile.

I know all the tricks. Don't bother with the polite, shy bit. It's not what most birds go for—though I have had to put on the witty, good-guy act to win over a few. I'm willing to play whatever role will put them in their comfort zone—their ease leads to their nakedness. And nakedness is *my* comfort zone. It is what I seek.

Something soft brushes against my arm, and I look down to see the brunette from the other room sliding purposely against me as she edges through the crowd toward the drink counter. Our eyes meet and I give her a smile. She tucks her hair behind her ear and glances down before looking back up at me.

"Sorry," she says. "I'm just . . ." She points to the drinks on the other side of me.

"May I get you something?" I ask.

She stares for a moment, as if my voice and accent were unexpected. Her chest is pressed against my upper abs, and the crowd jostles us together. A cloud of red surrounds her, and I open my senses to let in the peachy scent of her pheromones.

Right. That'll do. I'm ready to shag her. Thankfully I'm a pro at this next bit. Getting someone into bed is an art. A dance. It's crucial not to misread her.

Without asking, I whisk her cup from her hand and turn to make a fresh drink. In moments I hand her a full glass, ice clinking.

"I hope rum and Coke is all right?" I already know it is because I smelled the remnants of her drink with my supernatural senses.

Her eyes go wide. "That's what I was drinking!" Her smile is huge, as if this is a sign that I am her Mr. Right.

"Brilliant. What's your name, then?"

"Brittany. And you're Kayden, right?"

I smile. Nobody can seem to spell or pronounce my name. I'm used to this. "Close, luv. It's Kaidan."

"Oh, sorry." She tries my name out the right way, *Ky-den*.

"Sounds lovely when you say it." Taking her by the elbow, I gently lead her away from the crowded kitchen. "Were you at the show?" She was. I saw her.

"Yes. Ohmigawd, it was *so* good. You guys rock."

"Ah, thanks. Mind if we go out back? It's hard to hear you." I'm already opening the back door and she gladly exits. Her aura pushes outward when I touch her waist and lead her away from the smokers outside. We find a wooden bench swing to sit on. It's dark out, and the light from the back porch is now dim.

We glide back and forth. Her aura is jittery and I need to relax her.

"Are you in school?" I ask, though I don't care.

"Yeah. It's my first year at Georgia Tech. You?"

I shake my head. "No college for me." I'm going to be what they call a senior in high school, but she doesn't need to know that bit.

"Not to be rude, but you're nicer than I thought you'd be," she says. "Most good-looking guys are . . ."

"Pricks?" I supply.

She nods and takes another drink. Her aura is a nervous gray as she asks, "Do you . . . um . . . have a girlfriend?"

Bingo.

"No," I say sadly. "I'm not the settling-down type."

This shouldn't make her happy, but it does. I see it in the way she bites her lip against a smile. Her aura is excited. "I think everyone's the settling-down type eventually. You just have to find the right person."

Gotta love delusional romantics.

"I'll never settle down, Brittany." It's the truth, but I say it like an unfortunate mantra.

"You never know," she whispers, angling toward me.

She wants to be the one who settles me. They all do. I've been honest with her, just as I am with all of them. I can't help it if she wants to fool herself.

I turn my head, catching a glint of the night's stars in her eyes.

"What do you want from life, Kaidan?" she asks.

I want to stay alive.

I take the drink from her hand and set it down. "All I want right now, Brittany, is you."

Today is my birthday, and I'm prepared to use that fact as

13

a wild card, but it's not necessary. She is mush. Her aura is on spin cycle. I slide one hand around her waist and pull her hip to mine. I ignore her guardian angel, who has gone frantic above her. She lets out a whimpering breath and I kiss her. She molds to me, ripe to my touch. Things escalate more quickly than I expected—I thought I'd have to be the initiator, but her hands are all over me. She is clearly ignoring her guardian angel's whispers to run, run, as fast as she can. Most people aren't in tune with their angels, and that works to my advantage. Her hands are everywhere.

"God, Brittany, I need you."

Her chest heaves as she takes in air. "Where can we go?"

Hell yes.

I look up to the house and focus my hearing on the upstairs bedrooms. All occupied. Shite. Then I catch a conversation in the dining room. . . .

"I can't find her. Derek says he saw her go off with the drummer. He said that guy's bad news."

"Oh, freaking great. Just what we need. She finally breaks up with Douchebag and now she's gonna get her heart broken by Mr. One-Night Stand."

Fantastic. The vigilante friend patrol. And they know their little Brittany well. They'll be out here any moment.

"I know it's not ideal, but we can go to my car if you'd like."

She nods. I take her hand and we walk quickly around the side of the house. I've parked my SUV away from everyone else—you never know when you'll need a bit of privacy.

I click the button to unlock the doors, help her into the massive backseat, and step in behind her. We pick right up where we left off. Soon we are both in our comfort zones, naked. She suddenly hesitates.

This is where most blokes bung it up. Many girls experience a moment of moral hesitancy when their blasted angel's whispers faintly break through, causing them to face the reality that they just met me and this might not be the best idea.

"I've only been with one guy," she tells me, breathing hard. "We were together a long time. I don't usually . . . you know . . . this is not like me."

Most fellows push, pressure, guilt, whatever. But this is where I'm golden. I nod as if I respect what she's divulged.

"We don't have to, Brittany," I say as I begin nuzzling against her, giving her a preview of my strong hips, my ability to move them. "We can stop." I begin to pull away.

"No!" She nearly panics, clutching me close. "Don't stop. I just . . . I need you to know."

"I understand," I whisper against her lips. "You're a good girl."

She kisses me with renewed passion, as if I have seen into her soul and understand her like no one else.

And so I keep going, and I make it worth her while. I give her plenty to tell her friends tomorrow, though it'll likely be followed up days later with tears when she realizes I'm never going to call—that I won't acknowledge her when she shows at my next gig. Because she's not "the one." I tried to warn her.

"The one" does not exist for Kaidan Rowe.

Only the right now. Only feeding the urges. Only my survival matters.

* * *

I'm surprised to see a limo in the driveway when I return home—I had thought Father was staying in New York for work. Being the vice president of Pristine Publications means nonstop parties with models, actors, and various supporters of the rich and famous porn industry. I wonder for the millionth time why he chose to live in Atlanta rather than New York City, and then with a twist of my gut I'm reminded.

Madame Marissa.

I hear her nauseating, lazy laughter when I push my hearing into the house. I want to turn my car around, but I know Father has heard me by now. He's always listening. He's the one who taught me to be constantly on the lookout. He's the one who taught me everything I know.

He's the Duke of Lust. Known to demons as Pharzuph. Known to humans as Richard Rowe. And he chose to make his home near the most sinister human bitch that ever lived— leader of the largest sex trafficking ring in the Southern states. The two of them go way back, having met in the U.K. Father even brought her and several of her older girls over to help with my carnal training when I first turned eleven.

I've never hated someone as much as I hate Marissa.

I grit my teeth and take my sweet-arse time getting out and trudging in through the giant doors.

I want to go straight down to my room in the basement, but I'd be smacked in the skull for slighting our "guest." So I paste a polite expression on my face and enter the heated sun porch beside the indoor pool. The room is as lush with plants as a damn jungle and smells like chlorine and tropical flowers.

There are plenty of lounging chairs, but Marissa is sat on Father's lap. Her guardian angel looks resolute, if not a bit worn, beside her. I actually feel bad for the spirit, especially since a peevish demon whisperer is circling it like a giant gnat.

Marissa's black hair reaches her hips, and her giant breasts are about to tumble out of her black scoop-neck dress, a sight that does nothing for me. Bloodred lips match her creepily long nails, and she gasps when she sees me.

"Look at him, Richie . . . he looks more like you every time I see him."

Father nods, looking me over and tipping his nose up, probably to check the air around me, to be sure I'd done my job for the night. His sense of smell is astounding.

I nod back. "Father. Marissa. I hope you're well."

"It's only two in the morning," Father says. "Early night for you. How many'd you get?"

Damn it. "One," I admit. I would have stayed out if I'd known they'd be here.

"Not much of a birthday celebration," Marissa says. Of course she would remember my "special" day.

Father looks from her to me. "Is it March thirty-first already?"

Marissa laughs and swats his shoulder before looking at me again. "Seventeen looks nice on you. And you'll only get better as you age."

I choose to ignore this. "Mates threw me a party last night since we had a gig tonight," I lie.

Marissa stands and saunters toward me on high heels. She's in her late thirties. She's pale as porcelain. Avoiding the sun has been good for her skin. If she weren't so evil I'd think she was hot.

She comes too close and looks up at me with a pout. I

know what she wants. She fancies a kiss, which I never voluntarily give to her. I lean down to quickly peck her cheek, but she grabs the back of my neck with viper claws and takes my mouth with a satisfied sound. No tongue, thank God, but she takes my bottom lip between hers and suckles it. I'm certain her lipstick is all over me now.

Father chuckles at the ridiculous display, as if Marissa is an auntie pinching my cheeks, not molesting my mouth.

"Madame has a job for you, son," he says from his lounging position.

This causes Marissa to release my lip and turn for her purse. I take the opportunity to wipe my lips with the back of my hand and school my face to hide the revulsion I feel.

"I've a new niece coming from Hungary in a couple months." Marissa has taken a photo from her purse, and she crosses her arms while she explains the fate of a girl who was either stolen from or sold by her desperate family. "A valued client has requested a virgin, so she is to stay innocent."

She hands me the picture and I blink several times, rocking back on my heels. The girl can't be older than eleven. She hasn't even begun developing. She's frail and tiny with stringy blond hair and big doe eyes. Father watches me with expectancy and Marissa clicks her long nails together, a familiar sound that follows me into nightmares.

For the first time ever my disgust overrides my fear.

"She's a bloody *child*," I spout without thinking.

Father sits up, his forehead pinching at my minor outburst.

Marissa snatches the picture back, but her eyes are amused. "She is old enough."

Father stands and walks over now, taking the picture. "She's not *that* young. And her age is not your concern." I hear the edge of warning in his voice, a sound that feels like shards of ice. He'd kill me in a second. I have no doubt of that.

"We're not asking you to have sex with her," Marissa croons. "We just don't want her too terrified when her new owner touches her. Some buyers like that, but not this one."

Ugh! I don't want to touch her *at all*.

When it comes to girls my age and older women, I'm down for anything. But this is disgusting. Father deals with lust of all kinds—he's into the sickest shit out there—but I cannot, I *will not*, physically force myself to be attracted to a child.

"Looks like your boy's more plain vanilla than you thought," Marissa mutters.

"He'll be fine when the girl arrives, luv," Father assures her, eyeing me. "He'll do what needs to be done."

Fuuuuck. Will I? I think of the little girl's face again, and my stomach cramps.

No. I won't. This is not good. I've crossed a lot of lines in my life to make Father happy and prove my worth, but this is different.

Maybe the picture is old. I can only hope, because I don't want to find out what consequences he has in store if I lose my usefulness to the demonic cause. I should have known breaking hearts wouldn't be enough.

"Yes." Devil woman runs her nails down my arm. "He always does what needs to be done."

CHAPTER TWO

STRANGE GIRL

"My devil loves your angel, you can't take that away . . .
See if she'll take her halo off, if only for today."
—*"Devil's Love Song" by Tishamingo*

I am still pissed off when I get to the club. When we parted this evening, Father's face was tight as he reminded me it's now May and the child will be arriving soon. In the two months since I turned seventeen and showed defiance about the young girl, Father has been pushing me. Testing me. Nothing is good enough.

We stand backstage and Raj is adding more gel to his fauxhawk, staring in the mirror and pinching the tips of his hair. His eyes are bloodshot from the spliff he just smoked. "What's wrong with *you?*" he asks.

I shake my head and look away. I can't exactly tell him my father's a demon, that he expects me to do horrible things. No humans know what I really am.

I'm still trying to scrub the image of the enslaved girl from my mind as we take the stage. It does me no good to think about her, or the hundreds of others like her who I've hurt already.

Don't feel.

Don't think.

Don't acknowledge it's real. Just go through the motions, like always.

I slide onto my stool and twirl the drumsticks, savoring the familiar feel of the cool, smooth wood between my fingers. Deep breaths. Time to clear my head in the only way I know how. Sitting behind the drums, I am myself. The real me. Even during sex I cannot completely let go—I am hyperaware. Music is the only way.

I look out at the packed house. Girls screaming, jumping up and down in front of the stage. Loads of skin on show.

This I can do.

Starting with feather taps and working my way across the set, I rip a line of beats to warm up. Immediately the energy in the room changes, heightens. Conversations hush and heads turn toward the stage, then voices buzz back to life louder than before. A wicked beat can change the entire atmosphere in a room. Michael, feeling it too, shoots me a grin before checking his cords and mic. I feel eyes on me, heating my blood. Yeah, a good beat is sexy. Makes people wanna move their bodies . . . their hips. . . .

Plain vanilla my arse.

Damn it. I have to stop thinking about that.

Michael throws his strap over a shoulder, electric guitar slung low. He picks off a few notes, eyeing Raj on bass until they both nod, satisfied with the sync.

When we're set, Michael motions the DJ, who tells the room to give it up for Lascivious. And they do. Nice and loud.

I purposely don't eye the energized crowd as Michael takes to the mic with the welcome. I have to focus. Can't be distracted by all the chicks and their curves.

Michael gives me the go with a flick of his chin and I raise the sticks above my head to count us in.

"One, two, three, four!" *Bam.*

First song is high energy, throwing me into a chop out and ending with muscle burn. All the shit in my life disappears and there's only the creation of beats—beats that vibrate from soul to soul across the room, bringing flesh to life, every cell thumping in a rhythm they can barely contain. We're on fire.

I imagine joy is something akin to this. Just letting go.

My forehead is already damp by the end of the first song. I push my hair aside and get set for the second song, which begins slower.

When the room settles I start on the warm cymbal, a shushing buildup to a quiet beat. Michael always makes it to second base with the microphone when he sings this ballad bit. And then the real fun begins—dramatic silent pause and stillness, followed by a raw, all-out punishment of the drums, screamed lyrics, and a high-decibel refrain loud enough to rip the rafters from the roof.

This is The Zone. The place where I can truly breathe.

My body takes over, and hit after hit falls just right until the *crash* of the cymbals. I whirl the drumsticks over my head with a flourish, then tuck them under my arm.

Damn, what a rush. I feel good. Focused. Until my stupid hair catches in my eyes and I can't blink it away. I swat it aside. We have a minute before the next song while Michael bullshits with the fans a bit, keeping them worked up.

Two girls in front shout my name. Mother Nature has blessed them both with perfect tits, and they, in turn, bless us all by wearing tiny shirts. Such kindness deserves a grin. Maybe they'll make it backstage later. I shift on the stool as I imagine it.

Argh. *Stay focused.*

The third song begins. Raj picks the tune on his bass line, and then I come in strong, willing myself to get lost in the intricate details. When it ends I quiet the tinging cymbals between my fingers. With a tilt of my head I flick the hair from my eyes and grab my water bottle from the floor.

I scan the crowd, attempting not to check out the gorgeous cleavage display for the time being, hoping to avoid the faces of a few girls who've been stalking me. But my scanning skids to a halt at the sight of a fresh-faced blonde staring right at me. She's a complete doll with a wild mane of long hair and a spicy red aura. But the bit I notice next sends an iced razor down my spine.

Bloody hell . . . is that a *badge* on her chest? I stare in disbelief at the small, round supernatural burst of light emanating from the core of her torso. It isn't black like most badges—it's a dark yellow swirled with white. I'm suddenly stiff and on guard, imagining the knife in the ankle of my left boot. I search around the strange girl, looking for a possible guardian angel, but she has none.

Shit. A bloody fucking Neph is at my gig. Sent by my father, no doubt.

SHIT!

I try to swallow but can't, so I force down a few gulps of water. For half a moment I forget where the fuck I am. Then Michael is giving me the go for the next song. I drop the bottle to the floor and pull the sticks from under my arm.

I've lost all focus. I don't know how I stay on beat. I glance over to keep an eye on the Neph, but she's gone, pushing her way through the crowd. What is she up to? It takes every ounce of self-control not to abandon the band and follow her. She goes into the loo, but it's likely a ruse. I thought I knew every Neph close to my age, but I've never seen her. I'd remember that face. That hair.

I silently curse the song for being so long, but at least it's our last before the next band comes on. I shove my auditory senses over the massive crowd and straight into the girls' loo. I listen, trying to make sense of the silly conversation while thrashing out the backbone of the song.

"I heard that guy Kaidan has gonorrhea."

I miss a beat and my bandmates shoot me questioning glares. I can't remember the last time I've dicked up a song, but I'm too concentrated on the bathroom drama.

Gonorrhea?

Clearly the Neph is trying to keep the other girls from coming backstage to meet me. Fewer obstacles in her way as she attempts to find me and . . . do what? Kill me? Test me somehow for Father and the other Dukes?

And now what is she going on about? She's taking back what she'd said about me and apologizing? What the . . . ? This doesn't make a bit of sense.

Finally the blasted song is wrapping up and I can put an end to this rubbish.

The blond Neph heads back into the club just as we're rushed off the platform. I keep my hearing tight around the girl as I walk backstage. She meets up with some guy called Jay. Their conversation sounds ordinary. She's a good actress, but she can't fool me.

Anna. He calls her Anna.

Jay is taking "Anna" backstage. Perfect. I feel the weight of my knife in my boot as Michael, Raj, and Bennett high-five down the hall and bump shoulders next to me.

Time to play, little Neph.

Ah, cripe. Three local models are waiting for me backstage. I forgot I'd invited them. My mind is too preoccupied to fully appreciate the females encircling me as I sense the Anna girl walking in with two human boys.

The girl next to me lifts a cigarette. I have a matchbook out of my pocket and lit before she can reach for her lighter—a pub talent I'd perfected at age fourteen after seeing my father do it. But I can't pretend to be more interested in the girls—I'm too distracted by Anna as I watch her human boys leave her there, looking out of place and uncomfortable in her own skin. And her aura! Her emotions are on display all around her. Why the hell is she letting them show like that? Some sort of trick to confuse me, no doubt. Can you trick your body into displaying false emotions?

The models chat me up and I reply absently, but I can't for the life of me take my eyes off Anna. And then she raises her eyes to mine, giving my pulse a punch.

Her aura goes berserk, and she drops her eyes abruptly, as if shy. *As if.* Does she think I'm a fool? She looks back up, and I swear she appears terrified, which irks the hell out of me. She thinks she can play me? *Balls to the wall.* Time for confrontation.

A slender hand grabs my arm and calls my name in a whine. I raise an index finger and excuse myself.

The Neph's eyes dart all around as I approach, which only makes me stare harder. What is the point of this frightened, innocent act? I don't know what she's playing at but she's about to lose.

Finally she holds my eyes, locked.

"Who are you?" I ask.

Her mouth pops open. "I'm . . . Anna?"

Trying to be cute, eh? Not buying it. But damn, she *is* cute. Fifteen. Maybe sixteen. Legs and arms are a bit too thin in the denim skirt and tank top, but she'll fill out as she gets older, no doubt. Her long, honeyed hair falls smoothly to her waist and her face has lovely symmetry. Brown eyes that tip slightly downward at the corners. Small nose. Rosebud lips. The wholesome, all-natural look is quite brilliant if she's trying to put me at ease, but I'm not buying it.

"Right. Anna. How very nice." I lean closer. "But who *are* you?"

"I just came with my friend Jay?"

She begins to babble and fidget as I stare at her nervous aura and that amber-and-white-swirled badge at her lower chest. I've never seen a Duke with an amber badge, and white is unheard of—the light of angels. Anna crosses her arms where I'm staring and I look up.

Her lips are pursed like she's offended . . . and she has the loveliest beauty mark at the top edge of her lips. God, I want to touch it . . . to kiss her mouth and lick that dark freckle. Naturally, that thought leads to imagining her naked, silky hair falling all around her. She wouldn't be able to keep up the innocent act in bed with me. I'd have her true vixen side showing in no time.

Hey, arsehole, she's likely here to gather intel that could lead to your death, I remind myself, clearing my head and shifting before my body has a chance to take over. I have a firm "no Neph" rule.

This girl is strange, no doubt, but I can't help getting closer. If she's pretending to be human, I want to see how far she'll take this impromptu act.

"Where's your angel?" I ask.

"If you mean Jay, he's over there talking to some man in a suit. But he's not my boyfriend or my angel or whatever."

She seems genuinely flustered. If this is all a charade, why are her colors jumping around like that? Light gray, medium gray, fuzzy, sharp, and yeah boy . . . a nice swirl of red. She wants me, but I can tell she's not happy about it.

Completely baffling.

Why doesn't she just show her hand? Tell me what she

wants? Why play this game when she knows I can see she's a Neph? I've even seen her gazing at my badge. I step back as a thought occurs that freaks me the fuck out. What if she doesn't know what she is? What we are?

No.

That isn't possible. Perhaps back in the day when Dukes had countless offspring there could have been unaccounted-for Neph orphans. Everything is tightly regulated since the Great Purge a century ago, when the Dukes wiped every Neph from the face of the earth. Thousands of us were killed because our numbers overwhelmed our demon fathers. Apparently the Neph were growing out of control, not being careful with their powers, and even sliding under the radar when it came to working. Now there were only a hundred something Neph children, and the Dukes were careful not to overpopulate again.

Someone *has* to know about this girl. Perhaps she's been kept hidden from other Neph, to be used as a secret weapon against us—to confuse the hell out of us and then go for the kill.

I wonder how far she's willing to take this before she fesses up. I glance over at the humans she came with.

"Not your boyfriend, eh?" At this, she appears angry. "Are you certain he doesn't fancy you?"

I grin and she juts out her chin, standing a little taller, which isn't very tall at all.

"Yes, I am."

"How do you know?" I ask.

She seems to ponder this question before spouting smartly,

"I just know, okay?" Her arms are still firmly crossed over her chest.

I lift my hands and laugh in the face of her adorable show of sassiness. Perhaps I'm having a bit too much fun with this whole thing, but I can't help myself. It's just so ridiculous. I'm determined to out her by any means. Intimidation hasn't worked, so it's time to turn on the charm.

"I'm terribly sorry, Anna. I've forgotten my manners. I thought you were . . . someone else."

I stick out my hand. "I'm Kaidan Rowe."

She pulls a hand away from her side and takes mine. Hers is soft and cool and seems right at home in mine, which is an idiotic thing to think. This little Neph is having bizarre effects on me. I stare into her eyes wondering how she can hide her deceit so well.

I'm about to pull my hand away when hers suddenly warms . . . and she full-out blushes. Un-fucking-believable. How did she get herself to do that? I've never seen a Neph blush in my life. Her aura is going mad again, lust winning out as the dominant color. And just to be sure she isn't simply an expert at mind games, I open my sense of smell and let it surround her.

Oh damn. Definitely giving off pheromones.

She smells divine. Like a fresh pear. And some dainty flower I can't put a name to. That's gonna bug me.

Right. I chuckle at the craziness of it all and slowly take my hand back. I'm about to tuck my sense of smell away when I get an idea. One more test to see if I can get her to admit to being Neph. I search down the street, bypassing foul city scents until I find what I'm looking for.

"Ah, smells good. There's nothing like American hot dogs. I think I'll have one later."

She looks at me like I'm crazy and says, "I don't smell anything."

"Really? Lean toward the door some. Breathe a bit . . . *deeper.*"

I can tell she knows what I mean. Her face tightens in concentration and her little nose slightly flares until I know she's smelled it. One mile away. I wait for her to try to deny it, but she only shakes her head and blinks at me. *Yeah, that's right. . . . I can do what you can do, so let's cut the shite, shall we?*

"Hmm. I suppose I was mistaken then," I say with a healthy dose of sarcasm.

This has gone on long enough. I need to get some answers, out of the public eye.

One of the abandoned models takes this inopportune moment to approach, stepping between us. I whisper what she wants to hear—that I'll be over in a moment to take them home, and then we'll have all night. She walks away satisfied, while I feel anything but. I can't get out of work to chase this Neph girl, especially if I'm under some sort of surveillance. But I will find her. Her human "friends" are over there giving their information to our road manager. I'll find out where they live, what school they attend, what parties are happening in their area. . . . I have resources, and people give out a plethora of information on their social media accounts.

"Maybe I'll see you around, Anna. I'll be sure to give your boyfriend Jay's songs a listen."

30

As I turn to walk away, I hear her say, "He's not my—" but I don't stop to listen. My beautiful dates are waiting none too patiently.

I listen from across the room as the bloke Jay goes back to her, inquiring about me. I almost spit my bourbon through my nose when he says, "Man, y'all looked like you were gonna rip each other's clothes off!" and she hits him. Instead I make eye contact with Anna one last time and wink at her. Damned if she doesn't blush again before turning quickly to leave.

She deserves an Oscar, that girl.

I try to give the models my full attention, but all I can think about is Anna. I listen to her conversation as they drive away. She's just about to ring someone named Patti when they exit my range of hearing.

"Freesia!" I say aloud when the name of the flower finally comes to me. She'd smelled of pears and freesia.

The models give one another funny looks and giggle.

I shake my head. "Sorry. Don't mind me."

They laugh now and I grin, feeling like an idiot—an unfamiliar feeling for me.

Intrigue like I've never experienced floods me, and I don't like it. Everything about her screamed of innocence, but that's impossible. Her sudden appearance in my life will drive me to distraction, something I cannot afford. Still, I know I will replay our meeting for days—the images—her all-natural appearance, her open expressions and colors, and her seemingly authentic friendship with a human boy.

Either this Neph has some twisted, ingenious plan to

entrap me, or she truly doesn't know what she is. If that's the case, it means serious danger for her. Not that I should care. Not that I *do* care. I'm intrigued is all—enough to know that I won't rest until I find out more about this mysterious Anna.

CHAPTER THREE

MORE CONFUSED THAN EVER

"Burning mud in my eyes,
Blinding me from the truth."
—*"Long Way Down" by Robert DeLong*

I'll admit, I've been stalking the hell out of the bloke called Jay. I cannot find a trace of Anna online, other than a list of choir award recipients from two years ago. But Jay has accounts on damn near every social media site available.

Today he posted: *Raise your hand if I'll see you shaking your stuff at Gene's party tonight!*

That started a quick strand of comments—*I'm so going! . . . Gonna be tight. . . . I've heard his lake house is awesome! . . . Everyone's invited! . . . Anyone know the address?*

Bingo. Someone posts the address and I lock it into my mobile.

That night, with my bandmate Raj at my side, we roll up

to the house on Lake Allatoona with nearly every other high schooler in the Atlanta area. Raj immediately heads down the stairs toward the smell of marijuana. I search the party with my hearing and find Jay—he's loud and surrounded by laughing girls—but there's no sign of Anna.

As I walk into the kitchen and glance out the window, I see why. She's outside talking with a bloke.

"Hey."

I look in the direction of the husky, sexy voice and see the speaker next to me. She's got a drink in one hand, her other elbow leaning back against the counter. She's a rocker girl with a streak of pink in her hair and plump, hot-pink lips. She's wearing all black, in fishnets and boots.

She looks fun.

"Hey, yourself," I say. I glance out the window again. Anna and the kid appear to be stargazing or something. Her aura is blasting a nervous gray with orange bursts of excitement. So strange.

Rocker girl doesn't smile. Her aura is fuzzy, so she's either been drinking a good bit or smoking downstairs, but she doesn't wobble or show any signs of being impaired except for her heavy-lidded eyes draped in silvery-gray liner.

"Never seen you before," she says. "I'd remember." She reaches up a hand with chunky rings and flicks the hair above my eye. "I like your hair."

I look at her neon-pink streak, a stark contrast to the black locks around it. "I like yours more."

She keeps a straight face, too cool to smile, but her eyes momentarily glint. She reaches up again, and this time runs her fingers along the side of my hair before scratching behind my ear. I want to wag my tail for her, but I'm too distracted. I glance out the window again and she drops her hand.

"That chick is weird," Rocker Girl says. She's looking out at Anna now, too, and she sips her drink.

"How so?" I ask.

She shrugs. "I mean, she's nice, I guess. Just kind of . . . freaky. She stares a lot. Doesn't talk much."

Interesting.

"You're in school together?"

"Yeah, for, like, *ever*. Anyway—"

Raj bursts through the crowd. "Yo, Kai. Got us some goods." He holds up his hand with some pills and bumps Rocker Girl's arm.

"Hey, watch it!" she says, holding up her drink and wet hand.

"Sorry . . ." He looks her over. "Damn, you're hot."

Without looking away from her, Raj thrusts a pill my way, probably X, and I slip it into my pocket.

"What's your name?" Raj asks her.

"Mandie."

"Cute name. I'm Raj. Bass for Lascivious."

She appears unimpressed, but I can see the swirl of orangeish-red attraction and excitement in her aura. "That's a band, right? Yeah, I've heard of you guys." Rocker Girl takes in his black fauxhawk and the myriad of piercings on Raj's face and ears. She bites her black thumbnail between her teeth, as if considering him. Again, her eyes are alight, but she won't crack a smile. Raj looks at me with his eyebrows raised, asking permission. I nod and turn back to the window.

Anna and the bloke are gone.

"Shite," I mutter. I lean forward to see more of the back deck, but other people are spilling outside now, and I don't see her anymore. I leave Raj and Rocker Girl, and Raj's laughter follows me as I push through the crowd. I stop and lean back against the entrance of the main hall when I catch sight of Anna's long, honeyed hair heading down the basement stairs. I won't lose her again. I bubble my hearing around her and I spot the guy she was with, standing at the kitchen island.

Several things happen in the next few minutes that I cannot make heads or tails of. Anna seems genuinely freaked out by the drug use downstairs and she hurries back up. The kid she's with slips a powdered ecstasy tablet into her drink. When he gives it to her, she downs it as he watches in smug enthusiasm. She *has* to know the drink was drugged. Any Neph would have been listening to their date and gathered that much. But she allows him to think she's clueless.

When she and her mates walk my way, heading toward the dance room, I think about hiding, but part of me hopes she sees me. Her friend catches me staring, but I pay her no mind. Anna's eyes are glazed and her colors have faded to a thin, blotchy mist of confusion. I resist the urge to grab her by the arm and pull her from the party.

She's only working, I tell myself. I've been blitzed out of my mind countless times while working. So why doesn't this feel okay?

I glance into the dancing room, where the music is blaring. It's dark enough in there to need my night vision—my pupils expand and I take in the sight of Anna dancing. She's willowy and graceful, and most definitely high. I can't stop watching her.

They walk past me again on their way back, and once again Anna does not look my way. Clearly the Neph girl is ignoring me. Her focus is unnerving.

The kitchen is too bright for me to remain hidden, so I stand around the corner and listen.

When Jay finds Anna, he is *not* pleased to find she's not sober.

"Are you drunk?! What the hell, Anna?"

"Jay . . . Please don't be mad at me!"

He's been trying to score with a different girl all night, so I don't think this is romantic anger he's feeling—it's a friendship thing. I don't get it.

And then her date comes back, his aura a mix of purple pride and red lust. Everyone laughs at everything he says, and looks at him like he's a demigod. Mr. Popular, no doubt. I want to take him outside and dunk his head into the lake a few seconds too long.

I watch as he takes Anna by the hand and leads her down the hall, past the dance room, up the stairs. I stand at the bottom of the stairs using my extended hearing to drown out the high volume of music and voices surrounding me. The bloke takes Anna into a room and closes them in. It sounds as if they're climbing onto the bed.

My heart is beating faster than normal, and there's a sour feeling when I swallow. I don't feel right. This *night* doesn't feel right.

Anna let herself be drugged and taken to a room—perhaps that's how she works, pretending to be the innocent victim and allowing dodgy gits to believe they're taking advantage of her. So why are my instincts screaming at me to go up there and intercept her?

I stand at the bottom of the stairs, leaning against the railing and pretending to look at my mobile. I feel girls looking my way, brushing purposely against me as they pass, but I ignore them and focus on the conversation in the upstairs bedroom.

"Everything feels so soft," Anna is saying in a dreamlike voice.

"When I'm on E," Creeper says, "I always think everyone should be naked. Just like Adam and Eve."

A burst of laughter escapes me. Did he just use a biblical reference to get laid? That was the absolute worst line in history.

But Anna gives a breathy laugh and says, "Just completely natural and happy." I roll my eyes. I've been high on ecstasy and I know how sensitive your skin feels, but she sounds like Snow White or something. I wish she'd stop humoring little Dopey.

I'm getting impatient.

"You know, Anna," Creepy-Dopey says. His voice has taken on a false silky quality. "It wouldn't take much for you to be more, I don't know, popular or whatever. . . . I mean, you're pretty, but you could be, like, *hot*. You know?"

Damn. Burn. Is he serious?

She sounds inexplicably sweet, not offended, when she responds. "I'm sorry, Scott, but even if I had the money, I just don't care about those things. I want people to like me for who I am. Isn't that what you want, too?"

I'm halfway up the stairs before I realize it.

Things are not adding up. This plonker's words, plus what Rocker Girl said, and Anna's friendship with Jay—what Neph chooses the "Unpopular" role? Especially when they're as gorgeous as she is?

"Have you kissed many guys?" Creepy-Dopey is asking.

I'm at the top of the stairs now, heart slam-dancing against my ribs. I don't feel right.

"I've never kissed anyone," Anna says. I nearly snort with laughter at the lie, as sincere as she may sound. There's no possible way she's never been kissed.

"Not even Jay?" he asks.

"No way. He's like my brother."

I've found their door and I'm standing in front of it.

"How long will this last?" Anna whispers. "This feeling?"

"About four hours. Then it takes a couple of hours to come down." She makes a sad sound at his answer, and he says, "Anna?"

"Huh?"

"I want to be your first kiss."

I grit my teeth and grip the door handle.

"Okay," she whispers.

First kiss or fiftieth, doesn't matter—this guy's not getting any satisfaction under my watch. I wrench the handle down and kick the door open. They bolt upright on the bed.

"What the—" Creepy begins, shielding his face from the hall light, but I'm only looking at Anna, feeling a strange sense of relief. She squints at me.

"Ah, there you are, luv. Let's go, then." I motion her toward me with the flick of two fingers.

She stares, mouth open.

"Can you walk, or will I have to carry you?" I ask.

The guy finally sprouts a tiny pair of balls. "What are you doing, man?"

"I need a chat with Anna." I'm watching her. She sort of smiles, dazed, then slides off the bed to stand.

"I'll be back," she says to him.

Like hell she will.

"I wouldn't count on it, actually." I enter the room and take her by the hand. We leave the bloke sputtering and red-faced with anger. He shouts at me, and I give him one hard-ass glance to shut him up before I slam the door behind us.

I hold her hand and lead her down the hall, down the stairs, through the party, onto the back deck, and down the steps leading to the dock and the water.

I am confused.

I don't enjoy being confused.

I pull her faster down the dock, where we can be alone. But when we get to the edge of the dock, I'm at a loss. I sit, and she carefully sits next to me. I can feel her eyes browsing me, and I let her. I stare out at the moon's reflection on the water.

I've never met a Neph who doesn't act like one. She doesn't hide her colors. She is kind to people, even when they're deceptive to her, and there seems to be nothing in it for her. She appears to have a true friendship with a human, Jay. She says and does things that no Neph would dare say or do. And then there's the part about her having no money, which can't be true. Either she doesn't know what she is or she's got the most twisted and ingenious working profile I've ever seen. To have two completely opposing possibilities is mind-bending.

A breeze blows across the water and Anna shivers.

"Who are you?" I ask, just as I did when we first met.

She pauses. "I don't know how you want me to answer that." It's almost like she feels bad about this. Then very suddenly, she gasps violently and her hands curl around the edge of the dock.

"What is it?" I ask.

"I think . . . It feels like it's starting to wear off. But he said four hours!" She stands on shaking legs and begins to pace, hugging herself around the middle and hunching over.

It takes me a moment to realize she's talking about the drug. She's coming down from the high, but she seems almost panicked about it. I stand and block her exit down the dock so she can't run. I need her to focus on me. Perhaps she'll be more open while she's still high.

I grasp her chin and lift her eyes to mine. We'll start with Neph basics. We never get ill.

"Have you ever been sick?" I ask.

She holds herself tighter. "Sick . . . ?"

"The flu. Tonsillitis. Anything?"

Her eyes grow larger and for that second she stands a bit straighter as she stares at me. Then her body spasms and she bends at the waist, grabbing her knees. It seems as if she's in true pain, but if it's an act I will not play the fool.

"Maybe this little sweet will help you." I hold up the pill Raj gave me, and Anna swipes for it, fast as a damn cheetah. But I'm quicker. Her eyes are flashing and eager with need.

"Answer all of my questions first. Any illnesses in your life-time?"

"N-no," she stammers.

Good. We're finally making progress.

"How far back can you remember?" I ask.

She stops shaking and stares up at me. Her mouth opens, then closes. She's afraid to answer. I step closer, my heart beating uncharacteristically fast. I feel as if I'm on the edge of a discovery.

"Answer the question," I say.

Her hands grip her sides and she drops her eyes as if embarrassed. "Fine. All the way back. My birth and even before that. Happy?"

I'm never happy, but I'm at least satisfied she's finally admitting to her Neph traits. Our memories are vast and clear from the moment our souls entered our bodies.

"Now for the important part." I step closer. "Who is your father?"

I've never seen a Duke's badge of that color—dark yellow amber—and I definitely haven't seen white—that's an angelic color.

Her jaw quivers. "I-I don't know. I was adopted."

"Bollocks," I say through gritted teeth. "You must have some idea." I raise my arm so that my hand with the pill is above the water.

She gasps and raises her hands in horror as if I'm threatening to drop a baby.

"There was this one man . . . ," she says. Finally, some bleedin' answers. "I remember him from the day I was born.

Jonathan LaGray . . . he's in prison now."

Holy shit. "Yes, of course." I'd completely forgotten about the Duke in prison, as I've never met him. The Duke of Substance Abuse—addiction—hence Anna's desire for more of the drug. "I should have guessed from your behavior tonight."

She closes her eyes and I stare at her. She knows she is different. From the way she is shaking and battling this drug lust, I can only guess this isn't something she deals with often. As if she's never been trained. But of course, if her father's been in prison . . . but wouldn't he have gotten someone else to train her? Neph are taught to control themselves, not lose themselves to their sins this way.

Anna sticks out her hand. "My pill." Her face is pale and drained. There's no way I'm giving it to her. If her reaction is this bad coming down from the first pill, it will be worse after the second.

"You mean this one?" I ask. I know I'm cruel, but she comes across far too kind. I want to force her claws out. "Sorry, luv, just an aspirin," I lie. I toss the pill into the water with a *plunk*.

"No!" She damn near dives in after the stupid pill, and I grab her by the arms. I need to calm her before she does something stupid.

"How long ago did he give you the pill?" I continue holding her tightly.

"What?" Her eyes dart around as she tries to focus. "I don't know. Maybe thirty, no, forty minutes?"

"It should be out of your system very soon. You'll be fine. Just sit here and try to calm yourself."

When I let her go she sits obediently and grabs around her

knees, burying her face and rocking back and forth stiffly. She looks tiny balled up like that, and her long, straight hair lifts and blows in the wind. A foreign tug of sympathy invades, and I look away from her.

I want to believe her, but I'm still wary. I don't want to be entrapped by the mystery surrounding her. I can't afford to care.

I sit down on the edge of the dock while she rides it out and sobers up.

After ten minutes she scoots closer to me, watching my face with a newfound carefulness. Her colors are back: gray and orange.

"Why did it come and go so fast?" she asks. I'm happy she's worked up the nerve to open up and ask me something while she's sober.

"Our bodies fight anything foreign. Germs, cancer, disease, the whole lot. Drugs and alcohol burn through quickly. Hardly worth the effort. I tried smoking. Spent days coughing up black tar."

"That's attractive," she says, brushing something invisible off her knee.

I snort with the irony of her comment. "Precisely. Can't afford to be unattractive."

"So . . ." She's still being careful. "Are you like me?"

"Yes, and no, it seems."

Her head cocks to the side as she's observing me. As if *I'm* the one who needs to be figured out. I want to ask her so much, but I don't. There's still a quiet, untrusting voice in my head warning me away from acting too interested. Neph are not supposed to give a damn about other Neph, or anyone, for that matter. In fact, we've probably spent enough time together tonight.

I push my hearing up to the house to see if Raj is looking for me, but he's not. He's out in the car smoking a joint with Rocker Girl, no doubt after taking his hit of X, as well. He'd better take it easy or he's likely to show Rocker Girl a poor backseat performance.

Tut, tut.

"Why don't you have one of those cloud thingies around you?" Anna asks. She's eyeing the air around me, and I shake my head. What on earth is she talking about? Then, I realize she must have just turned sixteen and gained the ability to see guardian angels.

"Cloud thingies?" I sputter. "You can't be serious." Surely, surely she knows that humans have guardian angels. That is the most basic of Neph basics.

As I'm pulling my hearing in I stumble upon a scuffle inside the house—shouting.

"Do you know what I'm talking about?" She sits up straighter, and looks like she might grab at my shirt. "You do, don't you?!"

Inside the house, Jay and Scott are fighting. Seems as though Jay is drunk and defending Anna's honor. Brilliant.

I stand up, asking, "Are your senses back now?"

She opens her mouth, clearly wanting to know more about the "cloud thingies," but I've thrown her off and she blinks.

"I think so," she says.

"There's a fight in the house. I think you'd better listen."

She stands up and closes her eyes, looking pained as she strains to hear. Then her eyes pop open. "Oh, my gosh, Scott and Jay!" Yep. Jay just landed a nice-sounding *crunch* and Scott is howling.

Anna takes off running and I watch her go. She's got nice form. And a great arse.

And she's *still* a possible enemy, although it's taking more and more effort to convince myself of that. If this girl has been sent by the Dukes to test me, I cannot let myself be reeled in by her spectacular act.

I take my time walking back up to the house and going in. I listen, further baffled, as Anna defuses the situation and gets the drunken Jay to her car. She cares for him with patience and tenderness. The only Neph I've ever seen act like that is the twin Marna, but she's only like that with the few of us Neph who are her friends, never with humans.

I stand in the nearly empty kitchen—everyone has made a mass exodus to the front of the house for the fight. As people filter back in, I hear Anna whisper something in her car, seemingly to herself.

"I'm not finished with you, Kaidan Rowe."

It's like a puppy threatening a cobra. A grin flashes across my face and I quickly wipe it away before saying to the air, "Likewise."

Two seconds later Rocker Girl is standing in front of me with her hands on her hips, looking unamused.

"Uh-oh," I say. "Has Raj overindulged?"

Her eyes narrow in annoyance. "He says his hands weigh a thousand pounds and he can't lift them."

We stare at each other for two beats, and then we burst into laughter. Rocker Girl covers her mouth until her mirth subsides.

I twist the strands of her pink hair in my fingers, and she looks up at me with a tough face, pretending she never showed that moment of humor. Then I lean down and whisper into her ear. "You're fucking sexy when you laugh, Mandie."

I'm not sure if it's my words or my breath against her skin that makes her shiver. She hooks her fingers into the belt loops of my black jeans and looks up at me.

"What's your name, anyway?" she asks.

"Kaidan Rowe."

Her mouth drops open and she bats her eyes. "Shit. Wow. I totally didn't put two and two together when Raj said he was in the band. You're the drummer. Kai."

I nod.

Her fingers tighten on my loops and she pulls me closer. "Your reputation precedes you."

"Oh, yeah? And what reputation is that?" I slowly back her against the counter, amidst all the people.

Her voice goes even huskier. "I've heard you're a very, *very* bad boy."

I shrug. "Good. Bad. It's all subjective, right?" I grind my hips against hers, and her eyes flutter back. I lean down to her ear. "You have two choices. There's a room upstairs or the empty boathouse."

"Boathouse, all the way," she says breathlessly.

I take her hand and say nothing more, but as I'm opening the back door to the deck the hairs on the back of my neck stand up. A dark whisperer swoops in and snarls with glee at the partygoers. I tense for half a second, glad Anna is away from the party now. When the demon spirit flies my way, I acknowledge the savage being with a nod, hoping it will leave off, but it doesn't. It cackles and dives toward Mandie, whispering harshly in her ear as her guardian angel pushes and fights it. She's unaware she's being whispered to, but her aura darkens and I squeeze her hand. A pit opens in my gut at the thought that I'm on the same team as that evil thing.

It finally leaves off and I pull Mandie outside. She looks away from me purposefully and reaches across to scratch her wrist. In the porch light I see the silvery reflection of scars up her arm. Cut marks.

Fucking whisperers.

I won't ask about those lines. Nor will I stick around to chat about it afterward. But tonight I'll try to take her mind off it, even for a moment. What happens afterward is up to her.

CHAPTER FOUR

MEETING DADDY DEAREST

"You're way too young to play these games,
But you better start, but you better start."
—*"I'm Not The One" by 3OH!3*

Anna has me turned completely around, arse about face. It's been days since I saw her, and I feel as if I will not be able to tell up from down until I figure out if she's for real.

Am I naive to think she's genuine? I cannot figure out why she would lie about not knowing her heritage, other than to entrap me for the Dukes' dark purposes, to question my loyalty.

While I'm out of Father's hearing range, I call Blake, the son of Duke Melchom, demon of Envy.

"Ever heard of a Neph called Anna? Daughter of Belial?"

"Huh?" he asks. "He's Substance Abuse, right? I don't think he has any kids."

"Yeah," I say. "Neither did I."

"What's going on, brah?"

I shake my head. "Nothing. Take care, mate."

I know I roused his curiosity, but it can't be helped. I have trust in Blake, a rarity among our kind, but I can't say too much over the telephone.

The first knock comes from upstairs. My bandmates are spot on for our practice time. I hear the door open, and voices spill down the halls and stairs. Feet tromp down to my basement, where I sit at the drums, ready to go. Ready to clear my head. A group of girls comes down behind the guys, laughing and smelling of perfumes and hairspray. Raj and I bump fists, and Bennett slaps my palm before turning on the keyboard. There's enough hair product between Michael, Raj, and Bennett to keep the gel companies in business forever.

I sometimes wear an earpiece at large gigs, but in my basement I have to wear headphones to keep the sounds from echoing. It's a relief to put them on, do our sound checks, and get started.

We rock out for nearly two hours. I am refreshed and tired in the best way. The only thing I need to top off this feeling is a bit of soft skin against mine. I lock eyes with a redhead in a miniskirt who I hooked up with months ago. We haven't had sex yet, though, and I plan to remedy that.

I give her a nod. Poof goes her aura, as red as my shirt. I'm so in. I jerk my head to the side and she gives me a smirk like only hot girls can do. She comes to stand between my legs, eyeing me sexily.

"Oh, so you're going to give me the time of day now?" She tries for nonchalance in her voice, but her colors are screaming like a fireworks display.

"What are you on about, babe? I haven't seen you in ages."

"I've been at, like, a ton of gigs since that night."

I widen my eyes as if surprised, and lazily push the curls off her shoulders with the back of my hand, touching her bare skin. "You should have come backstage."

"See ya, Kai," Raj calls. I raise my chin to say bye to the guys as they leave with a bunch of girls. One chick stays behind, the redhead's friend. She sits in an oversized chair, texting.

"They wouldn't let me backstage! I tried and tried to catch your eye. And I've called you."

"Ah, my stupid phone," I say. I widen my knees and take her by the waist, pulling her closer. But before we get started, I scan the property with my hearing. The voices I catch in a car outside make me freeze.

"... *want me to come with you?*"

"*It might be better if I talk to him alone.*"

"*That's cool. There's this instrument store . . .*"

Anna is here. Jay's brought her. She's come for me. I somehow know this is the moment of truth where she will finally show her true self. I have to be ready, because there's a huge part of me that will be disappointed if she's an enemy. I steel myself against it and prepare myself for the worst.

I quickly stand and drop my hands from the redheaded girl, backing away. Her eyes flash with shock. *Bugger.* I do not have time to deal with angry girls.

"Er, look, I'm sorry, but I need to work on these songs a few more times by myself. I'll give you a ring to hang out later. All right, then?"

"Are you serious?"

"I'll let you show yourselves out." Her friend is staring at me, mouth dangling open to show the chewing gum inside.

Yep. I'm a prick. Don't care. They need to go. Now.

Redhead lets out an angry growling sound and proceeds to gather her belongings and stomp off. Her friend glares at me before they finally leave.

I put my headphones back on and force myself to relax. This Neph will not beat me. If the Dukes think they can send a tiny, beautiful actress to throw me off my game, they are mistaken.

I release my crazed anxieties on the drums but keep her in my peripheral vision when she enters the basement. She gently closes the door and looks around the room in awe before her stare lands on me. As she watches, a cloud of lust practically glows in red around her, and it makes me play harder.

Call me moody, but if I'm expecting a shag and it falls through because a possible enemy decides to show, it puts me on edge. Especially when this possible enemy is hot for me and I refuse to touch her. I've never had such ambiguous feelings for someone. I'm a paranoid, confused mess, and that irks the bejesus out of me.

Enough of this. The game ends now. I slam the final beats and then stand, throwing down my headphones.

"Well, if it isn't little orphan Annie," I say.

A hurt look crosses her face, and navy sadness slices through her aura. I refuse to feel bad. I get myself a drink and decide to call her out. Take this to the next level.

I take out my knife. Open it. Twirl it. All the while

watching her fear and confusion. I want her to speak, but she doesn't. So, I move closer. Get right in her face. Cage her in against the wall.

Now she's the one feeling ambiguous—torn between lust and fear. I keep my knife steady in my hand, out at my side where she can see it. I am primed and ready for a fight, expecting her to reveal secret ninja skills at any moment, but she doesn't. She merely melts back against the wall.

"What do you want?" I ask.

"I just want to talk. You don't have to try to scare me."

Her voice shakes. The darkness of her fear is overridden by a puff of red as my hips graze against hers.

"There's hardly any room for fear when you're so bloody turned on."

A blade of near blackness slices through her lust. I'm making her mad. Good on me. Perhaps if she's angry enough she'll finally blurt out what she wants.

"Ah, there's anger now . . . and a bit of embarrassment."

"I know what we are now," she says in a shaking breath. The sound of her voice rakes against my cold heart. *What we are* . . . is it truly possible she didn't know? Obviously she knew she was different, but could she have been ignorant about being the daughter of a demon? Possible, but not probable. It has to be a bloody lie.

"Congratulations." I consider kissing her, just to see how she'll react. Just to see how those pretty little lips feel.

At that thought I push away from the wall, berating myself, as I send my small dagger flying at the dartboard with a hard throw.

Bull's-eye.

I make it smoothly to the couch and turn, not wanting my back to her for too long. I sit and wait for her to explain why she's come, but she simply stands there at a loss. Heavy doubt clouds my mind. Did she come here to talk to me about what we are? If she didn't know before, how would she have found out? I want to ask, but if it's all a wicked hoax, I can't fall into her trap.

Something inside me twinges—I hear something outside, but everyone should be gone by now. I push my hearing through the house and down our curved driveway.

A smooth-engined car.

My father's velvety voice as he talks on his mobile, schmoozing someone, chuckling.

Of all the bad fucking timing . . .

I look at Anna, but she doesn't appear to be listening. Does she know he's coming? Is this a trap? I wait for a smug look to cross her face, for the act to drop, but she's the very same Anna, standing there in a cloud of hurt feelings.

Sudden clarity smacks me and I feel the strangest sense of protectiveness over my mysterious Nephilim girl. I know I've been contemplating whether or not she's working with Father and the other Dukes, but in that moment my gut feeling overtakes me.

I don't think she is. Deep down, I think she's legit. Call me a damned fool, but the idea of keeping this girl in the room with my father is like putting a speckled fawn in the path of a wolf.

I have to hide her.

Father is saying his good-byes on the mobile now, and the driver is walking around to let him out. It's likely that Father has already heard us, but if he was on the phone he mightn't have. If I attempt to take Anna out a back way, he will hear both of our footsteps and wonder why I'm avoiding him. I have about one minute to dupe him into thinking she's a hookup.

I jump from the couch and lunge at Anna, grasping her shoulders hard and pressing my lips to her ear. I whisper as softly as I can.

"My father is here."

She stiffens under my hand. Yes, she knows what we are, therefore she knows Father is a demon. Be afraid, Anna.

I pull her to the couch and fling her down. Thank God for female blouses with buttons. I rip it open, needing the scene to appear real. When she sucks in a shocked breath I press a finger to her lips. Her aura is a swirl of gray tones, both fear and embarrassment. This is not the time for modesty. I can't have her appearing terrified if we're supposed to be going at it. So I toss a throw blanket at her and rip my own shirt over my head. I point to her shirt and she starts rolling her shoulders to get it off.

God, she is sexy. Even in that innocent white satin bra. Let's just hope I haven't been a fool and she doesn't shove a dagger in my spine. I lower my body over hers and taste the skin at the base of her throat. I move upward to the curve of her neck and shoulder, and let out a low moan. Our skin touches and she moves underneath me in a sultry way, grasping the nearby pillows in her fists.

I suddenly want all her clothes off.

The sound of Father coming down the stairs erases that thought from my mind. He knows by now I'm with a girl, but he has no notion of privacy.

When the door opens, Anna's body jumps under me and she lets out a squeak. I turn my head to the door where Father stands, smiling, inching farther to the side to get a better look at Anna. Damn. I can't hide her any further without being obvious.

"My apologies, son. I didn't realize you had company." He is still moving casually across the room, staring.

Before I can say a word, the politeness slips from his features and his eyes flash red. I look down at Anna, who has foolishly allowed the blanket to fall enough to give Father a side view of her badge. I hold my breath. They definitely do not seem to know each other.

"I never imagined you'd care to entertain female Nephilim," he grits.

Not good. Not fucking good. Neph can work together, but they are not to play together. Especially in the one-on-one way.

"I don't normally." I stand and move away, as if coming to my senses. "She caught me while I was bored and alone after practice."

His face sours as he scents the air. "You will come up for tea. Both of you." He leaves, and I ball my hands. Close my eyes. I want to punch something.

Anna is *my* problem. *My* mystery. I don't want to share her with anyone, especially not the wolf upstairs. It's clear now they weren't working together. The blood has drained from Anna's face as she clutches the blanket to her chest. I simultaneously feel sorry for her and want to shout at her. She's a stupid, stupid girl for coming here.

She reaches for her shirt and tries to put it on, but there are buttons missing from when I went all Incredible Hulk. I toss her my red T-shirt and she puts it on.

No girl has ever worn my clothes before, and it's the embodiment of sexiness. I imagine her wearing it the morning after we've had an all-night shag fest.

I shake my head. What the hell is wrong with me? Father is waiting.

I lead her up the stairs to the sitting room, and I lean against the wall to watch helplessly as the wolf licks the fawn.

She maintains her norm of complete innocence as Father questions her. I listen and learn all the things I was too afraid to ask, though I'm still unsure how she came by the information. She has no idea her demonic father's name is Belial or what he does. Belial most likely doesn't know she exists. She and I met coincidentally at a gig, and she's just learning what she is. My head is spinning with thoughts when I hear Father say to Anna—

". . . you reek of innocence. Yes, that's right. I can smell it—your *virginity*."

I nearly topple over in surprise, and Father laughs at the look of horror on Anna's face. There is no way she's pure. No. Way.

Father smacks his knee in astonishment. "A sixteen-year-old Neph virgin! How do you expect to be a bad influence on humans if you aren't behaving badly yourself?"

Anna says nothing, but her eyes dart around nervously. I'm still gaping in shock at the revelation. Father informs her she's the daughter of the Duke of Substance Abuse, and I am so floored, so gobsmacked by her innocence, that blood rushes inside my ears and I can hardly concentrate.

She was never out to kill me or test my loyalty. My God, she was truly drugged by that human boy! And probably was telling the truth about never having been kissed. How is this possible? It's just my luck that I'd stumble upon her. If I'd known, I could have urged her to move far away from Father and other Dukes, but I was consumed by my own paranoid assumptions. I mean, really, what are the bloody chances?

Oh, fantastic. Now Father is pulling out his bag of recreational drugs, and Anna is practically shivering and drooling as she looks at it all. I want to warn Father that Anna and drugs are not a pretty combination, but I clamp my mouth shut.

I can't let myself feel bad for her. Father knows about her now, so she's no longer my problem. It's too late for "should haves." Anna will have to work now like the rest of us. It's her legacy to push drugs and alcohol. As a Neph, she has to be a "bad girl" by society's standards in every way but still recognize when to be seemingly docile to stay out of trouble. Her ability to tempt others will be wrapped up in a blend of her sensuality, tolerance for substances, and a personality that makes her sin appear fun and harmless. Neph learn from an early age that sex, drugs, and alcohol go hand in hand. It's what's expected by the Dukes, so Anna cannot remain a virgin. She'll learn and she'll be fine. She will grow to enjoy it.

I will *not* feel bad.

My head snaps up when I hear Father say my name. He's still talking to Anna.

"Kaidan will take good care of you. He'll have you working to the best of your abilities in no time at all. Don't take too long about it, though. Learn what you need to, and get to work." He turns to me and I stand straighter. "I'm expecting company this evening and you are to join us. Marissa is bringing one of her nieces."

Acid rises in my throat. "Yes, Father."

Anna is staring at me with curiosity, and I have to look away.

My mind is whirling when I return home from taking Anna to her apartment. So much has happened in the span of a few short hours. I can't believe she's lived with an adoptive mother all these years, a woman named Patti who loves her fiercely—even *I* took to the woman straightaway. And I can't believe what I've agreed to. I've gone completely mad, but the thrill of it is all-consuming.

Her words tumble through my mind as I let myself in the front door of my house.

"What will happen if I don't, you know, do all the stuff your father told me to? Because I'm not going to . . ." "I want to wait until I'm married . . ." "My mother was an angel . . . A guardian angel . . ." "What does it mean to be Nephilim?"

The girl is half angel, half demon. An anomaly. I'd laughed and told her she's a walking contradiction, but truly I'm mesmerized. I keep wondering what it must be like to be both. It's unheard of. And to be raised and nurtured by a human . . . wow.

And though it's all fascinating, her stubbornness against changing her ways cannot possibly last. Now that Father knows about her, she belongs to the Dukes—at least her body does. And they expect her to use her body for their purposes. Tomorrow morning I'll be up bright and early to begin teaching her the ways of the Neph—

My thoughts are interrupted when I pass the sitting room. I stop dead in my tracks, shocked at myself for forgetting. Father is standing beside the leather sofa, where Marissa sits with a small girl at her side. The girl I've been dreading.

Fuuuuuuuck.

No, no, no. I want to scream and rail. This cannot be happening.

She is just as young as the pictures.

"Come in, Kaidan," Father says.

I do as he says, and I see Marissa put a hand on the girl's leg when she whimpers. I can't bring myself to look the child in the eyes.

"Kaidan, this is Marissa's newest niece, Viktoria. We were hoping you could help ease her into her new life." His words are so casual. I've heard them a thousand times. Though I've never liked this aspect of my "job," I've never been repulsed like this.

I grab the back of my neck, trying to steady myself.

"She doesn't speak English," Marissa says. "But some things are universal, yes?" She and Father share a smile. "She is to remain a virgin, of course."

I allow my gaze to flicker to the girl, whose eyes are red-rimmed. Her light hair is pulled into loose pigtails. Her feet dangle, not touching the floor, in worn Mary-Jane-style shoes. I step back, causing Father's eyes to glow like a stoplight. Marissa and the girl do not have the ability to see his eyes redden, and I wish I didn't either.

"Is there a problem?" he asks through clenched teeth.

The answer should be "No, sir." I could try to force myself. I could try to think of someone else. Anna's face flashes through my mind's eye. She would cry if she saw this. I look at the little girl's feet again, and I can't. I just bloody can't.

"Kaidan," Father whispers, and that one word is laden with warning.

I dare to lift my eyes to his and open my mouth to speak the words. "I will do anything you ask of me that's in my physical power, Father. You know that. But I cannot force my body to react to a child. It's just . . . not my thing." I grab the back of my neck again as he stares at me. I've never defied him.

"Shall I get you a Viagra?" he asks. I nearly scoff. Oh, yes, that's just what I need. Artificial lust. Marissa cackles in mirth at his cruel teasing.

"Anything but this," I whisper.

"Are you morally against it?" He edges toward me, fire in his eyes. "Do you think the services Marissa is providing to hardworking clients are beneath you?"

"Of course not," I lie.

"Are you like the other prudes in society who think their brand of lust is the only acceptable one?" He is right in my face now, and my heart is racing.

"No, sir. Lust is lust."

"Then what is the problem?" he shouts, and spittle forms at the edges of his mouth.

Marissa is grinning, and the girl Viktoria begins to cry. Marissa pulls a fucking sweet from her purse and gives it to the child, crooning, "There, there."

Father continues his tirade. "Did you not tell me you can feel lust for anyone?"

Shite. I should have never told him that.

"Not anyone, sir. Only those who lust for me first."

Yeah, nasty little fact about me. Anyone, and I mean *anyone* who blazes a red aura for me . . . I will find something to fancy about them as well. Sexy ankles, full lips, shiny hair, you name it. It's as if my body is hardwired to do my job with no excuses. But this child has a few years before she'll know what lust is.

Father huffs through his nose, nostrils flaring. This is it. This is where he'll give me an ultimatum. Take the girl to my room this instant or dig myself a nice burial hole somewhere out in the woods. I can't believe it's come to this.

Marissa stands and saunters over, placing a hand on Father's shoulder.

"Darling, let him be." She pushes herself in so she's sandwiched between us, her arse against Father and her heavy chest against mine. Father growls and takes her hips as she runs her hands over my shoulders and down my arms. Her aura goes red as she stares up at me with bloodred lips and black-lined eyes. My stupid body reacts.

Marissa laughs and rubs against me. "He can't help it if he prefers grown women."

I hate her.

"I will train the girl myself, luv," Father says against her ear.

I hate him, as well.

Father snaps his fingers twice in the air and shouts, "Raul!" In a moment the driver stands in the doorway. "Ready the car for Marissa."

"Yes, sir." The driver bows his head and hurries off.

Father glares at me and then flicks his hand to tell me to get out of his sight. As I turn to go I glimpse the girl with the sweet in her cheek and the sad eyes.

I hate my life.

CHAPTER FIVE

Road Trip with a Nun

"Come and take a walk on the wild side . . .
'Cause you and I, we were born to die."
—*"Born to Die" by Lana Del Rey*

After the events of last night, I need to focus on protecting myself and staying alive. Nevertheless, here I am, humoring this girl who refuses to do what's best for her. Driving her across the country to meet her demon father for the first time.

Yeah, there's no part of this arrangement that's smart, is there?

Patti, although she seemed to loathe the idea of Anna meeting Belial, thinks he will somehow be able to help and protect Anna. When Patti adopted Anna, she was told by the orphanage to find Belial and return to speak with a nun named Sister Ruth when Anna got older. There's more to this story than I can guess, and I'm too damned curious to walk away now. Plus, I feel a foreign sense of obligation for her. I could have offered to fly us—I certainly have the funds—but a road trip will allow me more time to figure her out. Alone.

I turn up the stereo, but my thoughts are louder.

It's like Anna's a stray I stumbled upon, and she'll be crushed by a damn car if I let her out of my sight. I've never met anyone so filled with bloody goodness. She practically glows. When I'm with her I feel . . . different. Lighter or some shit.

I glance over at this girl, this naive Neph, void of ego, and I shake my head. We drive with the music blaring. I expected my playlist to be too hard-core for her, but she seems perfectly content, even humming along with some of the songs. When "Sex and Candy" by Marcy Playground comes on I see her listening intently. She meets my eye at the chorus, a splotchy blush running up her neck, before she quickly turns to stare out her window. I look forward again and grin, keeping an eye on the skies for evil whispering spirits.

Although the landscape is boring, she stares out the windows like she's never seen anything so beautiful. As if she's on some incredible adventure with me. She's clueless about the dangers. Even after I've told her, straight up, that she can't fuck about with the Dukes. They are ruthless, evil bastards and they will kill her. She acts as if she's safe with me. As if I can protect her from them.

That causes some idiotic thing inside my chest to swell and strengthen.

I think Anna Whitt is bad for my health.

The thing is, as adorable as her innocence might be on the surface, it would be foolish of me to allow her to stay that way. She's not open to being trained, other than a mention of wanting to learn how to hide her colors. She refuses to see the necessity of losing her virginity, or at least *pretending* not to be so good. It's only a matter of time before the Dukes start sniffing around, but she just doesn't get it. She has no self-preservation instinct. I have to help her out.

But I have to be smooth about it. I have to win her over. For both our sakes, I need to shag her like mad by the end of this road trip.

Anna will be my toughest conquest yet. From what I've seen so far, she's the queen of self-control. A nun in training or some shite.

There's only one way to get a girl like Anna into bed before marriage, and I'm not looking forward to the amount of work it will require. She's not the kind of girl who goes for the bad boy, so I must be on my best behavior. But in order for her to appreciate my best behavior, she needs to think she's causing some positive change in me. I'll need to make her think I'm letting her into the deep, dark places of myself. Essentially, I have to make Anna fall in love with me and believe I'm in love with her, as well.

A twinge of guilt fills my bowels, but it's fleeting, gone before my next breath. It must be done. Eventually she'll thank me.

Day one goes well, I think. And I manage to get her to agree on a single room at the motel instead of separate ones. She's into me. Drawn against her will. And I gladly take advantage of it.

I get comfortable on my bed, enjoying the way she stares at me when she doesn't think I'm paying attention, and how easy it is to make her nervous when I play with my blade.

After some uncomfortable chitchat, in which I talk about my childhood and Father's horrible parenting—all true—I proceed to make her jealous with the texts I'm receiving from other girls, which is adorable. So far she's playing directly into my hand, but her questions and need for knowledge eventually sidetrack my efforts. She seems fascinated that I'm always using my supernatural abilities. Her hatred of her Neph senses is baffling. She needs to be proud of her heritage, to understand the benefit of her extended senses. I go over and sit next to where she's lying on her bed, and she gets skittish, trying to scoot away.

"No, stay lying down," I say, touching her arm. "I want to show you something."

I want to show her a lot of things, and I daresay she knows this by now. She narrows those little brown eyes at me, and I have to laugh.

"Calm down, luv." I find that I say "luv" a lot more since I moved to the States. American girls go crazy for it. Not sure it's working on Anna yet, but it's worth a try.

"What are you going to do?" Her sweet voice and light Southern accent go straight to my crotch, and I'm glad she's at an angle where she can't see.

"Nothing that will compromise your virtue and have Patti hunting me down. Now close your eyes." I'd promised Patti I'd bring Anna home safely, with her virtue intact. I plan to keep only the first part of that promise, even though I quite like

Patti. What neither of them realize is that Anna's virtue is the very thing that will put her in danger.

What I'm planning is a simple exercise to build her trust, to show her I'm more than a sex fiend. I want her to see that her senses can be pleasant. And maybe I want to touch her, just a small bit.

At first I don't think she's going to play along. Then she lets out a huff and lies back.

Good girl.

But God, she's stiff as a board.

"Now, I want you to relax and concentrate on your sense of touch. I'll be a good boy. I promise."

I *am* planning to be good.

I watch as she exhales and relaxes. I can imagine the tingling she feels as she opens her nerve endings to full exposure. And I remember something cool that my Neph friend Marna once showed me when we were younger. Without touching any other part of her, I press my fingertip into the palm of her nearest hand.

I smile when she gasps. "I can sense your fingerprint!"

Wicked. Wait until she feels what's next. I scoot down and take her foot into my hand. I watch Anna's face soften with bliss as I knead and press my fingers against her sole. Then I move up to her ankle, and suddenly her eyes pop open as she wrenches her knees to her chest.

What'd I do?

"Wait," she says. "Not my legs. They're . . ."

What is she going on about? "They're lovely." In fact, they're killer.

"No, please. I didn't have time to shave this morning."

I throw my head back and laugh. Call me sick and twisted, but it takes a hell of a lot more than a little hair to bother me. Her paranoia is adorable, though.

"All right, fine, no legs. But you're missing out. I'm not through with you. Roll onto your stomach and relax again."

She obeys immediately, and I'm so relaxed I forget to mentally prepare myself for the sight of . . .

"Mmm." I don't mean to moan. It just sort of slips out. But her arse . . . blimey, it's fucking perfect. I bite down hard on my knuckle.

"What?" she mutters into the pillow.

"Oh, nothing." Except I can't think straight. "It's just that you've got quite a nice little—"

Damn, she moves quick. She's glaring sharply and I hold up my hands. Little Ann can be feisty when she wants.

"Sorry! A guy can't help but notice. Truly—best behavior—starting now." I want her to hurry and lie back down so I can stare at that arse again. This is far too fun.

She rolls back over, slowly and warily, and then—hello, perfect bum. Would it be okay if I touch it? Just once?

No. This is Anna Whitt. It would decidedly not be okay to touch the bum. I recognize that my self-control is unwinding bit by bit. I'm unaccustomed to looking and not touching. Sampling and not devouring. This moment is pushing my limits. I must stay calm, moving us to the next level. My voice comes out low and husky when I talk.

"I need you to trust me and stay relaxed. I'm just going to raise your shirt a bit so I can get to your back."

Is she buying this? She doesn't move, so I take that as permission to gently pull her shirt upward and expose her soft, creamy back. My breathing goes a bit wonky. Angel girl is letting me see her skin. She's going to let me touch her. She's trusting me.

My fingers sink into the soft skin and muscle on her lower back, working slow circles.

Holy Mary, I'm all but panting. Get it together, Rowe! This is the least sexual thing I've done in ages, and it's turning me on more than a bloody van full of naked girls.

I run my fingers across her back until she's covered in goose flesh. She is reacting to me, and I need to touch her with more than just my fingers. My hands press down, massaging harder, gripping her waist in my hands. I need more.

I try to shake the rising fog from my head, but it's no use. My own sense of touch begins to open itself, my skin buzzing with neediness. She feels like silk.

I need more.

My hands go farther, past her satin bra, up to her shoulders. I might rip her shirt, and I don't bloody care. I am nearly beyond thinking. Her pheromones and red aura encircle me, grip me.

I am need.

I am greed.

And I take what I want.

Her skin calls to me, and I'm above her, moving her hair aside and breathing in the warmth of her neck. I have to taste her or I think I will die—implode—explode—something terrible will happen.

I home in on the spot under her ear, and my desperate lips

finally touch her . . . this is my heaven. Her neck is heated, and she lifts her chin, allowing me to kiss further. Her body slightly twists, angling toward me. I open my mouth, dragging my tongue along the silk and salt and sweetness of her. Up to her jaw. And then she's turning, her hands are in my hair, and she's leading my mouth to hers.

I am overwhelmed by this kiss. She must be using angel voodoo on me because I can't think. I can't. I'm trying, but all I can feel is her lips. I'm more lost to the world than I've ever been. I want to let go and never come back. Lose myself in her for eternity.

I need more. I need all of her. Her stomach is so smooth. The satin of her bra is filled with a mouthful of flesh that's sure to be the most succulent—

Abruptly, Anna shoves me away and I feel as if I've been doused by fire.

WHAT THE FUCK WAS THAT?

Bloody hell, my heart is pounding like an amateur's. I cannot let her know how freaked out I am.

She's panting. "You promised to be on your best behavior." Her aura is a mix of grays and red. I'm suddenly furious we're not still kissing. Why would anyone put a halt to such epicness?

"*You* kissed *me*, Anna," I remind her.

"Well, *you* started it by kissing my neck."

Mmm, her neck. It'd been so warm and inviting. "True. I hadn't planned that."

She paces the room, attempting to fix her hair, but she's too angry and lustful. She's shaking.

"Why did you stop?" I ask.

"Because you were moving on to other things."

What other things? Oh . . . I suppose my hand did wander a bit, didn't it? "Hmm, moved too quickly. Rookie mistake."

Judging by the way she crosses her arms, it probably would have been best to keep that thought inside my head. I'm still not quite thinking straight. Why is she having this effect on me? And for the love of all things holy, *why aren't we still snogging?*

It was slightly amusing at first when she stopped us, but now that I know she's serious, I'm starting to feel a rise of panic. My body has not and will not shut off or calm down. This could get ugly.

"I can see you still want me," I say. It's true. She's only being stubborn. Is this some kind of cruel angel punishment? Now she wants to be pissed off instead of lustful? "Oh. There it goes. Mad instead. Well, sort of. You can't seem to muster a really good anger—"

"Stop it!"

"Sorry, was I saying that out loud?" She really hates when I read her colors, so I do it as often as possible. And right now it's better to be cheeky than to let her know I'm frantic on the inside. My demand for relief is growing.

"I can read people, too, you know." Here she goes again with the feistiness. "Well, not you, but at least I have the decency not to notice, to give them some sort of emotional privacy."

No doubt, because she's a bloody nun. "How very decent of you."

She grunts with frustration and throws a pillow at me. It's

probably the angriest she's ever been in her life. I raise an eyebrow to see how much madder I can make her. "Pillow fight?"

She wants to scream. I can see it in her rigid, huffing demeanor, but she takes a cleansing breath and deflates a notch.

Nice trick. If only I could do that. I've got some parts that could use deflating.

"Get off my bed," she orders. "Please. I'm ready to go to sleep."

That's a load of bollocks. She's not tired. She's as filled with passion as I am, but she's too bloody good to embrace it. Her self-control burns me up. I want her to throw a wobbly and break things. Then pounce on me.

But seriously. We should be naked.

I get off the bed and wave an arm toward it. She climbs deep into the covers and puts her back to me. I try to bring her back to life by reminding her that I saved her from the plonker who drugged her at the party and almost stole her first kiss. But she doesn't take the bait. Doesn't leap from the bed and jump my bones. Doesn't even turn to face me.

Then I remember—*I* had her first kiss—that's right, *me*, and I want to beat my chest like an ape.

"So that's it, then?" I say. My lust is still working at full-throttle-rocket mode, but there will be no countdown to launch. I'm torn between disbelief and a rising ache deep in my abdomen. It hurts like hell. It takes everything in my power not to be the caveman my father wants me to be and ravage this girl senseless. "I always wondered what it would feel like."

"What *what* would feel like?" She finally looks at me.

"Rejection." It would be humorous if it weren't for the pain element. I've never felt this before.

"What are you saying? That *no* girl has ever told you no?" She needn't sound so shocked.

"Not one," I say. I won't tell her I seek out those who show interest to begin with.

"And what about you? Haven't you ever stopped or said no to a girl?"

Pfft! "Why would I do that?"

"Lots of reasons," she mumbles. "Never mind, just go to sleep. We have a long day tomorrow."

She rolls back over, making all sorts of ruckus as she settles. I've never had much cause to hate my lustful heritage. I've always been able to sate the beast. But at this moment all I want is this mad need for her body to disappear. It's more than just pain now. It feels as if a black cloud is consuming me, fogging my mind and vision. I attempt to blink it away.

I think about Anna's last question, and suddenly my childhood mate Ginger's face fills my mind. That awkward, terrible night when she hit on me in front of Blake comes rushing back. "I suppose I did refuse one, but she doesn't count." I'm babbling now, but talking seems to help. Will this feeling pass?

"Why not?" she asks.

"Because she was Neph." My stomach tightens when I think of Ginger. She was my friend once. My closest friend.

Anna says nothing, and I'm left standing there with a rather large problem. The feeling is not passing. I desperately need to have sex or I may have to curl into the fetal position and howl. I adjust myself while she's not looking. How do regular blokes deal with this torture when they're turned down all the time?

"This must be the part where I take a cold shower?"

Can't she sense my need? Doesn't she care at all that it feels as if I've been racked by a giant?

Apparently not. "Good idea" is all she says.

Cold. Hearted.

I trudge stiffly to the bathroom and climb into the shower, but it does nothing for me. I cannot believe this is happening. I shouldn't have lost control while we kissed. I should have taken my bloody time and gotten her so hot she was begging for more. How the hell did the little nun get the upper hand over me? I am reduced to showering with myself, which is an inadequate substitute for what I need. But then I remember the girl at the hotel desk who checked me in. Midtwenties. Bored out of her gourd. Completely hot for me.

Brilliant.

I dry myself and walk into our room stark naked, but she doesn't even peek. The girl is infuriating. I quickly dress, find a room key, and open the door.

Anna perks up from her bed. "Where are you going?"

Look who suddenly cares. I frown at her, hoping she feels a bit of the pain and frustration I'm experiencing.

"I have to work," I say.

"Have to? Or want to?"

Anger and indignation rip through me. This girl has no clue, and she has the nerve to try to make me feel bad? She's never feared for her life. She's never given in to her dark side and then experienced the physical impossibility of ignoring it ever again. I cannot stand here and listen to her.

"Why should that matter, Anna? I'm going now."

"Where will you go?" she all but shouts. She sounds a bit desperate, which gives me some amount of satisfaction.

I'm glad to tell her, and I hope it makes her share a bit of my agony. "I'll go visit the girl at the front desk, just as she suggested. So unless you've changed your mind . . . ?" I give her one last chance, and I watch as envy and sadness fight for space in her aura. But she only shakes her head.

"Didn't think so," I mutter. Then I flick off the light and shut the door, checking to be sure it locks behind me.

Her words ring in my ears, but I shake my head to rid myself of them. I enjoy my work most of the time. And tonight I definitely will.

I walk with purpose down the pavement to the front office, where I can see the girl through the glass window. She's on her mobile. When she catches sight of me her eyes go wide and she quickly hangs up, smoothing her curls down. She greets me with a big smile and a heavy Southern accent.

"Hi there . . . Mr. Rowe, right? Everything okay?"

"Yes. Just Kaidan, please." I swish damp hair from my eyes. I'm not really in the mood for a detailed seduction. I'd prefer to make this quick, so I delve into my bag of douchery. "I'm trying to give my sister some time to herself in the room. Our grandmother just passed, and she's taking it hard."

The girl puts a hand against her chest, and her aura fills with sadness. "Oh, bless her heart. And yours. I'm sorry about your grandma."

I nod, looking sad, which isn't hard since I'm feeling rather strange in general. I lean against the counter and wonder if

Anna's okay in the room. I do a quick auditory scan, but it's quiet in there. I don't see any demon whisperers about, doing their rounds for the Dukes.

"Hope I'm not bothering you . . ." I look at her name tag. "Vanessa."

"Not at all!" she says brightly. "You can call me Nessa. It gets boring here, so I'm glad to have company. I work for my uncle. This place is kind of . . ." She sticks out her tongue and makes a face.

"A job is a job, right?" I lean against the counter, crossing my arms. I cringe against a bout of needling pain. "I'm glad to have some company right now, too. It's been a rough week."

We lock eyes and I hold her stare until her aura lights up, bright red, then I brazenly let my eyes drop to her lips, down to her chest, back up to her eyes. She is besotted, holding her breath, lust thumping through her. I let out a dry chuckle and run a hand through my hair. "What's the most fun you've ever had here at work, Nessa?"

"Um . . ." She laughs nervously. "I don't know."

"Because I could really use some fun right now if you're up for it."

"I . . ." More nervous laughing. "I mean, what kind of . . ."

I've taken a huge gamble that I might overwhelm or frighten her, but so far she hasn't run screaming. She's nervous and excited, probably wondering if I mean what she thinks I mean. She licks her dry lips and glances over her shoulder at the small office with the door ajar.

"That your uncle's office?" I ask.

"Yeah." She grins.

I slowly walk around the front desk, our eyes locked, and her aura jumps with orange and red when I reach her.

She licks her lips again. "Just so we're on the same page, Mr., I mean, *Kaidan*, what kind of fun are we, um . . ." I step closer as she babbles. "Talking about?"

"The kind that will take my mind off everything, and make you very happy," I say in a low voice. I hold back the beast with all my energy and wait for her to give me the go.

"Oh," she breathes. She tentatively touches my forearm, and lets her fingers travel down to my hand, where we join fingers.

My relief is palpable.

"Thank you," I whisper. I bring my mouth down to hers, this lovely girl whose face I won't remember after a week's time. I'm hoping for that epic passion to hit me like it did in the hotel room, but it doesn't. We're moving toward the office door, groping and snogging as we go.

I kick the door closed behind us with my foot.

She moans as I lift her onto the desk. "I can't believe this is happening."

I silence her with my mouth, and focus. Though her hair is curly, not straight, and she doesn't smell of pears, I let my need take over and I give her the best night of work she's ever had.

An awful thought occurs as I walk back to the room.

Had Anna listened to my office romp?

Wait a bloody minute—who cares if she did? Perhaps it would do her some good. Stubborn girl. But still . . . I feel oddly *off*. I can't put my finger on it, but the sex with Nessa didn't offer me the satisfaction it should have. In fact, it left me feeling empty, like a husk, needing something more.

What I need now is a good night of sleep to shake off the rejection from Anna. She's got my brain muddled is all. I knew she'd be a hard sell, but this is worse than I'd imagined. I hadn't expected to sleep with her the first night, but I definitely hadn't anticipated a firm stop sign when I'd barely reached second base. I'm accustomed to getting what I want.

I shake my head as I let myself in the room. Anna is quiet and still, but her breathing is too shallow. She's still awake. I go to the bathroom to wash up and brush my teeth.

Then I strip naked and climb into bed. I prop a hand behind my head and wonder what the little nun is thinking about. I should go to sleep, but I can't help but get under her skin one last time, the way she's gotten under mine with her angel voodoo.

"Anna?" I'm not surprised when she doesn't answer. "Did you at least enjoy your first kiss?"

She's quiet a second more. "Just go to sleep, Kaidan."

It's not a "no," which makes me smile in the dark. I learned a valuable lesson tonight about how to win over Anna. Tomorrow I'll be on my A-game. I let out a deep breath and fall straight to sleep, semi-satisfied.

CHAPTER SIX

PEARS AND ORANGES

"I keep a sinister smile and a hold of my heart.
You want to get inside, then you can get in line, but not this
time."
—*"Hero/Heroine" by Boys Like Girls*

Winning over Anna means walking a fine line. In many ways she's like other girls—she giggles and blushes and is flattered when I flirt—but only to a certain extent. Unlike most other girls I've met, Anna is an "old soul." She's like a proper old woman in a hot, young body. She can be a downright prude biddy, saying things like, "Do you think you could try to be a gentleman . . . and maybe wear shorts to bed?" and "This is going to be a long trip if you give girls the bedroom eyes every time we stop."

I'll admit, I love to shock her. I stood there nude this morning, wanting her to see exactly what was available for the taking. But cripes, I hadn't expected her to scream like a banshee. And that's the problem: I'm not the only one doing the shocking here. She continues to render me speechless with nonchalant admissions, like "I can sense pregnancies" and "I can *feel* other people's suffering."

Exactly how powerful is this girl? She can bloody well do *angel* things. And her angel voodoo has other power, as well, such as the power to make me open my mouth and say entirely too damn much. She's just so selfless. So genuinely interested. There are brief moments when I feel . . . I don't bloody know how to explain it . . . but I don't feel myself.

I'm supposed to be making her fall for me. I'm supposed to be reminding her that I'm badass, and then crafting moments of comfort and openness. Well, that's exactly what's happening, but I'm not crafting shite. Instead I'm feeling it. *She's* using *her* skills on me.

This girl is dangerous.

She's got the talents of a cookie-making nana, a world-renowned psychologist, and a seductive succubus all in one. And the most mind-bending part is that she has no clue about her effect on me. It's only been two days and I'm torn between wanting to throw her to the wolves before she infects my mind any further or hide her and keep her all for myself.

And now she's asking me about other girls. About my motives when I work. She is digging too deep and assuming I'm some sad chump who feels bad for what I do.

But I don't.

Yet it's not to my benefit to announce what a heartless bastard I am. It *is* good she's talking nonstop, though. In our quiet moments all I can think about is having sex with her—pulling over behind an oversized road sign, or lifting her onto my lap as I drive.

And then as I drive she says something that throws a spanner in the works.

". . . I care about you."

Her words reverberate through me and fill me with a sense of terror.

"Don't say that," I snap. I am shaking on the inside. This is what I wanted, right? For her feelings to grow. But it's not how I thought it would be. It's far more complicated, because now *I'm* feeling things I didn't anticipate, like guilt, and I can't understand why. "You shouldn't say that, about *caring*. You hardly know me."

She's too foolish. Too open and trusting, watching me with those fawn eyes. Damn it, she *needs* to know the constant danger she will be in for the rest of her life. She *needs* to understand how I live and breathe that danger every day. She needs to lose her virginity, to convince the Dukes she's one of us. If she doesn't embrace her life as a Neph, the Dukes will end it for her.

"And you hardly know me, but here we are," she says. "You offered to take me on this trip. You've answered my gazillion questions. You haven't forced me to do anything, and you haven't exposed me to your father. I'm glad to be here with you."

No. Stupid feelings. I will not let those warm, chocolate-chip-cookie words soften me. I hold the wheel tightly and stare at her.

God, she's pushy. Question after question. Not satisfied with half answers. Searching for what she wants to hear—that I'm a "good guy" underneath.

"Why are you trying so hard to make me think you're a bad person?" she asks.

Just like the human woman, Patti, Anna won't be satisfied with anything but the truth. So I'll give it to her.

"Because it would be best for you to have a healthy fear of me so you can't say you weren't warned. I'm not like the boys at your school. Think of the pull you feel toward drugs. That is how I feel about sex."

Her face slackens with understanding. That's right. We both live with an insatiable beast inside.

"Starting to get it now? Let me be even clearer. I can feel someone out within five minutes of conversation to know what I would have to say and do to lure her into bed. That includes you, though I admit I was off my game last night. With some people it's a matter of simple flattery and attention. With others it takes more time and energy. I do whatever it takes to get their clothes off, and then I attempt to make it so they'll never be with another person and not think of me. I know secrets of the human body most people don't even know about themselves. And when I leave, I know they're ruined when they're begging me to stay."

It's my legacy. I have no regrets.

As Anna watches me with wide eyes, gray zaps of fear burst inside her aura. She understands.

"It's about time," I say.

***

83

New Mexico brings more awe-filled staring out the windows at the passing scenery, and more questions about the hierarchy of demons and Neph. It's insane how much she doesn't know. She wants to learn, even though the details sadden her to tears. Hopefully this knowledge will allow her to begin seeing the dark, whispering spirits, which she *should* have been able to see for years now. It has to be her innocence that keeps her from seeing them. She needs to know what they're up to so she can stay safe when I'm no longer around.

When we stop for night two, I'm surprised that Anna allows us to share a room again. Naughty possibilities immediately fill my mind, and I have to tamp them down. I will not lose my head again.

I stand on the second-story balcony with my arms crossed while Anna talks to her mum on the phone. And yes, I use my powers to listen through the glass. I listened to all their conversations in Georgia, as well, and they knew it. Sue me.

"Just be careful not to let your guard down," Patti says.

Good advice. Only Anna doesn't have a "guard." She is an unshielded open book.

"Okay. Love you," Anna says in that sweet voice of hers.

"I love you, too."

Anna makes a kiss sound, and Patti does it back, and they both laugh.

Their relationship fascinates me. They say those three words *every single time*. And I get a fucking shiver down my spine each time I hear it. What is that like? To know someone feels that way for you, no matter what, and would do anything for you? Everything I've seen about love is fickle. People don't work for it. They take it for granted. They abuse it. But these two . . . they embrace it.

I listen as Anna lets herself out of the room with a soft *click*. Her footsteps down the carpeted hall. The whir of a vending machine dispensing. Minutes later she is opening the sliding door and standing behind me. I wonder if she'll touch me. I wait for it, wanting it. But instead she steps to my side and presses cold water against my arm. She got one for me, of course. Always thoughtful.

"Thanks." Our arms touch, sending a rush of heat through me. I think about kissing her again, right out here in the fading dusk of light, but I know it's not time. Her aura is unsure. She's both happy and nervous, but not lustful, as we lean against the railing together.

She looks sweet in a ponytail that began high this morning but now droops loosely as if it's had enough of this traveling business. I want to run my fingers through it, let it slide heavily over my hands, maybe give it a tug to make her gasp.

Cripe. Bad Kai.

Anna flinches a little and sniffs, and for a moment I wonder if she can bloody well read thoughts, because she leaves me to go back in the hotel room. I listen as she walks into the bathroom, and it sounds as if she's touching my toiletry bag. Perhaps she needs to borrow a razor for her legs. Ha.

I smile and go inside. What I see in the bathroom makes me accidentally chuckle. Anna Whitt is sniffing my deodorant.

When she hears me she startles, dropping the deodorant into the sink with a clatter and a scream. Everything about this amuses me. And turns me on. Because, yeah, she's touching and smelling my stuff. I can't help but laugh.

"Okay, that must have looked really bad," she says as she fumbles to put my things away. "I was just trying to figure out what cologne you wear."

Ah. I see. This is an interesting turn of events. She's caught my scent.

I cross my arms and move into the room, trying not to show how much I'm enjoying this. "I haven't been wearing any cologne."

"Oh." She clears her throat. "Let's just forget about it."

Not a chance.

"What is it you smell, exactly?" Ginger told me what my pheromones smelled like when we were younger, and if that's what Anna is detecting, that means she's been opening her senses unknowingly. I move forward, wanting her to look at me, but she won't. That's okay. Judging by her mix of anxiety, excitement, confusion, and lust, I'm affecting her just fine.

"I don't know," she says. "It's like citrus and the forest or something . . . leaves and tree sap. I can't explain it."

Ginger said I smelled like sour kumquats and dirt, the cow. I think she just enjoyed saying *kumquat*. "Citrus? Like lemons?"

"Oranges mostly. And a little lime, too."

I like her description a lot more than Gin's. I flick the hair from my eyes. Things are about to get serious.

"What you smell are my pheromones, Anna."

Her laugh is a shrill, nervous burst, as if she doesn't believe me.

"Oh, okay, then. Well . . ." Anna tries to leave the bathroom, but I shift to block her. We are not finished yet.

"People can't usually smell pheromones. You must be using your extra senses without realizing it. I've heard of Neph losing control of their senses with certain emotions. Fear, surprise." Wait for it. . . . "Lust."

Embarrassment rises up, but there is still a hint of red lining the bottom of her aura as she babbles a lame excuse about her senses. She is far too adorable to be trapped in a bathroom with the likes of me.

"Would you like to know your own scent?" I ask.

Her eyes widen as they dart around the bathroom. "Uh, not really. I think I should probably go."

I think not.

"You smell like pears with freesia undertones."

"Wow, okay." She clears her throat, and her aura pops with lust. "I think I'll just . . ." She presses herself against the sink to inch past me, as if touching me will set off a bomb. I hold up my hands, far too amused.

She rushes about the room, stuffing her feet into sneakers. If she thinks to escape me, she'd better think again. I'm not letting her out of this hotel without me. And she can be in denial all she wants, but there *will* be more snogging tonight.

"Going somewhere?" I ask.

"Yeah, I'm going for a run."

Not alone you're not. "Mind if I join you?"

"Only if you'll do something for me."

My eyebrows go up.

"Teach me to hide my colors," she says.

Eh, not exactly what I had in mind. Very well, then. Skills now, snogging later.

I watch her arse as she climbs the rocks ahead of me, and I'm glad I'm wearing loose shorts. I need to calm down before we get up there. It's a bit easier when she reaches the top and sits, successfully obstructing any view of her backside. I give myself a moment, then pull up next to her and lie down. I stretch out on the warm, lumpy rock surface, staring up at the sky.

Trying not to think about sex.

Last night's escapade was not enough. Even with all I divulged to Anna today, I daresay she's not ready to sleep with me yet. Perhaps I'm going about this all wrong. Perhaps I should pretend to be smitten. Is that what she'd prefer? Maybe if . . .

What is she doing? I go completely still as her hand tentatively touches my knuckles and her fingers slide between mine, soft and warm and small.

She's holding my hand.

Why is my heart beating so fast? And why does it feel like we're going entirely too fast and too slow all at once? I search the skies for dark whisperers, stretching my senses in a wide arc, but there's no sign of spirits.

I let myself feel her hand in mine, even though Kaidan Rowe does *not* hold hands. The gesture is so simple. So lovely that it rocks something deep inside me. I contemplate pulling away, but decide to let it continue, telling myself it's all an act, and that two hands touching is not a monumental event.

We lie there a bit longer, holding hands and chatting. She

pays close attention as I explain how I visualize the hiding of my aura, and her eagerness draws me in. I find myself wanting her to learn—wanting to assist her. An hour flies by. I'm shocked and relieved by how quickly she catches on. Think of all the other things I can teach her.

That thought sends a shot of lust straight to my groin, and I shift.

Damn it. Focus. We're not finished working on her aura.

Hiding emotions is much more difficult in real terms. I need to see how she handles disguising her feelings under duress. I need to rattle her. Naturally, lust is the first thing that comes to mind, so I let my instincts take over.

"You know, for the record, Anna, I won't think any less of you if you change your mind about doing the things my father expects."

Please change your mind, I silently beg. *Let me train you and have your body just once.* Then maybe this ridiculous craving for her will go away.

I touch her ankle and let my fingers and palm slide up the back of her smooth calf. She is frozen under my touch, trying not to let it affect her. I can see the concentration on her face when her small throat flexes with a swallow. I watch her chest heave in shallow gasps as my fingers meet the bend at the back of her knee, running across the soft crevice. Words pour out of me, an insatiable need growing like a live thing inside me.

"It's just you and me right now, Anna. I felt you come alive when we kissed, and I know you're afraid of that. Afraid to unleash that other side of yourself." I don't realize how true the words are until they're out of me. Her eyes are wide. "But you needn't worry. I can handle her."

I can and I want to. I'm not interested in taming her. Together we could be a wildfire, out of control, feeding off each other's breaths. Wanting, needing, taking, consuming. God, it could be so good.

My hand moves farther up, cupping the muscle of her thigh. I want to keep going, but her hand firmly locks around my wrist to stop me.

I search the aura around her, desperate to see a shock of red. I lean in, ready to devour her mouth the moment her lust shows, but it never does, and the disappointment I feel is palpable. It's a kick to the sack, physically, but mentally I'm torn between being proud of her acquired skills and yet dying to see her colors again. I need to know what she's feeling.

"No," she says. I marvel at how her voice can be soft and firm at the same time. Our eyes lock, and there's so much stirring in her depths. Her long, blond ponytail hangs lazily over one shoulder, untamed wisps of hair escaping. That hair, the way she always ties it back, it's like a symbol of her wild beauty kept under wraps. I want to let it loose. I want Anna to come undone in my hands.

It's only lust, I tell myself. But seducing Anna is proving to be a different sensation—something foreign and distinctly dangerous.

It's because she's Neph, I reason.

It's because she's your most difficult conquest yet.

It's because her angel voodoo is fucking with your head.

Yes. All of it.

I break away from her and bend a knee to block my body's

reaction to the lust test. She watches my face closely, always searching.

"Sorry, I had to play dirty," I tell her, and she sort of nibbles her lip. "Some people work better under pressure. Now, if you don't mind, I should probably walk it off."

Yeah, I need to get away from her. I jump down from the rocks and pace, breathing in the night air. When my body is finally under control, I find Anna waiting patiently atop the rock. My stomach stirs with a strange feeling at the sight of her, and I want to stab myself for being so weak.

I reach up to help her down, saying, "Come on." She takes my hand without hesitation, and we walk silently to the hotel.

I'm relieved she's learned to hide her emotions. We're one step closer to having her trained. Now all I have to do is bang the innocence out of her, deliver her to her demon father, and find out what that nun lady wants with her. Then I can deliver her back to the world in good conscience, and never have to see her again.

I'm halfway through my shower when it becomes glaringly obvious that I cannot go an entire day without being sated by another willing person. There is no way around it. I was careful tonight not to lose myself to the beast, but it's always there, under the surface, starving for another fix no matter how well I tamp it down. I've always simply accepted it, and for the first time ever, I'm resenting this urge.

What I really want to do is go into that room and claim my place directly between Anna's lovely legs. But I know she's not having any of it. Yet. And I don't have time for a long seduction. I cannot focus. The painful ache is returning to my abdomen, a dense tugging, and I need sex *now*.

I come out of the restroom in cargo shorts, and Anna's eyes flicker over my bare chest. I look for her aura before remembering she can hide it now. But her eyes say enough. She likes what she sees. If only she'd act on it.

I pull a shirt from my bag and finish dressing. It's time to go. I clear my throat, suddenly nervous, which is shite. I cannot possibly care what she thinks. I'm being an idiot.

"Right, then," I say. "I'll just, um, be out for a bit."

Her entire being slumps with disappointment, and I feel as if she's kicked my chest.

"Don't go," she says. Another kick. Where is this coming from?

This is who I am, and I refuse to let her make me feel guilty. Anger rises instead, and I grasp it, feeling more at home in its prickly embrace. Where I really want to be is here, tangled with her, but I know that's not going to happen, which pisses me off.

"I have to work, Anna. Either out there or in here."

Tell me to stay, little Ann. Crook your finger and beckon me over.

"It wouldn't kill you to take a night off," she says, jutting out her tiny chin.

It's kick number three, and anger is giving over to a strong flood of fury.

"Is that so?" I tell myself to relax, but her self-control and judgment and lack of understanding make me want to shake her. Words drip from my mouth like venom. "Says the little doll who's never had to work a day in her life?" She is not being what she's supposed to be. *I am.* She doesn't know that once you give in to the beast there's no going back. You must feed it.

But she keeps pushing me—keeps talking about shite she can't comprehend—keeps trying to make me feel bad for what I am.

"It's not like demons are monitoring your behavior," Anna says.

She cannot see the demons, the whisperers. She does not know how they network, how quickly I can be spotted "not working," how they'd rush to turn me in. She doesn't know what it means to live in fear of them showing up at any given minute. But I'm too enraged to communicate any of this.

"Don't push me, Anna," I warn, grasping for control. "You don't know what you're talking about."

Nobody has ever made me feel this way. I can see she's worked up, too, her face pink and her eyes intense. I have to leave. As I turn to go, she shouts, "You can make it one night without sex!"

Rage blinds me like a white flash, and my body reacts. Her next words are drowned out as a need to destroy something bears down on me, and I swing at the nearest lamp, sending it flying. It smashes against the wall with a satisfying *crash*, leaving my ears ringing. I point hard at Anna, who needs to get a bloody clue and stop pushing my buttons.

"You. Don't. Understand!" I am panting with an overflow of emotion. She appears ashen, staring at me like I've kicked a kitten, and it's all too much. I drop my arm. I'm out of here. "Don't wait up this time."

I nearly steamroll an ancient couple when I burst into the hallway. I leave them tottering there as I take the stairs down to the first floor. The hotel has a bar and it's hopping with a dance area.

Ah, bloody hell. They're square dancing to country music.

My eyes dart to a bored-looking woman at the end of the packed bar, nursing a margarita. Early thirties. Gray business suit. Black hair waving to her shoulders. No time to waste. I sidle up next to her, waiting to catch the bartender's attention. I feel the woman watching me, so I glance over. She quickly looks away, a fizz of orange excitement in her aura. My eyes drift to the cleft of cleavage exposed at the top of her blouse. I check out her ring finger. Bare. Possibly divorced? Her nails are manicured and she takes good care of herself.

I give a nonchalant nod. "Hallo."

She smiles and confidently brushes her hair from her shoulder. "London?"

I nod, sweep my eyes over her. She looks away again, and her body language says she's not interested, but her aura says otherwise. I hope she'll not play hard to get.

"I'm Kaidan."

"Celeste. And I'm way too old for you," she says, as if that will put an end to my interest. I laugh at her openness and stick out my hand. She eyes it a moment before shaking it, and turns her attention back to her drink.

The bartender finally comes over. I hand him my fake ID and say, "Jack on the rocks."

I feel her perk next to me as she takes in the exchange; hopefully she believes I'm twenty-one now.

"Celeste. Mind if I sit?" I motion to the stool next to her.

"Free country. Do as you like." She absently stirs her margarita as I sit. Methinks Celeste is a tad jaded. But I can work with that. I can work with anything.

"Staying at the hotel?" I ask.

"Real estate conference. You?"

"I'm here for the night. Headed to L.A." A blast of pain in my gut urges me on. *Keep her talking.*

She takes a long drink. "What's in L.A.?"

"My band," I lie.

"Let me guess," she says sarcastically. "Lead singer."

I laugh and throw back half my drink, relishing the burn, before setting it down and looking at her again. "Drums."

"Mmm." A flash of red trots into her aura. She finishes off the margarita. I order her another.

"You didn't have to do that," she says.

"I know."

She sips her margarita, licking a touch of salt from the rim. I watch her tongue, the beast growling inside me.

"How old are you, Kaidan?"

I'll never understand why women are so obsessed with age. I level her with my gaze, getting serious. "Old enough to bring you more pleasure than you ever thought imaginable."

Celeste's eyes widen a fraction, her aura blazing red before returning to a gray of distrust. "Those are big words," she says.

I chuckle. "Good thing I can back them up." I throw back the rest of my drink and set the glass down hard.

"Look, you're wasting your time here. There's a girl over there with her eye on you," Celeste says, nodding across the dance floor. "Maybe you should go talk to her."

I don't even glance where she's pointing, because I'm invested now. I love a challenge.

Without looking at Celeste, I say, "I prefer women to girls," signaling to the bartender. He pours a new drink and slides it in front of me.

The music gets louder, and if possible twangier, making people cheer. I send my hearing up to our room and find only silence, then a rustle as Anna turns over in the bed. Her breathing is even, slow. Is she asleep already? She's not upset about my show of temper? Isn't she at all curious what I'm up to?

Beside me, Celeste lets out a small laugh, shaking her head. "Do you know how long it's been for me?"

The margaritas are catching up with her.

"No idea, but I'd be happy to remedy that for you."

She shakes her head like I'm full of shite and asks, "Why?"

"Because you're sexy."

She narrows her eyes. "Like I said, you're wasting your time."

"I don't think I am, actually."

We nurse our drinks in silence. After a few minutes of this, she sighs. "You're not giving up, are you?"

"No, Celeste. I'm not." I turn to her.

She thrums the bar top, staring at her hand. "I don't have condoms."

My insides jump, but my face stays passive and confident. "I do."

Her face turns up to me and we stare. The beast claws at the ground in anticipation.

"Fine." Celeste tries to look bored, unaffected, but her aura is a dazzling display of the opposite. "We can go to my room. . . ."

I nearly close my eyes and sigh with relief. That was the longest forty minutes of my life. I praise the forwardness of older women who know exactly what they want. I throw money on the bar and lean forward, my face inches from hers.

"Brilliant, Celeste. You're an angel."

The word *angel* catches on my tongue. The relief I'd been feeling suddenly wavers and I curse Anna as guilt shoves its way back into my consciousness. For a fleeting moment I imagine telling this woman I've changed my mind. I imagine what it would be like to ignore the throb of pain and go back up to my room to be near Anna.

It's a completely pointless and idiotic thing for me to ponder. There is absolutely no reason not to do this. I place my hand on the small of Celeste's back and lead her out of the bar. I want what I want, and I'm going to get it.

CHAPTER SEVEN

Sold

"I'm starting to want you, more than I want to . . .
I just want to make you go away, but you taste like sugar."
—*"Like Sugar" by Matchbox Twenty*

Anna doesn't stir when I slip back into the room in the dead of night and take another shower. Her heavy sleeping is a sign of her overly trusting nature. She is never on guard, never listening, completely unaware of her surroundings. It's infuriating. I don't want to have to worry about her safety once this trip is over. I don't want to have to think about her at all.

And yet, as I fall asleep she fills my dreams.

We begin to square dance together to that horrid badonka-donk song, and we're both quite good. But it's one of those dreams that's so fucking weird you wish you couldn't remember it. In my dream, Celeste cuts in on our dance. This angers Anna, who slides over to the bartender, snogging him to make me jealous. I wake early, flustered and frustrated, and I realize I've been going about this all wrong.

I've been trying to have my cake and eat it, too. I'm not doing myself any favors by letting Anna know I'm sleeping with other chicks. Jealousy often helps get girls right where you want them, but not Anna. She's not going to offer herself up just to keep me from going to another. I vow to be nicer for the rest of the trip. And when I leave to work at night, I will pretend I'm doing something else. What a bloody knobhead I've been.

I'm feeling bright and chipper at breakfast after my revelation, especially after I realize Anna has long since forgiven me for my Hulk Smash moment with the lamp. I flirt with her, teasing her, giving her every bit of my attention. I watch her blush and listen to her giggle. I'm determined to win that body over if it's the last bleedin' thing I do. I even let her drive.

I don't expect Anna to have such a lead foot, and naturally her need for speed turns me on. I play game after game on my mobile to distract myself.

"Do you mind if we stop?" she asks.

I look up at the small Native American reservation, which piques my interest. "Not at all."

New Mexico is hot as hell—a dry heat that reminds me of the western Cape of South Africa. The reservation has an old-world feel that gives me a false sense of ease. Anna is in her element, flitting around like a butterfly and smiling at everyone.

I watch her examine jewelry, spending an especially long time staring at a turquoise necklace. It's the perfect piece for her, shaped like a heart. She turns it over, holds it up, practically pets it, then looks at the price tag. She quickly sets it down and steps away. Curiosity tugs me to her side. She obviously adores it—why doesn't she buy it? Then I recall her and her mum's money problems, which are unheard of for a Neph. I catch sight of the price tag and feel indignant on Anna's behalf. She should be able to have whatever she wants.

"See anything you like?" I ask.

I think I startle her because she jumps a little and moves even farther away from the necklace.

"Yeah. It's all beautiful, isn't it?"

Strange feelings wrestle around inside me. She won't admit she likes the necklace, as if she feels shameful for coveting it.

"Can I . . . get you something?"

Her neck and cheeks turn bright pink. "Oh. No. I don't need anything, but thank you."

It's baffling. She'd probably rather die than ask me to buy it for her. But I really want her to have it.

Whoa. I blink, desperately needing to examine the reasons behind this feeling.

Girls like gifts.

It will make her think I care.

This little gem could get me laid.

Those are my only reasons. Right? Right.

Sold.

But not in front of her. I don't think she'll allow it, and I don't want a scene. So I send her out to cool off the car while I buy drinks. The old whittling bloke gives me a knowing nod as I present the necklace and drinks.

"For your love," he says in a dry, crackly voice.

My stomach swoops in an arc. I let out a dry laugh. "No, no. Nothing like that."

He gives another knowing nod, accompanied by a grin this time. I want to tell the old fool to take back his cursed words. Now I feel jumpy. I pay and get out of there as fast as I can. I hope Anna wasn't listening.

She's clueless when I climb in and hand her a drink. My brain is a flurry of blurred activity as Anna drives away, chatting merrily. I feel like smiling for no good reason when I think of the stupid necklace in my pocket. I want to punch myself in the face and remind myself this is all part of the plan. I needn't have so much fun with it. The fun will come when she's finally naked.

"Will we be passing the Grand Canyon?" Anna asks. "I've always wanted to see it."

That'd be brilliant. I pull up the map on my mobile, but the search leaves me disappointed. We can't afford the extra time.

"It's a bit out of the way. More than an hour." Her father's not going anywhere, but the nun she needs to see is apparently on her deathbed. We can't waste too much time. "But how about this? We can go on the way back, since we won't have a time crunch."

That seems to make her very happy, and I'm far too happy at the moment, as well. Probably because it feels like I'm winning her over bit by bit.

But I can't seem to rid myself of this light feeling, even as we talk about serious things. When it gets quiet for a bit, Anna snorts out a giggle.

"What's up with you?" I ask.

"Are you *sure* it's not possible for a Nephilim to have the influence?"

I narrow my eyes at the strange question. Dukes are powerful enough to influence humans through their words, and even by pushing thoughts to them. They can't force them to do anything, but they can strongly urge them. It would be amazing to have that ability.

"I've never heard of anyone having it except a Duke, and trust me, I've tried. It doesn't work." Still, my assurance leaves her looking skeptical.

We stop at a convenience shop for the loo, and as I approach the door to leave I get the most bizarre urge to spin around on one foot. So I do.

Wait just a damned second . . . I just did a ballerina move. In public. *What the hell?*

I look up and see Anna dart into an aisle, nearly falling over herself with laughter.

No way. No fucking way. My mind reels. She cannot possibly influence people like one of the Dukes. Can she? But then I remember she *is* different. She has two angels as parents, not just one, so who knows what else is possible. I'm overwhelmed with pride on her behalf, and sheer jealousy. Plus a bit of shock that she'd use it on me.

"Oooh, so not funny." I leave the shop shaking my head. When she climbs into the vehicle trying not to laugh, I have to physically hold myself back from grasping her and giving her payback, Kaidan style.

I'm having more fun than I can ever recall having. It's a heedless, stupid feeling, and I can't let it go. She starts making me laugh and I can't stop. We laugh together over the stupidest shit, and I stop trying to remind myself that it's all part of my plan. I tell myself I'm just trying to win her over.

But then I just let go of all thought and give in to the mood.

In those moments something happens I can't explain. All I know is that it feels right, and I can't hold it back. I don't want to.

I let myself feel. And it's good.

CHAPTER EIGHT

A NEW CRAVING

"I can feel you watching even when you're nowhere to be seen,
I can feel you touching even when you're far away from me."
—*"Voodoo Doll" by 5 Seconds of Summer*

We make good time. As we near L.A., I consider going straight to a hotel, but I'm not quite ready to throw us into another awkward situation.

"It's still early," I say. "Let's drive through L.A. or Hollywood."

Anna agrees, and moments later she squeals, "Oh, my gosh, Kai, look! The Hollywood sign!"

God, her excitement is cute. Every little thing. It's amazing. And then I replay her words.

"You called me Kai." It's the first time, and it feels . . . big. I have no idea where all these pansy-arsed feelings are coming from and how I keep letting them slip in so easily, or why it feels less and less important for me to block them. It's like I'm rebelling against my own damned self.

"What are your friends like?" Anna asks. She's turned toward me, practically bouncing in her seat to learn more about me and the people in my life. My vision darkens at the reminder that my friends are Neph. I am Neph, and Anna is Neph. I cannot forget that, no matter how far removed I might feel from that life at this particular moment.

So, I decide to be honest about each of them—Blake, the son of the Duke of Envy, Marna and Ginger, the daughters of the Duke of Adultery—they work, just like me. They understand this life.

I can see from Anna's frown that my explanations disturb her and her ideas of right and wrong and justice, but she needs to know.

And then there's Kopano, son of the Duke of Wrath. He is more difficult to explain. My feelings toward him are a tightly wound bundle of admiration and jealousy.

Kope was trained at eleven and worked several years until having an extreme change of heart. As a young teen he defied his father and refused to work any longer. With anyone else, this would have resulted in death, but Duke Alocer turns a blind eye to his son's defiance. None of the Dukes know about Kopano's resistance of his wrathful nature. Only our small group knows.

To make matters more insane, Kopano not only suffers from the sin of wrath, but he's also inflicted with the sin of lust, which his father promoted hundreds of years ago before my father was brought to earth to take some of the load. I am the only Neph who knows this, because I figured it out on my own. How he fights against two urges is beyond me.

To be honest, I'd prefer to never be around Kope, because his presence is maddening. So bloody noble he makes me ill. I try to keep my voice even as I tell Anna about Kope. I'm careful to leave out the lust part.

Anna is watching me too carefully as I explain Kopano's situation, and I wonder if I've sparked too much interest in him. The two of them would make the perfect saintly Neph pair, a thought that sends a burn through my chest. I wait for Anna to say something like, "If he can go against his nature, why can't you?" or some shite that will send me off the deep end again. It's just not that simple.

"Kope is a mystery," I quickly say with finality.

I'm relieved when she lets it drop.

A lot of lust lives in Hollywood, along with every other sin. Some areas of the city are a cesspool of funk and desperation. An ugly part of me stirs when I think about diving headfirst into what's being offered, but I shake the dark thought away, afraid Anna will be able to sense it. Then I look over and see that she's pressed back into her seat, her forehead tense.

Oh, no. Is she *feeling* all of this? The thought that Anna, with all her positive energy, is taking in all the negativity given off by these people makes me want to roll over all of these convertibles and get her the hell out of here. I have no idea where this protective instinct has come from, but I can't control it.

"Is it too much for you here?" I ask.

"It's hard," she admits. "But not because it's Hollywood. Even Atlanta is hard for me sometimes."

She's downplaying it.

"I'll get us out of here," I say. When we stop at a light, I scroll through my mobile's GPS for the best side street to get us off the main road.

I hear a click and zip and look over to see Anna opening her wallet. What the? Tell me she's not giving money to one of those celebrity home tour scammers. I peer over and see who she's staring at. An old, homeless woman.

Don't, I think to myself. That kind of giving act makes blokes like me squirm with discomfort. It's too much.

"You're wasting your money," I say. The woman's probably a drunk or something.

"Maybe," Anna whispers. "Maybe not."

I hold my breath and watch in awe as Anna rolls down the window and the woman makes her way to the car. The way they stare at each other sends a chill down my spine.

"God bless you," the woman says to Anna as she takes the money. Her aura is clear and grateful, which means she's not high or drunk, as I'd suspected. Before she can turn to leave, Anna is opening her purse and dumping out all of the money into the woman's hands.

I'm an outsider watching their intimate exchange, but I can't look away. I've never seen anything like this happen between two strangers. Complete openness. Selflessness. Thankfulness.

I feel strange. The woman walks away and Anna rolls her window up. She seems at peace for a moment, and then she looks back down at her wallet and her face falls.

"I'm sorry," she says. "That was presumptuous of me. But she—"

"What on earth are you apologizing for?" My eyes roam

her beautiful face, her tied-back hair, her swirled badge. She drops her eyes and I realize she feels bad because now I'll have to cover her expenses. It must've given her some sense of comfort to know she could pay for something if necessary.

I tear my eyes from Anna and back to the road when the light turns. My hands tingle, and it's spreading. My heart is beating entirely too hard as unfamiliar feelings swell to an alarming size, filling every available space of my body and soul.

I'm nervous and excited all at once. I want her. I want Anna with every hot-blooded cell of my body, and I wish I could say it was only lust. Lust is familiar. What I'm feeling is huge and frightening and altogether unfamiliar. I want more than her skin and touch. I want *all* of her—all the madness that goes along with a female—the small touches and laughter, the talking after the hookup, the phone calls and hand-holding. I want it more than I've ever needed sex.

Bugger. Shite. No. This is too much for me. I am freaking out.

And then I nearly slam on the brakes and shout. Up ahead on the boulevard is a shadowy demon spirit. It takes all my control not to panic and bust a U-turn in the middle of Hollywood Boulevard, bunging up every car in my path, but that would draw even more attention. So I keep calm as I speak.

"Legionnaire." I hold my hand down and point in the direction of the demon whisperer. Anna sucks in a breath and stares around blankly. She still can't see them! I explain what the spirit is doing. "Whispering to that man in the blue suit. If he comes this direction I'm going to ask you to hide. Be ready to move."

She slides lower in the seat and we both watch the contact between a man and a prostitute. I wish Anna didn't have to see this. I'm prepared to order her down to the floor, but when the couple walks off, the whisperer flies down an alley and is gone.

I grip the wheel and grit my teeth to keep from shaking. Bringing Anna into Hollywood was royally stupid. I mumble angrily and get us out of there, wanting to bowl down every slow pedestrian in my path. What had I been thinking? I'd been so keen on wanting to watch her experience life that I forgot about the myriad of negative experiences to be had as well.

When had I *ever* forgotten that before now? Never. It's usually the other way around.

I am so deeply ensnared in her angel voodoo. I know I should run. I should drop her at the nearest hotel and leave her far behind like the ticking bomb she is, but I feel as if I physically can't. A new craving has taken root and the deepest part of me salivates for it. I can't leave her yet.

Just a bit longer, I tell myself. I promised Patti I'd get Anna to this nun and to Duke Belial, and then I will leave her for good and get my mind right again.

However, for now I think I'll let myself indulge in this new sensation while I can. I feel as if I'm carrying some epic secret, and the only reason I'm safe is that nobody else will ever know. It's so rare to feel anything different, anything *positive*, and this is most definitely out of the ordinary. Shiny. New. Amazing.

Temporary.

In our room I change into basketball shorts and flop onto my bed.

"We could go for a swim," I suggest.

"Didn't bring a bathing suit," she tells me.

Damn. I don't suppose the hotel allows skinny-dipping.

"Kaidan . . ." Her sweet voice sails over me, relaxing me. "What happened to all of the Nephilim? Why are there so few of us now?"

So much for feeling relaxed. She will not let this subject go until I tell her. Yes, she needs to know our Nephilim history, but I hate seeing how it affects her. Female tears are one of my least favorite substances in creation.

I sigh and move to sit next to her. She listens raptly as I explain the Great Purge—the killing of every Neph on earth over one hundred years ago—and the measures the Dukes have since taken to keep our numbers at bay.

Anna covers her mouth in horror as it sinks in. "They sterilize them?" There's shock and question in her eyes.

"Yes, me too," I say. "All of us had the procedure." I'd been eleven when Father flew a Neph doctor from India to our London home to give me a vasectomy. My body had burned through the pain meds faster than the doctor could administer them. I cringe as I recall it.

Anna becomes angry and indignant now. She jumps to her feet to pace and turn away from me, but I can see in the way she wraps her arms around herself that she's crying. I lie back against the headboard.

"I knew it would only upset you," I say with regret.

"Of course it upsets me! Doesn't it upset you?"

She looks right at me, full of passion about the things I don't let myself ponder.

"There's no use wasting time thinking about things that can't be changed."

She comes back over and sits next to me, pulling her knees up to her chin and sliding her feet under the blanket. I want to comfort her with my arms, because I don't have the words to make any of this right. I move closer, talking low, and take her hand into mine.

She watches our hands together—the way I trace her small fingers and thumb. I want her to look up at me.

Look at me, lovely Anna.

We're so close. I want a redo on our kiss. I want to do it properly this time, and stay in control of the beast. I want to own that gorgeous mouth for as long as she'll let me. I want to roll around the bed with her, completely clothed, testing the limits of my control for this girl until she's ready for more.

Her heartbeat is visible in the soft skin at her neck—fast and hard. I'm making her nervous. With disappointment, I raise her hand to my mouth and kiss the pad of her thumb. Then I let her go and stand. I'm shocked by how good I feel, even with the low rumble of constant pain plaguing me.

"Get some rest," I say.

She scrambles under the covers and hides her face. I wish I could see her colors.

I climb into my own bed, though I'm not at all tired. My skin is prickling with energy and the low throb of pain pulses in my abdomen. Can I truly go a whole day without feeding the beast? Today, I feel as if I can fight it. I feel like I can take on the world. For the first time ever, I want to attempt not to work.

"Kaidan?" she whispers.

My pulse sprints. "Yes?"

"I'm not trying to judge. I'm just curious. Um . . . are you going out tonight?"

The concern and jealousy in her voice send a thrill to my core and I bite down and swallow. "I don't think I will."

She says nothing as my heart pounds, and I'd do anything to see her colors again. Is she happy? Is she proud of me?

I'm not ready to fall asleep. Tomorrow is a big day for Anna. The day she meets her father. The plan was to meet the nun first, but when Anna called the convent, she was told Sister Mary was not well enough to visit yet.

I know she's nervous, but I don't know how to help her with that. What is special to Anna? People. Her spirituality. I've seen her pray over meals, silently. It freaks me out a bit, I won't lie. Inviting the Maker into one's thoughts . . . I shudder at the idea. But it's part of her, and I need her to know I accept it.

"Ann?"

"Yes?"

"It won't bother me if you need to, you know, properly pray, however you do it."

"Oh." She sounds surprised. "Okay, thanks."

She pulls her arms out of the blankets and clasps her hands under her chin.

She's really going to do it, right now. It's so bizarre. Her eyes close and her face calms in meditative peace. My eyes dart about the room, expecting a beam of light or something, but the room remains calm and comfortable.

Anna is talking to God. I could never do that. We are so different. Opposites, really.

Her eyes open and I realize I'm staring like a total creeper. What the hell have I become? I want to laugh at the complete lunacy of my turnabout. It's like I'm a bloody woman or something. Next thing you know I'll be petting puppies and cooing at babies.

Ugh, no. Babies is where I draw the line.

"Good night," Anna whispers. I nod, slightly discombobulated, as she turns out the light, bathing us in darkness.

CHAPTER NINE

First Time for Everything

"Don't wanna let you down, but I am hell bound."
—"Demons" by Imagine Dragons

I wake with a low, underlying ache in my gut.

I am not right in many ways at this moment. I slept so hard last night and this morning that I didn't even hear when Anna woke before me. I only just opened my eyes when I heard the shower cut on. Whisperers could have been swarming the room and I wouldn't have known. I drag a hand through my hair.

The feelings I developed for Anna yesterday haven't gone away—they're still there, glaringly bright and agile inside of me—but a bit of the idiocy has worn off and I can see straighter.

I feel as if this trip has been a joy ride at our own private theme park, teetering dangerously above reality. I'm still on that ride, but the end is in sight. This cannot last forever. On one hand my chest drops into my stomach when I think of being apart from her, and on the other hand I'm eager to get us back to safety, apart from each other. It's stupid to tempt fate, to endanger ourselves.

Just another day or so of this ride, and then it's back to reality.

Speaking of reality, my body is right furious with me. The ache thuds as I imagine Anna in the shower, covered in slick bubbles, her hands sliding over every peak and valley and . . . *ugh, damn it.* I have to stop.

I stand and yank on a pair of cargo shorts and a T-shirt, modifying myself in a way that makes my issue less noticeable. I lean my fists against the side table and squeeze my eyes shut, breathing through the pain like a fucking woman in labor. Then I order room service, because Anna will need her strength when she finally meets her father, Duke Belial, in a few hours.

I haven't let myself think much on their meeting. Now, as I lie back on the bed, I feel dazed at the thought of what might become of the little half angel after this day. When I met Anna's adopted mother, Patti told me she believes Belial has Anna's best interests at heart based on what she was told by the nun, but I am skeptical. He is a demon, and they can be quite convincing.

Nevertheless, there's no hiding for Anna now. My father knows about her. If she tries to hide she will be hunted, found, and killed. I'm doing her a favor by bringing her to Belial. If he tries to make her work, she'll be upset, no doubt, but she'll be alive. My gut twists as I imagine her refusing, and I curse myself for not training her better these two days. Yesterday I selfishly coddled her innocence and soaked in her nurturing spirit, rather than attempting to show her some Neph survival skills, like how to pretend you don't give a shit. Yeah, I should have done things differently, but now it's too late.

Anna comes into the room looking fresh-faced with damp hair, and the beast inside me growls. *I know, boy*, I tell him. *She's bloody gorgeous, isn't she? Ah, the things we'd do to her. . . .*

As I lie there watching Anna braid her own hair, her fingers moving deftly through the smooth, wet locks, I have to bend a knee to block the effect she has on me. I expect my Neph curse to hit with unbearable pain, but it doesn't. Just a steady, low cramp. I can only assume it's because this strange *other* feeling makes me stare at her with an even deeper longing for something far more powerful. I shake off that thought. It can't last. I allowed myself one day of ridiculous thoughts yesterday, and it'll have to be enough to last a lifetime. Playtime is over.

When our food arrives, Anna is too nervous to eat. I wish I could take her fear away. I do have something that might take her mind off it for a moment, though, and for once I'm not talking about sex. I reach in my pocket to feel the smooth turquoise stone there. My heart jumps at the thought of giving it to her, and I need to stand.

I move to the window, still staggering from the madness I feel inside. So many thoughts to muddle through. I want to escort Anna into the prison to meet Belial, but they won't allow me. She is on her own, and I can't protect her. My only consolation is that she and her father will be surrounded by other people.

One way or another, after Anna meets her father today, she will be changed. It's inevitable.

"You've gotten scruffy," comes her soft voice. Her hand is suddenly against my face, her touch pulsing through me. I grasp her hand and shut my eyes. Why do I feel this way? I am not myself when I'm with her. I long for this simple touch far too much.

When I look at her, she tilts her head like the timid fawn she is, searching my soul. I wonder if she sees the blackness there. This is our last day, and then this has to end. I let her go and cross my arms, staring from the window.

"I have something for you," I say.

She brightens and perks up at these words, and I'm suddenly nervous as hell.

Going for nonchalance, I pull the necklace from my pocket and hold it out, but she doesn't take it. She only stares, making me more nervous.

"I saw you looking at it and thought you liked it." Does she remember?

Her face slightly pinches and she blinks. I'm feeling like a fool here.

"Have I upset you?"

"No! I'm not upset. I'm just surprised. I can't believe . . ." Oh, bloody hell. She's crying. "I mean, I *love* it. Nobody's ever given me anything like this."

Oy, she's making a huge deal of it. I've never been a gift giver. Gifts mean something to the giver, even more so than to the receiver most times. I should know. I receive loads of gifts that go straight into rubbish bins. But I'm afraid this means as much to Anna as it does to me, and that's not a good thing. I drop the damned necklace into her hand and curse, shoving my fingers into my hair.

What have I done? I know I wanted to make her fall for me, but she is clearly a romantic. Here I am buttering her up just before she goes to meet her demonic father, who will probably be in shock when he sees just how innocent Anna is. Not that he should be too surprised, considering he slept with a fucking angel to conceive her, but still. I've changed my mind about letting Anna fall for me. It would not be good for her. It's bad enough that I'll likely pine for her like Peter Pan after Wendy. I don't need her doing the same.

"This was a mistake," I mutter.

"No." Her voice is full of emotion when she takes my arm. "It wasn't."

"Don't read into this, Anna. It would be a mistake to romanticize me."

"I'm not," she assures me. "It was a nice gesture. That's all."

Is it? If she believes that, we are both fools.

She wears the necklace to meet Belial. I have to remind myself it's just an inanimate object. An accessory. Not a big deal. But she keeps reaching up and touching it as she stares off, deep in thought.

I have bunged things up royally, and I haven't a clue how to turn it back. Nothing good can come of this, especially once she meets her father. I want to give her a list of warnings—don't tell your father about me, don't let him know how good you are, guard yourself and be careful what you say—but I can't say any of this because we're in the prison parking lot now and Belial could be listening.

The visitor doors open and I swallow hard. "You're up," I say.

I feel ill when she enters the building and leaves my sight. I remain still and listen carefully as she makes it through security, moves into an echoey room, and sits. Soon there are sounds of chains and feet shuffling. I cannot move. I feel paralyzed with helplessness. I'm listening so intently I can hear the shake of Anna's breath. I nearly jump when a guard tells "LaGray" to sit. I didn't know Belial's earthly name.

"I can't believe you're here," says a deep, scratchy voice. I assume this is Belial, and I'm momentarily floored by the gentleness there. He goes on, *". . . I wanted you to have a normal life."*

"There was never any chance of that," Anna says softly.

She doesn't sound scared, and I feel my own fear subsiding. Especially when Belial asks, *"Have they treated you well, the people who raised you?"*

His voice is filled with concern. And as I continue listening for a bit, realization soon hits me—he loves her. Of course he does. Patti was right. I'm certain Belial can sense the depth of her goodness, just as Duke Alocer can sense the goodness in Kopano. *They* are the sort of Neph who can soften even the hearts of demons. *They* are the kind of Neph who deserve love.

A knot that cannot be swallowed forms in my throat. Knowing Anna is safe, I start the car and drive away.

* * *

I peruse L.A. like a sightseer for a couple hours, but I don't really see anything because my mind's a disaster. I don't understand the things I feel. I've always been a moody bastard, but this is beyond my normal scope. I go from rage to tenderness to terror to happiness in a few blinks. Anna's angel voodoo is a dangerous tonic. This is worse than being piss-arsed drunk—it doesn't seem to want to burn off.

I return to the prison with only minutes to spare—L.A. traffic blows.

I push my hearing through the walls of concrete and steel until I find that gruff voice once more, "... *might be different for you. Your mother's good might cancel out my bad. We don't know ...*"

I let out a full breath. She's fine. For the first time ever I feel strange about eavesdropping, so I pull back and ponder his words. I wonder if he's talking about what I think he is: hell. And the fact that Neph are sent to hell after death, no matter what kind of life we've lived. Yes, perhaps it will be different for Anna. Her soul is too good for that kind of darkness. It would be the ultimate injustice, and I'm deeply disturbed pondering her suffering.

I step from the car and lean against it, waiting. From what I can tell, Anna didn't get a verbal beating from her father, and I'm glad for her. When the doors open, and Anna filters out with the others, all the madness I felt today disappears. My blood rushes at the sight of her. But as she gets closer, the look on her face halts my thoughts.

Something is wrong. She ignores me and climbs into the

car. I go around to the driver's side and get us out of there. I want to ask what he did and what he said, but we're still within his five-mile hearing range.

When we're far enough away, I'm about to ask how it went, but she buries her face in her hands and cries the most pitiful, heart-wrenching tears I've ever heard. I have no idea what to say or do to make this better, which makes me feel weak and powerless.

Have I mentioned I hate when girls cry?

Thankfully, after five minutes of this she gives a loud sniff, wipes her eyes, squares her shoulders, and swallows away the rest of her tears.

"Were you listening?" she asks in a thick voice.

"A bit at the beginning and end, to make sure you were all right."

She nods and proceeds to tell me every detail of their conversation. I usually zone out when girls talk this much, but I'm completely rapt with Anna's storytelling. She pulls one knee up and turns her body toward me in the passenger seat, talking fast. I listen to the story of her parents' epic, forbidden love—how they were soul mates in heaven before the Fall, and how he became a Duke to search for her on earth, finally finding her working as a guardian angel. Anna's mother, Mariantha, broke all heavenly rules to inhabit her human charge's drug-sickened body and be with Belial. He never cared about hurting humans, though he pushed drugs to keep his position and he was good at it. But all along, he only cared about Mariantha. For the first time ever, I find myself relating to a Duke.

When I get to the hotel we just park and sit there while

she gets it all out. She hides nothing—making her joy, love, sorrow, and disappointment plain. Her father clearly loves her, but he'd been brutally honest about her fate on earth and afterward. She would have to at least appear to be working for the dark cause. She had to toughen up. I'd been wondering if her father would have positive news about Anna's afterlife. He didn't. She's as hell-bound as any other Neph, as far as Belial knows. A sharp pang rips at my chest at the thought of that doom for her.

It's not right. It's not fair.

I shake my head and turn off the ignition. I haven't worried about whether or not something was "fair" since I was a small child. It hadn't taken long to realize nothing was fair in life. That bloody word shouldn't even exist. But it's the thought that continues to blaze through me—a soul like Anna's should never be confined to hell. How could the One who made her even consider it?

Yet another thing to fill the churning pit of anger that fuels my daily life.

I'm incredibly edgy when we reach the hotel room. So much so that I stand in the doorway while Anna goes in, her arms crossed, lost in thought.

"This hotel has a gym," I tell her. "If you don't mind, I think I'll get in a workout this afternoon while I can."

Physical exertion is exactly what I need.

Anna nods absently and stares at her luggage. "I think I'll do a load of laundry or something."

"I can tell them we'd like laundry service when I pass the front desk."

She gives me a puzzled expression. "Oh, you mean have the hotel do it? No way, that'd be way too expensive. There's a Laundromat right across the street."

I cringe. "You mean with the crackheads?"

Anna snorts and shakes her head. She's already gathering her dirty clothes, and she even reaches for mine, but I step on the shorts she's grabbing.

"You don't have to do mine." I'm a bit appalled. How can she be so casual about this?

"Oh, just let me." She yanks the shorts out from under my foot. "I've had to use a Laundromat lots of times, and it's perfectly safe. It's mostly just moms. I'll just, um, need some money. If that's okay. I mean, not much, just a couple—"

I whip my wallet out in a flash to erase the embarrassed blush staining her cheeks, and thrust a bill at her. "You're sure it's safe? This is L.A., not backwoods Georgia."

"Ha-ha." She snatches the ten and stuffs it in her pocket.

"I'll be listening," I tell her.

She rolls her eyes, but then whispers, "Thanks."

I keep my hearing locked around her for the hour plus that I run on the treadmill and do a series of push-ups and sit-ups. I'd prefer weights right now, but this poor excuse for a gym has none.

Anna's been so quiet at the Laundromat that I decide to see if she's all right with my own eyes. The place is completely dodgy from the outside, but when I walk in it smells clean and there's a calming whir of washers and dryers going. Two old women are power-napping in chairs on the opposite side of the room from where Anna stands with her back to me, folding clothes.

She bends to pull my T-shirt from the dryer, and within two seconds flat my beast sniffs the air and smacks his lips. Anna is far too cute in those shorts. She raises my shirt in front of herself with a flap and does quick work with her fingers, ending with the shirt in the form of a perfect, flat rectangle. Should I be this impressed?

I've moved across the room until I'm just behind her, and I swear she's so focused and lost in thought she doesn't notice. Even after meeting her father and knowing fully what dangers are out there, she is still too trusting. It's a damn good thing it's only me creeping up behind her, and not some dangerous bloke.

And then I remember I *am* a dangerous bloke where Anna is concerned. I still plan to keep her safe from my father by taking her virginity at the first possible opportunity. It's for her own good. The fact that I'll enjoy the hell out of it is inconsequential. The thought of being that close to her sends a stream of heated adrenaline and need through my blood.

Before I can advise myself otherwise, I'm reaching for her waist. She startles at my touch, and I pull the back of her closer into me.

"Just me, luv," I say. I shouldn't let myself get this close, because I can hear the lust in my own voice. I wonder if she can hear it, as well. I wonder if she's feeling the same. There is barely any space between us now, and I'm breathing in her scent from behind like a fiend who can't get enough. Why must she smell so lovely?

"Kai . . . you shouldn't . . ."

No, I really, really should.

I feel her tremble in my hands. "Unless you're going to be my boyfriend, you shouldn't touch me like this."

Boyfriend. I go still, and for a heartbeat I want to smile. Would she want to be attached to me in such a way? Never once in all my life has the word *boyfriend* had a smiling effect on me. *Boyfriend* and *girlfriend* are the most useless, flimsy labels out there, yet people put such stock in them. They trust those labels to mean so much more.

But hearing Anna say it is rather charming and ironic. Like a lethal poison in a candy shell. She has no idea. None at all.

"The Neph are not permitted to be in relationships," I say against her hair. "Especially not with one another."

She's quiet for a moment. "Nobody has to know. Just us."

I am a maelstrom of emotion, spinning too quickly. I want to embrace this moment, have something all to myself, hide her away where she can remain as she is and say these sweet things to me all she wants. I'm filled with a longing far stronger and deeper than lust, and it makes my heart race. I'm out of bounds. Out of my territory. In a perilous place where I cannot afford to be. Ever.

"It can never happen," I say. And I wonder if I'm saying it to her or myself.

Her body stiffens and her chin rises as she gently pries my hands from around her waist. I want to thank her for doing the thing I couldn't do myself. I'm glad one of us is strong enough.

I leave her, taking deep breaths the entire way to the hotel room, attempting to shake off the odd sensations. This has gotten out of hand. I've allowed myself too much leniency where Anna is concerned. It began with harmless fun, but now it's got to stop. Both our lives are at stake, and it's time for me to control the reins.

Tonight, I will take things one step further and show Anna how good it tastes to live on the wild side. I'll buy some alcohol. She's such a lightweight—she'd be seeing the world differently after one wine cooler. I need for her to embrace her fate.

I'm primed and poised when Anna returns. I go for casual, lying on the bed with my feet crossed and a hand behind my head, pretending to watch the telly. She puts the clothes away and rummages through her bags, finally plopping a large book onto the opposite bed. I ignore her scowl.

"What are you getting into?" I ask.

She shoots me a suspicious and rather annoyed glance before saying, "English."

Brilliant. Father made me study the great "romantics." While Anna was memorizing Bible verses in Sunday school, I was memorizing Shakespeare and Byron, and any other rubbish that might get me into girls' knickers.

I flick off the television and go to Anna's bed, opening her book as I lie down. I wonder if she'll be impressed with my skills. I am English, after all. I flick through the pages, and Anna sits as far away as possible. Hm. I'll need to remedy that. I land on the sonnets but am quickly distracted when Anna begins to unbraid her hair. With each wavy strand that is freed from its binding, the book and all of our surroundings disappear.

Anna Whitt's hair is bloody amazing. It's a sin she keeps it held back all the time. It's like heavy, golden silk falling around her, and her face is in absolute bliss as she runs her hands through it.

Must touch it . . .

Hot, raging longing fills my every cell. Blood pumps so fiercely in my ears that I cannot hear the beast pawing the ground, but I know it is, because I'm salivating. When she glances at me I quickly look down. I think she might've caught me.

She flicks through some pages and I can't make out what she's muttered.

"What's the matter?" I ask.

I'm afraid she's about to order me off her bed, but instead she goes on about the summer poetry assignment. Passion is spouting from her pores and I sit up. I can't wait to throw my poetic genius at her.

She goes on and on, oblivious of her own beauty as she waves her fists and purses her lips in indignation. "The beauty of poetry is that it can mean different things to different people at different times. . . . It's wrong to dissect poetry like this!"

She throws down her paper, breathing hard, and I suddenly cannot recall a single line of poetry I've memorized. All I can think about is touching her. Taking a chance that she might slap the shit out of me, I cup her face, surprised how hot her soft cheek is in my hand.

But she doesn't smack my hand or move away. She stares at me, and I stare back.

This girl.

I am no match for her.

"Seriously," she whispers. "You're doing that bedroom-eyes thing again."

Bloody right I am.

All at once we're both crossing the space, crashing in a blaze of lips, ready and seeking, needing and wanting. God, it's that epic feeling again. Like I will die if we can't devour each other and become one. I'm awash in her pear and freesia scent. It tantalizes my every sense.

Our mouths embrace. I'm losing myself, just as I did the other night, and I can't stop it from happening. This is like no lust I've ever experienced. It is all-consuming the way her tongue licks at mine, greeting, teasing, inviting me in further. And so I go.

She kicks her school things to the floor, and I know this is happening.

I must have more of her.

My mouth pulls away, landing on the slight saltiness of her neck. The moan she lets out swells inside my ears and I am flipping her, cradled so perfectly by her legs, ready to own her. There's hunger in her dark eyes as she feels me pressing on all the tender places where no other bloke has ever been. She's gasping and making the sexiest little noises.

I'm surprised when Anna starts to pull my shirt up, but I quickly help, reaching over my head, grabbing it and yanking it off. I go for the top button on her shirt, and when she doesn't stop me I hurry through them, desperate to see and feel as much of this girl as I can. Her shirt and undershirt are finally off in a flick of arms. I'm all but growling as my chest and stomach touch hers, hot and smooth, and our mouths meet once more. I want to savor every moment. She feels incredible underneath me, skin to skin.

The feel of her hands grasping at me—knowing she wants me as I want her—is incredible. I am going to take my time with her, and it's going to take all night.

And then I remember with a pang of disappointment. "What time will Patti be calling?"

"Not for an hour," she whispers.

Far too soon. "That simply is *not* going to be enough time." I don't want any distractions, but I'll take what time I can get. I flip us again so she's on top and I have better access to remove her clothing. I'm leaning partly against the pillows and headboard, and Anna sits across my lap. She takes my lead so perfectly on everything, letting me be in control. Trusting me and going with it.

I have to be careful on this next part because she freaked last time I went near her chest. I will not go for the grab. I concentrate on her shoulders, kissing the smooth skin, and working her bra straps down. Going slow is driving me mad. I want her naked ten minutes ago. I can't remember the last time I've gone this long or wanted something more.

I feel for the back of her strap but then decide to leave her bra on. As much as I want her completely naked, I've known since the night we met that she's self-conscious of her chest size. Completely ridiculous, of course. I'll leave that discovery for later.

When Anna scoots down on me and curls her hips against mine, I go momentarily blind with lust. My control is slipping much faster than normal. Time to meet the arse I've been desperately dreaming about.

One hand goes around her back and I lift my hips, turning us over so she's lying on her back again. I move down, kissing a path along her breastbone, down to the soft mound at the top of her bra. As if begging me not to stop, Anna's hands push into my hair.

Ah, God, this is unbelievable. At every moment I keep expecting her to stop me, but she never does. I move down her stomach to her gorgeous belly button, kissing and tasting every inch. When I get to her shorts I look up and her eyes are shut. Her whole body is fluid, squirming and ready for me.

Take her.

But . . .

Does she know what she's doing? She mightn't be thinking clearly. . . .

Doesn't matter.

My body is screaming. I'm so close. This is what I've wanted. I won't stop now.

With one flick, the button of her shorts is undone. My hands slide under her back and she arches for me. I love the responsiveness of her body, so completely in tune with mine. I lick the skin I've just exposed and she sucks in a massive breath.

This is nothing, I want to tell her. *Wait until you feel what's next.*

She has no idea what she's in for, and though it's all good things in my mind, I feel a sudden unwelcome pang of guilt just as I'm about to unzip her shorts. My defenses go up. I've no reason to feel guilty. I warned her. She knows who I am and what I'm after. So why do I feel the need to warn her again?

"My parents were soul mates in heaven," she'd told me. She'd been created in love by an angel and a demon who were separated because of others' lies and deceit. She is nothing like me. She gives all her money away to needy strangers, and has a heart for the downtrodden.

Who cares? Keep going, you bloody fool, before she changes her mind!

I never let myself think of how the girl will feel afterward while I'm working, but this doesn't feel like a job. I don't *want* it to be a job. I shove my inner work voice aside and give her one last warning.

"Now would be the time to stop me, luv. You're about to be undressed, and trust me when I say it will be too late after that."

She's going to stop me now. I know it, and I feel a sense of relief. I kiss her stomach one last time while I can, so grateful to be this close to her for these fleeting moments.

And then she says in a sultry voice, "No, Kai. Don't stop."

I freeze. She's giving permission.

Don't stop.

I have to kiss the mouth that said those words. When I do, our bodies move together, and she's clinging to me, rocking me from the inside out. And though there's clothing between us, it's the most sensual and satisfying thing I've ever experienced.

My chest swells with an abundance of that feeling only Anna can give me. It overpowers the beast inside me with its luminescence. A single thought echoes through my mind: it's time to stop. I don't even understand why. Clearly, Anna is ready. She has told me as much, and her body is screaming it, rubbing against me in a way that makes me want to explode.

It's time to stop.

"We . . . ," I mumble. "Baby, I . . . we have to . . ." Stop.

I am baffled by this thought. It's as if it's coming from a greater power outside me. With sudden clarity I know Anna will regret this spontaneous decision to sleep with me, for reasons I can't begin to understand, but I *know.* Something will not be right if we do this. The sureness of it is enough to scare the shite out of me.

I shake my head. My entire body goes stiff and I try to lift myself, but Anna has ahold of me, and she's whimpering for more like a needy little vixen.

I have to momentarily close my eyes against the sight of her.

"We can't," I whisper.

"Kai?" The sound of the surprise and hurt in her voice kills me. I want to give her what she wants—what we both want.

It's time to stop.

I want so badly to ignore this stupid fucking feeling of intuition, or whatever the hell it is, and take this girl with every ounce of strength in my body, but I don't dare. I've never had a feeling this strong and clear. When I attempt to move off her, she tightens her hold around my waist. Her back arches underneath me again, lifting her hips to mine in the most agonizing way. I am about to lose all control.

"Damn it, Ann, please! Don't. Move."

Our gazes collide, and we're both panting with unsated need. She's gorgeous and so bloody hot for me that I have to look away.

And move. Quickly. I get my arse off the bed, and immediately that overpowering sense of intuition leaves me, and it's just me and the beast. Scorching pain racks me from thigh to stomach, and my head gives a giant throb. I grab my hair, pacing—I can't stay still. What have I done to myself? It feels as if I might die. I try to shake away the excruciating headache that makes me barely able to open my eyes, but it's no use.

"You don't want me." Anna's small voice shoots straight through my ears and down to my core, making me groan with animalistic longing. Her eyes water and she looks lost.

Can she not see how I want to ravish her like the devil I am? I like to think of the beast and myself as separate entities, but I'm fooling myself. We are one and the same. Right now I want to give in to my darkest urges, throwing caution and gentleness aside, shredding every scrap of cloth between us, and overpowering her body with mine to see how loud her sweet voice can get.

"Don't do that," I struggle to say. "That was the single most difficult thing I've done in my entire life."

I stand, trying to clear my head.

"I don't understand, then," she whispers.

No, no she doesn't. And neither do I.

"You didn't do anything wrong, okay? And don't think for a second I don't want you—" I push my knuckles against my pounding forehead. "But it shouldn't be like this."

"Like what?" she asks.

Everything is wrong. I don't even know how to explain it. I'm so bloody frustrated. Why is she asking me these questions? Is she blind to the kind of person she is, and the kind I am? None of this is good enough for her.

"Uncommitted," I say. "In a hotel room."

"Then commit." Her voice is resolute. As if it's that simple.

I throw my arms out, at a loss. "I can't!" That is not my life, and will never be. She can try to slum it with me all she wants, and fool herself into thinking it's okay, but I know the difference between us. Eventually, she will, as well.

"I'm not taking your virginity," I tell her. "You would regret it."

I lean my forehead against the wall, but the pain in my gut is too powerful to stand. I turn and slide to the floor, elbows on my knees, face in my hands. My abdomen contracts in anger as I force myself to breathe.

I hope she understands. I hope she can forgive me and move on with her life, realizing how narrowly she escaped being ruined by the biggest bastard she'll ever meet. I will take her to that convent and then we must go our separate ways. She and Patti can move to the middle of nowhere and she can attempt to live in peace. It's good that we didn't have sex—this way she'll be able to forget about me, and she'll be okay.

I look up at her, feeling a sliver of hope for her, and that's when I see it.

She's staring right at me, and floating around her body like a grand cotton-candy swirl is the pink of love. For half a second my heart rejoices—*she loves me*. And then I realize . . . I've ruined her anyhow.

I shut my eyes and lose all energy.

In a perfect world I would stand and take her in my arms. In a perfect world I would be her stupid boyfriend and make love to her all night without worry. In a perfect world I'd tell her the words I've been too afraid to admit to my own self.

As quickly as my heart swells, it seizes in terror. Anna doesn't know the stories of Neph who fell in love and attempted secret relationships, only to be executed in horrific public displays as warnings to other Neph.

I will not allow that to happen to Anna.

I hear her moving about the room but cannot bear to open my eyes yet. When the phone rings I still don't move, but I listen to her conversation.

Holy shite. The nun is dead.

CHAPTER TEN

ONE-WAY FLIGHT

*"I'm the devil's son straight out of hell, and you're an angel
   with a haunted heart.
If you were smart you'd run and protect yourself, from a demon
   living in the dark."*
—*"Save Yourself" by* My Darkest Days

I'm not accustomed to hanging around once things get awkward. I know Anna expects me to say something, but I can't. I take her to the convent to get whatever this nun has left her, and then take her back to the hotel room. We sit on her bed and I use my knife to open the box. I won't lie, I'm dying of curiosity—but what we find inside takes me completely by surprise.

I stare down at the shimmering hilt. Every major pulse point in my body is pounding erratically. This cannot be what I think it is. . . .

"May I?" I ask.

"Go ahead." She nods toward the mysterious sword hilt.

I pick it up with care, and it's warm in my hands. The metal feels solid, but just under the surface it seems to swirl as if made of liquid.

Blood slams inside my ears and head. "I don't believe it," I whisper.

"What?" Anna asks. "What is it?"

Could it be a heavenly relic? I quickly drop it back into the box and close my hands into fists. Anna reaches for it, and the second her fingers touch it she gasps and yelps, yanking her hand away as if she's been stung. This confirms everything I need to know.

"What is this thing?" She stares at it with distrust.

"It clearly wasn't forged on earth. I think— But it's impossible. A Sword of Righteousness?" Saying the words out loud sends a wave of cold over me. I've heard tales of these weapons, but I've never heard of one being on earth.

"What's that?" she asks in awe.

"They were used by the angels in the war of the heavens." Used by angels, feared by demons.

"But why is she giving it to me?" Anna asks.

Why, indeed? Was this nun truly human?

"Only the angels of light could use them. The old legends say the blade will appear when needed if the wielder is pure of heart. Anna . . . it's the only known weapon that can take out a demon spirit."

We stare at each other, and her eyes are wide when she asks again, "And why is she giving it to *me*?"

Isn't it obvious? Anna is good and pure and full of innocence, like an angel. The Sword of Righteousness reacted to her touch. But in my sordid hands it was useless. There have always been major differences between us, but in this moment it's as if stone barriers are erected around her.

OFF-LIMITS.

She is destined for something I cannot fathom. Something I could easily ruin if I stay near her. Today I had a freak moment of strength, but I can't guarantee that will ever happen again. I need to get her to safety, away from me.

Her eyes have gone a bit foggy with shock.

"I need to clear my head," I say absently as I grab my wallet and keys. I give Anna instructions to call Patti on the room phone, and I rush out.

My hands are shaking and my stomach churns when I climb into my vehicle and start the ignition. I drive two miles away and park in a shop's lot. It only takes a few minutes to do a one-way-flight search. It's already after dark, but I'm hoping I can get Anna on a late flight tonight.

No such luck. Damn it. I slam my palm on the steering wheel. I don't want to chance another night with her, but I also feel ill at the thought of having her out of my sight. I book her for the earliest flight back to Atlanta in the morning, and then my gut twists as I make a more difficult call.

"Miss Patti?" I say when she answers. "It's Kaidan Rowe— before you ask, everything is all right." She lets out a huge breath. "Erm, have you spoken to Anna yet?"

"Yes, we just got off the phone. Are you okay, Kaidan?"

"Well . . ." I clear my throat and gather my wits. "I've just run into some issues and I won't be able to drive Anna home after all, so I've booked her a flight."

"Issues? Are you in danger?" Her concern makes the back of my throat burn.

"No," I lie. We're always in danger. "Nothing like that. Let me give you her flight information."

She takes it down, and when we hang up I get out, keeping a constant watch for demon whisperers. Remembering Anna has no money for her trip home, I stop at a corner ATM and take out cash for her. Then I walk. I can't go back to her yet.

It's a busy street with two nightclubs and a bar. I must be giving off pheromones like a champ because heads are swiveling my direction as we pass and red auras are popping up, even through the haze of drunkenness here and there. For once I'm unfazed, despite the needling ache deep within.

I need to walk it off. Or run. Or pound something with my fists. Because for once in my life I want something—truly want something—that I cannot have.

"Hey, you," murmurs a girl in a black dress who's getting out of a car with her friends. She touches my arm, but I keep walking, slipping right past her. I pinch the bridge of my nose.

Lust is the groveling cousin of love. It's the house made of straw and sticks. It cannot compare. I was a fool to think chasing lust forever could be enough. That is not a life. I would take one moment of love with Anna over a lifetime of meaningless lust, but I can't. That's not my fate, and it hurts worse than anything I could imagine. God, if my father could see me now. He would have my balls for tea.

I walk and walk until I'm craving Anna's presence so strongly it sends me jogging back to the lot where I left my car. I half expect to be pulled over as I speed back to the hotel, but L.A. cops are too busy to worry with me.

I run up to the room and am blasted with Anna's scent when I open the door. I practically tremble as I breathe her in. A stab of abdominal pain hits me, but I ignore it as I walk into the room. She's restless in sleep, and I want to climb into her bed and hold her. I'm a fucking mess as I sit on my bed, longing like a heartsick boy for the girl on the other side of the room.

I set the alarm for four thirty, but there's no hope of sleep for me. This could be my last time with Anna, and I just want to experience these hours of being in her presence.

Four thirty is a right bitch. Anna is confused and groggy when the alarm goes off and I tell her we need to get an early start. I don't have the heart just yet to tell her I'm taking her to the airport. Our grand adventure is over. That bubble has popped, and reality is glaring into my face, as hideous as ever.

Like the good girl she is, Anna gets ready and climbs into my car without complaint. I feel my mood plummeting to wicked depths as we approach the airport.

"Where are we going?" she asks sleepily.

My heart picks up speed with nervousness.

"You're going home today. Everything's been arranged. Patti will be waiting for you when your flight arrives in Atlanta."

"Why?" She sits forward a bit so she can look at me.

"Things have gotten too complicated."

"Do you mean because of the sword or because of me?" she asks. She doesn't sound happy, and I'm afraid this will get ugly. Why must I constantly explain the danger we're in? Why is she unable to grasp these facts?

"It's you," I say. *It's everything about you.* Everything I'm not. Everything I can't have. Anger at the injustice of it all rises up to suffocate me.

"Is it so unbearable to be around someone who cares for you?" she asks.

Let's not beat about the bush.

"I'd say you're feeling a bit more than 'care' for me, Anna. I could see your emotion popping around you like pink bubble gum last night."

"So what?!" she yells. "I haven't tried to *say* it to you. I'm sorry I lost focus for a second and let you see it!"

I grit my teeth and take the airport exit. This entire situation is driving me mad. The sooner she's away from me, the better. "Don't be dramatic about this."

"You don't call this dramatic? Abandoning me at the airport before daylight?"

Abandoning? As if I'd leave her in an unsafe situation.

"I'll see that you're in safe hands before I leave."

"Don't bother!" She's seething, and her angry passion stirs me. But then everything shifts as her chin trembles. "I've never even been on a plane before."

I desperately hope she doesn't cry. I prefer her anger to her tears.

"You'll be fine," I say.

"I want to stay with you."

Don't cling, Anna, please don't cling. Don't make this harder for me, when all I want to do is cling, as well.

"You can't," I say. "Your father was right. You should get home as soon as possible. I don't trust myself with you."

"Don't trust yourself? Or don't trust me?"

I'd thought about this all night. I'd imagined dozens of scenarios where we'd run away together. I imagined what it would've been like if I'd ignored that intuition and kept going when Anna told me not to stop. I imagined a life in Atlanta where we'd sneak to be together when my father goes to New York each week. And every single imagining ended the same way.

In our early deaths. Watching Anna be killed. *Reality.*

This is clearly not what Anna sees when she imagines us. She still envisions rainbows, kittens, and fucking unicorns.

Frustration ignites. I explode. "I don't trust either of us! We can't be together in *any* capacity *ever* again. It's a damn-near miracle you're still a virgin now. If that Sword of Righteousness is intended for you to use, then you should want to stay away from me, too, because I promise I could not resist if you told me to pull the car into that parking garage right now." I inch closer, daring her. "Could you resist a drug if I repeatedly placed it on the tip of your tongue, Ann? Could you? We're playing with fire!"

Her eyes are wide and filled with realization. She now sees how hard last night was for me, but pity isn't what I want. Nothing I say has the effect I need it to have. I glance up at the outdoor check-in desk, which blessedly has no line.

"So, what are you going to do now?" she asks. "Go back to doing your father's work and pretend you never knew me?"

That's exactly what I'd intended, though it sounds so pathetically depressing when she says it. I sigh and let my head hit the headrest. "What would you have me do?"

She pauses a long while. "You have to work." Anna's voice is full of emotion, and I wish for the millionth time that she wasn't so soft for the things of this world. I need her to be tougher, more aware. I need her not to love me. I need her to let me go.

"Do you know what my father said when I came home the night after he met you?" I say quietly. "He said God was a fool to put you in my path. And he was right."

"No. Your father was wrong! And how do you know it wasn't *you* who was put in *my* path? There's a purpose for you in all of this, too."

I want to laugh at her naive view and the ridiculous notion that I can be used for anything good, but I can only shake my head. She thinks all I've done is seduce a few girls for a bit of fun. The only reason she fell for me is because she doesn't know everything about me. It's time to remedy some of that.

I tell her about Father's relationship with Marissa and watch as her eyes narrow in horror when I mention an underground prostitution ring in Atlanta. *That's right, sweet Anna*, I want to say. *I'm involved with sexual slavery. What do you think of me now?*

"The girl they brought me the night before our trip was the youngest ever. She couldn't have been twelve. For the first time ever, I refused him, told him I couldn't."

143

She shakes her head, face pale as I release some of the demons that haunt me.

"You put thoughts into my head that Neph shouldn't have." I look away from her, out the window. I've never shared any of my fears with anyone. I should tell her to get out of the car and go, but now that I've opened these cursed floodgates, I can't stop. She's the only person in the world I can talk to, and I have to make her understand. "He'll be watching me now, testing me. I can't afford to have anything more to do with you."

"Kai . . . I know you're freaked out. I am, too. But maybe this sword is a sign that something's going to happen. Something good for the Neph."

I feel my shoulders slump. This might be her most naive thought yet. If anything's to happen with that sword, it's nothing to do with me or the Neph. Nothing good can come to us.

"You felt power when you touched the hilt, didn't you?" I ask. I look at her and she nods. "Well, I didn't. I'm not worthy to help with whatever plan they have for you. So just go back to your sweet and innocent life and stay away from me."

"Please," she begs. "Don't push me away. We can be friends, and—"

This is heart wrenching. I take her face in my hand, forcing her eyes to look straight into mine to make her understand. "We can never be just friends, Anna. Get it through your head now. There can be *nothing*."

I let her go and get out of the car, but she doesn't follow. So I approach the counter and get her boarding pass. Then I open the door to let her out. I want her to leave without another word. This is maddening, and I'm drained. She climbs out slowly and stands before me. I take out the cash and push it into her pocket, thrilled by the small touch.

When she leans her forehead against my sternum I nearly pull her back to my SUV and drive us away. It would mean our doom, but we might have a few more days of fulfilling enjoyment before we were found and brutally killed.

I clench my fists at my sides and resist the urge to touch her. "It's time for you to go."

"Wait." She gazes up at me with those brown eyes. "Remember at the beginning of the trip, when you said you always know right away what you'd have to do to get a girl into bed . . . even me?"

Ah, shite. I don't like where this is going. I bury my hot hands in my pockets and give a tight nod.

"What would you have to do? For me?"

This is dangerous territory. "Let's not go there," I warn.

"Tell me. Please."

I look into her sweet face, at that freckle at the corner of her mouth, and I clench my jaw. Perhaps it will be good if she knows the truth about my plan to seduce her. It will be better if she doesn't know how I feel. It will make it easier for her to get over me and move on. It's bad enough that I know what I'm going to be missing. She doesn't need to know it, too.

"I'd have to make you believe I loved you."

Her eyes drift closed and her face scrunches in pain. Knowing I've hurt her makes me want to gouge out my own eye.

"I wish, just once, that I could see your colors," she whispers.

My sweet and lovely little Ann. This is good-bye.

I swallow hard. "Well, I'm glad you can't. And I wish I'd never seen yours."

What Anna does next fills me with pride at her strength, and as much as it stings, it gives me hope that she'll be okay. She simply picks up her bag, and without a backward glance, she walks away.

CHAPTER ELEVEN

OFF TO WORK I GO

"Do you still consider me . . . the boy you laughed with or that you learned to live without?
. . . You wouldn't get me on the phone, and you couldn't make me not alone."
—*"Logan to Government Center" by Brand New*

I am obsessed. I believe this is what they call "getting a taste of one's own medicine," and it's a bitter flavor.

I didn't work on the way home from Los Angeles. I drove like a zombie with hardly a wink of sleep. It wrecked me to see Anna's number calling my mobile and not be able to answer.

That was over a week ago. Since being back in Atlanta I've thrown myself into work with a flourish, determined to get her off my mind. Surely another person's body will make these thoughts of her go away.

No?

Right then, two people.

Three . . . ? New bodies day and night. Different smiles on different lips. Different arses, different hips. I've even been writing songs, much to Michael's bloody delight.

Music, sex, pot, bourbon. Vast quantities of all of the above at once.

Nothing. Fucking. Works.

I get into trouble when school starts, which pisses Father off, as if I'm some human boy who gives a shit about his senior year and his future. He just doesn't want to play nice with the humans when they call with their concerns. It's not high on Father's to-do list to pretend to care for his troubled son who comes to school with bloodshot eyes and sleeps through history lessons.

Although he has seemed otherwise impressed with my performance outside of school. Good on me.

Because not one bit of this makes Anna go away. In fact, with each girl I abandon and each arsehole thing I say and do, I'm filled with shame. I see her face at every party. In every car I pass. She is everywhere, but I cannot have her. I'm constantly surrounded by people, but I've never been more alone.

I'm not sure how long I can sustain this level of self-abuse, but I cannot stand to be sober, and the more I fuel my lust, the more I seem to need. I am a disgusting disaster, but there's an apparent "tortured soul" appeal about me, because chicks have never been so keen to have me. I'm getting more action than James Fucking Bond. My bandmates joke that I'm a god.

And yet, I've never been less fulfilled.

Each time Father leaves I listen to Anna's voice mail

messages. I shouldn't. It's stupid for many reasons, but what can I say? I have become an idiot. Like that time this week when I called Marna, blasted out of my mind, and mentioned I'd met a new Neph named Anna, daughter of Belial. I figured word would have spread about her from Father by now, but Marna was obviously shocked and overly interested. Gin was in the background shouting questions.

"What's she like? Why haven't we met her? How old is she?"

"Erm, she's a year younger than me. Father asked me to help train her up."

"Train her up?" Marna asked. "What for? Isn't she trained and working already?"

"I meant, we work together. Or something."

"Or something?" she asked incredulously.

Even in my drunken state I knew enough to cut the conversation short.

Today, I make another idiotic phone call. This time to the band's manager.

"Ay, it's Kai," I say.

"Rowe! What's up?"

"Couple months ago this bloke called Jay gave you a CD of his songs. Think I can come by an' give 'em a listen?" Cripe, I'm drunk. Hope I'm not slurring.

"Hold on, let me look." I hear him shuffling around through his things. "Is it Jay Thompson from Cartersville?"

My heart rate spikes. "Yeah, that's him."

"Haven't listened to this one. He a friend of yours?"

"Just an acquaintance. Can't make any promises."

"No problem. Come in when you can. Oh, and did Michael tell you the news about L.A.?"

Bile rises in my throat at the thought of my L.A. memories, but we're only going there to make a record.

"Bloody brilliant news, mate," I say.

I give the alcohol twenty minutes to burn off, then hop in my car.

It turns out one of Jay's songs is incredible. Upon my urging, our manager gets on the phone to see about allowing permissions for a cover. When Jay says yes, my manager claps me on the back, probably thinking I'm grinning about discovering a new song, but all I can think is that when we cover it, Anna will be there to support him.

Bloody hell.

Now who's playing with fire?

We learn Jay's song in record time, excited to have new material for our next gig. When the night comes I down three shots of Jack to calm my nerves in the half hour preceding the show. The house is packed. When we take the stage I find Jay straightaway in the front row. He's with that curly-headed bloke who wrote the songs with him. My heart feels like it's slipped off a ledge. I look all around the dim room and cannot find her.

Why isn't she here? Has something happened?

After the show I head backstage, knowing Jay will come. I'm immediately bombarded by fans, but I can't focus on a single one of them. When Jay comes in I go straight for him. I try to be polite, because for once Jay is not smiling at me. I hold out a hand and he's slow to take it. His aura is orange under-neath, probably leftover excitement from the show, but it's gray with his misgivings for me on top. I wonder how much Anna told him.

"Nice work on the song, mate," I say. A bit of the gray fades.

"Thanks, man. You guys freaking rocked it. I mean, holy wow, dude!"

I grin. "So, uh . . . where's Anna?"

The gray is back, full force, when he says, "She's at home."

"Oh." I hadn't expected her not to come. There's a clench-ing and churning as I wonder if she's over me already. "How is she?"

"Well, she's been better, man." The way he says it is a harsh jab to the ribs. All I can do is nod. And for the first time since I returned to Atlanta, I head home without a substance in my system or another body at my side. I've only bitter disappoint-ment to keep me company.

I lose track of days and have lost all sense of time. I'm damned lucky our manager texts group updates when we have practices and gigs.

When a reminder about tonight's gig sounds, I have to untangle my naked body from the silky sheets where I've been passed out hard. Someone rings when I'm in the shower. When I get out, toweling off my hair, I call my voice mail and freeze at Ginger's words in the message. . . .

"Oy! Arse-face! We're at your little girl Anna's house. Ring me back straightaway."

My pulse goes ballistic. What the hell are they doing at Anna's house? The thought of her with the other Neph is like my two worlds colliding. I cannot imagine them together. What are they saying about me to Anna? Gin's probably scaring the ever-loving shite out of her.

I ring her back, on edge. I don't think Father bothers listening to my telephone conversations, but you never know. He's right bloody upstairs. Granted, he's gathering his things to leave for the weekend, but I won't relax until he's long gone.

"Is Pharzy home?" Ginger asks in a fake nice voice that raises the hair on my neck.

"Yes," I say through clenched teeth.

"Drats. We'll stay here for now, then."

"What do you think you're doing?" I ask.

I must come off sounding defensive, because she says, "Don't worry. We haven't tortured the poor girl. She's the one trying to torture us with American iced tea."

Damn it, Gin. She needs to be more careful what she says. Obviously she hasn't taken to Anna or she wouldn't talk about her *at all* knowing Father is home and could easily listen.

"Don't think you can weasel out of seeing us," she says when I don't respond.

"I'm busy. I have a gig at a club called Double Doors."

"When, tonight? Hold on."

I hold my breath as Ginger and Anna converse and Anna refuses to agree to go with them. And then a deep voice rumbles through the phone.

"*Come,*" he says, and my blood slows. What is Kopano doing there? I would've thought he'd be too busy at Harvard to take a bloody break. Has he talked with Anna? I can't help but wonder what she thinks of him.

"*Please,*" Marna pleads.

There's a long pause and then Anna whispers, "*Okay.*"

I am buzzing when we hang up. I'd like to think Anna agreed to come because she likes Marna, and she wants to see *me*, not because Kope has seduced her with his smooth voice and good-boy charm. The very thought makes me want to rage.

I'm the one she loves, I remind myself. She'll see me again tonight and remember that.

I dig through my dresser until I find the red T-shirt Anna wore home that night after she met my father. She was so bloody sexy in it.

At the sound of Father's footsteps coming down the basement stairs, I drop the shirt and wipe any sentimental look from my face.

He barges into my room in a tan suit, looking around and sniffing the air before coming to me.

"I'm leaving for New York."

"Enjoy yourself, sir."

He nods. "I always do. What are your plans?"

"Gig tonight, then work the backstage crowd."

"You've been busy lately." He says it with an ounce of pride and takes my bare shoulder in his hand. Then he runs the back of his finger along the small patch of hair at my sternum. "We should have this lasered off. Doesn't your generation prefer less body hair?"

"Yes, sir," I tell him, though I definitely haven't received any complaints.

He gives my bicep a squeeze, and his eyes slide down to my stomach, studying my body. "You could stand a bit of bulking up, as well. Abs could use more definition. Time to hit the gym harder, yeah? Make the girls resent those paunchy men of theirs."

He laughs and pretends to punch me in the abs, so I play along, bending with an "oof," and I laugh, as well. Gotta love quality father-son time.

I'm immensely relieved when he leaves.

Just like at the last show, I have to take three shots of Jack to calm my nerves. This time I know Anna will be here, and I'm in knots. Before we go onstage I bounce on the balls of my feet, shaking out my arms and loosening my neck. Raj looks at me like I'm crazy, because I'm usually leaned against the wall at this point, calm.

Thing is, I've been listening to Anna's voice since she arrived at the club. Hearing her after several weeks has pumped me full of the angel voodoo that makes me go a bit insane. I even feel like smiling.

We take the stage and I look straight up, hungry for eye contact, but she's not looking.

SHE'S NOT LOOKING.

I'm consumed by paranoia—is she over me so quickly? Has she fallen for another? Is she still mad at me? I shake my head at my own questions and grab my crotch to remind myself I'm a man. The goods are still there. I need to chill the hell out.

Her attention is on Jay as we start his song, and I force myself to focus on the drums. She's being supportive of her best mate, 'cause that's how she is. That's all. I'm not going to look again.

During the brief guitar instrumental where I have to pause

a measure, I totally look up again. This time she's staring right at me. It's as if the entire room goes silent and disappears. Her eyes are warm. It's all still there between us.

Marna pulls her away just as it's time for me to pick up in the song. I feel relieved enough to focus on the music now. Anna seems to be getting on well with the others. I lose myself in the next song, feeling a bit of enjoyment for the first time in weeks.

And then the song ends and I look up again, like a fool.

Anna and Kope are facing each other, leaning against the rail, looking bashful. I shoot my hearing up to them.

"*. . . very much like to know your story,*" Kopano is saying.

Oh, I bet he would like to know her "story." On the outside, Kope is a smooth-talking picture of perfection, but I know what he's like on the inside with his rare double curse. He's bound by both lust *and* wrath. I'll just bet he's thinking he's finally met his flawless match and he'd love to unleash all that withheld aggression on her.

When they stare at each other, standing far too close, and she doesn't move away, I am overcome with deranged jealousy. Naturally she looks down at me at that very moment and I'm unable to school the expression from my face.

She sucks in a breath and looks down at her hands. My eyes move to Kopano as he looks at me, and I glare back. Disappointment seems to flash across his face as he catches my "back off" vibes.

That's right, mate. Back. Off.

I'm all too keen to get to the party after the gig so I can stake my claim. Before I get out of my car I pull a fifth of Jack from under my seat and drink a healthy bit to hide any bond Marna and Ginger might see between Anna and me. It's none of their business, and I don't want to hear any ribbing.

I think of Anna's voice mail as I approach the party, and I imagine her running up to me, throwing her arms around me.

But it doesn't happen that way, does it? Girls run up to me, but none of them is Anna. I spot her through the crowd and what's she doing? LEAVING THE ROOM WITH KOPE.

Bloody hell! The cheek of him!

I am wound tightly with fear and anxiety as the worst possibilities overcome me; did she come tonight, not to see me, but because the others forced her? Worst of all, is it possible she no longer loves me, and she fancies Kopano instead? After all, he's everything I'm not. Would Kope plan a trip to seduce her, and then toss her off at the airport the moment things get heated?

No.

I don't want to listen, but I feel compelled. I shove my hearing through the walls and hear Anna and Kope bantering, and then he's telling her the story of how he abandoned his life as a Neph and got into Harvard.

God damn it, I feel ill. I need a drink.

I'm greeted at the kitchen counter by a platinum blond with a bottle of tequila. That'll do the trick. The tequila, I mean. It's loud in here. I glance through the crowd to see Anna hanging on Kope's every word in his oh-so-charming African dialect. She glances up and sees me as I take the shot handed to me. Then she turns her back to me as if I mean nothing, and my vitals plummet.

I can't believe this is happening. I can't believe I let myself care this much for someone. I should be glad she's out of my hair. She can be Kope's problem now, not mine, but I'm not glad at all. I'm so fucking sad it's pathetic.

On the heels of my sadness comes anger, crashing through. I never would have expected Anna to be so fickle. To love me one week and forget about me just as quickly.

I'm going to need a bit more tequila.

"Mind if I take this for a moment, luv?" I ask the blond.

"Only if you promise to come talk to me later." She smiles up at me.

I touch her chin and say, "Deal." Then I grab the bottle, lime slices, and shot glasses, and head across the kitchen to where my mates are gathering with Anna and Kope. When I'm standing right next to her I'm struck again by a sensation of betrayal. She's acting sweet and innocent here with Kope, but I've seen her high and desperate for more drugs. I've heard her begging me to keep going. I *know* her. I know her when she's sweet and I know her when she's salty. I notice the way her eyes dart to the bottle with longing, because unlike the others, I'm watching for it.

"Tequila, anyone?" I say to her.

She squirms uncomfortably as others call for drinks and I hand them out.

"Kope?" I say, because I haven't forgotten how he ignored my warning to back off. "Anna?" I want to call them both out for pretending to be perfect when they're just as fucked up as the rest of us.

They just stare at me, clearly unhappy. Good.

"Oh, that's right," I say. "I nearly forgot. The prince and

princess would never stoop so low. Well, bottoms up to us peasants."

I've made everyone uncomfortable, and I don't care. I want to laugh. It's all a big joke, isn't it? This thing called life, where we hurt, where we work so hard not to care, and then a bit of feeling creeps in and people use it to hurt us further.

We take our shot and it burns through my chest. I can see Anna gripping the counter, trying not to look at me as she craves the liquor in my hand.

"How's your soda, princess?" I ask her.

"You don't need to be hateful," she whispers.

Her words are like a sharp pin to my inflated chest, and I feel like shite for half a second.

"If you ask me, I'd say the princess prefers a dark knight," Ginger says.

If I'm the dark knight, Gin is wrong. "She only thinks she does," I respond, but I'm not so sure she prefers me over Prince Kope at all. I can't even look at Anna's reaction.

We end up out back, and I tip up the bottle, chugging the pungent alcohol when nobody's paying me any mind. I leave the empty bottle on the deck and head for the yard under the trees with the others. I sit heavily in a flimsy lawn chair and lean back, switching my gaze between Kope and Anna, who won't look at me. If the two of them want me out of the picture, I'm not going to make it easy on them. It's not how I work. I'm not a gracious loser.

Marna suggests a game of Truth or Dare, so I decide to cut to the chase.

"I'll go first. I dare Kope to kiss Anna."

It's like a monk kissing a nun. Brilliant. I lean back and

cross my arms, enjoying their shifty-eyed embarrassment. Anna suddenly stands, I'm assuming to get far away from me, but instead she heads straight for me and kicks my chair up. I lose my balance and topple backward like an idiot. But when I look up and see her standing over me with eyes ablaze, I can only grin.

There's my girl. I'm relieved I've made her feel *something*.

Ginger and Blake are cracking up as Anna storms away. Jay goes after her, and then Marna trails him. I try to push my hearing out, only to realize I'm too drunk to do so.

Kopano is glaring at me hard. I get to my feet.

"Is there a problem?" I ask him, holding my arms out. I sound like my bloody father. Kope only sighs, as if disappointed.

Before he can respond, Marna is yelling my name. Excitement clutches me as I forget about Kope and head for the side of the house. Marna and Jay pass me, but I ignore them because all I can see is Anna standing there with her arms crossed and her head down. I move to stand in front of her, and my anger is smothered by a blanket of her softness. I'm at a loss. I know I've been a prick.

"Sorry," I whisper, shocking myself.

"I'm sorry, too, about the whole chair-flipping thing."

"No, I deserved it."

She looks at me, and the world clears a bit. Just standing here, the two of us, makes me feel secure. I know it's stupid and fleeting, but I can see in her eyes that she still feels for me, and that is all I needed.

I can't let myself sober up while the twins are around. I can't allow anyone to know how I feel, so I pull the flask from my pocket and take a long drag. Ugh, bourbon and tequila are not a good combination.

I'm not quite as drunk as I was ten minutes ago, but I have to keep a good buzz going. I walk with Anna back to the group. When we sit, I get a strange sensation up the back of my neck, and I turn to look for whisperers. The others are laughing and playing Truth or Dare for real, but I can't shake the feeling something's off. My hearing is still wonky from the alcohol, but I hear a girl near the back door say my name, and when I look up I see the platinum hair through the window.

She's looking for me, and I don't want to deal with it right now. So I get up and move to hide behind the tree while Blake tells her I'm not out here. That's a good boy.

I expect the strange feeling to pass, but it doesn't, so I keep alert.

"Everyone cheats," I hear Ginger say.

"That's not true," I mumble without thinking. They all stare at me and I could kick myself for saying something so pure out loud. I can only shrug. "Well, it's not."

Ginger likes to think everyone cheats because she can get 99 percent of them to do it, but in fairness she only goes for the ones who seem dodgy anyhow, just as I go for the ones who are showing signs of lust for me.

"What the hell do you know about it?" she snaps. I hate my life as much as the next Neph, but Gin is poisonous about it.

"Nothing, I suppose." I'm feeling prickly, like I need to do a perimeter check for whisperers. I don't want the others to worry, but that sensation of being watched will not go away. "I know I need another drink."

I send my hearing around me in a circle like a radar as I walk to the house. But when I get inside the feeling dissipates. It's something *outside*. I go back out and freeze at the edge of the deck.

No. Blood slams through me as a giant dark spirit circles Anna. I can't make out his features, but he looks vaguely familiar. Everyone is still until the whisperer flies off. Marna quietly sends Jay away. As he comes up to the deck, I make my way down the steps at a jog.

This is not good.

"I would swear it was Azael," Marna says. "But what was he doing?"

My ears ring as everyone talks. Azael. Satan's messenger spirit. My world flips and I feel as if I'm dangling in midair. Please, not this. Not her.

"What are you not telling us?" Ginger demands.

My eyes lock with Anna's. I need to get her out of here. I stretch my hearing in a farther radius and catch booted footsteps beside the house. My heart rate goes berserk as I realize it's too late to run. I slowly turn my head to the sound of the footsteps as a big-ass man steps out and walks toward us with casual, even steps. He's bald and broad with a goatee, and he's got a thick, amber badge at his sternum.

Belial.

I'm immediately relieved that it's him and not one of the other Dukes, but I still don't trust him, no matter what Anna says. This brute can definitely snap a neck with no remorse if it suits him. And when he sees me and glimpses my badge, that's exactly what it looks like he wants to do.

"You're a hard one to find," he says to Anna. Damn, his voice is even deeper and more intimidating in person. I want to know why he's come and what he plans to do with her. I feel the weight of my knife in my pocket, and I will not hesitate to use it, no matter how big he is.

Then Anna introduces all of us. When she gets to me, her father cuts her off.

"Son of Pharzuph." He sneers, and it's clear there's no love between him and my father. My stomach turns and I'm filled with self-loathing from the look in Belial's eye. I am not good enough for his daughter. I nod and drop my eyes.

"You're leaving with me, girl," he says to Anna. "Time to start your training."

It takes all my power not to look up and shout my first reaction of *No!* I don't want her submersed in this life, but it's too late.

Anna goes compliantly to his side, as if he's asked to take her to the park. She gives me a small smile, and I know she's telling me she'll be okay, but I'm too nervous. I can't let anything happen to her. I stretch my hearing to follow them, but they don't speak. And then they're out of range. Gone. And I cannot keep her safe.

CHAPTER TWELVE

TRIANGLE THING

*"I'd never dreamed that I'd meet somebody like you
I'd never dreamed that I'd lose somebody like you."*
—*"Wicked Game" by Chris Isaak*

A few minutes of stunned silence pass after they leave, and then I reach in my pocket for my keys. Ginger grabs my arm, digging her fingers in when I try to pull away.

"Where do you think you're going?" she hisses.

"I'm off to work a different party."

"Bollocks!"

She eyes me suspiciously, and I level her with a stare. She always could read me too well. Blake removes her claw from my arm and says, "It's all good, brah. We'll catch you later."

Marna pushes past them and squeezes me around the waist. It takes me a moment to relax and hug her back, and then I'm off. I don't even look Kope's way.

I just need to be sure Anna makes it home all right, I tell myself. I get on the highway and push my hearing as far up the road as I can, threading through each car, but none of them are Anna and Belial.

I don't calm down until I'm within a mile of Anna's apartment complex. I throw the vehicle into park in the lot of an abandoned petrol station and listen. I can hear her moving around her room. The shuffle of clothing and linens. Is she going to bed? She starts humming a song by Pink, and I nearly laugh at how she's at ease while I'm on edge.

It's one in the morning. Anna is safe. I've no clue where Belial's gone. Did he truly show up at the party just to nab her and take her home? I'm not buying it. It's too bizarre. I'll just stay for a bit to listen.

It's hard not to doze when Anna falls asleep, because the sound of her breathing is so comforting and even. At some point my chin falls to my chest, and I startle myself awake as an early autumn wind whistles through the darkness. It's just after three. I should go. I shuffle my extended hearing back up the road and into the apartment one last time. Then I nearly jump out of my skin.

Anna and Patti are both shrieking.

I fumble with the keys and finally crank the engine, peeling out of the pebbled lot.

Shite! How could I bloody well fall asleep? I knew something was up!

It's chaos at the apartment, with Patti yelling and Anna crying. I accelerate. I cannot figure out what the hell's going on. A knock at their door ratchets my pulse higher, and rain splatters the windshield, muddling my hearing.

"This is my friend Kope," I hear Anna say, and I go cold all over.

What. The. Hell.

That scheming pretty boy must've been right outside her neighborhood!

"Whisperers were here!" Anna says to him. *"I could see them. . . ."*

Whisperers? Wait . . . she could see them? My poor girl—her voice is trembling. I turn too quickly into the apartment complex, going up on the damn curb and probably killing a flower bed.

Don't care.

I am seeing red. The raging bull kind.

Why are the whisperers haunting her? Who sent them? And why is Kope here?

I park across two spots and leap out, taking the steps three at a time, and burst into Anna's apartment. She screams and claps her hands over her mouth. I jump and reach for my blade when a raspy voice behind me says, "What in God's name is going on over there?"

Bugger, just an old neighbor. Anna pulls me in and shuts the door.

"What are you doing here?" she yells at me. She's wearing a threadbare fitted T-shirt and fuzzy blue shorts and has adorable bedhead, ponytail askew. I want to shove Kope from the room so he can't see her like this.

From the corner of my eye I spy movement, but it's only Patti. My heart warms a bit when she seems relieved to see me.

"They could come back any second and see us together and tell your father!" Anna is still yelling at me. "Go home!"

No, I want to know what happened. I want her to tell me about the demons and what they did to her, the way she told Kope. I look over at him with his arms crossed, and something inside me cracks. He doesn't look smug, only resolute, as if he's not budging from his place as protector. And why should he? Anna's not telling *him* to leave.

"Yes, I'll go," I say with a measure of bitterness. "You've got help."

I slip past her halfhearted attempt to stop me, and she doesn't come after me. I'm too angry to listen anymore. I don't want to hear them talking, even though I'm dying to know every detail about the whisperers.

The footsteps coming down the dim stairs behind me are too heavy to be Anna's. I flex my fists as I turn to face Kopano at the bottom of the stairs. Rain is falling in torrents around us, and we're barely protected by the edge of the stairwell's awning.

"Let us go somewhere and talk," Kopano says.

"We can talk here. She never uses her senses." It feels good to throw that fact at him—there's loads about Anna he doesn't know.

"Do not be upset, Kai," he says calmly. "I feel only concern for her."

Right. If by concern he means attraction and awe. "I'll bet you do."

"Even you are willing to risk yourself for her, brother."

Okay, so he can tell I feel attraction and awe, as well. So

what? "That's because I actually know her. What's your reason? I suppose you'd like to get to know her, too?"

"You have made it very clear that she is not available in that way." And yet, he has pursued. "Be reasonable. There is plainly more at stake here. I only wished to help."

Bullfuckincrikey. How is he going to help? By being her shoulder to cry on? He's just as powerless against the Dukes and whisperers as I am. He can lie to himself, but not to me. He wants her. "There's nothing you can do, Kope!"

He tries to calm me, which makes me more furious.

"There is no stronger weapon for Pharzuph to use than your concern for each other. If he learns you were here to console her, you will lose all leverage with him. Do not fool yourself into thinking he will not discard you."

"Yes," I say with pure malice. "Some of us have to worry about such things. Thank you for the reminder."

I've been taken off guard by this conversation, and I catch the sound of heavy footsteps too late. Kope's eyes widen as he peers over my shoulder, and I spin, whipping out my switchblade with a *zing* and holding it in front of me where Duke Belial stands mere feet away, looking lethal as a bomb.

He smiles down at my knife, water dripping from his face. "Put it away, boy. Sorry to break up the testosterone party."

With a shaking hand, I slide the blade back in and slip it into my pocket. Anna comes racing down the stairs barefooted and stops herself just short of us.

She looks up at Belial and yells, "Dad!" Her hands cover her mouth as she looks between us. When Belial faces her full on, her hands fall to her side and her face goes slack.

"It was you," she whispers. "You sent them."

My head snaps to Belial to see his jaw set. Everything suddenly makes itself clear, and I nearly sag where I stand. He sent the whisperers to haunt her. Anna is not under suspicion, and her father does not want to hurt her. He's trying to smarten her up. He's forced her to acknowledge and see the demons. It's admirable and heinous all at once.

Belial turns on me and Kopano, stepping closer, and we both stand taller under his intense scrutiny. This is obviously a man who wants to protect his daughter, and right now he's staring us down like we're threats. Shame burns me as I realize what fools we were, standing out here arguing when larger issues are at stake.

"This little thing," Belial says, pointing between Kope, Anna, and me, "isn't gonna fly. Don't worry yourselves about Anna anymore. You hear?"

I nod, but there's no way in hell I can stop worrying about Anna. I'm in too deep.

"Then get on out of here," he says in that low voice. "And keep your heads in the game."

Anna is watching the ground where the rain falls next to us. I don't look at anyone as I turn to leave, climbing into my vehicle, driving straight into the storm, head on.

"Love Letter" by Kaidan Rowe

Staring at this paper
Tryin' to write a "love letter."
This is not my thing,
Yeah, it's just not me.
My mind turns instead
To a wicked beat in my head,
And I bang out the lyrics to a song.
Yeah, I bang out the lyrics to a song.

You're soft to my hard,
You're sweet to my salt.
If we both end up naked
It'll all be my fault.
Yeah, I'll take the blame,
That's it, say my name.
You're gorgeous, you're stunning,
Let me win at this game.

CHORUS:
Gimme, gimme, gimme,
I'm Greed when you're near.
I want more, I need more,
Ignore all of my fear.
Heat me, scald me, burn me,
I'm Lust for your touch.
You kill with a smile
And I refuse to be rushed.

How's this for a love note?
Do my words rock your boat?
If not, I'll try harder
Take things a bit farther.
You bet your ass I'll do that,
Raise the bar, sexy cat.
So step closer to me, turn up the AC.
You'll be singin' the chorus in 1, 2, 3 . . .

CHORUS

Roses are red and violets are blue,
That played-out shit isn't for you.
I got your love letter right here in my eyes.
If you look deep enough, you'll see through the lies.

CHAPTER THIRTEEN

GOOD WITCH, BAD APE

"Baby, you're beautiful, and there's nothing wrong with you.
It's me, I'm a freak."
—*"Whataya Want from Me?" By Adam Lambert*

I've always lived life like a game, moving my piece along the board, taking pleasure where I can, but feeling otherwise numb. Until a surprise came along and fucked it right up. Life is still a game now, only the rules have changed. Each move I make lands me on a mystery space, and I'm forever unsteady.

Over and over I imagine her as she was that night, sitting on the bed in the hotel room, like a still shot captured in my brain—her fluorescent pink aura, shockingly beautiful, surrounding her skin as she held a pillow to her nearly naked chest.

That image. It does me in every time. It slices me to pieces. She's safe now, in her father's care—or as safe as a Nephilim can be. I resist the urge to drive over and check on her each time Father leaves for New York. I remind myself the whisperers could see us, and I've already tempted fate enough by spending far too much time with her in the past. It's made me careless.

I only work the days Father is in Atlanta. I know it's bloody dangerous to limit myself to only a few halfhearted hookups a week, but Anna has ruined me with a craving for something far more substantial. She possesses the only thing that can fill the deep void within me, and nothing else comes close.

It's been over two months since I've seen her. When I caught sight of Jay at a party last week I was caught in a moment of desperation.

"Heard about the Halloween field party, mate?" I'd asked. Good ole Jay lit up at the invitation, just as I'd counted on. I'm not certain he'll bring Anna, but it's worth a try.

She probably won't come, smart girl that she is. Halloween is one of the demons' favorite nights of the year to whisper their sweet nothings.

I didn't let Father see the Halloween costume I'd rented. It's the ultimate way to hide from people. Only one girl will be able to recognize me in this giant gorilla costume. She'll see an ape with a red badge.

Halloween has always been my favorite holiday: people dressing in ways they normally wouldn't dare. Inhibitions down, even without drugs and alcohol, and dark exhilaration in the air. Tonight is no different as I scan the field of laughing people, but I don't feel the buzz I normally do on this night.

The gorilla head smells rank, and it's hot inside this

damned thing. Between my nerves and the lack of ventilation, I'm sweating. I look through the mesh eyes at the crowd. There must be several hundred people there to see the five bands play. Not our band tonight, though I'm certain Raj, Michael, and Bennett are around here somewhere.

I focus my eyes, pulling each face into clear view from across the field. I wonder what Anna'll be wearing. I imagine her in a sexy angel outfit—the irony would be our secret.

My gaze halts on the fuzzy blond head of Jay with an eye patch, and a fake parrot propped on his shoulder. Next to him is a small green witch wearing a ratty black wig and pointy hat, with a badge at her sternum only I can see. I grin to myself inside the mask as cool relief floods my system.

She's here.

I won't approach her. I don't know how she feels anymore. A lot can change in two months, especially when I've done my best to push her away. She deserves better.

I feel the burn rise when I think of Kopano. Makes me want to rip off the gorilla head so I can breathe easier, but I'm not in the mood to be recognized by anyone other than Anna.

Kope is quite possibly the only man on earth worthy of Anna, but I'll be damned if I'll let him have her when her love's the only thing I've ever wanted. Impossible thoughts plague me. Impossible desires. Dangerous dreams.

I watch Anna now as she glances down at herself, then crosses her arms, looking self-conscious of her chest in the tight black dress. I have a spanking good view of Anna's side profile. My gaze outlines the curve of her back down to her waist, landing on her round arse. A deep, intoxicating stir is triggered within me. Good thing this ruddy costume is roomy.

My thoughts sober and my pulse spikes when I realize she's looking at me now, recognizing me. I don't move. We stare for what feels like forever before she finally waves. I'm overcome with joy at this simple acknowledgment. I lift a paw and chuckle at Anna's greenness. A girl I hadn't noticed before grabs Anna's hand and says something. I focus my hearing on them.

"—Who are you waving at?" the girl asks. She's dressed like a provocative Minnie Mouse.

"Um, that big monkey," Anna says. "I think he's staring at us."

Correction, dear. I'm only staring at you.

They both watch me expectantly, so I lift an arm and scratch the furry armpit, which makes them laugh. I think I recognize the girl as the one Anna was dancing with at that lake party ages ago. I still love thinking about how I stole her away from that wanker in the bedroom that night, and the look on his face. It's one of my few prized memories.

Anna turns away from me and starts chewing on her nail. She's not coming over, the stubborn thing, but I'm too greedy not to see her face-to-face while I can. I won't talk to her for long. Just a moment. Just to get my fix. And then I can leave.

I walk to them and pull off the costume head, shaking out my sweat-dampened hair and sucking in the fresh night air. Both of the girls' eyes widen. Minnie's white polka dots temporarily cover over with a red aura. Anna frowns when she notices. The girl has a slight bump in the arch of her nose that gives her face a certain seductiveness, though she probably hates it. Girls are like that when it comes to their bodies.

I look at Jay and say, "Arrgh, matey." He laughs and sticks out his hand for me to shake, which I do. Nice bloke.

"What's up, man?" he says.

I throw a drummer joke at him, since he always likes to lay them on me.

"What's the difference between a drummer and a savings bond?" I ask.

His grin is huge and his aura bright yellow. "I don't know. What?"

"A savings bond matures and eventually makes money."

He laughs and reaches out for another appreciative hand slap. When we turn to the girls, Minnie's colors have settled back down.

"This is my friend Veronica," Anna says in a level voice. "And this is Kaidan."

"Oh, I've heard all about you," Veronica tells me with a big, knowing smile. I raise my eyebrows with interest. Girl talk. Brilliant. I find nothing more amusing than eavesdropping on girls in conversation. They give blokes a hard time for things we say behind closed doors, but girls are just as bad.

I focus my attention on Anna now and decide I don't like the green face paint. It covers over her freckle. And what is that blob on the end of her nose? A wart? Only Anna would try to make herself less attractive.

"Nice wart," I say, then flick the dangling thing off. She gasps, and both her friends laugh.

"I told you it was stupid," Veronica gloats.

But Anna's a good sport. She rubs a finger over her nose

to even the paint, going adorably cross-eyed in the process. I fight back a smile.

Anna and I lock eyes. I used to be uncomfortable under her gaze; the way it made me feel vulnerable. Now I welcome that feeling, even for a moment.

She crosses her arms and says, "Your hair's grown a lot."

"So has your bottom," I respond without thinking.

Ah, shite. I know better than to make "growth" comments to girls, or anything indicative of size that could be deemed unflattering, but it just sort of slipped out. Her friends burst into laughter, and there isn't enough paint in the world to hide the shock on Anna's face.

"Dude, you can get away with anything," Jay tells me.

"I meant it as a compliment," I say honestly.

Veronica is still laughing when she grabs Jay by the hand and leads him away. He shoots me a serious look of warning as they go. I respect him even more for his protective feelings over Anna. Especially now that I know he's never fancied her, which is insane to me.

I flick my head to the side to get the hair out of my eyes while Anna shifts, biting her lip and staring at the grass.

Say something, you git.

I haven't a clue what to say, though. Should I apologize for the bum comment?

"My dad gave me a cell phone," Anna says in that sweet voice of hers, looking up again. The green paint and night sky make her brown eyes even darker.

I pull my own mobile from the ape pocket and blow a piece of lint from it. When I raise my eyebrows she starts giving me her number, but the damned costume is not cooperating. Without asking, Anna takes the phone from me and programs her number. That small act of familiarity, as if she has every right to touch my things, makes me even hotter for her. I want to throw her over my shoulder and carry her into the woods to claim her.

Right. She's staring at me in that way that makes it seem as if she can read my mind. I clear my throat.

"How did things go with your father and the training?" I ask.

"It went fine. I guess." She answers quietly, crossing her arms again. "I know my drinking limits now and all that."

I try to imagine Anna drinking. Is she a silly or a sad drunk? I kind of hope I'll never find out.

Anna moves closer and my breath stops. "I understand what you mean now about the dangers of being together. I didn't get it then, Kai, but I do now."

I can't breathe. She gives me her trademark look—the one that drains me of all strength and makes me want to give her anything she wants. I'm too weak. I turn toward the stage, where the music begins, and try to regain my momentum, but she keeps talking, moving closer.

"I know it's risky to see each other, but we could talk on the phone when your father's not around. If you want."

If I want. She has no clue how much I want. But I can't simply have a tiny slice of Anna. I'm no masochist. It has to be all or nothing, and "all" would ensure the death of us both.

"That's not a good idea," I say.

Even now, since we've been standing here together, I've not

once looked around for whisperers. She turns me into a single-minded idiot every time.

I turn from the stage toward a group of loud people behind us, but I can't concentrate on a damn thing.

"I think about our trip all the time," she whispers, her words sinking into my bones. "Do you ever think about it?"

Every day.

"Sometimes."

With a feminine grunt of frustration, Anna grabs hold of the front of my costume with her little fists, shocking me. I look anywhere but at her.

"Why did you invite Jay to this party?" she demands.

To see if you still love me. But I won't let her pry my feelings from me. It'll only make things harder. Ironically, isn't that what I'm trying to do, as well? Find out if she loves me so it can be difficult, all over again?

"I don't know," I grind out. Who am I kidding? I am a complete masochist seeking out pain, and a sadist as well, the way I keep hurting her.

She pulls harder on my costume, and the amount of passion in her tiny form fills my body with a buzzing need.

Her voice quavers. "I can't keep living like this, Kai. I need to know how you feel. I need to know one way or another so I can have some sort of closure."

It's clear she still cares, but she doesn't want to. I have to stop doing this to us. I have to stop thinking about her, and make her stop thinking about me, no matter how it hurts.

"I thought you'd be over it by now," I say harshly, making the mistake of looking down into her eyes, lively even in the darkness.

"It doesn't work like that," she says.

I stare down at her in desperation. I need to burn this bridge—to deceive her into believing I don't give a shit. But haven't I tried that already? Hasn't she seen through me like no one else ever has? Damn her see-the-best-in-people ways.

Smoke from a nearby bonfire blows over us.

"Don't invite Jay to any more parties, Kaidan. If there's even the slightest chance you'll be there, I'm not going. It hurts too much to see you."

Even when she's being tough, she's too sweet, grabbing me by the heartstrings and twisting.

"So why did you come?" I ask.

Her green face bears an expression of sad turmoil. Reaching up, she pulls off the tangled black wig and I feel like the wind had been knocked from my lungs. Her long, natural, honey-colored hair is gone, replaced by bright blond streaks and a sexy chopped style. A wave of sadness and loss rocks through me. She's had to change. With or without me in her life, she is a Neph, and there is no escaping it.

I gather my strength and say, "You should go then."

Don't go. Don't bloody leave me. Throw your arms around me. I don't care if you smear my face with paint, Anna. Tell me you love me. Show me you still want me. Torture me a bit more. Oh, God . . . she's walking away from me. Just as she'd done at LAX.

I should let her go, but I'm shaken.

"Wait," I shout.

She doesn't stop. My pulse rockets into overtime. I push past people and run forward, wrapping my hand around her tiny wrist and spinning her to face me.

Fuck! How can she turn away like that? I yank her closer,

fully aware I'm acting like an absolute psycho, but I'm too weak to do what needs to be done. She is mine. Doesn't she know that? Because my body and soul are screaming it—demanding me to make her mine in every way.

Her eyes stare up at me with a mix of fear and hope, reminding me what an arsewipe I am to keep doing this to her. Once again, I've royally screwed everything up. I need to let her go, but instead I find myself touching her face with a stupid paw, cursing the costume for getting in the way of feeling her soft skin, cursing her green paint for hiding her face from me.

With a furry thumb I wipe the paint from above her lip and she yanks back.

"What are you doing?"

"I . . ." There it is. The perfectly round brown dot, at once innocent and sexy. "I wanted to see your freckle."

The inside of my costume is a sauna at this point. I want more than anything to kiss her. One last taste.

Don't do it, you evil bastard. Don't make it harder on her. Just push her away.

"What do you want from me, Kai?" she whispers.

Isn't it obvious? I want everything. Why can't I control these feelings? And why should I have to? It all fills me with a raging fury of injustice. I grip her tighter.

"For starters?" I growl. "I want to introduce myself to every freckle on your body."

I feel her tremble in my hands, sending my body to its boiling point in the ape suit.

"So, just something physical, then? That's all you want?"

I hate myself for my inability to let her go. If I can't push her away, maybe I can force her to push me.

"Tell me you hate me." It would be so much easier if she did.

"But I don't hate you. I couldn't."

Her breath smells like bubble gum. Everything about her is too sweet for me.

"You could," I assure her, pulling her tighter. "And you should."

She's fighting tears when she says, "I'm letting you go, but only because I have to. I need to move on with my life, but I'll never hate you."

Yes. Let me go. Move on. Then maybe I can do the same.

I force myself to open my hands and let her go. She stumbles back, shooting me one last heartbreaking, wide-eyed stare. And then just like at the airport, she turns from me and walks abruptly away, her matted blond hair falling against her shoulders. And just like before, she doesn't turn back.

I roughly yank the gorilla head over my face. It smells as sour as I feel.

Damn the Maker and the Deceiver. Damn them all.

CHAPTER FOURTEEN

ANNA'S TEST

"I really miss your hair in my face
And the way your innocence tastes."
—*"Better Than Me" by Hinder*

We've been good. We've stayed away from each other since Halloween—two months exactly. But still, we are not safe. Always, threats lurk, and this one snuck up.

All the fear I've known since meeting Anna seven months ago has led to this night. She is under suspicion. I could have helped her avoid this fate. I could have put aside my own selfishness and properly trained her during our road trip. But I didn't. Instead, I've played games, pushing her away and reeling her back in for the past seven months. And now she's forced to go against her personal morals to save her life.

Honestly, I don't know if she can pull it off. The other Neph and I have given her as much information and advice as we possibly can. We'll be at her side tonight, each of us work-ing, but she has to do her part on her own. I'm more nervous for her than I've ever been for myself.

"You all right there, babe?" Marna asks, leaning up from the backseat. My knuckles are white, and I force myself to loosen my grip on the wheel.

"Yeah," I say. "Fine."

Blake claps my shoulder from the passenger seat. "We got this, brah."

"Just don't do anything stupid," Ginger mutters at me from the back, where she's applying another coat of eye shadow. "Like that bloody awful haircut."

I ignore her, running my hand over the buzz cut I gave myself while wasted on eggnog.

"I like it," Marna says. "It's cute. He looks a bit like a crimi-nal."

Blake turns in his seat. "Criminals are *cute*? Dude, whatev. Girls are weird." At this, Marna giggles.

I catch Kopano's eye in the rearview mirror. He was in the wrong place at the wrong time, hanging with the lot of us here in Atlanta for holiday break when Father and the other U.S. Dukes met at my house and called us all together, suggesting we work together as a group this New Year's Eve for maximum damage to the humans. We didn't know at the time Anna was under suspicion. Thankfully Belial tipped her off. She'll most likely be tailed by whisperers all night, who will report back to the Dukes about whether or not she's a suitable worker. Her life depends upon being a bad girl tonight.

Kope will be working for the first time since he was fifteen, and I know he's doing it for our sakes. For Anna's sake. I'm grateful.

We park at the hotel and I chug from my flask before I get out. I straighten my tie as we walk, and feel the heavy slap of my wallet's chain against my thigh. I try to concentrate on these small details so as not to freak the hell out. Thankfully no whisperers are in sight. Yet.

It takes me half a second to find Anna when we walk into the darkened ballroom. She's dancing with that Veronica chick, in true Anna fashion, as if this were an ordinary party and not a test in which her life is the prize.

My worries are momentarily sidetracked as I watch the way her body moves with fluid grace—the way her arse shakes in perfect time to the beat. I reach down to adjust myself through my trousers, and Ginger huffs next to me, mumbling, "Oh, gawd."

Whatever.

Anna is smiling and fanning herself when the song ends. And then she sees me and stops. I want to go to her and remind her of everything we told her about dealing with the whisperers. I want to shield her and protect her and take this burden from her, but she's got to do this on her own. I cannot be a distraction, so I will make myself scarce; however, I'll be listening and watching when I can.

It doesn't take long for the whisperers to show—two of them—and they stalk her like the creepers they are. I want to tell them to back off and give her room to breathe. She's completely rigid when they first take to her, but to my surprise she heads straight for the bar and shakes off the stiffness with determination.

Knowing she's okay for now, I find a brunette in an emerald dress to talk to in a corner where I can see Anna from across the room. I manage to keep up a conversation, answering, nodding, even making the girl laugh, but she's only got a small portion of my attention.

I'm more than a little proud of the way Anna handles herself at the bar, but I'm worried her friend Veronica is going to be an issue. I think she's together with Jay, and . . . oh, fantastic. Marna has him in her sights. What is she thinking? She should not be working on Anna's friend and causing unnecessary drama for her to deal with when she's trying to bloody concentrate! The moment Marna breaks away, I excuse myself and head over to her.

I catch Marna near the poker tables. "What are you doing? Not Jay, okay? Leave him be so Anna can focus."

Her eyes are sad and she whispers, "Sorry." Ah, shite. I think her play for Jay was less about work and more about her possibly fancying him.

Ginger marches up, frowning at me. "She's got nothing to be sorry for. She's working the way *you* should be. Come on, Marn."

She takes her sister by the elbow, and Marna casts an apologetic glance over her shoulder at me before they walk through the room, making eyes at all the guys who're coupled up. I shake my head and catch sight of Kope at a poker table. The blokes he's with are all edgy, their auras stirring with gray. We give each other a nod.

I grab two wines from the bar and head back to the girl in

the emerald dress. I don't care for wine, but she's a chardonnay type, so I suck it up. Anna finally finishes with the Veronica/Jay drama and is making her way to the bar again. She's only got one whisperer flanking her now. I duck behind someone when Anna's eyes move in my direction.

Loud chaos ensues and suddenly people jump up, running to see. I stretch my hearing and nod to myself when I realize what's happening.

"What's going on over there?" asks the girl I'm with.

"Fight at the poker table," I say. She stands and shifts side to side, trying to catch a glimpse.

The room's energy zings and auras are fading as more alcohol is consumed, along with other drugs. The music gets louder. The brunette finishes her drink and eyes mine.

I push it toward her with a grin and she smiles up at me, running her pearl necklace back and forth between her fingers. The last thing I want to do is talk to a girl right now. I can scarcely concentrate, but with whisperers about, I can't afford to stand here and watch Anna all night.

When I glance toward the bar again, I can't quite believe what I see. Anna is quite the little entertainer, working the bar crowd and throwing back shot after shot. I hope she still knows her limits.

"You seem distracted," says the brunette as she sips my chardonnay.

"Sorry, luv," I say. "I'm here with my cousin and she's quite the lush. Just trying to keep an eye on her."

"Aw, that's so sweet." She gets off her stool and moves closer to where I sit, fitting my knee between her legs. My arm goes around her back automatically, and I fight to keep my eye on her instead of turning to the bar again. Especially as people whoop and cheer.

"I had to break up with my boyfriend last week, because he cheated on me. Now I just want to have fun."

"That right?" I ask. Declarations like that used to make me rejoice. Her hand rubs my shoulder, and she angles slightly sideways. She's way tipsy.

Hollers blast from the bar area, and the brunette peers over my shoulder. "Uh-oh. Is one of those your cousin?"

I turn. Anna, Marna, and two other sauced girls have climbed onto the bar and are dancing. The whisperer is going crazy, dancing its own nasty jig all over the patrons. The bartenders stand almost directly under them, staring up their dresses, pretending to be there to catch them, no doubt. The wankers.

"Yeah," I say absently. "The, uh, brown-haired one on the end." Marna.

"Aw, they're just having fun," says the girl. "Don't worry about her. She's fine." The girl begins to nuzzle my neck, and two other immaculately coiffed girls approach.

"Tasha, we're going up to do a linc. Wanna come?" They look me up and down approvingly. "He can come, too."

Tasha, the brunette in emerald, looks at me. "Come with?"

"I can't." I nod toward Marna, thankful to have an excuse.

She shakes her head at her friends. "I'm staying with Kaidan."

They give her knowing smiles and leave us. Damn. I was hoping she'd go, too. She slinks over to face me.

"You know," she says, "we could go to my room. Your cousin's a big girl. She'll be okay."

"Er . . ." I look over. Bloody hell, Anna is so sexy in that little dress, completely letting loose.

I feel someone staring at me and catch Ginger at a table with a guy. She's frowning at me and throws her thumb over her shoulder, telling me to take the girl to her room. I narrow my eyes to tell her to shut up.

The brunette runs a finger along my jaw, leaning forward as if to kiss me, and I have a moment of paranoia that Anna will see. The whisperer is in sight, and more could show at any moment, so I can't very well ignore Tasha's advances, but there's no way I'm going far from Anna.

"Come on." I take the girl by the hand and lead her from the ballroom, going the long way around to avoid the bar, where the girls are being helped down. I'm just going to snog her to pass the time and make it seem as if I'm working toward more. No offense to Tasha, but I'm ditching her the first moment I know Anna's safe and we can go.

My emerald-wearing brunette turns out to be drunker and randier than I thought. The moment we're out of the ballroom she flings her arms heavily over my shoulders and goes up on her toes to smash her mouth against mine. People walking past us in the hall snigger and one guy yells, "Get a room!" I flick him off behind Tasha's back, and the group laughs.

I can't unhook her from around my neck, so we sort of swerve and stumble our way to the empty supply hall near the bathrooms. I shove my hearing back into the ballroom while experiencing the wettest kiss of my life. Before I can find

Anna's voice in the mass, I feel a prickle on my neck and the space around us darkens.

A hair-raising cackle sounds in my mind, cutting off my extended hearing, and I nearly flinch. A whisperer is on us.

"Oh, God, yes," says Tasha as the demon whispers in her ear, shoving away her guardian angel, who fights against it.

Time to work.

I kiss her back now for real, taking control of the show and putting that sloppy mess to rest as I push her back against the wall. She moans and lets her head fall back into my hand. She grabs my lower back and pulls my hips flush against hers. After a minute I think the whisperer leaves, but I can't stop to look.

Tasha hikes her leg, and I grab it, feeling the dress rise. Her hands are pulling out my shirt and finding their way to my bare back, where her nails dig in. My hand slides higher until it's under her dress and she's going wild.

My body works, but my mind is not in this hall. I go still at the sounds of familiar voices nearby. My head jerks around. No whisperers in sight, but I see the back of Ginger.

"What's wrong?" slurs Tasha.

"I think I hear my cousin," I whisper, still not moving.

She groans with disappointment.

Their voices are clear.

"Stop. That's not fair," says Anna.

"Fair," snorts Gin. "You're no better than the rest of us."

"I never thought I was."

My heart goes still. Of course Ginger would be a complete cow to Anna. I drop the girl's leg.

"I'm so sorry," I say, tucking in my shirt. "I've got to take care of something." Oh no, I think Anna's running to the loo to be sick. Tasha tips to the side and I right her. "Perhaps we should ring your mates, yeah?"

"Wait . . . you're leaving?"

"I have to go." I don't feel too bad leaving her, since she's staying in the hotel. I'm sure she'll find her way. But just in case I pull her mobile from her small purse and put it directly in her hand. "Call your friends."

She nods. Then hollers at my back, "Wait, what's your number? We can hang out later!" But I don't turn back.

In the hall I shove past Ginger and she shouts, "Hey! You can't go in there."

I turn on her. "Stop trying to police the lot of us!"

She glowers. "What the hell's gotten into you, Kai?"

If she only knew.

I turn away and march straight into the ladies' loo. "Anna?" I see her feet in a stall at the end. My heart is pounding and filled with worry at how she's feeling after a night of whisperers on her back. "Ann?"

"I'm fine, Kai," she says, but she doesn't sound it. I need to see her. Help her.

I go to her stall and touch the handle. "You're sick. Let me in."

"No. I'm fine now."

"Shall I send Marna, then?"

"No. I just want to be alone. Go away in case the spirits come back."

I feel a burst of pride, followed by sadness, to hear the

190

caution in her voice. She will forever be aware and more careful now. I didn't want her to have to learn this way, but it is what it is. I'm certain she's feeling shame and regret, but in my mind she did nothing wrong. It's the life of a Neph. It's all muddled and gray for us. Whether we enjoy it or not is neither here nor there.

"You did . . . well tonight."

"Go," she says. I think she might be on the verge of tears, and I want to demand that she let me in so I can hold her. "I want to be alone. Please just *go away!*"

The pain in her voice guts me. I lean my head against her stall door as sounds of the countdown to midnight ring through the hotel.

"Happy New Year," I whisper, and I leave.

CHAPTER FIFTEEN

New Year's Day in the Big Apple

"The fragile, the broken, sit in circles and stay unspoken . . .
Everybody wants to go to heaven, but nobody wants to die."
—*"Hospital for Souls" by Bring Me The Horizon*

At some point I will learn to stop feeling relieved. When one thorny situation passes, something worse inevitably rises in its place. Hours after Anna's test has ended, an emergency summit is called in New York City.

Anna has failed her test. There's no other explanation for the summit. Neph are not called to attend unless one of us is to be dealt with. I thought she did well, but apparently she let her true nature show at some point last night. Father sends his jet to get me, Blake, Kope, and the twins. I'm sick to my stomach. I can feel the others looking at me during the flight, but I can't stand to meet their eyes and see the pity there. Or the mutual fear.

I can only assume Anna's father will bring her to New York, or attempt to escape with her. But if they run, the demon lot will give chase, and they'll be found. Either way, Anna is doomed.

I am twisted up inside like a rope in intricate, nonsensical knots, so full of anger and hatred I can scarcely hold it in. I don't know how I'll make it through this night. I don't know how I'll be able to watch what torture the Dukes have in store for Anna.

All day I've tried to put on my straight face and close off my heart to any feelings, but this is too big. I can't numb myself. I can't block it out. I don't even know how she feels for me anymore, but it doesn't matter. I know how I feel, and watching her suffer will kill me.

On the way to the hotel I stop at a spirits shop and use my fake ID to buy bourbon. I have to keep a tolerant buzz tonight in order to hide any possible bond that might show between me and Anna. Only the twins' father, Astaroth, would have the ability to see it, but that would be enough to have the both of us killed. The five of us take a cab to the hotel and sit silently. Waiting. The tension in the room is like static electricity. I'm pouring bourbon into my flask when Kopano gets a call from Belial.

"Pick up Anna on your way to the summit. She's in room 433. Same hotel as you."

"Yes, Duke Belial," he answers smoothly.

Of course Belial would ring Kope to collect her. I stare at the wall and shake my head.

We leave soon after that, sliding into our coats and winding scarves about our necks. My body is heavy as we take the lift down to Anna's floor.

Kopano knocks on her door, and she opens it slowly. She smiles hesitantly when she sees it's us. Nobody but Marna smiles back. Anna looks fit in a pair of black trousers with black heels and a puffy gray coat. Her hair is down and she's exuding such a sweetness I have to look away before she meets my eye.

We leave to walk to the comedy club where the summit will take place—fucking demon humor. The six of us are the only people in Times Square who aren't laughing and talking, plastered, or nutters. My fists are shoved tightly into my jacket's pockets, and I cannot unclench them.

I keep Anna in my sight, and each time I feel her eyes on me, soft and warm, I want to close my eyes and savor it. Instead I lock my jaw and let the flavor of hatred roll around on my tongue.

I wonder if Belial has told her the rules about a summit— how Neph are not to speak unless asked a direct question. I wonder if Belial has taught her to lie with confidence when the Dukes question her. I wonder if—holy shit . . . is Anna still a virgin? My father will know. My fists clench tighter.

When we turn down the street where the summit will take place, I fall back to walk beside Anna. My eyes scan the area for immediate dangers. I've been listening out for Dukes all day, trying to catch any snatches of conversation that might give clues about what they're after tonight, but it's all bollocks. They say nothing of importance, so wrapped up in their own enjoyments.

Being next to Anna soothes me, and I can finally relax my hands and take them from my pockets. I want to look at her, but I'm afraid I will grab her and run.

It's a cruel fate that Anna showed up at my gig that night last summer. It's cruel that I opened my heart for the first time in my life to the one person who could so utterly annihilate me with her goodness. It's a cruel fate that I pushed her away to keep her safe, only to lose her anyhow.

But she does have the hilt—the Sword of Righteousness that the nun gave her. I wonder what kind of damage she could do with it tonight. How many Dukes could she kill before she's taken down? Does she have it in her?

We're momentarily halted by a load of people spilling out of a club. Anna's arm brushes mine, and I feel the back of her hand against my palm, then her pinkie winds around mine, deliberately connecting us while it's too crowded for anyone to notice.

I am flooded with a blinding sense of joy at this simple contact from Anna—this small gesture that shows I still mean something to her. Recklessness overcomes me, and while the street is too crowded for anyone to notice, I pull Anna by the pinkie and she follows easily. I'm holding my breath, so hungry for this moment I can hardly stand it.

I lead her quickly into a small alcove stairway where we rush down, away from the others. It's dark and smells of damp earth as I turn her to face me and press my mouth to hers. She doesn't push me away; she pulls me closer. She meets my fierceness with her own, and together we heat each other in the icy air. Our frozen noses and cheeks thaw. Even the air around us steams with warmth. We cling and taste and breathe each other's breaths.

This stolen kiss tells me everything I need to know. Anna still wants me. Still cares for me. Still needs me.

We break the kiss and I press my forehead to hers. Our breath clouds around us, too hot for the winter air. I watch her as she touches my face, and I can't understand how anyone could want to hurt her. I don't want to live in a world where someone like Anna Whitt is in danger for being who she is.

I would trade places with her if I could. In fact, if Anna is to die tonight, so will I. I won't let her die alone.

When Ginger orders us up from the stairwell, back to reality, everything is a blur. I take a long draw from the flask, relishing the burn and how it dulls my senses. Is this what it's like, when you know you're going to die? I'm a zombie as we make our way down into the comedy club for the summit. A dead man walking.

The six of us sit as far from the Dukes as possible. The Aussie Neph guarding the door doesn't find the knives hidden in the compartments of my boots. I bend down at our table while everyone's busy and take them out, sliding them into my pockets. Blake notices, his jaw tightening. He won't look directly at me, but he's blinking and I know he wants to ask me what the hell I'm thinking.

I lace my fingers over my abdomen and lean back. When the time comes, I don't want him involved. I don't expect anyone to try to save me.

I drink more.

Father takes the stage and I stare without expression as he cordially welcomes the Dukes and Legionnaires and Azael, the personal messenger of Lucifer who might've been the spirit circling Anna at that party before Belial showed—still don't know what that was about. Father welcomes Rahab, the Duke of Pride, to the stage, and I feel the burn of bile and bourbon rising as Rahab reminds all of us Neph of our place in the world.

"Your life is not your own. You were bred to serve us. . . . There is one among you who has been warned, and yet still chooses poorly."

Has been warned? Was Anna ever warned? I wait for the bomb to drop, but Rahab never even looks toward Anna. He stares toward a middle table full of Neph.

"Gerlinda. Daughter of Kobal."

Bloody hell. My eyes shoot around the room as it all becomes clear.

It's not about Anna. They're after another Neph.

I school my body and my face not to react. I must not exhale loudly or slump with relief. I sit rigidly and take a celebratory sip of bourbon, though I'm quite buzzed enough to block any bond from showing.

I lean forward and steal a glance toward Anna, and the look on her face punctures my heart, deflating my relief.

She is staring at the stage and the Neph Gerlinda with unguarded horror, as if she might scream or cry as the Dukes begin to heckle.

No, Anna, I want to say. *Sit silent and be grateful. There's nothing you can do to stop it. You don't even bloody know her . . .* but since when has that mattered to Anna? She is a bleeding heart for injustice, and I know it will scar her to witness this. I don't particularly want to view this show myself, so I know it's a million times worse for her.

Shite, she needs to just stare at the wall and try to block it out or something. But every time I glance down she's fervently watching, even moving her lips.

Please, Anna, please. For the love of God, keep your damn mouth shut.

She is making me so nervous. If she can just make it through this, we'll all be all right. I know it's cruel of me, but I don't care about Gerlinda or what's happening to her onstage. I can block it out. I can only hope Belial has taught this skill to Anna.

I'm beginning to sweat in this stupid button-up shirt. It's freezing outside, but a thousand degrees in here. I undo the next button on my shirt and take another drink. Gin shoots me a "stay still" glare.

The entire room tenses and I look up for the first time, allowing myself to fully see what's happening. Rahab has raised the gun to the Neph woman's head. I've never seen anyone die before. I start to shift my eyes away when I hear a lovely voice call out from several seats down, and my heart stops.

"No!" Anna shouts.

Oh, my God. Her voice rings in my ears, echoing. *No, no, no . . .*

Everyone turns toward our tables, staring in shock. Rahab yells, "Which of you dares to speak out at this sacred summit?"

This cannot be happening. Why, Anna, *why*? Why can't you be a silent bystander just once?

The room begins to spin as they bring Anna to the stage. My stomach rolls. I move to the edge of my seat, and I see

Kopano grip the table edge in front of him. All eyes in the room are on Anna, but Belial slightly turns and eyes our group of Neph in the corner. With one hand at his side he cups it downward and presses down as if to say *Stay seated.*

Does he have a plan?

It's taking every ounce of my energy to remain seated while Anna is up there under Rahab's scrutiny. I have no idea how she can manage to appear both fragile and strong all at once.

Father waves a hand in the air, and my stomach drops when he speaks. "Good Hades, Belial! She's still a virgin!"

The room gasps in unison. Blake flinches next to me, and Kope scoots forward. Marna covers her mouth, but Ginger slaps her hand quickly down.

The Dukes argue about how to deal with Anna and why she is still pure. All I can do is stare at her face, at the fear in her creased brow. By now, Rahab is furious that his show's been interrupted by an insolent Neph, and he's ready to punish her with or without her father's permission. He shoves Gerlinda out of the way and hits Anna in the side of the head. My hand is in my pocket and I'm halfway to my feet before Blake grabs my arm like a steel vise and yanks me back down.

Anna gets up again, standing strong as she takes yet another hit. The sound of her involuntary cry makes me struggle to take in air. I want her to reach for the hilt and murder him. I want him dead. Why isn't she using the sword?

Rahab points to the gun on the table and snarls at Anna. "To make amends for disrupting our session, you will complete it for us. You will kill her yourself."

Shite. She will not pull that trigger. And he knows it.

Everything with these bastards is a test or a game. And the rules are always stacked to ensure our failure.

"Raise the gun," Rahab tells her.

I know with sudden clarity—this is the moment we'll both die. Only a miracle can save Anna now.

Only a miracle . . .

My vision blurs for a split second, and a foreign urge stirs deep within me. I have never spoken to God. Never asked Him for anything. But for the first time ever . . . I want to pray.

As Anna stares down at that gun, a silent prayer stutters its way from my heart.

Save her. Please. I'm begging You. You're the only one powerful enough. I will do anything. If I live, I will stay far away from her. Please, just don't let them kill her. Take me instead. Don't let her suffer. . . .

"Last chance," Rahab says. He raises the gun to Anna's head and cocks it. When I hear the click, I'm on my feet and my knife is out. Rahab will be dead before he has a chance to pull the—

What the bloody hell is *that*? A gigantic light splits the back of the room and sends out a glow. Did someone open a door or turn on a spotlight? I look at Anna and find she is the only one not looking at the light.

She's looking at me. And then Kopano, who's standing two seats down. She gives her head an almost indecipherable shake, and I feel an overwhelming urge to sit. It takes me a moment to realize she is using her silent compulsion, and I want to scream.

The room brightens further and Rahab lowers his arms.

All of the attention has turned away from Anna, to the light. I squint as I try to look at it. Abruptly, I fall back into my chair and stare.

Angels. The Maker sent angels. Is this . . . did He answer my prayer? Or is this coincidence? I begin to shake, overcome by the beings pushing into the room. The Dukes are falling back and scrambling to move away. Neph jump up and run, huddling against the walls in fear. The angels eye the room sternly and I have no doubt they would gladly take out every one of our stained souls if the Maker gave the order. I want to run onstage and snag Anna away, but the angels move forward.

"It is not her time," says the angel in front, nodding to Anna. "She will serve as a test to many souls."

Not her time . . . I exhale in a rush. They really are here to save her.

Oho, Rahab is livid. A purple vein has taken prominence in his forehead. To see the Dukes crapping themselves might be the highlight of my life.

"Fine," Rahab says with a deadly smile. "It is not her time now. But it is *hers*."

The bastard raises his gun and shoots Gerlinda in the face. Anna shrieks as the girl tumbles back, dead. The angels rise up in unified indignation, and I lift a hand to block the brightness.

Chaos breaks loose as Rahab orders everyone out of the room. Neph push and shove to get to the exit. Where is Anna? As the angels retreat and the light fades, it's turned into a damn near trampling spree.

I search for Anna, working my way through until I see her

golden head. I call out to her, and she tries to press back into the crowd to get to me. I don't know why it's so important for me to touch her in that moment, but I need to feel her, to prove to myself she's alive. We finally link hands near the exit, but Belial pulls us apart. He practically carries her out and shoves her into a cab, where she is whisked away. Anna and I watch each other through the back window until she's out of sight. She's safe. Adrenaline still charges through my body. I turn and walk briskly with the running crowd, getting as far from the Dukes as I can.

After an hour of wandering, I sit on a park bench in Manhattan and stare down at my shaking hands in the glow of a streetlight. I don't know where the others have gone. I simply stare at my hands, in shock that there's still blood of life pumping through them. My breaths are still hot against the cold air. My boots are still solid on the ground.

When you're certain you're going to die and then you live, it's a strange sensation. But I don't dare feel relief. I don't dare feel anything. I don't even startle when a hand comes down hard on my shoulder and I look up into the face of Belial. He jerks his head for me to follow him, and turns to leave without waiting. I shove my hands into my pockets and follow a few feet behind him.

I follow him into the underground, where we take the train to the end of the line in New Jersey. I follow him until we're at a packed bar in Hoboken, clear of the Dukes in New York City. And then I sit in silence at the end of the bar as Belial orders five shots of Wild Turkey and throws them back one after the other, before sitting on the edge of the stool beside me.

He puts one giant hand on his thigh, and the other arm drapes along the bar beside me. He leans forward, boxing me in, and talks under his breath in a low, lethal tone.

"I saw you tonight. If any of the others had seen your little show, you'd be dead."

My jaw is clenched. He must not appreciate my I-don't-give-a-shit expression, because he points a hefty finger at my face.

"You listen to me right now, kid, and you listen good." His eyes. He is beyond furious about what happened tonight. "You stay the hell away from my daughter. You understand me?"

I swallow hard, but my throat is still dry. "I was planning to, sir."

"You're no good for her."

Stab.

"I agree, sir."

He narrows his beady brown eyes as if searching for sarcasm. I am too numb to manage any sort of sarcasm or wit.

"You think you're in love with her?"

I don't answer this, and he plows forward.

"You think she loves you? That she's meant for you? Wrong, lover boy. My girl's meant for bigger things. She loves everybody and everything. You're just a stray she'll eventually forget about. Understand?"

Everything he's said is true, but that doesn't mean my insides aren't ripped out. It doesn't mean there's not a part of me that somehow hoped I was wrong and that Belial might see whatever good thing Anna sees in me. But Belial sees the real me. The unworthy me.

My lips move, "Yes, sir," but only dry sound comes out.

"You are not a safe option, not as a friend, and not as anything else. If Anna wants to pal around with Neph, it sure as hell's not gonna be you. She can fall for that son of Alocer all day long, but I'll be damned if I let the son of Pharzuph fuck with her heart."

I grit my teeth. It feels as if a boa constrictor has encircled my chest. I give a tight nod.

"I know you thought you were cute tonight, playing Romeo like a God-damned fool, but the bullshit ends right now. If you ever endanger her again—if you dare to contact her or so much as *look* at her, I have friends who will make your death look like an accident. Am I clear?"

To see myself through his eyes—to be reminded so sharply and clearly of all the reasons I'm unworthy of Anna . . . it's like a series of stinging slaps across the face. Belial's eyes bore into me and his nostrils flare. I give him another nod, my neck stiff. He rubs his goatee down and pushes back from the bar.

Belial leaves me there in Hoboken, where I sit until they kick me out. I walk the streets in darkness, hoping to be finished off by drug dealers or gangs, but it turns out the bad guys are never around when you need them.

Perhaps I should pray for an angel of mercy to put me out of my misery. No, I will not pray again. I'm thankful Anna was saved, but having my own life spared feels like a fluke, and I dare not remind the Maker I'm still here. Still, I will make good on my end of the bargain.

I walk.

At six in the morning I ring our lead singer, Michael, from a street in Jersey City.

"What the fuck, Rowe?" he grumbles.

"I'm in."

It takes him a moment to catch my meaning, and then he chuckles. I've been the only Lascivious member who hasn't yet agreed to make the suggested move to L.A. We can focus on our music full time. I've been holding out, wanting to remain close to Anna.

"Hell yeah, baby." His voice is raspy with sleep. "You been up all night?"

"Yeah," I say.

He laughs again. "We're gonna rock that shit in L.A. Wait and see how much ass you get out there, man. You won't regret it." He yawns into the phone.

I feel none of his enthusiasm. I feel nothing. "Go back to sleep, mate."

"Yep. Later."

We disconnect and I hail a cab for the Newark airport, wondering if I'll ever feel anything again.

CHAPTER SIXTEEN

POSTCARD

*"It's like somebody stole the biggest piece of me,
I may never see it again, I may never see you again."*
—*"Before the Fall" by The Rescues*

I should have hired movers, but I didn't trust anyone to touch my drums. I leave behind my bedroom set but take everything else from the basement with the help of Michael, Raj, and Bennett. I don't think Father is thrilled about not having me under his thumb any longer, but he approves of my continuing on as a musician. I haven't told him I plan to drop out of school when I turn eighteen in March.

When we're loaded up and the guys leave, I trudge to Father's office to say good-bye.

He doesn't get up from his oversized leather chair, but he lifts his eyes, scrutinizing my long-sleeved T-shirt and jogging bottoms slung low.

"Change into something more attractive before you go."

"Yes, Father."

"You're still expected to come to Atlanta to help Marissa as needed."

My already tight muscles clench further. "Yes, sir."

"I can't believe you're going to drive that monstrosity across the country yourself like a bloody commoner." I look down at my hands as he continues. "I still expect you to work along the way."

"Without question, sir."

"I have very high expectations of you in California. I'm sure you won't mind if my Legionnaires or I pop in now and again."

"Of course not, Father. I look forward to your visits."

He stares at me as if trying to detect my bluff, and I stare back, unblinking. Finally, he nods, finished with me, and then turns in his chair to face the lewd images on his computer.

I nod to myself and turn to leave.

I drive the same route I took with Anna, only I can't go faster than fifty-five miles per hour because I'm pulling the SUV behind me and the damn thing swerves back and forth. So I take my time, blasting my music to drown out my thoughts.

Anna is everywhere. She is smiling at every landmark and showing kindness to every stranger I encounter. She is laughing at every silly billboard and humming along to my music. When I reach Arizona and my route changes, she is with me as I stop and walk to the ledge of the Grand Canyon. She is staring in awe at the magnitude, feeling small and fragile.

She is with me because she's inside me and I cannot rid myself of her.

I've made too many mistakes when it comes to Anna. I endangered her because of my own selfish motives and desires. I wanted her for myself, even when I knew I wasn't good enough.

I want to be good enough.

I shove my hands in my pockets and kick a rock. It goes soaring off the ledge and I never hear it hit. I've been waiting for something from the outside to change me—to kick me, to force me into a different life. But after watching Anna at the summit, grabbing her beliefs by the horns despite the dangers, I've realized it won't be some outside power that changes me.

It has to be me.

Anna and Kopano have control over themselves. Only I can control me. And it's time to make a change. I've always lived as if I had no choice, but it's not true. There is always a choice, no matter the consequences. I can't live Father's lifestyle any longer. I can't love Anna and continue to be with other people. I'm tired of hating myself. I'll never be good enough for Father or Anna, or God, for that matter. But if I can be proud of myself, for once, that will be a bloody good start.

I turn to go back to the van but stop when a bird flies past my face, landing in the gravel at my feet. I swear the damned thing is staring up at me. It even cocks its head to the side. I nudge my foot toward it, trying to scare it away, but it only bristles a little and hops closer. He puffs his feathers at me and coos.

It's a dove, I realize, and a lump rises in my throat. My own personal peace offering.

"Sod off, stupid bird."

It coos at me again and my palms begin to sweat. Just because I reach out to Him with one blasted prayer and decide to change my life, the Maker thinks I've suddenly switched sides?

I look up at the heavens and shake my head. "This is nothing to do with You. You want peace with me? Get rid of the demons, and then we'll talk peace."

When I look back down, the bird is gone. I let out a rattling breath and jump into the van, throwing the thing into drive. My hands are shaking and I accelerate too hard, spitting up gravel under the tires. I pull off at the visitors' center, and lean my head against the steering wheel, trying to shake off the bizarre bird episode.

Inside the little shop, I imagine Anna flitting along the rows, admiring all the baubles, and my chest feels as if it will cave in.

I never got to say good-bye.

In the aftermath of the summit, we'd sought each other. She'd wanted me at her side. Does she know there's nowhere else I'd rather be? That it's killing me to stay away? That I love her in a way I never believed possible?

I reach for a postcard and a pen at the counter. I've memorized her address. There's too much I need to say. I stare at the postcard so long the lady at the register starts to look at me funny.

Finally I scratch, *I'm sorry.*

I'm sorry I found you and introduced you to our cursed world. I'm sorry you fell in love with me. I'm sorry we can't be together.

I'm sorry for everything, Anna.

PART TWO

SWEET PERIL

CHAPTER SEVENTEEN

LOS ANGELES

"They're all around me, circling like vultures.
They wanna break me and wash away my colors."
—*"My Demons" by Starset*

I'm racked with severe pain every day that first week. I get the fucking shakes like a junkie when anyone lusts for me. It doesn't help that we're not in the studio yet. I hit the gym twice a day, for as long as I can stand it. Then I return to my apartment and blare my music as loudly as possible. At night all I want to do is drink myself into oblivion, but I'm trying to stay clean. When I'm drunk or high my finger hovers above Anna's name on the screen of my phone. I cannot afford to do stupid things. I changed my number to keep her safe from me, and I have to stay strong.

I check out all the hot spots with my bandmates, meeting loads of industry people and sexy groupies, but my heart's not in it. I'm filled with constant loss. The only time I talk to girls is when a whisperer is lurking. And when the demon spirit leaves, so do I.

This is no life. Even with the changes I've made, there is no satisfaction. Only emptiness, and fear that lingers like a bad habit I can't kick.

Michael, Raj, and Bennett have a house together where I keep my drums, but I opted for an apartment alone. We practice every other day, but it's never long enough for me. Michael is confused the day I stay after to see the songs he's working on. I've never taken an interest before, but I can't stomach going back to my place, where my thoughts eat me alive.

One of his discarded songs is only one stanza, but it fills my head and keeps going with new words of my own. I grab one of Michael's chewed-up pens and hunker over the paper, writing furiously. When I'm done Michael snatches it up.

I feel strangely nervous. I tap the pen against my leg and watch as Michael's head begins to bop back and forth and a grin stretches across his face.

"Dude, this is hot."

I shrug. "I don't want credit for that. Just a one-time thing, mate." The lyrics hit way too close to home. I can't have anyone knowing I penned it.

"What else you got?" Michael asks.

I shake my head and lie. "Nothing."

"Yo, Raj! Bennett! Getcha asses in here and listen to this. I think we got a winner."

We finally get to visit the studio and learn the ropes. I've no clue if we'll get a recording contract, since it's so competitive, but our manager is frat brothers with some bigwig's son, so he says he's got an "in." We'll see.

We've decided to record the single I mostly wrote, but Michael is more than glad to take credit.

We're taken into a room where a girl with straight, honey-blond hair is setting up mics and checking the sound. She's incredibly cute and has a kind contentedness in her aura that stabs at my lungs. She looks up and beams when we walk in.

"Hey, guys! You're right on time. I'll bring you some waters, and you can let me know if you need anything else. I'm Anna Malone, by the way."

The ground seems to rock under my feet. Bloody hell . . . why does the world hate me? Why?

She shakes the other guys' hands, and when she gets to me her aura flares bright orange with a red streak. Her eyes search every feature of my face and then she blushes. I quickly let her hand go and stuff mine in my pocket, looking away.

This is fantastic. Just what I need.

She leaves us and Raj punches my stomach. "She wants you, dude."

Michael raises his chin. "Told you you'd be getting all the ass you want here."

I shake my head. "I'd rather not mix business and pleasure."

"For real, though." Bennett snorts, and musses his blue hair. "We don't need any Kai stalkers up in this studio."

"Exactly," I mutter.

Anna, the studio girl, ends up being one of those girls with more male friends than female. She's all natural with a great sense of humor. She's the type of chick you don't mind hanging around. Well, the other blokes don't mind, but I keep my distance. It becomes harder when she begins spending more and more time with us, coming to frequent practices and ending up at the same clubs. Raj has a definite thing for her, and though she flirts innocently back at him, it's me she's got it for, no matter how I avoid her.

It'd be easier if she weren't so bloody nice. Or if I didn't have to see her nearly every day. Or if she didn't remind me in so many small ways of my Anna. Or if I weren't craving sex like a deranged mad dog.

Seriously. I keep hoping it will become less difficult to deny my body, but it hasn't. It's a constant ache. It would be so easy to give in. To give myself release with the dozens of willing girls who light up with lust for me.

And then I remember how I felt last year when I'd slept with all those women after coming back from our road trip. I'd been riddled with guilt and self-disgust. I never want to feel that way again. This is the first time I've ever challenged myself, and I need to win this.

If Kope can bloody well fight his temptations, so can I.

After six months, I have to admit, I'm so damned proud of myself that I want to shout it to the world: *I haven't shagged in six months!*

On second thought, I don't think anyone would be that impressed. Except Anna. And she's the only one I truly want to tell. I almost ring her so many times, especially when our first single hit local airwaves and we were invited back to Atlanta for a signing.

I love you. I only want you.

And then an image of Belial's face fills my mind and I'm reminded of all the reasons why I can't have her. A pang of dreadful fear pierces me at the thought that Anna might be over me. I can't hold it against her if she stops loving me, but I will never stop loving her.

My plan to stay away is ruined when Anna shows at the Atlanta record store. I should have known Jay would hear about it and tell her. The moment I sense her, I attempt to rapidly build a fortress of stone around my heart, shoving my emotions deep within the keep. But her brown eyes penetrate my barriers, as always, and I can't help but notice she's . . . changed. Intricate piercings line her ears. A short skirt shows off her sexy legs. Her look no longer screams innocence. Except those passionate eyes.

I'm filled with familiar rage, at everything. My anger and sarcasm rain down on Anna. The more she shows love and desperation, the harder I push her away.

I don't care, I tell myself. She shouldn't have come. She knows as well as I do. This is a mistake.

When we leave, she sees me being picked up by Marissa's driver. We're only having dinner tonight, no new nieces to train, thankfully, but Anna doesn't know that. I see the heartbreak in her eyes as she's reminded once again of all the reasons she shouldn't love me.

We are cursed. And my fortress is useless against her. I return to L.A. emptier and more broken than ever.

It's Friday when Anna Malone approaches me at the studio, holding her hands together in front of herself, her aura both excited and nervous.

"Hey, Kai. Um, I'm having people over at my apartment tomorrow night. Just a small party. . . ." She bites her lip and her eyes go round. She really is quite attractive.

I flip through different excuses I can use, but I know the other band members will expect me to be there.

"Sorry, but I'm visiting an old mate of mine in Santa Barbara this weekend."

"Oh!" She smiles, but disappointment fogs her aura. "No problem. Hope you have fun."

"Yeah, you as well."

Now I just have to ring Blake and let him know. He's been trying to get me to visit for months, but I haven't wanted him to know I'm not working. Well, no better time than now.

"Dude. Brah. Compadre. Cut the shit." Blake and I are sitting on bar stools under a tiki hut on a crowded beach where I have gently rejected the advances of three girls in the past hour. Blake is ogling me in disbelief. I continuously search the skies for whisperers.

"Don't make a big deal of this," I say.

His eyes drop to my glass of water then rise to my face. "I *will* make a big deal of it, because it *is* a big deal. You don't need to do this, man. You got nothin' to prove."

"I've got plenty to prove. To myself."

He closes his eyes, shakes his head. I didn't expect him to understand.

A blond bombshell saunters up to us with mile-long legs and mini black shorts. She has a posse of manicured beauties following behind her. Blake sees me looking over his shoulder and turns.

"Ah, hey, baby!" he says. The blonde smiles and stands between his legs, wrapping her flyaway arms around his neck and kissing him.

She's magazine material. A few men glance at Blake with envy.

"How's my man?" the girl asks, leaning her forehead against Blake's.

"Helluva lot better now that you're here."

She turns to me and blinks with big eyelashes.

"Oh, hey," Blake says. "This is my boy from way back, Kaidan. This is my girlfriend, Michelle, and her J-Pack of friends, Jessica, Jamie, and Jen."

Girlfriend? Apparently I'm not the only one with secrets.

We shake hands, and I say, "Nice to meet you, Michelle."

Her eyes widen at my accent, and her friends move forward, all their eyes on me, auras zinging with red. I shake each of the J-Packs' hands and sit back.

"Hey now," Blake says when Michelle has stared at me a beat too long. "Don't be looking at him. He's gay."

I fight back a grin.

"Oh," Michelle says, eyeing me differently now.

"Just kidding," says Blake. "He's bi. Sometimes we get it on."

Her face scrunches when she realizes he's teasing her, and she slaps his shoulder. Her friends laugh and smile at me.

"Wait," says the friend Jamie, with a hand on her hip. "So, are you gay or not?"

"He's whatever you want him to be," Blake tells her. "Straight, gay, bi, tri. My boy here does it all. He also likes to watch. So you girls go ahead and put on a show."

I keep a straight face as the girls laugh at Blake's antics and swat at him with their clutch purses.

"What are you girls up to tonight?" Blake asks them.

"We're going to the movies," Michelle says. "Want to come?"

"Not tonight. I'm taking Kai out on my boat."

Michelle's face lights up. "I want to come!"

"I mean the fishing boat," he backpedals. "We're going fishing."

"Ew, never mind. You guys have fun."

Blake winks at me. He and Michelle kiss again and the beauty posse leaves, sending a few backward glances my way.

"You have a girlfriend," I say.

"You're not working," he retaliates.

We search around us to be sure nobody has heard, then Blake tosses back the rest of his rum runner. "Look," he says. "My pops is making me, okay? It's not enough for me to date. I have to be able to land the big one and take her off the market. Trophy wife and all that."

"Shite," I whisper.

"Yeah. Don't say anything to anyone."

"I won't."

We look around again, paranoid. I wish we had a way of talking without worrying about anyone eavesdropping. I take a drink of my water and think about it.

"We should learn Sign," I say.

"Sign language?" Blake scoffs. "We can't be caught doing that. They'll know we're being secretive."

"No shit. We'd obviously only do it when nobody's around."

He thinks about it and nods. "Yeah, all right. I'll let Gin

know, and she can tell the others to learn too. I hope it's not too hard. Ain't nobody got time for that."

I do. I've got all the time in the world these days.

I end up spending a lot of time in Santa Barbara to keep my distance from the other Anna and to give Blake time from Michelle. I've never truly had a best mate before—someone I can be myself around. Our fathers approve of us "working" together, so it's a brilliant setup.

We've spent a lot of time learning Sign and trying to talk to each other. I had to dig a bit online to find all the swear words, though. Blake let the twins know, and they also want to learn. They've got a bit of time away from their father to safely practice now that they're both airline attendants.

All is well until the autumn afternoon I get a call from Marna.

"Hallo?" she shouts. "What is that noise?"

"Music." I'm stretched out on my bed with a hand under my head. Rage Against the Machine is blaring through the room: *The microphone explodes, shattering the molds . . .*

"Well, I can't bloody well hear you!"

I flick it off with the remote and silence falls.

"Honestly, Kai. You're likely to go deaf." When I don't respond, she sighs. "You alone, then?"

"Yeah. You?"

"Just me and Gin. Father's up north."

She sounds nervous and it puts me on edge. "What's up?"

"Something."

I sit up, waiting, but whatever it is, she won't say it over the phone. My heart picks up speed.

"Everyone all right, then?" I ask.

"Yes . . . we've just had visitors. I'm sure you'll hear everything soon."

Visitors. She's dying to tell me—I can hear it in her voice.

"Did 'A' visit?" I ask.

"Mm-hm."

Something's up, and it involves Anna. I stand and begin to pace. "Who else?"

She clears her throat. "K."

I stop.

"They're taking care of some business, that's all," she says. "But you should be on the lookout."

"Did someone send them on this business?"

"Yeah. B."

B . . . ? Oh, Belial. I have no patience for these riddles we have to use.

"What are we talking about here, Marna?"

"Tell him not to get his knickers in a bunch," Ginger pipes up in the background. "They're both too proper to be anything more than *friends*." She says the word with disdain.

"They're traveling together for business purposes."

What the hell is going on? Why has Belial sent Anna and Kopano traveling together?

I let out a low growl and Ginger mutters to her sister, "Told you not to call him."

"I'm sorry," Marna whispers. "Don't be upset, Kai. It's not bad."

Not bad. "I've got to go."

I hang up and pace the floor, growing more and more unsettled. I switch the music back on, letting it rattle my eardrums. For whatever reasons, good or bad, Belial has Kopano and Anna working together.

I can scarcely breathe. I bend into a crouch, grabbing my hair in my fists.

I can tell myself over and over that I want her to stop loving me, but it's a damn lie. The only thing that's gotten me through the past ten months has been my hope that she's thinking of me at night, as I'm thinking of her.

My phone rings again and I snatch it up, hoping it's Marna. But it's Blake. I hesitate, then switch off the music again and answer.

"Yeah."

"You okay, man?"

"Fine," I say through gritted teeth. Marna obviously called him to check on me.

"Don't go jumpin' to conclusions, brah. I'm sure it's nothing."

I can't help it—it's my nature to go straight to the worst-case scenario. "Do you know anything?" I ask.

"Nope. Same as you. Freakin' weird, though, right? They've got me curious as hell."

"Yeah," I mutter. "Swear you'll tell me if you hear anything. No matter what."

"I swear, Kai. No worries, though. I'm sure it's fine."

I'm not sure at all. And I know it's going to kill me, waiting to find out.

CHAPTER EIGHTEEN

PARTYING WITH PHARZUPH

*"Now the son's disgraced, he who knew his father when he
  cursed his name . . .
But it broke his heart, so he stuck his middle finger to the
  world."*
—*"Let It Rock" by Kevin Rudolf*

It's never good to see your demon father's name on the mobile ID. I haven't spoken to him in ages.

"Is your band available in two weekends?" Father asks.

"I believe so, sir," I say, wondering what this is about.

"*Pristine* is having an Oktoberfest party to celebrate our new fall and winter models. Someone mentioned hiring a band, and I thought of Lascivious." He says this as if it's a brilliant idea, and he's doing me a great favor. My chest constricts.

Pristine—the world's leading pornographic magazine. Father. Models . . .

I know what happens at these parties—I've been to plenty.

I rub a hand down my face, thinking of my ten-month streak coming to an end. I force a response.

"Thank you, Father. Sounds excellent. I'll speak with the band, to be certain."

"I'm sure you can work it out—shuffle your schedule if needed. I'll send the jet."

We hang up and I launch my phone across the room. It smashes against the wall and falls in several pieces. Damn it. I don't feel like visiting the wireless shop.

I collapse back onto the couch, pressing the heels of my hands into my eyes. The pain of not working has finally simmered into a dull daily thrum that's bearable. I don't want to ruin my progress. I don't want to work and start all over. I don't want to be with anyone but Anna.

I dig my hands in harder.

Under Father's eye, I know I will work, because I don't want to die. Not on his terms. Not for this. Dying at Anna's side is different.

A voice in my head whispers . . . *Kope would refuse* . . . and that thought infuriates me.

How the fuck is he so perfect? Why am I so weak? The absolute worst part of this—the bit I don't care to admit—is that a small part of me is rejoicing at what awaits.

The scents. The softness. The sounds . . .

My heart races and the beast raises its lazy head after a long hibernation.

It's not in my power to end this curse. I hate myself.

* * *

Michael, Bennett, and Raj are so loud on the jet, so hyper, the pilot has to ask them to keep it down. We've killed the chilled bottle of champagne and moved on to beer Father supplied us. I keep a steady buzz and laugh at their antics, but I don't say much. I'm resigned to my fate. That momentary guilty excitement I felt after Father called has long since diminished, replaced by a sense of numbness. I know what awaits.

Once the party gets rolling, there will be no boundaries. No modesties. No privacy. No saying no. By tomorrow morning my bandmates will have seen things they can't unsee. They'll have done things they can't undo. This will not be like the parties they are used to.

When we arrive in New York City, a limo is there to meet us. Full rock-star treatment.

Acid is churning through me by the time we arrive at the building of Pristine's penthouse suite. The guys completely geek out the entire way up.

"Are the models going to be walking around naked and shit?" Raj asks.

"Possibly. Or nearly."

He and Bennett high-five while Michael rubs his chin, grinning.

"Seriously, man," Bennett says to me. "How easy will it be to score?"

I shrug. "Depends. Loads of rich men show at these things. It helps that you're in the band, but you've got to calm the fuck down."

All three of them stand taller, taking deep breaths, schooling their faces like cool cats. Better.

The lift opens and spills us into the sounds of laughter and tinkling glass. Women are walking about in those German Oktoberfest getups with tiny hats, loads of skin on show. The doorman looks us up and down and says, "Ah, the band. This way, please." He leads us around a corner to the larger room with chandeliers sparkling above a raised platform. Our instruments are set up and ready. Through the crowd of suits steps Father in a navy designer suit, with four gorgeous females at his heels. They're all wearing indulgent smiles and tiny black skirts with string bikini tops, covered in different-colored gems for the fall.

"Bad. Ass," Raj whispers as they approach.

Father comes straight to me, an award-winning smile on his face, and takes me by the hand, pulling me in to clap a hand on my back. His affection is all for show, but it's convincing. His hand grips my shoulder.

"I've been bragging on you to our Harvest Girls here," he says, turning to wave a hand at the four models. "They didn't believe I had such a handsome and talented son."

I grin, but not too big—more like a smirk. The girls look me up and down, taking in my black jeans, boots, and gun-metal-gray fitted shirt.

"God, he's practically your mini-me," says the girl with dark red hair and brown-tinted jewels.

"A little Richie?" says the platinum blonde with burgundy gems. She steps closer to me. "I wonder how much of you is like your daddy?" Her pink tongue touches the corner of her shining red lips.

"You'll just have to see for yourselves, luvs," Father says.

The girls laugh, gazing up in adoration and touching him with open intimacy—they've all clearly been with him. Now they're looking to me. My soul sinks, but my body stands tall.

I catch the eyes of my mates, ogling for all they're worth. I clear my throat.

"This is Raj, our bass; Michael, our lead singer; and Bennett, keyboardist."

Father shakes their hands and introduces the girls.

"We've got one of every fall flavor," he says. "Catherine was our September girl." He points to the blonde in burgundy. "Emily did October." The redhead in brown tones smiles. "For November we've got both Fátima . . ." The black-haired Latina in yellow-gold. "And Alina." He motions to a girl with creamy brown skin and chocolate-colored hair, wearing orange stones. "They'll shoot together."

Fátima and Alina share a small kiss. Raj makes an involuntary sound beside me.

Amateur.

I'm more than a little glad when Father motions to the stage for us to take our places. I can't see his colors, but I know he'd be dripping in the purple of pride when he introduces us to the room. All eyes are on me, filled with intrigue, as I take my place in front of the drums.

The son of Richard Rowe.

We begin playing, and I wish I could slam these sticks against the drums all night. I don't want to think about what I'll have to prove to these people later. Though I've attended my share of these events throughout my teen years, this one feels different. As I look out at the women dancing in front of us, I realize this party is no different than the others. It's me who's different now.

I try not to think about Anna, and what she'd think if she could see all this, but it's impossible. She's in my every thought, and this party would make her sad. Everything is artificial, eye candy. Things that aren't okay by normal standards, like the objectification of women, are made acceptable and enjoyable within these walls. But it's all temporary and shallow and fucking depressing.

Yet, I know it will feel good at the moment. I know too well.

Hours pass, and my arms burn at the finish of our last song. The room erupts into cheers. I look at my mates, flushed and sweating as they stare out at the sea of bodies, the breasts that defy gravity, the carefully crafted perfection of bodies there for the taking.

The sickening pit inside me deepens.

Father approaches, beaming at the crowd as he holds an arm out toward us. They cheer wildly again. He ushers us off-stage and a horde of women surrounds my mates and sweeps them away into the party. The Harvest Girls are on all sides of me, having lost their bejeweled tops somewhere along the way. My eyes are locked on Father's knowing grin as acrylic nails run down my arms, and extended eyelashes flutter up at me. But beyond all of the fakeness is warm skin, and that is real.

My chest is tight. Father thinks he owns me, but he cannot control my mind. I choose to work tonight, because I refuse to give him the power of ordering my death.

Anna believes there is a purpose for me, but I'm not certain.

I used to think *this* was my purpose, jobs like this, but I was wrong. I don't know why I'm here, on earth, other than to love her and protect her if I can. I can't do that if I'm dead.

So, I know what I must do. I must let the beast have complete control. I must live another day.

CHAPTER NINETEEN

THE CHILL OF WINTER

"When you're living a life that you gotta deny,
When you feel how we feel, but you gotta keep lying."
—*"Secret Love" by Hunter Hayes*

In spite of the sunny southern California weather, it's possibly the worst winter of my life. I'm filled with self-loathing over my work in New York, I'm missing Anna like mad, and I'm certain she and Kope are together now. I expect a call from Marna any day to give me the bad news.

At Christmas I get the call I've been waiting for—the one I'm certain will break me for good. But to my surprise, the call is from Kope himself. My initial thought is that something's happened to Anna, and my innards plummet.

"Hallo?" I stand in the middle of the television room, gripping my mobile.

"Brother Kaidan." His voice is too smooth. Too bloody calm.

"Kope. Is everyone all right?"

"Yes. Everyone is fine."

Then why the fuck are you calling me? I nearly rail at him, but I contain it, needing to match his proper tone. I ask, "Then to what do I owe this pleasure?"

He pauses and I want to reach through the phone and wallop him.

"Anna says you will not speak with her."

I stand there, momentarily stunned. Who is he? Her *BFF*? The last person I need to explain myself to is Kopano.

"What is your point?" I ask tightly.

"My point . . . she still cares for you. I wish to know how you feel for her."

I nearly laugh. My head falls back and I stare up at the ceiling. I know what this is. Kope is asking permission to make a move.

"That's none of your concern." I feel something deadly seeping through me.

"I am concerned because she hurts," he goes on. "If you care, you should let her know. And if you do not care you should release her."

The snake. I bloody knew it. I love how he's trying to make it all about her, not himself.

"So you can have a go at her?" I ask. My heart and lungs have gone haywire.

"I will not pursue her if you do not wish me to. But you must tell me."

The room goes spotty. This is really happening.

I can barely unhinge my jaw to speak the next words. "It's

not my permission you need, Kope. Talk to her father." Perhaps if he asks Belial, he'll get the same heartwarming pep talk I received. Then again, this is Kopano, perfect and safe, with a father who's not interested in killing Anna—not set on making her work.

Kope wants to make her happy. Is that what she wants from him?

"Please, Kaidan." He sounds weary, and I wonder where he is and what they're up to. "I do not wish to quarrel."

"Tell me: Does she know about you yet?"

He falls silent and I slowly grin without humor—I've reminded him he's not perfect.

"No," he finally whispers.

I think about him unleashing himself on Anna. Who knows what would happen if Kopano actually let loose? "Be careful," I say.

"I am ever aware, brother. And now I need your honesty. What are your feelings for her?"

A laugh escapes me, but I'm not amused. Not one bit. I feel like an animal backed into a corner by his persistent pushing. I hate Kopano at this moment more than I've hated anyone. He knows I have no right to keep her from moving on. She is her own person, and I'm not allowed to see her. If I've truly let her go the way I swore I would after the summit, I cannot hold on to any part of her, even from afar.

Perhaps to the outside world it looks as if I don't care about her anymore, but I believe Kope knows the truth. He's taking advantage of my inaction.

As much as it kills me, I have to wonder if this is my true

test of self. Can I do what's best for Anna if it means she'll be with Kopano? If they are meant for each other, can I stand aside and let them be together?

I squeeze my eyes shut and try hard not to crumble as I say the next words. "I've made it clear to her there's no future for us, mate. So have at it. Best of luck to you."

I wish I could say I spoke those words with a gracious heart. I wish I could say I'm happy for them. That doing the right thing feels good. But I can't, because my heart is full of malice, and I'm afraid it will eat me alive.

I want Anna to be happy. I want her to have what I can't, even if it murders my heart every day of my life.

Come February, Blake and I are still in the dark about where Anna and Kopano are traveling, and why. It's taking every ounce of self-control I can muster not to call Anna and ruin a year's worth of self-control. It is work staying away from her, knowing her feelings have likely changed. It's the only self-less thing I've done in my life, and let's just say I'm not happy about it.

I'm a right bear to be around.

No sex, plus no Anna, plus Anna with Kope, equals the recipe for one mad chap.

I've been in two fights this month already, which hasn't happened in ages. The second was yesterday in Santa Barbara with some knob who does motocross with Blake. So I'm not surprised today when Marna rings me.

"Babe, you've got to stop this. I mean it."

"Stop what?" I fall back on my bed, rubbing my forehead. "Everything's fine."

"They're only friends. I swear to you."

"I've no clue who you're talking about, but good on them." Bloody well hope her father's not listening.

"I'm out of town," she says, as if reading my mind. "About to make my next flight."

"He asked me to be with her," I blurt.

"Eh? Don't know anything about that. But it's not happening. Believe me."

She sounds certain, but I refuse to hope. "Was there a bond when you saw them?" I can't believe I'm asking. My chest shakes when I exhale.

"No relationship bonds," Marna says. Then, because she can't help herself, she rushes on. "Perhaps a *slight* attraction, but you know how fickle that is. Nothing to worry about."

I grunt.

"I mean it! Be careful, you. And chin up."

I grunt again and she sighs before hanging up.

They're only friends. I swear to you.

A bit of the dark cloud I've been living under lightens.

I haven't truly worked in four months, since the party in New York. It's been brutal restarting my sensual fast. If this is what Kopano feels like all the time, I feel sorry for him. And I hate him even more for being so calm all the damn time, making it seem easy.

Every interaction is difficult for me. In my muddled mind, a simple "How are you today?" turns into a purred "How do you want it, baby?"

But still, the only person I want in my bed is Anna Whitt. And that will never happen. Hence, anger and frustration.

These sour feelings are compounded when Father rings me on February 13, saying I'm needed in Atlanta the very next day. He gives no details, but my blood runs cold. Working in Atlanta can mean only one thing: Marissa. I suppose I should consider myself lucky this is the first time he's called me to Georgia in the fourteen months I've lived here. Still . . . it's one call too many.

Then one tiny spark of light fills my mind. I'll be close to Anna. So very close.

I can't see her—I've been strong, staying away all this time, and I can't ruin my efforts now. And I don't need Belial tracking me down to make good on his threats. However, being so near to her just might give me the fix I need, which goes to prove just how pathetic I've become.

It's not until I'm breathing frozen Georgia air and see the sedan waiting for me outside the airport that I allow myself to think on my purpose for being here. I half expect exhilaration to hit me at the prospect of being physical with a girl again, but it never comes. I don't want this. I ruined my first-ever streak of goodness in October, and I've been an angry shell of myself ever since.

I feel ill the entire way to Father's house. Over and over I stretch my hands open and close them into tight fists.

Do I dare refuse him about a niece of Marissa's again? What if it's another child? How far will I go to stay alive?

When I enter the house I find Father and Marissa having tea. They both glance at me, and then continue talking business. In a chair beside them sits a tall girl with her hair pulled back. She looks around sixteen or seventeen, thankfully no younger. Father and Marissa are speaking in French, which I understand, but the girl likely doesn't. I don't listen because I don't care to hear whatever they're discussing. I stand in the doorway of the posh sitting area, grinding my teeth as they murmur. I stare at an ugly, abstract painting on the wall. I can feel the girl watching me.

When they finish, Marissa turns to me in her chair. "Kaidan." I force myself to look at her. "This is my newest niece, Iva. I am hoping you can keep her company today."

Marissa reaches over and pets the girl's head. Iva smiles at her shyly, and then at me, which makes me grind my teeth even harder. The girl has no idea what she's in for. I force a nod and my mouth goes dry as I search for a way out of this. I devise a quick plan, though it's weak.

"I've heard there's a rave in the city this evening," I say, my heart thundering. "Thought I'd try to kill two birds with one stone. May I take Iva out with me this afternoon, and then drop her back at Marissa's on my way to the party?"

Shite. I didn't think this through. They're going to ask me where I'll take her. Lookout Point, perhaps? Father turns to Marissa and she shrugs, flinging her waist-long black hair from her shoulder and clicking her long fingernails together. Blast, that sound. I steel myself against a shudder.

"Makes no difference to me," Marissa says, reaching out to stroke the girl's cheek, "as long as the job is done and she makes it home to me safely. But keep her out of public." Marissa eyes me and says in French, "Teach her *all* the ways to pleasure a man. No need to keep this one innocent."

"*Oui.*" I nod tightly and try not to look relieved.

"You may take the BMW." Father tosses me the keys, smiling devilishly at Marissa, his mind otherwise occupied.

I look to Iva and jerk my head toward the door. The girl is quick to follow.

Aside from the young girl last year, I've never left a niece untrained before. This is the first time I've even considered it. I start the car and catch sight of the date on the dash. Valentine's Day. How apropos.

I drive in silence, tapping the wheel in nervous thought as the girl sits there with her hands clasped tightly in her lap. Her threadbare sweater is no match for the winter air. I crank the heat up.

When we're well out of the five-mile zone I take a deep breath and huff it back out.

"You speak English?"

"Yes," she replies in a heavily accented voice.

"Do you know why you've been brought to America?"

"Oh, yes. My brother tells me. I am to be married to handsome, wealthy man who will care for me."

I swallow. I usually have my guard up with the nieces. I keep myself numb and don't allow any thoughts in. But it's been too long, and my mind's been infected. I cannot ignore this girl's words. They seep into me.

Iva asks timidly, "Are you to be my husband?"

I shoot a glance in her direction and find her scanning my face with hope. I look back at the road and stare straight ahead as I speak the words that will shatter that hope into a million cutting shards. For once, I will tell one of Marissa's nieces the full truth without trying to sugarcoat it, downplay it, or glorify it in any way.

"Iva . . . I'm very sorry, but there is no husband. Your brother lied to you. He sold you. You're a slave now, and Madame Marissa is your master."

"I . . . What do you say?" Her voice shakes. I'm willing to bet she came from an extremely poor family. If her brother was the head of her household, her parents most likely died from illnesses because they didn't have the money for treatment. I'd seen this before, with too many nieces. Her brother probably squandered their small pittance of funds on drugs or alcohol. She's begun to tremble next to me.

I drive us to a state park, away from prying eyes and ears, surrounded by trees.

Iva's chest heaves with quick, frantic breaths. This is not uncommon. I need to calm her. I stop the car and turn in my seat.

"Please, sir," she says. "I don't understand!"

I'm filled with dread as I explain Iva's new world to her. I tell her what she will be expected to do, and what will happen if she doesn't. I make it clear that if she utters a single word of what I've told her, I will be killed.

"Why do you tell me this?" she asks, hugging herself around the middle.

I shake my head, staring off. "I want you to know the truth. I'm very sorry."

"You work for them, yes?"

"Not by choice. I'm kind of like you, Iva. I do as I'm told or I die."

It's the first time I've ever thought to make the comparison.

It's an excruciating afternoon in the car with the girl—me speaking calmly, her near hysterics. I answer all of her questions. I make it clear what is at stake for both of us.

"Are you a virgin?" I ask. Her eyes dart to the floor and she hangs her head—that's a no. "You don't need to be ashamed. I'm trying to see how much you know. I'm not going to do anything to you, but if you have questions . . . about men . . ."

She shakes her head frantically.

"We both have to pretend I've shown you what to do with these men, Iva. Do you understand that? We will both be punished if they find out we did nothing but talk today."

She jerks her chin up and down as tears stream from her eyes. "I know what to do," she says in a thick voice. "I don't want to go to that woman's house! Don't make me go. Please!"

She grasps my shirt in her thin hands and cries out. Nieces and conquests have cried in my presence more times than I can count, and I never reached out to comfort them. Never. Nieces must learn to self-comfort, and conquests must not be led on.

But that was before. Now, without hesitation, I pull Iva to me. She's far too thin. I put an arm around her as she cries into my chest.

"Please save me, sir, please," she sobs. I hold her tighter, swallowing hard.

I know better than to make promises I can't keep, but I dare to say, "I will try. I swear it. . . ."

Father knows people, and so does Marissa. They have ties to all areas of law enforcement—dirty cops and officials who've been bought off. If I try to uncover this operation, to expose it to authorities, I'll be killed. For now, I am powerless, and I'm at the mercy of Iva to keep my secret. But I swear to myself at that moment . . . I will be watching; watching and waiting for a time when I can expose Marissa and her abomination of a business.

My shirt is still damp with Iva's tears when I leave her at Marissa's, and I am hollow.

I'm feeling reckless after the encounter with Iva. It's too late to go back to being safe. There's no way to trek away from the edge of the choices I've made. I will forever be on this precipice I've climbed, staring over into the abyss of hell and waiting to be found out and shoved off.

It's only a matter of time. A certain peace comes with this knowledge.

It's that peace, paired with today's recklessness, that sends me toward Anna's town.

As I get closer, a light snow begins to fall. I push my hearing toward her apartment. I hear movement inside and my heart shoots into high gear.

This is foolish. I'm a fool. I shouldn't be here, but I can't stop now. My forward momentum is too fast. I'm parking and jumping out, searching around me. My quick breaths make clouds in the air as I jog up the steps to her door.

I listen as the person inside goes still, then tiptoes to the door.

"Who is it?" Patti asks. Her strong voice lifts me up and I smile.

"It's Kaidan, ma'am."

The door swings open and her eyes are wide, red hair wild.

Excitement and love burst from her aura and she throws her arms around my midsection. Holy shit, I'm getting choked up. I hold her tightly, swallowing and blinking away the emotion. I won't cry, but damn, this woman is shoveling something warm and golden into my hollow places. Just like when I'm with Anna, I can't help but wonder how someone so good can care for someone like me.

She pulls back and grabs my face to look at me, then hugs me once more and releases. "Anna's not here. She went for a run, but I'm sure she'll be back soon. It's too cold out there, the crazy girl!" She pats down her wavy hair, smiling. "Can I get you some tea?"

Disappointment tugs at my mood, because I should not linger.

"I'm sorry, miss. I'd love to, but I can't stay."

"I understand," she whispers. "But she'll be *so* upset she missed you."

Will she? This sends more golden stuff pouring into me, though the foolishness of my actions is starting to splinter through my reckless peace now. I *really* shouldn't be here.

Patti squeezes my shoulders as I bend to give her a quick kiss on the cheek and go. Her eyes are filled with moisture when I leave.

Nervousness invades my system as I walk quickly to the BMW.

Stupid, stupid, stupid...

I reach up and yank off my knitted cap to run my hand roughly through my hair, which I haven't cut in the fourteen months since I moved. It waves over my ears as I pull the cap

242

back on. I'm at the BMW now, opening the door. As disappointed as I am, I know it's for the best that Anna doesn't see me. I've worked so hard to—

I turn abruptly as something moves in my peripheral vision. I stand there and stare across the parking lot. From her light blue sneakers to her black yoga bottoms that fit every curve— bloody hell—to the thin jumper that can't possibly be warm enough. She's on the other side of the lot, her back to me. She stares up at the snow, oblivious to her surroundings. I want to shake her and yell, "I could have been a Duke or an axe murderer and you'd have never noticed me!"

But all I can do is stare. And then her name slips past my lips.

She freezes in front of her apartment stairwell and her head snaps up. Her cheeks, which were pink, go red as she stares back at me.

"Hi," she whispers, and it's so simple, so sweet, so Anna.

"Hi, yourself."

I should leave. I shouldn't have called her name. I shouldn't be here. I know all of that, and yet, I can't move.

"I hate Valentine's Day," she says.

My heart squeezes at the sound of sadness in her voice, but I grin at her blunt honesty. "Yeah, it's shite."

I want to tell her I'm fairly certain my father created this poor excuse for a holiday as a way to promote disappointment among lovers, but I don't want to mention him.

She rewards me with a small smile, then falls serious. "Is everything okay?"

No. No, everything is not okay. Everything has been awful.

But right now, in this moment, it feels perfect.

"I just needed to see that you're well. And it seems you are."

I want to go to her so badly that I grip the car door to keep from running. As we stand there, refusing to look away, it's as if each of the past fourteen months is stripped away, one by one, and we're back in that New York alley kissing. Any progress I've made to separate us is ruined. I know it, and she knows it, because she's moving toward me, and she's mirroring the need I feel. She's stepping off the pavement and walking my way.

That's right, little Ann.

I'm finally going to touch her again. Then I'm going to get to the bottom of what's going on with this "traveling" business. I'll worry about the consequences later. Right now, Anna is mine.

I move to shut the door and go to her when I feel the itch of a tingle across my neck. My eyes flash to the gray winter sky and I'm blasted with a sight I recognize well.

Two whisperers.

"Fuck," I whisper. I step back, and it kills me. Anna sees them and rushes between two cars, fear in her eyes. "Don't try to follow me," I tell her, because it's just the kind of thing she'd do. "I'm going to the airport." She nods her understanding that I'm not in town to stay, and her chin trembles.

My skin turns to ice in the cold air as I move to climb back into the car, leaving as quickly as I can, so as not to endanger her by being seen together.

That is why I cannot seek out Anna. Not even for a moment.

When I'm well enough away, I smack the steering wheel with my palms. I shout every obscenity I can at the top of my lungs. I rip my hat off and throw it on the floor.

We will never be safe. She can never be mine.

CHAPTER TWENTY

RAGE

*"The secret side of me I never let you see
I keep it caged but I can't control it, so stay away from me."*
—*"Monster" by Skillet*

Seeing Anna, even briefly, gets me through the next few months, though I can't concentrate for shite. My nineteenth birthday comes and goes without a blip on the radar except a text from the twins and a pity call from Blake.

I've always gone through the motions of life, doing what needs to be done and putting on a good show, but I've stopped caring about the show now. I can't even lose myself in the drums anymore. I'm too busy wishing for something more. The band knows something's up with me, and I overhear them talking. They think I've become a cokehead or some shit. I don't bother correcting them.

In May I start to feel the itch. It's been three months since

I saw her, and I know her birthday's coming up. I need to hear from her, to get my fix.

I'm sitting at a bar with Michael, Bennett, and Raj. When I see a group of girls watching me, then making their move to come over, I take out my mobile and dial Marna. I hunch into myself a bit while I talk, and the girls don't approach. They wait.

"Where are you?" I ask when Marna answers.

"Scotland, my lad." She sounds chipper.

"Any news?"

"Erm . . . no. Not really."

"Not really?"

"I meant no. Just no."

A prickle of apprehension heats my skin. "Are they still traveling together?"

"No."

Before I can ask another question I hear my mates greeting someone loudly, and the voice of Anna Malone rings out behind me.

"Hey, Kai! You're coming tonight, right?"

"Who's that?" Marna asks in a rush. "Is it the other Anna?"

"Hush," I say, turning to Anna. She's beaming at first, then cringes.

"Oh, sorry! Didn't know you were on the phone." She smiles and covers her mouth, turning to the bartender for a drink.

"What a cow," Marna mutters.

"Tell me what else you've heard, Marn."

She pauses too long. "Like I said, nothing."

My skin heats. As usual, I go for worst-case scenario. "Something's happened. Is anyone hurt?"

"No!"

Second-worst-case scenario. "Did they hook up?"

Marna pauses too long again, and this time pain alights along my skin as if I'm being eaten by fire ants. She lets out a fake laugh. "No . . . don't be silly."

Marna is lying. She always pauses awkwardly before she lies.

"I've got to go." I sound as deadly as I feel.

"Kaidan, wait!"

"You paused, Marna." I let this sink in.

She sounds frantic. "Please, listen. It's not what you think."

"It's exactly what I think."

"No, I mean it. There was just one moment, one *tiny* kiss, but they're not—"

"*Stop*," I whisper fiercely, squeezing my mobile. "I don't want to hear it."

I can't believe this is happening. In this moment I acknowledge to myself that I always held out a small hope that Anna would never allow it to happen, no matter how much Kope pursued. But she gave in, and for all I know maybe they've been together all along and the news just now got to Marna. They might've even been together when I saw her in February, a thought that wrings my lungs of air.

Within a matter of seconds, I rebuild the walls around myself that Anna Whitt tore down. The I-don't-give-a-damn-about-anything walls. My jaw clenches and I sit up straighter.

I don't care.

I don't feel.

Nothing can touch me.

"Kai?" Marna whispers on the other end of the phone. I scarcely hear her.

Anna from work stands in front of me, staring down at her phone. Her aura is gray with disappointment and she lets out an "Ugh."

"What's wrong?" I ask her. Marna tries to pipe up, and I say, "Not you, Marn. Hang on." I put the phone to my shoulder and look at the frowning Anna.

"My roommate is coming home and doesn't feel good— she doesn't want any people over." She pushes straight strands behind her ear.

A sickening sort of determination to prove just how much I don't care comes over me. "Brilliant," I say. Anna's eyebrows come together in confusion until I say, "Party at my place, then."

She slowly grins. "Really?" Her excitement makes my gut twist with nervous guilt, but I ignore it. I've put this girl off for too long. And for what reason? If my Anna is moving on . . . I shake my head. Not "my" Anna. She's never been mine.

Raj bounds over and slaps me on the shoulder. I put the phone back at my ear as word spreads that I'm having people over. My parties used to be epic, so the guys are stoked.

"Gotta go, Marn. Fun to be had."

"Don't do it, Kai. It's not—"

"Bye, then."

I hang up and my stomach turns. For the first time, I don't try to move away or escape when Anna talks to me, playfully pushing my arm or slapping my knee. She can sense the difference. I see it in the way she's searching my face, wondering if I've finally seen the light.

Yes. Yes, I have. And it's blinding.

She's filled with happiness and excitement, bright and shining.

I give her my attention, but my chest is filled with a hive of stinging hornets.

We waste no time moving the festivities to my place, and soon it's overflowing with people. The party fills the whole apartment complex as neighbors open their doors and filter over. Music blasts from my speakers loud enough to shake the floors, just how I like it. Everywhere I look people are drunk, high, dancing, snogging, falling on one another, laughing. Anna sits between Raj and Bennett on the couch, playing a drinking game with cards.

I lean against the wall, watching as people drift past. My rage has not subsided. It's still in my eyes when Anna glances up and catches my gaze. She appears taken aback by the intensity there, her aura zapping with excitement and trepidation. Her guardian angel sees this and starts whispering to her. I want to tell the poor fellow not to waste his spiritual breath.

I raise two fingers and beckon her to me. Without a word to the other guys, Anna gets up and makes her way through the crowd, nervous but determined. They watch her. She stands before me now, breathing faster.

"What's up? Are you okay?"

"No, actually."

"Um." She rolls her bottom lip between her teeth. "So . . . what's wrong?"

I've told Anna on numerous occasions I don't date people I work with, that I'm not dating material anyhow, and that I've got loads of crap going on in my life. It has been enough to keep her at bay so far, and yet here she is.

"A lot is wrong with me, Anna. But I think you've figured that out by now, yeah?" My hand snakes around to the back of her neck, and I feel the light vibration of her breathy moan as I pull her closer. Her aura pops with shock and elation. My body is steady, but inside I'm shaking, driven by everything I refuse to feel.

"Can I . . . help you?" she asks.

"I think you can."

For the first time in what feels like forever, I give my body permission to take over. My mouth covers hers. At the feel of her lips, months' worth of desire explodes through me. I back her roughly against the wall, and she grabs the back of my shirt in her fists. From across the room the entire band hollers their approval, but I can hardly hear.

I know I have to control myself, because I can and will hurt her if I don't. I break the kiss and take her by the hand, pulling her to my room. It's packed with people. I don't have the patience to wait for them to leave, so I pull her into the bathroom. She grabs my face the second the door is closed and we're kissing again. She doesn't protest when I pull off her shirt or strip down her jeans. And she definitely doesn't protest when I raise my own shirt over my head and drop it to the floor.

"Holy shit, Kai," she breathes, running her hands over my chest and stomach. "You should just walk with your shirt off all the time." Her eyes dart up to mine as if she's horrified she's just said that out loud. I kiss her again, but she keeps breaking the kiss to look at me, and kiss me again. For some reason I cannot take it—cannot stand being looked at right now. I turn her and press her against the bathroom door. It has the desired effect. Her palms are against the door, face turned to the side, hips pushing back against the front of me in a way that makes me grab her hips and groan.

I need more.

I reach around to her front and slide my hand down her stomach, and into her knickers. I use my other hand to hold her up, and it doesn't take long until she's squirming, moaning, out of breath, weak-kneed. I hold her up until she stills.

"I can't believe that just happened," she whispers between breaths.

The scent of her lust surrounds us, and the familiar sensation of emptiness begins spreading through me.

She turns to me and takes my face again. I close my eyes and let her kiss me slowly. Suddenly, moisture builds behind my lids, and I have the powerful urge to cry. I've had moments of emotion lately, but I haven't truly had the urge to cry like this since I was a child. My throat is dangerously tight.

"Kai . . ." She whispers my name against my mouth, but I cannot open my eyes. Her hands move down my sides to the front of my jeans. She undoes them, and touches me with a gasp. My hands are on her waist and I tighten my grip.

"Anna . . ." When I say that name I'm far away, and the

saddest, most heart-wrenching sense of wrongness invades me. This is not who I want touching me. I can't do this.

I gently grab her wrist, and wrench the word from my throat. "Wait."

I open my eyes and find her staring at me. I pull away, and with great effort manage to zip up my jeans. My abdomen clenches with a stab of pain.

"God," she says. "I'm sorry, I . . . What's wrong?" Her voice quivers. I lean my forehead against hers because she's such a sweet girl and she doesn't deserve to be dragged into my train wreck of a life.

In that horrible moment I know that no lie or feeble excuse will do. I clear my throat and stand straight to look at her.

"Last year, when I moved here." I clear my throat again. "I . . . there was a girl. In Georgia. She's sort of . . ." I am tongue-tied, having never spoken these feelings out loud.

"You love her?"

I search the wall over her head before I nod. "Yeah. And her name is also Anna."

"Oh." She snorts and crosses her arms, looking down. "No wonder."

"I'm sorry. I had an awful day and I'm an absolute idiot to have put you in the middle of it."

She shakes her head. "No, it's . . . whatever. No biggie." But her aura says otherwise.

She reaches for her jeans and I hand her her shirt. I snatch up my own and pull it over my head. As she's buttoning her bottoms with shaking hands I reach for the door.

"You're an amazing girl, Anna Malone. I truly am sorry."

Her eyes are watering when she looks up at me just before I leave her. I push my way through the crowded apartment. At the couch I ignore the jeers of my mates, and shake my head at Raj's offer to do a line of coke. Instead, I lean down and swipe Bennett's pack of cigarettes and leave the apartment. I walk all night and smoke the entire pack. I will spend the day tomorrow hacking up tar, but I don't care.

I just don't care anymore.

CHAPTER TWENTY-ONE

REUNITED

"She finds color in the darkest places,
She finds beauty in the saddest of faces."
—*"Walk Away" by The Script*

I know she's coming to California, the newly eighteen and graduated Anna. I've been warned by the twins, and I've prepared myself to be unmoved. She's only coming to inform us what's going on—the mystery we've been kept in the dark about for the good part of this year—and then she'll leave again. I'm certain Belial won't allow her to linger. The demons are having a summit in Vegas, so Anna has a short window of two or three days to travel unseen.

This is business, not personal, and I won't allow any emotion to interfere. Marna says Anna's traveling without Kope now, and I'm dying to know why, but I won't ask. Cool, calm, and collected.

This is all very easy to say until I see her standing at the railing of Blake's deck, overlooking the cliff side and beach where we've been surfing.

The moment I see her up there in pink and silver, blond hair blowing in the breeze like a siren . . . every feeling I've suppressed comes crashing over me, wave after wave. The emotion that trumps all others is anger. Seeing her makes me furious, and I know it's irrational, but I'm seething about how she's made me love her, how she's gone and fallen for *him*. I don't care what Marna says. I know Anna. She wouldn't hook up with Kopano if it didn't mean something to her. She's not impulsive like most people.

I wonder if she's truly happy with Kope or if she's just settling. I wonder if she enjoys touching him as much as she enjoyed touching me. I wonder if Kope is able to control himself now that he's finally being physical with someone. I wonder how it would feel to punch him in his perfect face.

We're quick to climb the steps to Blake's house. I want to tell all of Blake's friends to get lost instead of ogling her like the fine piece of arse she is. I mean, bloody hell, the girl fills out that outfit perfectly. She looks strong and toned, and she's as fresh-faced and shy as ever. I stand in the back while Blake tackle-hugs her and the other blokes try to flirt. I'm overflowing with loss in her presence. It hurts to look at her, so I grit my teeth hard and lean against the rail, staring out at the ocean instead.

Blake, smart lad that he is, sends the other blokes away, and it's just the three of us. Anna takes on the same position as me, leaning against the railing, staring out in thought, looking gorgeous. It's as if this is a holiday for her, while I'm over here in knots.

The anger is back, full force, along with an urge to lash out.

"Where's your boy?" I ask. When our eyes meet, I know she sees my anger. Fuck cool, calm, and collected. I want something real. I want to see her as mad as me. I go on. "I'm surprised he left your side. I thought Belial and Alocer would've arranged your marriage and you'd have a pack of adopted orphans by now."

The perfect little couple and their perfect little life. They probably talk about how they pity me and the others.

Blake tries to laugh off my comment, but I'm not going to let him defuse this. I want to see Anna blow up. I stand tall and face her. She starts to say something but is distracted at the sight of my body. I've bulked up quite a bit since she last saw me. I'm filled with animalistic pride at the way her eyes take me in and fondle me.

She finally snaps out of it and says, "We're friends. Just friends."

Bollocks.

"Do you snog all your friends, then?" I'm about to suggest she snog Blake, so he's not left out, but he takes off into the house.

Anna's eyes appear sad, but I'm not buying it.

"I never meant for it to happen, Kai. We were—"

"I'd rather not hear the details, thanks."

She is still too calm. I need to see her get angry. I need to know that I can still bring out the vixen in her the way she brings out the beast in me. I need to know I can make her feel something other than pity.

She tries to sidle closer and I move away from her. I need a drink and she needs a reminder that she's Neph, just like me—imperfect and cursed. I stride to the bungalow and toss back a cold beer. Her eyes are on me as her jaw locks. She's knows I'm attempting to stir her up. She comes right over, trying to get me to stop and talk, but I dodge her.

When she touches my arm I turn to fire. I fight back an urge to take her straight down to the floor where she can feel the weight of me on top of her. I pull away quickly. She doesn't get to touch me whenever she likes. Not anymore.

Anna follows me about the deck, determined to make me see that what she's done is fine.

"Is this all because of Kope?" she says to my back. "You're acting like . . ."

I turn, staring her down.

" . . . like I cheated on you or something." She finishes in a small voice that pierces my heart, as if she truly never knew she was mine.

I walk away, considering what a fool I've been. I toss the bottle in the air over and over, wishing I could smash it into a thousand bits. Anna still follows me.

"You really have no right to be upset with me," she says. "I heard what you told him on the phone."

Him. My stomach sours, but I laugh it away. Anna should know actions speak louder than words. Plenty of my actions have shouted my love for her, but she chooses to cling to flimsy words instead.

"Words are powerful, Kai, and so is a *lack* of words. You

wouldn't even talk to me anymore. I didn't know what to think! And then to hear you tell him that? How was I supposed to feel?"

I will not take the blame for her actions. Could she not sense the anger and sarcasm in my voice when I spoke to Kope?

"Nothing I said could've pushed you into his arms if you didn't want to be there."

She huffs. "Yeah, well, in one really bad, freaked-out moment, that's where I ended up, but it wasn't planned. It felt . . . wrong."

A chuckle escapes me at the malicious joy I experience over their kiss feeling "wrong." Is it possible there's something imperfect about Kopano after all? "Perhaps your boy Kope is just out of practice. Although some things should come natural for him."

She throws her arms up and lets them fall to her side with a defeated slap. "All right, you're being unreasonable. We'll talk when Blake comes back."

She looks away, too calm. What will it take to piss off this resilient girl? She walks to the edge of the pool, and my mind searches for something to push her buttons and bring her to life.

"It was inevitable," I say. I toss the bottle in the air again as she spins to face me, eyes narrowed.

"Inevitable?" she asks. I hold back a smile at the anger brewing in her eyes. "Like you and that Anna chick you work with?"

How . . . ? I miss the bottle and it clatters to the deck. "Shite." I pick it up, trying not to show my surprise that she knows. Fuckin' Marna. I tamp down the guilt I feel. I didn't touch another girl until after I'd heard about Anna and Kope. Still, though. I never wanted Anna to know, and it makes me feel like a filthy bastard when I think about it.

Flustered, I call to Blake to come outside. I failed to make Anna lose her cool. Point to her. I'm glad when he joins us, because together we're able to tease Anna. Tag team effort. It's brilliant, and I sit smug when we finally get her to blush, flushed with frustration.

"I don't appreciate when people are fake with me." She says this pointedly to me, and I frown. Is *that* what she thinks? "If you guys will sit down and shut up for a minute, I'll tell you what I came here to say, and then I'm out of here. You two can find someone else to make fun of."

I think she's bluffing about leaving, to make us feel bad, but I sit up straighter at the mention of her news.

"Remember that nun, Sister Ruth, who I was supposed to see on the road trip?" I nod. The one who passed away. "Well, she came to me as a spirit. It turns out that she was an angelic Nephilim. She descended from the guardian angel of the Apostle Paul. It's his Sword of Righteousness that she gave me."

My mouth is agape and so is Blake's.

"She found me so she could tell me a prophecy. The prophecy foretells that the demons will be wiped from earth forever, led by a Neph of both light and dark."

My heart is a bass drum in my chest. A Neph of light and dark . . .

"You," I whisper. Her eyes catch mine and hold them as she nods.

All I can do is stare as my mind reels. Anna is the center of a prophecy dating back to biblical times. I shouldn't be surprised—I knew she was different, but this is huge. Dangerous.

"Tell us the entire prophecy," I say.

Anna swallows, and rattles it off. "'In the days when demons roam the earth and humanity despairs, will come a great test. A Nephilim pure of heart shall rise above and cast all demons from earth, sending home to heaven those righteous lost angels with whom forgiveness is shown, and sending those lost forever to the depths of hell where they shall remain with their dark master until the end of days.'"

"Damn," Blake whispers. "You memorized all that?"

"I had to." She rushes on, telling us about traveling she did to gain Neph allies after learning about the prophecy last year. She met Zania, daughter of Sonellion, in Syria. Anna says that Z was a hard sell, having led a brutal life with the Duke of Hatred. Her job has been to stir hatred and distrust of women in the Middle East. Apparently she's gained an addiction for alcohol along the way. Anna thinks she'll come around to our cause when the time comes.

Next she met Flynn, son of Mammon, in Australia. He's a redheaded MMA prizefighter whose lifelong match has been fighting his nature of greed. He was more than willing to go against the Dukes.

I feel a pinch of jealousy that I wasn't chosen to go with her on these missions, but I understand the safety of having Kopano. As much as I don't want to admit it, I'm glad she didn't go alone, and I know there's no way I could've gone without Father somehow finding out.

Bits and pieces of the puzzle of the past year begin to fall into place, painting an important picture as we ask questions and piece it all together.

"We're just building the list of allies right now," Anna says. "We can't rush it. I think when it's time to act, there'll be some sort of catalyst to let us know."

She sounds wise and unafraid, and I marvel at how she's carried this burden for the past year, growing stronger instead of bowing under the weight. Of course Anna would be given some monumental task. This is more amazing and terrifying than I could have ever expected. This . . .

Anna abruptly stands.

"Where are you going?" Blake asks her.

She pretends to brush something off her shorts. "Home. I said what I came to say. It was . . . good to see you guys."

That's it? After dropping that bomb on us, she's going to run off? I stare at her from where I sit, but she won't look at me.

She and Blake hug.

"Don't go," he says.

"I really should," she mumbles.

So, she doesn't *have* to go.

"I told you she can be stubborn when she wants, didn't I?" I say to Blake. I try to appear relaxed, as if I don't care one way or another.

"I'm not being stubborn!" She puts her hands on her hips and I raise a brow, trying not to smile at how riled she's getting. She points at me. "And you have no room to talk. You're a mule."

Blake finds this far too amusing, laughing like a hyena.

"She just called you an ass, man."

"I *am* an ass-man."

Anna purses her lips, annoyed, and I'm quite enjoying it. I'll banter all day if it'll keep her here.

"Aw, c'mon, just stay," Blake whines.

"I don't think so," she says, and I want to spank the stubbornness out of her. She marches over to my chair and says, "Just get up and say bye to me, Kai." Again I raise my brow and she adds, "Please."

I get to my feet and look down at this girl, a mix of sexy, sassy, and sweet.

"Bossy, aren't you?" I ask. I'm not ready to let her go. She stares up at me, and I know she's not ready to leave either, but she won't admit it. "Right, then," I say. "You'd best cool off before you go."

She screams in surprise as I scoop her easily over my shoulder and run for the pool, jumping in.

When we come up for air, Anna is livid. I can see it in the wideness of her eyes and set of her mouth. She pushes me, but I grab her, and we start to wrestle. I can't help but laugh, just as Blake is in hysterics at the side of the pool.

"Let me go!" she yells at me.

"Not until you agree to stay." I look at her, feeling her body skimming mine as she treads water. She is still angry, and for once I want to calm her. I whisper, "Stay." *Please.*

"Fine," she says.

I let her go and she swims away from me. I'm right behind her. She climbs the ladder and her bum's right in my face. Blake yells something I can't hear because lust has caused the blood to rush through my body in a rapid *whoosh*.

Feeling lust for Anna is not like lusting for other girls. This lust is stronger, braided and twined with love, admiration, and all the pain she's capable of causing me. It's too strong, and I can't resist following her, desperate to know if she feels any of this or if I'm alone in my madness.

She bends over to dig in her bag and I swear I whimper. Her wet clothing clings to her and I can see the bikini lines underneath. Her body calls to me like a flashing beacon, luring me closer. She stands quickly and turns, colliding with me. Every place she accidentally touches me alights.

"For the record," I say, hardly able to speak through the lust that pumps through my veins, "I was more myself with you during those three days than I've ever been with anyone in my life. It'd be easier if I could be fake with you, but you bring out everything in me, little Ann. *All* of it."

The good and the bad. The hot and the cold. The lust and the love.

She stares at me for a long time before blinking and stepping back, bumping the deck rail. She's so filled with goodness, this girl the angels prophesied about so long ago. This girl who has no clue of the things I've done.

And because I can't help but compare her innocence with my dodgy past, because I don't deserve anything good, because it's in Anna's nature to care for the lost and aching, I begin to doubt the validity of what I feel between us. I doubt everything. And I push. Because, like her, I need proof. I need to hear it.

"However it is that you think you still feel about me," I say,

"I can assure you it's nothing more than a classic case of some-one who wants the one thing she can't have. If you had me and got it out of your system, you'd realize the good boy's the one you really want."

She eyes me hard. "Those are *your* insecurities, Kaidan, not facts, and I wish you would stop taking them out on me." She tries to step away, but I block her. I don't want her to leave.

"Excuse me," she says. "I need to change my clothes."

Her clothes . . . yes. My eyes drop. I can't fathom why she needs to change. Her clothes are right nice the way they are—wet enough to cling to every curve of her thighs, hips, waist, and chest. I memorize this image.

For a moment I think she's going to hit me, but her hands go to the bottom of her shirt instead. I nearly topple backward when she begins to wriggle from side to side, pulling the damn thing up and over her head, then dropping it at my feet. I stare at the white halter top and the small, perfect curves it reveals. Bloody hell . . . she's got a belly button ring. I can't . . . Her waist . . . her collarbones . . . her eyes.

That sultry gaze—she's enjoying this in a one hundred percent vixen sort of way. The killer look in her eyes makes the cauldron inside me boil. Whatever scrap of sanity I had is slapped away as she undoes her shorts and pushes them down to reveal her thighs, which I have never seen until this moment.

I am salivating.

There's a challenge in her eyes, making her the bravest girl I've ever met, because I will bloody well lay her down right here on Blake's deck and pick up where I left off in that hotel room. I will have that bikini off faster than she can gasp.

I am just about to charge forward when she turns and bends over, slowly picking up her clothes. My body seizes. She saunters away with half her damned arse hanging out of the sides of her swimsuit, teasing me as her hips sway back and forth, back and forth, back and . . . *oh, God,* this hurts.

I groan in agony, but she takes no pity. Anna is good at not looking back. As she and her edible backside disappear into the bungalow, I cram my fingers into my hair and crouch, feeling as if a horse has kicked me in the middle.

A chuckle comes from the back doors and Blake is standing there, arms crossed over his chest. "That was brutal, brah. You so deserved it."

With my head hanging, I manage to say, "Stay away or I'll kill you."

"You couldn't pay me to come near you right now."

I sigh and try to breathe. Blake laughs a bit more at my expense before leaving me alone in my misery.

CHAPTER TWENTY-TWO

LEARNING THE HARD WAY

"Sometimes I feel the fear of uncertainty stinging clear
And I, I can't help but ask myself how much I let the fear take
the wheel and steer."
—*"Drive" by Incubus*

The problem about being with Anna is she makes me forget everything else. She looks at me like I'm her hero, and I forget who I really am. She smiles at the world around her, and I forget it's an ugly place. She exudes comfort, and I forget we're in constant danger. I forget all the reasons I've stayed away from her, all the reasons it's better for her not to care about me.

I'm sprinting up the same stretch of beach Anna and I walked down less than an hour ago. I'm cursing myself, and swearing that if anything's happened to Anna, I will find those guys from the carnival and take care of them.

I am furious with myself on so many levels. I let it slip

during our walk that Anna's father demanded I stay away from her. I guilted Anna into showing me her gorgeous aura of love, and then freaked out and was an asshole to her all over again. I talked her into going on the Ferris wheel and got so completely carried away trying to kiss her that I never saw the whisperer coming. Then I got us cornered by a fucking gang, where she tried to use her powers of influence and ended up with a gun pointed in her face.

Score two for the angels who saved her arse once again while I stood by helplessly. I grit my teeth as I run.

She's with Blake now, who showed up at the carnival on his motorcycle to whisk her away. Though I'm certain she's safe, the band of fear around my torso doesn't loosen. The gang is long gone, down the strip in the opposite direction, but I don't stop running. I need to deal with Anna.

I still cannot believe a whisperer caught us nearly kissing. I'm sick to my stomach. I want to hurl onto the beach, but there's no time for that. I need to remind Anna of all the things she makes me forget, the most important thing being that it's my job to keep us aware. It's my responsibility to keep an eye and ear out, since I know she won't. I failed us today, and she made it even worse by trying to take on those gang members single-handedly.

Why would she think that's possible? She should have left them to me. Doesn't she know what it'd do to me to see her killed?

I race up the steps to Blake's deck, struggling for breath through the fog of overwhelming fear clouding my mind. I go straight to Anna, who looks afraid, and I take her face in my hands. I have to make her understand.

"Don't ever do that again."

"I know it was dangerous, but there were five of them—"

"I can bloody well handle myself, Anna!" I let her go, frustrated that she doesn't get it. Back and forth we go, little Anna thinking she's a warrior fucking princess or something, and I'm about to lose my mind.

"Give me your knife," she says.

"What?" What's she going to do with it?

"Just give it to me," she demands.

Oh, bloody hell. "No, Anna, I don't know what you're trying to do, but this is ridic—"

Anna comes at me, and next thing I know I feel myself going backward and down. I land hard on my back with Anna looking down at me.

"Give me your knife," she says calmly.

Blake whistles and I stare up into her face of fierce determination, framed in a tumble of blond hair.

"God, that was hot," I say like an idiot.

She holds out her hand, and now I'm curious enough to dig my knife out and hand it over. She turns her head, throws the damn thing with a strong flick, and it lands in the side of a wooden heron's head. Holy shit. I can't believe it. Lust bashes me like a sledgehammer, and I suddenly imagine her naked.

"Dude!" Blake yells, snapping me back to reality.

Anna stares down at me as if she's conquered me. "You showed your colors!"

"Did not," I reply quickly. But even as I say it, I think I bleedin' well might've.

"You totally let 'em out, brah!"

"Shut up," I say to Blake as I push to my feet. I will beat him later.

We're all standing now, and Anna's wearing a satisfied look. "I've been training. I'm not completely helpless anymore."

"I can see that," I say, but as impressive as that was, I still don't want her trying to take on every bastard she comes across, thinking it will be that simple.

She steps closer to me and looks up. "I get it now, okay? Everything you've always tried to warn me about, I get. Today was . . ." Petrifying? Eye-opening? She clears her throat. "I came here and said what I needed to say. Now I have to go. I mean it this time."

And I can see in her eyes that she does. She's been sufficiently scared by our encounter with the whisperer and gang. I'm sorry she had to learn the hard way. I'm sorry both of us have to be continuously reminded. It only takes one whisperer to report back to the Dukes. We won't always be able to weasel our way out of it like Anna did today, telling the spirit we were practicing our "work skills" together.

I listen as Anna changes her ticket to an earlier flight. She gathers her things, and Blake and I walk her to her car. She hugs Blake first. I rest my hands on my hips, resigned to be happy that I got to see her for one day. As horrid as certain events were, and as stupid as we were to tempt fate on that Ferris wheel, a bad day with Anna is better than a good day without her, and I've been without her so long. I'm pissed at myself for ruining half the day being an arse.

She scans the skies before approaching me, and I feel a

smatter of pride for her awareness. I don't expect her to touch me again, but when her arms circle my waist and her face presses against my chest, I'm immensely grateful. I scan the skies myself, but they're clear, so I pull her tighter. I let my chin rest on top of her head for two full seconds, and then she's pulling away, holding my hands. Her fingers slide slowly away from mine until we're no longer touching, and her eyes drop.

A cavern of emptying loss opens inside me as I watch her go. I realize I can shield myself against everything else in this life—but I will never manage to keep Anna out. She's under my skin. She's in my head and in my heart, stretching out and taking up residence. When she leaves, the imprint of her stays, as always, but it's not enough.

It's never enough.

CHAPTER TWENTY-THREE

Alive

"And up until now I had sworn to myself that I'm content
with loneliness.
Because none of it was ever worth the risk. Well, you are the
only exception."
—"The Only Exception" by Paramore

"Come on, man," Blake says. "We'll grab a drink."

We're still standing in his driveway, staring down the street where Anna's rental car has disappeared into the distance. When I don't move or respond, he hits my arm to get my attention.

"I'll be in in a bit," I say.

He gives me a funny look, trying to read me.

"That's some crazy shit she told us, right?" he asks. "About the prophecy?"

I nod, staring back down the street until he sighs.

"All right, fine. I'll give you a minute, but hurry up. We only have one night until my pops gets back from wherever the hell they are."

"Vegas."

"Yeah, whatev. Just have your moment and getcha self inside. I'mma kick your ass at Grand Theft Auto."

I know he's trying to cheer me up. While other blokes would be having a party or going out, our idea of non-parental fun is just the opposite.

He jogs to the house, leaving me to stare down his private drive. She's gone and I've no clue when I'll see her again.

"Come on, Kai!" he calls from the doorway. With stiff movements I force myself to go. He hands me a chilled beer and sits in one of his video game chairs in front of the giant screen.

I play and try to relax, but I keep thinking about the prophecy. At what cost will the earth be rid of demons? At the cost of Anna's life? I won't let her die alone to make this happen. I'll go down fighting with her. I'd die today for a chance to see them all sucked permanently into hell with me.

But I'd die with one regret. I'd die wishing I'd shown Anna how I truly felt. I'd spend eternity in hell wishing I'd had one proper moment with Anna where I wasn't scheming to sleep with her, or pushing her away.

One night with no games between us.

In that moment, I'm filled with a sudden panicked sense of urgency.

My car crashes and burns on the screen and Blake laughs. I jump to my feet, startling him.

"What are you doing?" he asks.

"I have to go." I know I must look deranged. That's certainly how he's looking at me, but I don't care. I run to the kitchen, where I think I've left my keys, and he jumps up to follow.

"Where are you going? We have one night to chill! Don't leave me hangin'."

I find my keys with the silver skull and drumstick crossbones, and I nearly run into Blake.

"I have to stop her."

He's still looking at me like I'm a lunatic. "Who, Anna? For real? But . . . you're always so careful, trying to stay away from her. What about her dad, man?"

"Fuck him."

He chuckles, but shakes his head. "This is a bad idea," he sings as I brush past him.

I spin on my heels and eye him as a sudden grin overtakes my face. "It's the best idea I've ever had, mate."

I turn and he grabs my arm, getting uncharacteristically serious. "Just tonight while they're away, Kai. After tonight you can't mess around like this."

"I know," I promise him. "Just tonight."

I must look like a wild mess when I approach the old fellow at the ticket counter. I've run from the parking lot and it's hot as balls out there.

"I need to get something to my friend," I tell him as I catch my breath. "She's on flight four twenty-eight to Atlanta. Can I see her? Just for a moment?"

"No, sir. I would suggest calling her if she has a cell phone."

"She's got it switched off. Can you page her?"

"I cannot. That flight is about to start boarding. I'm very sorry."

But he's not sorry. His aura is clearly annoyed. He's already looking past me like he's going to tell the next customer to come forward. I wave my hand. "Wait! I'll buy a ticket." I yank my wallet from my back pocket, and he jumps back like I'm pulling a gun when I whip out my credit card.

"Sir, they're about to begin boarding," he repeats. "You might not make it."

"Well then, I suggest you run my card quickly. I'll take my chances."

He grits his teeth and types, swipes, and prints the boarding pass. I snatch it and take off. I'm so thankful we're in Santa Barbara and not L.A. The security line isn't too awful, though I'm bouncing on the balls of my feet the whole time, making the lot of people around me nervous.

When I'm through security I sprint, counting down the gates as I go. My vision spirals down the hall to Anna's gate, but I can't see her.

Come on, come on! I weave through the slow people. When I get a bit closer they announce the initial boarding call. As passengers begin to stand and move, I spot the top of her blond head and I let out an airy laugh.

"Anna!"

It takes a moment, and then her head whips around. Her eyes are red and swollen. My first instinct is to run to her, but she may not want to see me now. She might refuse me—push me away as I've so often done to her. But I have to know. I stop at the edge of her row, and it's as if the people have made a path down the aisle, just for me, straight to Anna.

She seems to be in shock, sitting there at the other end, staring at me, and I seem to be stuck here at the edge of the aisle.

"What's wrong?" she asks me with fear in her voice.

"I—" I peer around for whisperers. "Nothing."

Her forehead scrunches. "How did you get through security?"

"I bought a ticket." I hold it up. The people in the aisle ping their attention back and forth between us like it's a rom-com tennis match.

"You . . . you're going on this flight?" she asks.

Clearly this is out of character for me, as she's quite confused. "No, but those buggers wouldn't page you, and your phone is off."

As it sinks into her mind that I'm here for *her*, she slowly stands and makes her way toward me. I'm so afraid she'll tell me to leave. I have to get the words out before she boards.

"I . . . I just . . ." Oh, bloody hell, I'm really not good at this. I could talk dirty to her all night, but saying how I feel is altogether different—too exposing. Saying these words is the ultimate vulnerability. Anna must know this. It's why she needs to hear the words from me so badly.

Bugger. *Say something!* I lower my voice.

"Anna . . ." Right. That's a start. What next? *Tell her when it all changed.* "The night of the summit, when you were saved . . ." She is staring up at me, hanging on every word. "It was the only time in my life I've thanked God for anything."

Her eyes flutter closed and I exhale. I know the words have hit home, because only Anna can understand how huge that was for me. When her eyes open again, we drink each other in. She takes my face in her sweet hands and doesn't look away.

"I love you, Kai."

Now it's my turn to close my eyes as I savor those words. It's the first time anyone's said it to me and truly meant it.

I want to say it back, but I'm overwhelmed. That damn urge to cry has hit again, and I can't allow it. I keep my eyes closed a moment longer and swallow away the burn. When I look at Anna again, I take her face in my hands and she grasps my wrists. I throw myself out there.

"Spend the night with me."

Her eyes widen. "Kai . . . We shouldn't." But there's no backbone in her words. She's begging me to talk her into it—to say more of the words she's hungry to hear. I want to give her what she wants, in every way.

"I'm tired of living like I'm not alive." I take her shoulders. "I'm bloody sick to death of it. I want one night to be alive. With you." I press my forehead to hers, and now I'm the one begging. "Please, Anna. One last night and we'll go back to being safe again. I need this. I need you."

I lift my head and look at her so she'll know I mean it, but I see worry in her eyes. I don't blame her for needing reassurance.

"I'll be good. I won't let anything happen."

As we stand there with our eyes locked, the wait is

excruciating. I need this so badly. I don't know what I'll do if she says no.

Anna's hands move down my forearms, and her fingers twine tightly together with mine.

"Let's go," she says.

She bites her bottom lip nervously as a grin spreads across my face. We both let out exultant laughs, in disbelief that this is happening. I grab her bag and we simultaneously search around us. No whisperers in sight. I never let go of Anna's hand.

For the first time in my life I think to myself, *So, this is what it feels like to live.*

For the first time in my life, I am alive.

CHAPTER TWENTY-FOUR

LET ME KISS YOU

"Our night is lit by the city moon, and I see myself reflect on
you.
I know what I was meant to do."
—*"Aviation High" by Semi Precious Weapons*

The whole day has been a disastrous embarrassment. First we show up at my flat, where I'm berated by Michael for missing another practice, then I realize the bloody flat is in ruin from my party on Thursday and Anna wants to *clean it herself.* Pardon me, but I'm disgraced by the thought of either of us cleaning. Then she finds the lyrics to "Good Thing" in *my* handwriting. Fantastic. And to add a cherry on top, Anna finds remnants of cocaine on my coffee table and goes all daughter-of-Belial on me. I shouldn't have found her so sexy in that moment, but when Anna gets possessed with any kind of desire it's fucking *hot*.

I'd rubbed her finger where she touched the powder and said, "The way this made you feel? That is what you do to me." It's so rare when I can make her understand the madness I feel for her.

If she hadn't fled the flat to clear her mind at that very moment, I would have had no choice but to do all the sordid things to her I've been dreaming of.

Now I'm standing in my room, staring at the neat piles of dirty clothes along my wall, all organized by color. I shake my head. I can't believe I allowed her to talk me into this. Anna should not have to clean any of this.

I lift my chin as I get a whiff of something divine drifting down the hall. Slowly, I follow the scents to the kitchen doorway, where Anna stands with her hands on her hips, surveying pots and pans that are giving my stove a workout for the first time ever. She's softly singing to herself, "I knew you were trouble when you walked in. . . ." I will forgive her for the Taylor Swift lyrics, because she looks so bloody adorable standing there *cooking*—creating something with her hands for my consumption. I don't think Anna will understand how intimate I find it that she wants to feed me. As far as I'm concerned, it's an act of foreplay.

It's been roughly eighteen months since I kissed her. Sinfully too long. When I begin to think of my hands on her, my mouth tasting hers, my body goes completely rigid with intense need, and my sight begins to fog.

Take her.
Take her now.
Right here.

Who needs whisperers when you have a mind like mine that makes completely devious demands of your body? I'm rational enough to know I cannot obey these commands, but I want to so badly it hurts.

Anna reaches out to stir a simmering red sauce and she freezes. Very slowly, she turns and sees me. She sets down the spoon and takes a step back.

Smart girl.

I have to touch her, and she knows it. I fight every urge that's giving me permission to be rough. With every step I take toward her, she takes a step back, until she's cornered against the sink and I'm inches away, hovering over her, breathing in the air she exhales. I'm taking great care, because I know she can see the beast in my eyes. I know she's both excited and frightened. I don't trust my hands right now, so I grab the sink on either side of her waist. I will not let go.

And then I lower my head and I take her mouth with mine.

Sugar. Salt. Soft and tender. Unmistakably Anna.

Oh, God, yes. This is what I have been missing.

Anna must think it's safe, because she suddenly goes wild. My vision turns white as I fight for control. She tastes and feels even better than I remember. Unlike me, she's not holding back. Her hands are in my hair, nails on my scalp and neck. She's feeling my shoulders and upper back. She's trying to pull me closer, but I've locked myself in this position and I dare not move. I kiss her deeper, letting my mind be taken to that epic place of beauty. Then I ease up and my lips linger over hers, covering them with small and gentle kisses until I have to go deeper again.

When her pear-filled scent fills my senses, my body urges me again to take her.

Anna grips my forearms and pulls her lips from mine, looking up. "Are you okay?"

She has no clue just how okay I am. I want to show my gratitude in a very big way. I told her tonight wasn't going to be about that, but apparently my body didn't get the message.

I push myself away from her and rake my hands through my hair.

"I need another bloody shower."

I'm proud of myself for the self-control I've shown, but the showers are getting old. My body knows when it's being duped. The daily pain I deal with is so much more defined when Anna is near.

I run the towel over my head one last time and I'm about to drop it on the floor when I remember Anna is here and we're trying to keep the place clean. So I hold up the towel and awkwardly fold it in half and hang it askew on the rack.

See? I can do this. I'll even take out the last bag of rubbish without her asking.

I'm feeling good when I run into Anna in the hall at the stacked washer and dryer. That is, I *was* feeling good. Now I see the look on her face and the paper in her hand.

Shiiiiiiite . . . shite, shite, shite!

It's the fucking note Anna Malone left me. I only remember one damn line from the whole thing—something about picking up where we left off. This is not good.

"I heard a rumor that you're not working," Anna says quietly. "Is that true?"

I wish I could say yes, completely.

"Mostly. I work if whisperers come around or if my father gives me a task, but even with Marissa's nieces it's not usually sex."

She pauses and I want to tell her everything—about how hard I've tried and how good I've mostly been, but the proof is right there in her hands that I've done something, sex or not.

"Were there whisperers here when you had people over?" When she asks this, I know what she's really asking. Did you hook up with her because you had to or because you wanted to? Emptiness fills me. I won't lie to her, even though I'd rather gouge my eye out than admit this.

I shake my head. "No." I wasn't working.

She crumples the note and turns away from me, back to the washing machine, and I feel as if I'm falling. I know how she's feeling. I know that sickening sense of betrayal, and now I'm feeling like a hypocritical prat for giving her such a hard time about a kiss with Kope when I'd done even worse. God, if Kopano had done to her what I'd done to the other Anna . . . I clench my jaw, then I get a grip. I have to fix this.

"Anna." She ignores me and goes about stuffing laundry in. "Ann, please. Listen."

How can I make this go away? She turns to face me and her eyes are wet. I shove my hands into my hair, wondering how I can salvage this night.

"It was after I'd spoken with Marna," I try to explain. "I believed you and Kope were together, even though Marna said you weren't. I was certain you'd fall in love with him."

I hate admitting that my own insecurities led me to doing bastardly things, but I have to come clean with her. Anna closes her eyes, and her face is pained, as if she's imagining the worst. I want to take those images from her.

"Did you sleep with her?" she asks.

"No." Though I don't expect her to be impressed, I need her to know. "It wasn't nearly as hard to stop as it had been with you."

She still doesn't open her eyes.

"I've mucked it right up, haven't I?" She looks at me now with sad eyes. "I'd been good for so long, Anna. You wouldn't believe how good." Eight months since I'd had to work that party in New York. Nothing besides that except snogs in bars if whisperers showed. I wonder if she's able to understand how difficult it's been, how much I've missed her. A set of tears run down her cheeks. I want to wipe them, but I don't know if I'm allowed to touch her.

"When I saw you on Valentine's Day I was going to tell you everything. . . ." I ramble on about how I'd found out about her and Kope. "I rang Marna, expecting another no, but she hesitated . . . and there was nothing worth being good for anymore."

I need to shut up. I'm digging myself a hole. Inexplicably, Anna holds out her hand to me. I stare at her offering for a moment before I take her hand in mine.

She pulls me to her and says with conviction, "No more. No more running in the wrong direction."

I exhale and feel the tension from my body release as she holds me tighter. It's going to be all right. We're going to work through this. I once again marvel at Anna's ability to forgive, to love selflessly. I only wish I could erase all the pain I've caused her.

"No more," I promise her. I start by gently kissing under one of her eyes, and then the other, and down her cheeks, soaking up the salty tears on my lips.

Her hands are strong as she reaches up to grip the sides of my face. "You run to *me*," she demands. And then she kisses me hard.

Her forwardness ignites me. I back her into the washer and dryer. My knee parts her legs until it's between her thighs. She is what I need. I know without a doubt I will never again run to another. "To you," I say against her mouth. "I swear it."

Our kiss turns frenzied and I fear I'll never be able to get enough. I fear my need will always overtake me. It's hard to control myself when she's wild like this, but if I focus on Anna and her pleasure, instead of my own, perhaps that will sate me.

I think about the striptease she did at Blake's and my mind goes berserk. Those thighs. If I can get *her* naked but keep my own clothes on . . . just for a moment.

My lips pull from hers and move to her ear. I'm strangely nervous. I don't want to scare her away. I grip her tightly.

"Let me see you again," I whisper.

"What?" she whispers back.

I don't ease up on my tight hold of her, and I nibble the freckle atop her lip. I know I'm being too vague, but I'm afraid she'll balk if I grunt, "Naked. Now," as I really want to. So I choose my words carefully, knowing I'll need to take this slowly, layer by layer.

"Let me undress you. Not all the way . . . just as you were today at Blake's. Please. Let me see you again."

Our cheeks are together, and after a moment I feel her nod. I don't hesitate. I pull the tank top over her head, and my pulse races at the sight of her pink bra and all that gorgeous, creamy skin.

She reaches for my shirt, and I almost stop her, but the thought of my skin against hers changes my mind. I let her take my shirt off, but that's it. When the cloth is over my head I smash myself against her, taking her mouth with mine and reveling in the feel of our chests, arms, and stomachs flush together. She is so soft, and when our skin touches, the temperature goes up.

I stop only to look at her, to make sure she's ready for the next layer to come off. She says nothing, only breathes rapidly as I feel around the edges of her shorts and slowly remove them.

There are hips, thighs, and legs in my sight now, and I am dying to be naked with her. I close my eyes, and my head drops back. *Keep your shorts on, Rowe.* I'm going to focus on Anna. Her pleasure will be my pleasure.

"Let me kiss you," I beg.

"Okay," she whispers.

"No." I look at her, needing to be clear. "I need to kiss your body."

Her mouth opens but it takes a second for the word "Okay" to slip out again. I think she knows *exactly* what I mean, and if she doesn't, she's about to find out. I need to kiss her absolutely everywhere.

"Don't let any more clothing come off," I warn.

"Okay." She's breathy, and I have to make sure she understands—if we end up naked, I don't think I'll be strong enough to stop again.

"Promise me, Anna."

"I promise."

Now that I know she'll be the strong one, I allow myself to let go. Her body is all mine, and I'm going to savor every single taste. She wriggles under my mouth as I slowly move along her shoulder and down over her collarbone. My hands encircle her waist and back, fingers splayed to hold her close. I examine her skin as I kiss it, finding each freckle along the way and making it mine. Her natural scent intoxicates me.

I make it to her breasts and run my thumbs under the edge of her bra, dipping my tongue as far under the material as I dare. When I reach back to undo the clasp she presses her back against the wall to smash my hand away, and I grin to myself. I will get to those later. . . .

Down I go over her ribcage until I'm on my knees, staring at a blue heart charm dangling from her belly button. Holy . . . A sizzle of heat bolts to my core.

"You are killing me." I lick around her belly button and she shivers, moaning. Her hands grip my shoulders and then sink into my hair as my mouth moves farther south to the edge of her low knickers. I start at one hip and kiss along the edge to the other. The sound of her rapid breathing urges me on. I open my mouth and lightly sink my teeth into the skin at her hip, making her gasp, then my tongue circles over the spot. I know I'm a fiend, but I want to mark her all over.

I'm ready to go further, but Anna's legs are pressed together. When I move a hand down the back of one of her legs to bend her knee, she lets me. I gently pry her leg open enough to expose her inner thigh. Her hands are tight in my hair now, and I love knowing I'm making her crazy.

This is the one thing I can give her. The one thing I'm good at. I've never been more eager to make someone experience such bliss.

I kiss the inside of her thigh, running my tongue over the silky skin there. Anna lets out a gorgeous moan and she quivers, sliding down the wall. I move my hands back up to her waist to catch her. My mouth comes down inside her thigh, even closer, and Anna exhales a strangled breath.

"Kai! I . . . I . . . you have to stop."

Bugger. I need to reassure her. I want to keep my face right where it is and show her just how okay this is, but I know better. I force myself to stand and look at her. To remind her it's just me, and I won't do anything she doesn't want.

Anna's chest is rising and falling quickly. Her cheeks are pink. Her pheromones are flooding the air and making my head spin like an aphrodisiac. I lean against her, dipping enough to align our hips and drive them together. Her head falls back as she feels me against her, and I know I can bring her pleasure just as easily this way as the other. But I want to be touching her with my hands if not my mouth.

My hand covers her warm stomach. "Let me touch you. Just on the outside. Let me make you feel good." She groans sweetly, a sound of need, and my hand trails down.

So close.

I keep my eyes on her face, though her eyes are closed. I love watching her reactions.

I don't expect it when she begins to shake her head. Or when she says, "No. No, we can't."

Something is wrong. I drop my hand. "What is it?" I step

away, worried I've upset her. "I'm sorry, Anna—"

"No," she says in a quaking voice. "I don't want you to be sorry. I'm not sorry."

I blink. My skin flushes from fire to ice as she bends and pulls her clothes back on. I'm not at all certain what's going on. She pulls me into a hug, and I have to remind myself she is prompting this touch, so it's okay. I let my arms go around her trembling form.

"You're shaking," I say, still confused.

"Yeah, well, my body is pretty angry at me right now." She laughs shortly, without humor. "But I don't want to take any chances when it comes to the hilt."

Any remaining fire is put out at the mention of that thing, and my heart gives a lurch. The prophecy says the Neph of light and dark has to be pure of heart, I assume to be able to use the Sword of Righteousness. I hadn't really thought about what that would entail.

"You think it's *that* sensitive?" I ask.

"I don't know. It's meant for angels, you know?"

Ugh, damn that stupid sword.

"Are you okay?" she asks me.

Actually, no. I don't think a moment of pleasure with the man she loves will render her impure, especially if she remains a virgin, but I understand her apprehension. A lot is at stake. I can't imagine the pressure she must feel.

I hold her face and run my thumb over her cheek. "Don't worry about me. I didn't mean to upset you."

"You didn't," she says. "I love you. I want all that with you. Maybe someday?"

I shut my eyes against her hopeful words. I dare not believe there is a someday. There is here and now, and we're promised nothing more. Especially with the prophecy hanging over us.

She stretches up and kisses me. "I think I need chocolate."

This gets a laugh from me. Only Anna.

"Will you make me some brownies?"

"Me?" She must've misspoken.

"It's *my* turn to watch *you* cook."

I can't help but grin. "I assume you actually want to be able to eat these brownies?" But Anna only laughs.

She takes me by the hand, leading me down the hall toward the kitchen. Her defusing tactic has worked, taking my mind off the disappointment of the moment.

And one thing's for certain—after tonight I'll never look at brownies the same way again.

CHAPTER TWENTY-FIVE

SAVING Z

*"This is our last night, but it's late and I'm trying not to sleep
'Cause I know when I wake I will have to slip away."*
—"Daylight" by Maroon 5

Tonight was the most extraordinary night of my life, but also the most difficult, psychically. I can't explain the monster that lives inside me, or the battle I wage against it.

I remember when Father called me a caveman to Anna the night he met her, and he laughed, but not because he was taking the piss. He laughed because he knows what I feel, how constant my longings are, and it's funny to him. Amusing that I fight for self-control every waking moment, that at any second I could turn into a raging Lust Hulk, never satisfied.

Only not green. Lucky me.

There were times tonight when my fraying willpower was nearly shredded by innocent touches, and it kept me on edge.

I know it was beyond stupid to chase her to the airport and beg her to come home with me. The smart move, the safe one, would have been to let her go back to Georgia. But as I hold her in my arms, in my bed, listening to the sound of her soft breathing, I can't bring myself to regret our one night together.

We'd both finally fallen asleep a bit ago, but I woke during the night, filled with familiar paranoia. It's worse with her at my side. Even though I know the Dukes and whisperers are in Vegas tonight, I can't stomach the thought of Anna being in danger. All because of my selfish desire to have her.

She is complex, my lovely Anna. All gentleness. A bleeding heart for injustice. A brilliant capacity for forgiveness. But despite her gentleness, I've seen how her hands ball into tiny fists when she's ticked off. I've witnessed the fire in her eyes when she's lost to the hunger of her demon side. I understand that hunger. That need to lose oneself completely to pure physical sensation with no regard to consequences. That urge to say fuck it all.

The only difference is that she wants to lose herself in drugs and I want to lose myself in skin.

But obsession is obsession. To each his own.

Anna mews next to me like a baby kitten and snuggles closer, her knee rubbing my thigh. And, oh, bugger me . . . her hand lands on my lower stomach. Just a few inches south, and I would be a happy man.

I look over at the Sword of Righteousness hilt lying on the bedside table. It's mocking me, I swear. I know it keeps her safe, but I kind of hate that thing. I feel like it knows what I'm thinking, all the things I'd like to do to its sweet Anna.

Things I daresay she's not ready for.

The hilt doesn't seem to give a shite that I love her. It only sees that I'm a greedy bastard who wants every bit of Anna for myself. I want to savor each moment she looks at me and sees past the lust in my eyes—sees the boy I once was, and the man who now desperately needs her.

I close my eyes and try to rest, but her hand is quite distracting. I lift it to my chest instead. In her sleep she prods her nails into my skin and I think it's the sexiest and most adorable thing I've ever experienced. Then again, I'd thought the same thing when she was cooking earlier. And when my mouth was on her thigh, her hands pulling at my hair. And again when she licked brownie batter. Let's backtrack to the bit about *her thigh* . . .

Don't think about that, mate.

Don't think about the scent of warm pears that surrounded you like cognac.

Don't think about the silk of her skin against your tongue, how close you were to that place of hers where nobody else has been.

Don't think about the sounds of her moans, how you were just about to blow her ever-loving mind, or how you couldn't wait to catch her when her knees buckled as her whole body trembled with pleasure.

Definitely do not *think of that.*

I shove the heel of my hand against my eye and will away the images.

Damned hilt.

No, I'm not perfect when I'm with Anna. I still experience thoughts about every filthy, sexy thing imaginable. That's everyday life for me. But she makes me wonder what it would be like to make love. She makes me want to take my time with every millimeter of her body in the most maddening way until she's begging for more.

I let out a quiet sigh.

She makes me want more from life. Things I'm not bloody allowed to want. Things I can never give her. I conceded tonight to be her boyfriend. Okay, to be honest, it was my idea because it's the one thing I *can* give her—my heart and my loyalty. I asked if we could be together, and the way she lit up about attaching that label to our relationship made me both joyful and sad, because she deserves more.

I took her to band practice with me tonight, which was awesome, aside from that awkward moment when Anna Malone got jealous and stormed out. Otherwise, it felt amazing to be out with Anna, sharing my life with her. But she deserves a boyfriend who can openly claim her on a daily basis, not just when the demons are away. And that is why fury will always live inside me. Anna might be too good, too measured, to be angry about our circumstances, but I'm not.

I crack open an eye and glare at the hilt for good measure. Then I hold my girl closer, glad we took this chance to be together. I won't think about tomorrow yet.

When I finally let myself relax again, sleep almost immediately pulls me under.

There is pure terror in Anna's eyes when her father rings at the arse-crack of dawn. I don't know if she's more afraid that Belial's sending me on a mission with Kope or that he's sending me on a mission *at all*. One of our Neph allies, the daughter of Duke Sonellion, has been thrown in prison for lewd conduct. It's not looking good for Zania. In the conservative Middle Eastern town where she's being held, she's likely to be publicly beaten and executed, or sold into slavery. Her father refuses to save her since she's given in to her alcohol addiction and seems to be of no further use to his cause.

I want to wipe the fear from Anna's eyes, but I can't make promises. I can't promise I won't punch Kope when I see him. Nor can I promise we'll be safe in Syria. I won't lie to Anna, and she's no fool. Getting Zania out of prison won't be easy.

I want to tell her how much it means to me that Belial has asked me to go, that he trusts me with this, but I'm not sure I can put it into words without sounding like a complete idiot.

Perhaps I should be afraid, but I'm not. I face the possibility of death every day. Life has been a perilous walk under Father's keen eye, his whisperers always watching. But this journey—this mission—it's dangerous in a way that's worthy of death. It's the first time I've ever been called to help others, rather than hurt them. A chance to die in a way that would bring honor is worth it. Her father's belief in me has filled me with so much pride it's embarrassing.

When Kope shows, the sight of him makes me so hot with anger I want to pummel him to a bloody pulp. And if I did, he'd probably just stand there and not fight back, infuriating do-gooder that he is. He brings out feelings of inadequacy in me that I don't want to acknowledge. *He* was chosen to be at Anna's side as she traveled the world. *He* was the one facing danger in order to find allies for when it's time to fulfill the prophecy. *He* was her protector and teammate. Not me. And I hate him for it.

I hate him for all the years he's denied the urge to dive into the bed of every woman who makes eyes at him. I hate him for not beating the shite out of every man who stirs his wrath. Why can't he fuck up, just once?

As Kopano stands before me in the living room, all suave and put together, Anna's the only thing keeping him in one piece. Her, and the reminder that her father wants Kopano to lead this mission into Syria. Frankly, I don't want to get on Belial's bad side.

A makeup artist shows, hired by Belial, to turn Kope and me into passable Syrians. She's even brought traditional Middle Eastern clothing. I shake off my anger and let the lady have a go at me.

Turns out I'm still sexy with a big-arse beard and brown eyes instead of blue.

Flying is relaxing—whisperers stay low to earth and don't bother with the friendly skies. I know I should be nervous about what's to come in Syria. Or annoyed by the looks other passengers keep giving me, thanks to my Middle Eastern clothing. I wonder if Kope is getting the same treatment where he sits in the back. I want to yell at all of them, "I'm not a bloody terrorist, so piss off with the crazy stares." *Wankers.* Instead I shake it off, close my eyes, and rest.

Anna's parting words at the airport fill my head: *It was always you for me. Only you.* And with that lovely thought floating through my mind, I sleep better than I have in ages.

As it turns out, Kope is a good man to have at your side in the Middle East. His Arabic is flawless. I know only a few phrases, so I keep my mouth shut and let Kope do the talking. We travel through Damascus to pick up our weapons from Belial's human contact, and then stop near a busy mosque to search the area.

My eyes scan the scene, searching for the other Neph we're to meet here. A bloke in a maroon head wrapping stands out with his boxy body type and the roundness of his face, though his skin's been given a bronze dusting and he's wearing a brown beard like me. The son of Duke Mammon, from Australia. I know him as the doorman for the summits.

"There," I say to Kopano under my breath. "Near the corner." The man looks over when I speak. I stretch my hearing and open it around him. "Is that you, Flynn?" I ask.

The man gives a single nod. " 'At's me, mate." He rubs a hand over his mouth to hide the fact he's talking, and in an Aussie accent. "I'll follow you out and keep my distance. I've scouted the area already, and there's a hill nearby where I can watch from afar. Maybe thirty minutes outside the city. I'll give a yell if anything looks suspicious. There's three guards outside the compound, and it sounds like at least two inside. I don't think they're treating their prisoner nicely, if you know what I mean."

Ah, shite.

Kopano goes rigid. "We must go," he says. "Now."

The two of us head for the car while Flynn climbs aboard a small scooter/moped contraption.

We navigate away from the busy area and head toward a smaller town on the outskirts of the city. It feels like it takes longer than thirty minutes on the dry, bumpy road. The city lights and sounds and scents of spices are long gone. The landscape is more barren, though beautiful in its own way. Far ahead of us, Flynn takes a dirt path that leads toward low hills. It's now dusk, and I feel the stares of suspicious eyes peeking out of squat shanties.

I keep a strand of my hearing in a flimsy line behind me, concentrated around Flynn, who's found a spot on higher ground, covered with trees, for his lookout. I can see the rise of his hill clearly as we take a potholed side street to a small, darkened building. A wire fence surrounds the compound, guarded by three men with semiautomatic guns slung across their chests. They all stand a bit taller at the sight of our car. We pull aside and park.

We'd decided before arriving that I would listen for warnings from Flynn while Kope focused on the mission Belial planned for us.

I don't scare easily, especially where humans are concerned, but these men with their weapons and dark gray auras appear stark raving mad. Not the sort of combination that puts a bloke at ease. I treat them like the Dukes, not making eye contact but keeping my shoulders squared as we step out, so as not to show weakness. I'm ever aware of the daggers at my ankle and waist and will not hesitate to use them.

Kopano stands tall, briefcase in hand, and walks forward without an ounce of trepidation. He could be a prince of Africa with the air of importance he's giving off. I'm surprised when he barks out a phrase in Arabic as he approaches them on quick feet, sounding bored and angry. Gone is his gentle spirit. I think I recognize the word *girl*.

The guards exchange glances and frowns. We stop in front of them. Before any of the gits can respond, Kope is barking again as if they're wasting his time. The three of them jump a bit, clearly frazzled by this seemingly powerful man pretending to hail from Egypt. Kope lifts the briefcase, snaps it open to reveal piles of foreign bills, then slams it shut and says something else in that badass deep tone.

And I can't help myself. I'm impressed. Maybe he took acting classes at Harvard. Whatever it is, he's bloody brilliant.

Finally one of the guards speaks. Kope responds, sounding annoyed, but then stands back and lifts his arms. He never lets go of the briefcase. They pat him down, taking a handgun from his waist. I reluctantly lift my arms as one approaches me, and I allow him to confiscate my knives. I feel naked as the weapons are stripped from my body—and not the good kind of naked. I take note when he puts the daggers in his left pocket.

We're in. Excellent.

They lock the gate behind us and rush into the building with guns in hand, strapped over their shoulders. Didn't anyone ever tell these minions not to run about with their fingers on the triggers? Unnerving. I'm ready to get Zania and get the hell out of here.

One of the guards shouts something to a man who stands as we round a dark corner. The new man looks us over, his eyes a little wild, then gives a hard nod toward a doorway. Kope marches past him and I follow.

Bloody hell . . .

My stomach sours, just as it does when one of Marissa's new girls is being trained into obedience. But Marissa doesn't allow the men to beat her girls to this extent. Zania is little more than a brown pile of bones on a dirt floor. Naked. And no, her nakedness does not rouse my lust. Not a bit.

One of the guards nudges her with his boot and yells something. Kope waves him off with a harsh swipe and squats beside her. He speaks to her in a rough tone and she curls tighter. At least it's a sign of life. Kope repeats the phrase, slower and more quietly this time, and I think I understand enough of the context to put it together.

"You belong to me now."

Kopano takes her wrist and turns it over. He feels her thin bicep, checking her condition. Then he turns his head and gives a curt nod to the bloke standing in the doorway. The man comes forward, sets his gun down with a clatter, and pops open the briefcase, counting. His eyes are bright with greed. He shouts something at one of the other men, who runs off and comes back with a black cotton dress. The idiot starts trying to dress Zania, shoving the opening over her head and yelling at her when she won't straighten her arms for him.

Kopano quickly waves the man away and lifts Z into a sitting position, frowning. He murmurs gruffly as he coaxes her arms through. She tries to scoot away, but he follows and ignores her groaning protests until she's completely dressed.

All the while I'm silently chanting for everyone to hurry so we can get the fuck out of this hellhole. In the loose pocket of my cotton bottoms I feel my satellite phone vibrate. I take a quick peek and silently curse. It's from Flynn.

Think I have a tail but they haven't come n sight. Also getting strange looks from 2 locals.

I give Kope the we-need-to-hurry eye and he nods imperceptibly.

Before the guy in charge is finished fondling the cash, Kopano scoops Zania into his arms. She tries to struggle, but he grips her tighter and murmurs in Arabic for her to be still.

The man on the floor lifts his gaze from the money to give Kopano an evil grin of satisfaction. Kope glowers and says something about our weapons. Another man comes in with Kope's gun and my knives. I quickly take them and follow Kope as he exits, passing the men on the way out. They're huddled around the cash, grinning like they've won the lottery. One man drags himself away to escort us.

I've almost forgotten about Flynn until distant sounds ring out inside my bubble of extended hearing. Arabic words, spoken in a questioning tone. The scooter starting up. Footsteps running against dirt. Yells and grunts. Sounds of fighting.

Shite! My palms start to sweat. I want to get out there and help Flynn, but I can't with this machine-gun maniac at our heels. Suddenly the fighting quiets and I hear the scooter zoom away in the opposite direction. Maybe Flynn's escaped.

We get out of the compound and into the car, where Kope lays Zania in the backseat. As soon as we're on the road I sign to Kopano that Flynn's been discovered. We're trying to decide if we should go to him as Zania begins to moan.

"Drink," she whispers in Arabic. Her voice is scratchy.

I unscrew the cap off a bottle of water and lean back,

fitting it into her hand as she lies there. She takes one look at it through her swollen, purpled eyes and throws the damn thing back at me. Water goes everywhere before I grab it.

Right. Not the type of drink she's after.

It's clear we can't go traipsing through the unknown hills searching for Flynn when we've got Zania to deal with. Kope and I agree that Flynn likely got away and will meet us later. We hope.

I look at Z's thin arms where she's curled on the backseat. She's emaciated. I pull a protein bar from my bag and open it.

"I need you to eat this." I gently nudge her forearm.

At my touch, she balls tighter and screams in heavily accented English, "Don't touch me!"

"Zania, I want to help you. Please. You need to eat."

"Leave me the hell alone!"

I hold out the food again. "I won't touch you again, I swear. But you need food—" She smacks the protein bar from my hand and it falls to the dirty car floor. I sigh and look to Kope, who's cringing at my failed efforts. Then I remember the pictures I took with Anna just before I left, for this very purpose.

I pull out my phone and hold out the screen for her to see. "Look, Z. Do you remember Anna? Here we are together. I am her ally, just like you. Just like Kope." She glances at it and eyes me suspiciously.

Kope picks up on this and begins talking to her in Arabic as he drives. I imagine he's telling her she's safe now. Reminding her who he is, and explaining who I am. I hear him say Anna's name.

She seems almost calm, until her whole body begins to convulse.

I curse under my breath. "I think she's having withdrawals or something."

Kope's eyebrows knit together and he drives faster. I've no clue what to do. She dry heaves over the side of the seat, but there's nothing in her stomach to purge. I watch helplessly.

"The hotel is near," Kope says. "Two minutes."

We get back to the seedy hotel, and Kope tells her she must walk on her own so we don't draw much attention, even though it's dark and not well lit. Her slow gait is painful to watch. Thankfully the small walk from the car to the side door doesn't earn any unwanted attention. We use our hearing to hide around a corner until our hall is clear, then we get her to the room.

The daughter of Sonellion is wrecked. She walks with a limp from her injuries, but she won't let us close enough to see what needs fixing. I run her a hot bath, but she sits on the floor of the bathroom shaking uncontrollably, begging for a drink.

"Maybe we should give her one—" I begin, but Kope cuts me off.

"No."

I wish Anna was here. Zania groans and begins a chattering murmur that rakes my ears. God, she's suffering.

"Just one fucking drink," I whisper to Kope, but he is adamant.

"In the end it will only make her want more. She has to make it through this."

Zania snarls at him in Arabic.

I squat next to her. "Please, Z. We need to get you out of here before your father returns. You need to eat something so you can be stronger, so you can heal."

She looks at me, really looks at me, for the first time. "One drink," she says softly. She's so pathetic. I want to give in because I'm weak and I keep wondering if one will really hurt. Perhaps it would calm her. But I can feel Kopano's eyes glaring down at us. What would Anna do? I attempt to channel her positive energy before I speak again.

"I know it feels like that's what you need, but it's not. We want to help you." I'm proud of myself for sounding so gentle and reasonable. I open my mouth to continue and she wallops me straight in the eye.

Bloody fucking hell, that stings.

I move away from the Neph girl, who doesn't appear as if she can lift an arm, much less throw a decent punch. It seems where there's a will, there's a way, because I'm fairly certain she's given me a black eye. Not the first time I've been hit by a girl, but it's the first time I didn't deserve it.

Still, I can't bring myself to be mad. Until Kope chuckles.

"Shut up," I say, standing. "*You* give it a go, lover boy."

He frowns at me as I stalk past him and check out my eye in the mirror. Yep. It's darkening.

I expect Kope to try a gentle approach, but once again he shocks me. He speaks to her with stern, dominant authority.

"It's time to bathe, Zania. We will leave the room and you will bathe yourself. Our flight to the U.S. is in less than five hours."

She wraps her arms around her stomach and cries, "You should have let me die!"

"You were not going to die," he growls. "Your fate was far worse than death."

"Just leave me here!"

"Bathe. Now. Or I will put you in the bath and clean you myself!"

She eyes him with malice. He takes a hard step forward and she scuttles back.

"Don't touch me! I will wash myself."

"When it's time to leave," he says, "you will be presentable. We cannot raise suspicion."

He barges past me and I follow, closing the door. It's not until he sits on the bed, gripping the edge with his eyes shut, that his strong façade cracks and he begins to tremble.

I want to tell him he's done well, but I can't bring myself. Instead I sit on the other side of the bed in silence. We both relax a bit when we hear Zania step into the water. Then she begins to cry a mournful sound, her teeth chattering as she shakes, and it guts me.

I hate the Dukes. I loathe them with every fiber of my being.

I allow myself to imagine Anna, fierce and lovely, stabbing each of them with the flaming sword as all of us Neph hold them down, until their souls are extinguished forever.

And then another thought smacks me and I'm struck with sudden anxiety.

Where is Flynn?

I whip out my phone and ring him, but there's no answer. Next I text Anna's father with the code he told us to use. Belial texts right back.

Get her?

Yes, I respond, but F is missing.

My heart pounds, waiting for his response.

Leave with or without him.

Damn, that's hard-core, but I suppose I get it. Better to have one missing than two. At this point, with so few allies, we're playing a numbers game.

Kope looks over, so I show him the texts and he nods. He's tense, and I understand. We won't relax until we're on a plane, far away from here.

I wonder if it's too early to call Anna. I try to imagine what sort of shenanigans Blake got her into last night. You've never partied until you've partied with the son of Envy.

I dial her number and lie back, grinning at the sound of her husky, hungover, half-asleep voice when she answers.

"Hello?"

I sigh and focus on her voice. I can't wait to get home to her.

The rest of the trip is a blur. After Zania bathes and dresses she refuses to speak to us again. Kope miraculously manages to get her to eat three bites of warm flatbread from his fingers.

I don't need to be a child of Duke Astaroth to see there's a bond between those two. I let him take care of Z for the remainder of the trip, only getting involved when absolutely necessary. He knows how to deal with her in the way that she needs, and I don't care for another black eye.

Flynn shows up at the Damascus airport, completely ragged, just before our flight. He's got a rip in his shirt, and the corner of his beard has started to peel off. I point him straight to the loo to fix himself, glad he's okay.

When we land in Amsterdam later that day we all change

out of our Arab getups into Western wear. Scanning for whisperers and seeing none, we clap Flynn on the back and he goes his separate way, off to do some traveling around Europe before returning to Australia.

Zania looks frail in her loose jeans, as if she can't manage to stand straight, but it's clear what a beautiful woman she'll be when she's well. Her arms are crossed and she taps her foot furiously as she stares into the tax-free store, her gaze locked on the bottles of liquor. Kopano steps between her and the glass, and she narrows her eyes, which are no longer swollen. They're now big and dark brown and full of fire. Kopano seems to be drawn to those eyes, though he's clearly not at ease with her dire need for alcohol.

They stare hard at each other, connected, as if they might break into a round of intense sex right against the duty-free shop. That'd be a show. I bite my tongue against the urge to laugh and tell them to get a room. Saint Kopano would die of humiliation if I said that.

I'm glad when our flight is called. One step closer to seeing Anna again.

During our flight, an attendant sees Zania hunched over, hugging herself, shaking and groaning. Kope tries to play it off as motion sickness, but the flight attendant still seems worried. It certainly looks like an emergency to anyone with eyes.

Kope even tries to rub her back to put on a good show, but Zania yanks away with a yelp. Yeah, these two are going to get this plane grounded if they're not careful. It's time for me to work my charm.

I smile up at the frowning attendant and beckon her nearer.

She's probably late twenties. European. She swipes her eyes over me, and a great deal of her worried aura lightens, suddenly forgotten. She leans down and I sit up taller to get closer as I whisper.

"Between us," I say, "I think my mate's lady is up the duff, if you know what I mean."

Her eyes widen and she pats her stomach with question.

I nod. Grin. "They haven't announced it yet, but I'm fairly certain. She's not been herself for a bit, but it's nothing to worry about, luv. She'll be fine."

I wink for good measure. Then wet my lips. Her aura pops red, and my body reacts without permission.

No, I remind myself, feeling guilty.

"Well, all right then," the flight attendant says, brushing a hand down my shoulder and arm. My body tightens and I'm holding my breath. "If you need anything, let me know." She dips closer. "Anything at all."

Go away, go away, go away, and for the love of all things holy don't touch me again.

I give her a nod and she finally turns to go up the aisle. A quick glance to the side finds Kope and Zania both glaring at me. I suppose they didn't care for the pregnancy bit, but oh well. They should be grateful. I exhale and close my eyes.

At some point Zania nods off, still bent over, and her head ends up on Kope's thigh. *Hahahaha,* the bloke is frozen as stone, trying not to be affected. I take advantage of the moment of peace and move to the empty row behind us. I lean my head against the window and soon fall asleep.

I'm woken sometime later from a vivid dream where I'm

obliterating Anna's innocence. It's quite a nice dream, but I'd rather not be having it in public. The sounds of Zania's crying and Kope's gentle admonishments usher me back to reality with an unwelcome jolt. The kind flight attendant has covered me in a blanket while I slept. I take the blue bundle and cram it over my misbehaving lap, thinking of things that are not soft and warm. Things that do not moan and arch and bend.

It doesn't help.

I press my fingers over my forehead as hard as I can. My knee bounces faster. I inhale a filling breath and pull out my mobile, opening the picture of me with Anna. I stare at it until the pilot tells the flight attendants to prepare for landing. Then, with a heavy heart, I delete the picture.

I can't wait to land. I want to see Anna embrace Zania—for her to fill that broken girl with the same positive energy she fills me with—energy that makes one believe they can fight both the demons inside themselves and the ones outside as well. Energy that makes one believe they can win.

CHAPTER TWENTY-SIX

WATER AND WRATH

"In the wreckage of a job well done I saw a place I'd never seen before, yeah,
And that moment I refused to close my eyes anymore."
—*"Worth Dying For" by Rise Against*

From the frying pan into the fire, isn't that how the saying goes? Almost immediately upon arriving in L.A. we got a call from Belial to leave the area. A group of Dukes were flying into LAX from Vegas with some women they met. Blake had the idea of heading for the marina and taking his boat out to his father's private island, where we'd be safe from the mainland.

Brilliant.

Blake told us to think of this as a "mini vacay," and after all we'd just been through in Syria, I wanted that far too much. Us blokes took the Jet Skis out, leaving the girls to chat on the island's dock.

Thing is, it's dangerous to relax and not give yourself an out. We know that, and yet we'd come to the one place with nowhere to hide. Just our sodding luck. Thankfully the messenger of Lucifer, Azael, is secretly in league with Belial. The dark spirit found us and warned us that the Dukes were on their way to the island.

Now, here we are. Kopano, Zania, and Blake are submersed under the boat dock. I am sitting on the edge with Anna, about to jump in. Why? Because we have to hide someplace where Father cannot detect Anna's scent of innocence.

Underwater.

After all we've been through, you'd think I'd no longer get scared, but where Anna is concerned there is always room for fear. My protective instinct for her has only grown, and I can hardly keep a straight mind when she's in danger.

I watch Anna as she stares down at the moving waters beneath us. Strands of hair around her face are wet from running around to prepare. She looks resigned to what's coming. When she turns her face up to mine, her eyes widen to find me watching her so intensely.

I still haven't told her how I feel—not in words. I'm cursing myself now for being too afraid, knowing how much it would mean to her. The Dukes are in hearing range by now. I can't risk speaking, but I have to tell her. If we're caught today, if anything happens to us, I will hate myself for not saying it. So, I give her the only thing I have. Silent words.

I raise a hand and make the combination "I" "L" "U" in sign language—*I love you*. She stares at my hand until her eyes water. She holds up her hand and mirrors mine, pressing her

311

sign against mine, mouthing the words, *I love you, too.*

I vow we will make it out of this.

She reaches out for me and I pull her against me, feeling her arms wrap around my back. I hold her close, wishing this night would be over soon. I don't know when the Dukes will arrive, or how long they will stay, but I know we're in for a long evening.

Blake reaches up and grabs our ankles, telling us it's time to get in. Anna and I both slide down, holding on to the planks, and she sucks in a loud breath of air as her body hits the water. The first bout of worry bombards me when I feel how the sea has chilled within the past hour since we were on Jet Skis. The water is always cold here, but Anna is so much smaller than me. She'll freeze if we're in too long, especially after the sun sets.

She gives me a firm nod that she'll be okay. I know she's a fighter. We quietly swim to the posts underneath the dock where Kope and Zania have grabbed hold. The damn things are slick with sea life, making them difficult to grip. The five of us look around at each other, ready to weather what's to come. I stare at Anna and she gives me one last brave nod.

Please, please, let this be over quickly. I hope the Dukes will get their fucking kicks and get the hell out of here. Surely they don't plan to stay all night?

I hunker down with the others and wait as the sea temperature drops. Zania seems worlds stronger after only a day under Anna's nurturing. She got her to shower and eat a bit. I'm glad, because Z'd never be able to survive this if she was in the same shape now as two days ago. Her quick Nephilim healing probably helped, as well.

It doesn't take long for the Dukes to arrive. They've even brought Flynn, which surprises me. His father must have called him to Vegas soon after we parted in Europe.

Father, Melchom, Mammon, and Astaroth came to the island to work, bringing married and engaged women, who they plan to ruin, to soil with adultery, guilt, and regret.

Hours pass, and it's bloody cold. Nearly unbearable. I can't stand to see Anna's lips turning blue and her body trembling uncontrollably.

At some point during the Dukes' exploits, Anna begins to lose it. She's shivering like mad. She lets out a squeak of fear, and jumps as if something's rubbed up against her underwater. Then she nearly laughs, delirious. I rush from my post, stiff and numb, wrapping my arms around her frozen body. I press a hand over her lips to remind her to be quiet and she slowly nods. I keep one hand firmly around her waist and hold the pole with the other.

We cling underneath the dock for hours, pushed and pulled by the Pacific tides, waiting for the Dukes to finish their bloody business so I can get Anna to warmth, but the night only turns worse. I thought perhaps the Dukes had brought Flynn along to be their bodyguard and lackey—to drop the anchor and fetch them wine—but their reason was more sinister than that. Much more.

They know Flynn was in Syria, and that Zania was bought by two "mystery men." They know there are traitors among them.

"What you don't know, son," Duke Mammon whispers

with malice, "is that Duke Sonellion borrowed one of Duke Thamuz's sons to keep watch over the transaction of the girl while he was away."

Kope and I share a shocked glance. Another Neph had been there in Syria with us. He'd seen Flynn get into the fight on that hill, seen his red hair when his head covering fell back. But it sounds as if he hadn't seen me or Kope.

"Tell me who you're working with!" Mammon shouts above us.

Don't tell them, I silently beg. *Stay strong, mate.*

Anna is shivering violently, and my worry has turned to panic. In the moonlight her lips are lavender, and I'm not sure how she's able to keep herself afloat. The only part of her that looks alive is her eyes as she watches the action on the dock through a chink in the wood.

"I will tell you nothing, old man," Flynn says.

Bloody right on him. He's ready to die for this cause. His father, Mammon, holds a gun to his head, but Flynn is unflinching.

"Last chance," Mammon says.

"I'll see you in hell," Flynn responds, and he sounds almost liberated . . . free.

I touch my fingers to Anna's cold lips and hold her tight as a gunshot splits the air. Her body jolts in my arms. I press my cheek to the side of her head.

For the second time in my life, I witness a fellow Neph murdered by a Duke. Unlike the first time, I am not numb. I feel the brutality of Flynn's death, and it hurts. It's personal.

I watch helplessly as our worthy ally's soul is pulled away

to hell by demon spirits, and my rage threatens to make us known. I watch as Z's teeth chatter and Anna goes limp with grief in my arms. I watch as Blake has lost all remnants of humor, and even Kope's face is desolate. I hate that we must sit here in silence, vulnerable and defenseless.

How much more can we take of this? How many more of us must die before we can act?

I've never been more relieved than when the Dukes leave the island. Anna's frozen stiff as I hoist her onto the dock with my weakened arms. My sore muscles ache as I pull her into my lap and bring Zania closer to Anna. Kope and Blake quickly leave us for the other side of the island, with the hope of retrieving Blake's boat as fast as possible. Anna and Zania's shaking has become violent, and they can hardly open their eyes.

"Shit—I think you have hypothermia." I rub Anna's arms, but she's soaked through. I know the wet clothes are supposed to come off, but I need to wait until she's in the boat. I surround her with my arms and she encircles Zania weakly. "It's okay," I say. "You'll be all right now. The boat is nearly here."

Hurry, hurry, hurry.

The boat finally docks and Kope jumps off. Together we rush the girls down into the cabin. My first instinct is to put them on the bed, but they're soaked. I set Anna in a chair, and Kope follows my lead.

"Can we get the heat on down here?" I call up to Blake. "We need to get them out of these wet clothes."

"I'm trying to figure it out!" he yells back. "I might need

some help up here. Can one of you guys find the extra blankets?"

I squeeze Anna's hand. "I'll be right back, luv. We're going to get you warm." With eyes closed and jaw rattling, she nods.

I take a running leap up the stairs and find Blake shivering at the panels. "The heat's not labeled. I've never had to use it." We try different switches until we finally figure it out. Then we run about readying the boat so it doesn't drift away while we're thawing. When I go back down the stairs I can hear the heater cranking, and I'm so ready to get Anna dry and warm.

What I see stops me in my tracks. Kopano is taking off Anna's shorts. His hand is on her calf. Anger rumbles through me at this blatant act of intimacy.

I can barely get the words out. "Get. Your. Bloody hands. Off her."

He freezes, caught. I am shaking all over now. It is *my* job to care for Anna. *My* job to touch her. Only me. All of my unvoiced fury over his betrayal comes back, full force, driven by the day's horrific events.

He always knew how I felt for her, and yet he still pursued. Even now he thinks he has the right to touch her.

Kopano moves away and stands to face me. The girls, like mannequins, open their eyes and stare blearily up at us.

"She is in the worst condition." Kope points to Anna. "The wet clothing must be removed—"

"Not by you! I can't believe you'd take advantage of this situation."

Deep down, I know the truth. I *know* he was not making any kind of advance, but the familiarity and openness he shares with Anna kills me. I want it gone once and for all. I can't handle her being close to any other man. Anna would point out my own insecurities, but whatever it is, I'm feeling irrational and I just can't stop. I need to be mad.

Kope's eyes slant at me, seething. "You go too far, brother!"

Seeing his wrath ignited thrills me. I move forward, and so does he. It would feel bloody good to throw a wobbler right now—to pummel each other until we're too tired and sore to be angry anymore. I owe Kope an arse-kicking, plain and simple, for kissing my girl when I couldn't be in the picture.

"You will never touch her again."

Kope's badge is pulsing dangerously. I'm ready, fists clenched, blood and adrenaline rushing through me at a dizzying speed. We are face-to-face, anger growing, until we're suddenly shoved apart and Blake is looking back and forth between us. His intervention causes my hearing to clear a bit, enough that I hear him say, "Go. Take care of Anna."

With sudden clarity I remember the reason for all this. Anna. Hypothermia. Shite! I am an epic idiot. I shoulder past the guys and rush to Anna's side. Zania helps shield her while I get her shirt off. Then I wrap the blanket around her and carry her to the bed. Her skin is like ice. I spread another blanket on top of her and she whimpers.

I wonder why no one else is moving into action, and when I turn, I see exactly why. My anger has been diffused and diverted, but Kopano is still standing there, battling his wrath within. His eyes are closed and his hands are curled tight. His breaths are labored. A pang of guilt stabs me. I did this.

Like the others, I stay very still, thinking of a way to make this better. I feebly consider apologizing, but I'm not even certain Kope can hear through the beast right now. I meet eyes with Blake beside me, and he gives a small nod, showing we're on the same page—the two of us might need to take him down if he doesn't calm on his own.

"Brother Kopano," comes a smooth, sultry voice. His stormy eyes open heavily. My head snaps to Zania in the chair across the room. She no longer looks frail as she sits slightly forward, chin up, gripping the edge, though she's trembling when she says, "Warm me?"

Kopano and Zania stare at each other, and for a moment I'm worried his beast will change from wrath to lust. His attention has narrowed singularly to Zania, and he seems to fight for control as he prowls across the small room to her. Kopano takes off his shirt to show his broad shoulders, and Z starts to take off her own. I shoot a look at Blake, but Kope manages to stay in control as he approaches her. He grabs a sheet to shield her as she removes her wet clothing. Then he carries her to the bed and he lies behind her, spooning against her back. He is still rigid. Still fighting for control.

He glares at me for good measure, and I hardly blame him. Then he snuggles Z and closes his eyes. The girls, side by side, give each other little smiles. Anna rolls over and fits her back against Zania's front, looking at me.

A tremble of deep cold shakes me as I try to relax. I lift

the covers and mold myself to Anna's curled form, where she buries her face against my chest. Blake climbs in and presses his bare back against mine, as we try desperately to warm ourselves after the hours submerged in frozen water.

The bed shakes with the tremors of five people. Anna, seeking more skin-to-skin contact, slides her knee between my thighs and I choke back a moan. This is not sexual, I tell myself. I scoot even closer, spreading my hand over her hip. She's okay. We're all okay. For now.

I close my eyes, letting myself remember the one good thing that came of today's dreadful events. I finally told Anna I loved her. Life is too short to live as a coward. I swear to myself at this moment that I will never hold back from Anna again.

I'm happy when Anna and Zania fall asleep. I kiss Anna's hairline and bury my nose in her neck. After an hour I finally feel warm again. I elbow Blake, who rolls out of bed behind me.

Kopano also rises, and sits on the edge of the bed with his back to us. Blake puts his wet clothes back on with a grimace.

"I'm gonna start the boat and get us out of here," he says. Kope and I both nod.

I pull my disgusting clothes back on, though they're bearable now that I'm back to normal temperature. Then I open another blanket and lay it across the girls for good measure. Kope dresses, too, and when he turns to leave the cabin, I grab his arm. His jaw clenches as we meet eyes. I drop my hand.

"I'm . . . sorry," I say lamely. I can't bring myself to say more. I just remember how he was in Syria, how I admired him as a friend, and I want to put this behind us—to get back to that place.

He stares at me, lips pursed, and slowly nods. "As am I."

We say nothing more. We both glance down at the sleeping girls and leave them to rest.

CHAPTER TWENTY-SEVEN

NO GOOD-BYES

"Sunshine upon my face, a new song for me to sing,
Tell the world how I feel inside, even though it might cost me
everything."
—*"Alive" by P.O.D.*

When we made it back to L.A., we brought Z to the convent where Anna was born. Belial thinks she'll be safest there. Then we took Kope to the airport, and saw Blake off, back to Santa Barbara. We tried to keep things light, but I know we were all thinking the same thing as we parted: the Dukes knew something was up. The prophecy could happen tomorrow or years from now—we had no idea what to expect or when we'd all see one another again. These were bittersweet thoughts, but for the first time in our lives we had a reason to hope for something more. Something different.

Something better.

Life without the demons.

I take Anna home with me, but Belial shows soon after. I grit my teeth as he struts in, remembering the last time we were together, and his warning to me after the summit. I respect Anna's father as much as I can, since he sympathizes with the Nephs' plight, but I refuse to grovel to him or any Duke any longer. When he walks in I remain standing, crossing my arms over my chest. If he tries to order me out of Anna's life again, he will not get the answer he wants, not this time.

Belial's face turns deadly when Anna tells him that the other Dukes know about the prophecy, that we heard them talking about it on the island, and how they suspect Anna could be "the one."

"Tell me exactly what they said," he orders. As Anna rehashes last night, Belial eventually sits, but his presence in the room doesn't get any smaller. His eyes are like darts and I can practically see the wheels turning in his mind as he works out possible strategies to keep his daughter safe.

"You're going to have to move, Anna," he tells her, and I hold back a nod of agreement. "I can't have you in Atlanta anymore."

He can't have her near my father is what he means, and I couldn't agree more. Anna's heart is broken at the thought of not living with Patti anymore. Belial looks like he can handle Anna's tears about as well as I can, which is not well at all.

"Everything I've done has been to protect you, Anna," he says. "Sending the whisperers to haunt you that night, this thing with the two boys, making you move. All of it. I hate to see you upset, but it's all been for the best."

I inwardly wince as Anna's ears perk up.

"What thing with the two boys?" she asks pointedly. She picked up on the exact phrase I was hoping she'd skim over.

Belial stares at her, then glances at me. "I thought he'd tell you."

"Tell me what?" Anna asks sharply.

I shake my head and drop my eyes. This is the last thing I want to deal with, especially now that I've begun to make amends with Kope. I want to move past it, and I know Anna will be hurt and furious when she finds out her father hoped and planned that she'd get over me and fall for Kope, so she could find love with someone safe.

Standing abruptly, her face ashen, she calls him out on it.

"You told this to Kai when you commanded him to stay away from me, didn't you?" she asks. My girl's eyes are blazing with indignation.

"Yes," he says unabashedly. "I told the son of Pharzuph—"

"*Kaidan*," Anna says. "His name is Kaidan."

No one has ever stuck up for me before, and I'm betting nobody has ever spoken to Belial like that. He stops and works his jaw side to side, speaking through clenched teeth.

"I told *Kaidan*. At the time, he agreed it was best for you."

"What was he supposed to say?" Anna shouts. "You're a freaking Duke!"

"No, Anna," I say heavily. "I did agree with him at the time." I'd become resigned to it. I had felt that Kope was safer and better, and I thought I could handle it, but I was wrong. Theories that work on paper don't always sit well in reality.

"Yeah, and you were *both* wrong!" Her chin pinches and

quivers, and I realize for the first time that I wasn't the only one tortured by this year and a half apart. From the look on her face now, her heart had been broken as much as mine had.

Was it worth it to try to keep her safe by keeping us apart? I'm not so sure anymore. There must be a better way. We're all trying to navigate this strange sea of danger, trying to suck some semblance of life from the salt along the way.

"Things are gonna change now," Belial says to us both. "I won't try to keep you two from communicating, but I will tell you this. You will only see each other when I tell you it's safe."

Slowly, I look over at Anna and we both nod. Though he's under suspicion, Belial will have inside information from ally spirits about where the other Dukes are at any given time. This could work.

Belial points at me, and my blood chills.

"I've been watching you," he says. "I'll tell you exactly what I told Anna. You've got to at least *appear* to be working. Get yourself out to the parties and bars three or four nights a week. Do not get comfortable. Work if you have to. Anna will understand. Won't you, Anna?"

He turns to Anna, whose face is all sadness. "Yes. I've already told him that."

I feel ill at the thought of either one of us even pretending to work, but I understand his reasoning. The dangers remain, prophecy or not.

"Can you keep up appearances, kid?" he challenges me.

I begrudgingly respond, "Yes, sir."

Belial stands when it's time to leave. He gives my shoulder a squeeze with his massive bear claw until I meet his eyes, which are surprisingly soft.

"You're not a bad kid," he says. "I see that now. You'll make a good ally." I swallow hard and he gives my shoulder a pat.

You're not a bad kid. . . .

Anna slips her soft fingers into mine and tugs me forward. I follow her into the kitchen, my eyes downcast, feeling strange. She starts cooking something, and I quickly snap out of my stupor when it's apparent Anna is wiping at her eyes. She tries to cover it up, babbling.

"You'll need fresh milk soon. And probably more eggs, too. Eggs are an easy thing you can make yourself. All these meals are labeled with cooking instructions. Remember how I showed you—"

"Anna."

She won't look at me. I stand and take her hand off the fridge, closing it, and pulling her into my arms. She lets me hold her until she calms.

We're going to be okay, come what may, but I don't pretend it won't hurt like hell when she has to leave.

We eat dinner and spend our remaining time entwined together on the couch.

"I love you," she says softly. And like every time before, the words spread over me like warm honey. I work up the nerve and open my mouth.

"I've loved you longer."

She pulls back from my chest and stares up at me. "I don't believe you."

I can feel an idiotic grin threatening to spread across my face, just talking to her like this. I bury my face in her neck and hair, and I tell her exactly how I first fell for her. I make her believe me. "You see the best in everyone," I say. "You drove me mad that trip . . . and then you gave that homeless woman all your money in Hollywood, and that was it. I was done."

Her eyes are sparkling as she angles across my lap, slips her hands into my hair, and pulls my face to hers. Her leg swings over so she's straddling me, and I let my hands move over her back, her waist, down to her hips. I'm trying so damn hard to keep my hands and the rest of my body on good behavior, but I let my mouth be as wild as it wishes. She doesn't seem to mind.

We pause to stare at each other, marveling like a couple of lovesick fools. I want to laugh, like I'm on the best kind of high, but then she's kissing me again.

"We're gonna be okay," she whispers between kisses.

"Better than okay," I say.

She grasps the front of my shirt and leans back as our lips come together again, pulling me so that I'm lying on top of her, between her legs. I move against her, just as I know she likes.

"I want to take you with me," she groans.

Ah, God, my little vixen underestimates my self-control when she's naughty like this.

"So you can drive me mad like this every day?" And use me for your plaything? I rather like that idea.

I snatch a glance at the clock and it's almost time for her father to come back. Damn it. I push my hearing outside, and sure enough, firm steps are sounding.

"I think someone's coming up the stairs," I whisper, although I know Belial could most assuredly hear me if he wanted to listen. I kiss the tender spot under her ear. She smells fresh and clean from her shower.

"No," she says bravely. "Not yet." She clings to my shoulders and arches her hips up to mine, and she feels so bloody good. I grind into her body one last time, and my head is spinning with desire for more.

Belial pounds on the door and we both go still. We're panting like mad. Nothing like a dose of your girlfriend's father to douse the kindled fires. Anna giggles in a very mischievous way and I grin.

My lovely little vixen.

Belial knocks again and Anna frowns. "I don't want to say good-bye."

"Then don't," I tell her.

"Hurry it up," Belial shouts through the door.

Anna looks sad now, so I pull her up, taking her face in my hands.

"All right, gorgeous. No good-byes. I'll talk to you soon." I press my lips to hers one last time.

Belial groans against the door. "Oh, for the love of—"

"Hush, Daddy," Anna says. She puts her hands over mine, which still cradle her face, and her eyes flutter closed. "All right. We'll talk soon."

I peck her lips one last time and hand her over to her father. I stand in the doorway as they head downstairs. That awful feeling of being left behind weighs me down. I have to trust that she'll be safe in Belial's care, and wherever he chooses for her to live now.

For the first time ever, when Anna walks away from me, she actually turns and looks back with a smile. That's how I know this time will be different. I lift a hand, and though I miss her like mad already, I feel stronger than I ever have.

We're stronger together than when we're apart. It's a state of mind. Just knowing she loves me, and she's secure in my love for her, makes me feel bloody invincible. I feel as if I've been given a second chance at life, and I'm grateful.

Yes, this time will be different, because this time, I am alive.

PART THREE

SWEET RECKONING

CHAPTER TWENTY-EIGHT

MOST IMPORTANT JOB

"Everyone's got to face down the demons
Maybe today, you could put the past away."
—*"Jumper" by Third Eye Blind*

The Dukes don't waste any time. They're after Anna already, and it's only been a few days since they discovered there are traitors in their midst, since they killed Flynn. Now I've learned from Anna that Father's sent someone to rifle through her dirty laundry so he can get his hands on her knickers—he's determined to find out if she's still a virgin.

Dodgy bastard.

It's been days since I heard from her, and I'm beginning to feel edgy. My heart leaps when my mobile dings, but it's a text from Blake.

My pops is going thru the changing of the guard. China.

He must be jubilant. To the world it will look as though his father died of a heart attack, leaving his mansion to Blake. In reality, Duke Melchom's spirit will be roaming his new duty station of China, searching for a new body to inhabit.

And I'm engaged.

I cringe at this. Should I send my condolences? My mobile rings and I assume it's Blake until I see Father's name. Great. I hesitate, but I can't *not* answer.

"Hallo."

His voice is posh, bored, and all business. "You're needed in Atlanta straightaway. I've sent my jet to L.A. It will arrive in four hours and you are to be there, ready."

I want to ask what this is about. If it's a job for Marissa or something else. But I don't dare. For all I know he could be suspicious of me already.

"Yes, sir," I say.

He hangs up without another word, and my stomach sours. I immediately want to contact Anna or the others, but it's too dangerous. If they've found a way to hack her phone, we're screwed. If he's calling to ask me to work, he's out of luck. That's never happening again.

I text Belial with the code we'd agreed on for when my father calls. **K-611**

I grab my bag and begin readying for the trip, wishing my knives could make it past security. I'll need to stop and buy one when I get there.

Bloody hell, I nearly forgot about the East Coast humidity. Thankfully I'm only in it a moment before I'm whisked off by Father's driver in a black sedan, AC blasting.

"Stop at the sporting goods shop," I tell the driver.

I buy a new knife and get back in the car. My heart beats a steady, fast rhythm the entire way to Father's house, and I match it against my knee with my thumb. My face is schooled into an expressionless mask, and I'm eager to find out what this is about.

As we near the house I push out my hearing and find sounds of two people going at it in the den. We arrive and I stand outside the door of the den until a maid with ample hips hurries out, flushed, smoothing down her clothing. She glances at me and rushes past.

Father sits relaxed in a recliner when I enter, one of his dark whisperers bobbing in the air at his side. Father doesn't get up or motion me to sit. He only scans me from head to toe. My straight face will not give away my nerves. I won't allow it. I hook my thumbs in my pockets lazily.

"I've come as you requested."

"You're looking well," he says. "Bulking up nicely."

"Thank you, Father."

He steeples his hands and runs his joined index fingers up and down his chin. "I've got a rather . . . strange job for you. But quite possibly the most important of your life."

I force myself to take slow, even breaths. "Anything you wish, of course."

"Of course," he drawls. For a moment his eyes are lost in thought, then he kicks the recliner closed and stands to move closer. The spirit circles the two of us.

"We've been dealing with a load of nonsense recently," he says. "Nothing we can't handle, but a nuisance nonetheless."

"I'm sorry to hear that." I know better than to ask questions. Father hates questions. Finds them pushy.

"Yes, well. We believe Duke Belial has turned traitor, and he's using his daughter Anna to work against us."

Bugger . . . I push my eyebrows together as if this is shocking and appalling news. *Keep it together,* I warn myself. He continues.

"We will find Belial and return him to Lucifer straightaway, but we need to find his daughter first. We must know if all of our suspicions are correct."

I nod, thrilled to hear news but terrified at the sound of Anna's name coming from Father's mouth.

"Do you recall she was a *virgin* when we last saw her in New York?" His whisperer makes a sound of disgust in my ear.

"I do recall, Father. Last New Year's."

He *hmphs* a breath through his nose, still annoyed, no doubt, that I didn't take her virginity when he sent me off to train her originally. "Well, we have reason to believe Belial is keeping her innocent."

I draw my eyebrows together again, as if the idea is absurd.

"If what we suspect is true, he has ulterior motives for keeping her clean, which you don't need to concern yourself with. All you need to know is that it's imperative the girl loses her purity immediately. I would ask you to kill her, but that pleasure will belong to the Dukes."

Breathe slowly. Nod.

"Your job is to find the girl and personally make sure there is not a trace of innocence left in her body. I will accept no excuses this time, Kaidan. If she is found to be a virgin after this, you'll be dead on the spot. Do I make myself clear?"

Darkness swirls behind my eyes, causing my fingers to tingle with numbness. "Yes, sir."

"Good," he whispers. "Very good." He steps closer and puts his hands on my shoulders. He feels the girth there and nods to himself, running his hands down my arms to examine my muscles. His eyes shift over me.

Do not ball your fists. Do not clench your jaw. Do not pull away.

"Shall I leave straightaway?" I ask.

This brings him back to the moment and he drops his hands.

"Yes. You'll take my BMW and head north." He picks up his mobile from a side table and swipes through it. "She was last seen on Interstate 95 in South Carolina, heading north. I will text you updates as I receive them. We've got Neph and whisperers tailing her for other purposes, but I won't trust this job to anyone but you."

"Thank you, Father," I say. "I'm honored." And truly, I'm grateful. If they had asked another Neph . . .

Do not growl.

"My whisperer Rafe will escort you."

My eyes go wide, and I quickly neutralize my face again, but Father catches the look and smiles.

"Is that a problem?"

Yes, actually, it's an enormous problem. "No, sir."

"Good. The spirit will report to me as soon as the job is done, and we'll retrieve her when we're prepared to deal with her."

"I understand. Would you like me to be in contact with the other Neph myself?" I ask. "To save time?" And to find out who's against us?

"I think not," he says with a half grin. "Not all Neph are to be trusted these days. It's best if we deal with all of you directly ourselves."

I nod, pretending not to care that his words clearly include me.

He pulls keys from his trouser pockets and I take them.

"Drive fast. I don't care how many bloody tickets you get. Find her and ruin her once and for all, Kaidan. Make me proud."

"I will, Father."

I turn away and head to the garage. When I'm out of his sight I clench my jaw and silently curse him straight to hell before his stupid minion spirit flies in and I fall into false relaxation mode again.

Leave it to my father to unknowingly sabotage the one good thing in my life. I have no bloody clue how to get out of this. I wish like hell I could contact Anna to tell her she's being tailed, and to let her know I'm on my way. I've no idea what I'll do when I get there.

On the way out of town I stop at a drugstore and buy an over-the-counter men's fertility test to make sure I'm completely sterile. Just in case.

I cannot have sex with her. She has to remain a virgin—it's the only way she'll be able to use the Sword of Righteousness. I'll just have to take this charade as far as I can until I can go no further. This could be it. This could be the thing that kick-starts the prophecy. Because when it comes right down to it, if I cannot find a way to fool them, I might have to take Anna away; I might have to run. I've told her myself that she cannot hide from the demons, but damn it, I cannot let them have her without a fight, either. If our only other option is to stay put and be captured, then we will run like hell.

CHAPTER TWENTY-NINE

Not Like This

"Keep my eyes open, my lips sealed.
My heart closed, and my ears peeled."
—*"Hurricane" by MS MR*

I drive through the night, stopping only once for petrol and coffee. Each time a text comes from Father I reprogram my GPS with the new information. I cannot wait to get to Anna. To see her safe, with my own eyes. I'm desperate to have her out of their sights. After a while I think something must have happened with the Neph tailing her, because the updates from Father simply stop and only whisperer sightings are being given now.

Father's whisperer has been a nasty thorn in my side for far too many hours now. It keeps whispering excitedly about all the foul things it wants me to do to the "Neph girl," things I've never done to anyone. I try hard to keep from shuddering.

"I'm not into Neph," I tell it. "I'm not planning to stay all day."

It begins a breathy whine in my ear. *"But—"*

"No. Just a quick job—nothing for your entertainment."

It proceeds to throw a tantrum, stiffly flying from the car and bashing into the earth, out of sight, then back up, kicking at cars and flailing its grubby arms at trees as it passes them. What an idiot.

As I'm driving through Wythe County, in the mountains of southwestern Virginia, I see a whisperer swoop down in the grassy median to relay something to the other. It then flies to me, right in my face. I lean to the side, keeping an eye on the road. I can't stand the cold sensation when they touch me.

"Blacksburg," it whispers creepily. I nod. I'm not too far from her now.

I've been trying to figure out for hours what I'll do when I get to her. How will she react? With the whisperer there, we'll have to pretend we hardly know each other. If Anna cries or tries to hug me, or does anything remotely Anna-ish, we're as good as dead.

Our biggest chance of making it through this is to somehow lose the whisperer, and based on how closely he's been at my side, that will be difficult. The only other thing I can think to do is get her under the covers and pretend to shag her. That, however, could be awkward for poor Anna, and very, *very* difficult for me, especially if we're naked.

You can do it, I tell myself. I just hope she'll play along with whatever I decide. I grip the wheel and take a cleansing breath as the murky whisperer leads me to Anna.

It's early in the morning. The sun has risen, but the town is still sleepy. I park outside the hotel and listen while the whisperer circles the car. Anna is stirring, her murmuring breaths sounding as if she's not sleeping very soundly. When the whisperer ventures away from me for a moment, like a dog sniffing around, I whip out my phone and pull up Anna's contact info: *Hot Chick From Gig.* Before I can type a word, the whisperer is back and I quickly close the screen.

"What are you doing?" it asks. Damn it.

"Seeing if I missed any messages," I mutter out loud. "But I haven't."

"Let's go."

Bugger. I hate being here, so close to her, under these pretenses. It kills me not to warn her. I get out of the car and note exactly where it's parked and where the nearest exit is. I walk with purpose, fighting to keep my cool as my spirit escort flies up and down beside me. His wing keeps swiping my back and I grit my teeth. I desperately search each room of the hotel with my hearing, but everyone is sleeping or doing boring morning things.

Then my senses snag on something in one of the first-floor rooms. Something that sounds like it's just getting started. Something right up this whisperer's alley. It's better than I could have hoped. I take the long way around so we can pass that room on our way. I take note of the number on the door: 108.

This is a long shot. My first instinct is to distract the demon right away, but Father will be extremely suspicious if he learns I sent his whisperer away before the job had even begun. The spirit has to see me with Anna. He has to think we're having sex. And then, if I'm lucky, I can convince him to leave, to take in the more exciting events of room 108.

I head up the stairs, my pulse at an all-time high, and I knock on Anna's door. Inside, I hear her go still. Abruptly, she begins scrambling and shuffling through her things like mad.

Don't be frightened, I want to say. *Trust me, Anna. Play along.*

Anna whispers suspiciously, "Who is it?"

"Kaidan Rowe. Son of Pharzuph." Impersonal. Formal. *Please take the hint, luv.*

I hear the quick pad of her footsteps to the door and I'm filled with fear that she's going to fling it open and jump into my arms. I'm immensely relieved when she stops at the door without opening it. "What do you want?" she asks. She's being smart.

"I need to speak with you. Open up."

When she doesn't open, the whisperer hisses a harsh curse in my ear and I'm filled with loathing for the stupid, impatient spirit.

"I'm not here to hurt you," I say. It comes out sterner than I meant it to.

After a long pause the door opens enough to show Anna's beautiful, fresh face. Her eyes soften just slightly when she sees that it's really me, then widen when she catches sight of the whisperer over my shoulder. She doesn't move.

Anna knows something's up. Good. Because it's about to get real, and I need her to put on a show. I need her to pretend with me, one on one. Enough to convince the idiot bobbing behind me, foaming at the mouth.

I grasp the edge of the door above her head and push it open, forcing Anna to step back into the room. I scan her when she's in my sight—from her messy morning hair to the knife and another thing clenched in her fists.

I first cover her knife hand with mine and pry her fingers open. She gives a slight gasp as I relieve her of the weapon and slip it into my pocket. Then I reach for the other hand . . . a torch? Or, rather, *flashlight* to Americans. It's hardly big enough to use as a weapon, but I suppose it's better than her bare hand. I drop it to the floor and close the door behind me, still moving her forward until I have her against the wall. She glances toward the whisperer, then back to me. I have to ignore the hurt and fear in her eyes and get her to focus solely on me.

Her breathing goes a bit ragged as she stares up at me. I remind my body this is not for real, but it responds excitedly all the same. She puts her warm palms on the rise of my chest, and pushes me back with a fierce look in her eyes.

"Back off, son of Pharzuph."

I feel a wicked smile spread across my face because she's figured it out and she's playing along. She's the most sexy and spectacular creature on earth.

Let's do this, Anna.

"I'm only here as a precaution," I tell her. "To be sure our little daughter of Belial is behaving properly."

It's vital that she knows what's at stake and that she trusts me for what's to come. Anna's breath hitches and her eyes widen as if she's frantically searching for something to say.

"I heard you don't even like Neph girls."

I laugh and jerk my head to the side, flicking the hair from my eyes. Then I close the space between us. "I don't. But I'm willing to make sacrifices for the greater evil."

Don't show innocence, I want to beg her. *Be hard. Be tough. Act like you don't care.*

"So, what are you saying?" she asks with attitude. "The Dukes don't think I'm working? Is that why they're sending every Neph to question me and fight me?"

Fight her? I was under the impression she hadn't had any contact with the other Neph. Bloody hell.

"Just covering all the bases," I tell her. "They know you're pushing alcohol, but you weren't exactly a well-rounded worker at that summit, yeah?"

Her eyes flash with indignant anger. "That was a year and a half ago. I'm *very* well rounded now."

"Prove it."

I press her hard against the wall and slant my mouth over hers. She lets out the tiniest yelp of pain, and I have to stop myself from backing off to see if she's all right. I wasn't being gentle, but I also hadn't been rough enough to hurt her. I move past the awkward pause and focus again on her mouth. Anna's hands go to my chest. Her nails dig in and grasp my T-shirt. *That's it, Anna.*

The side of my body chills like it's been hit by a cold breeze, and a wet, bubbling sound of ecstasy fills my head. Fucking demon. Anna cringes and I turn to glare at the spirit, who's right in my face.

"Bit of a turnoff when you do that," I say through clenched teeth. "Mind shutting up?"

I hope it will back off long enough for us to give a decent show before I attempt to send it away. I take Anna's warm mouth again, but I'm finding it hard to focus on the charade. I want to savor my girl, and I can't think like that right now. I have to think of this like a job. Like a random hookup.

I can't let myself feel for her right now.

I kiss her harder. She doesn't melt into me like she usually does, but she's not pushing me away, so I press on. Father's whisperer is not going to want me to take my time with Anna. I have to get to business.

My shirt comes off first. I'm craving her touch all over my bare skin, but she's acting sort of stunned by what's happening. When I reach for the hem of her T-shirt, her arms automatically lock down to her body.

C'mon, Anna . . . trust me.

With a resigned expression, she raises her arms and I tug the shirt over her head, then our bodies are together again. Oh, God. No bra. She's bare-chested. For the first time, I can feel the soft and taut parts of her touching my own skin. Her arms go around my neck, tight with tension. I release a series of curses in my mind. I want to look down. I know, I'm a pig, but I'm dying to see every bit of her. However, she's as stiff as a board, so I pretend her naked chest is no big deal to me—not worth checking out.

It's time to take this to the next level by removing more clothing. I continue to hope Anna won't throw on the brakes.

Just a bit longer, I want to tell her.

But the biggest part of this show hasn't even happened yet.

I kiss down her neck to her shoulder and slide my hot hands

down her back. My fingers easily push past the elastic of her sleeping shorts, and then her underwear, until I'm cupping her bare arse.

This is the most perfectly fucked-up moment of my life, because having her ass in my hands is heaven, and I should not feel that way right now. My body is so overcome I can't move. She's mine and I want her.

Then I remember that my most heavenly moment is being closely scrutinized by a demon.

Still overcome, I manage to say, "Take them off."

Anna freezes. We don't look at each other. We have about two seconds to make this look believable—two seconds before she reacts or I rip them off myself.

"You don't have to be such an ass!" she snaps.

That fiery voice is just what I need to hear. She is livid, but still playing along. Anna will not strip herself, so I will do it for her. A dark part of me is loving every minute of this—thrilled that I will finally be naked with Anna Whitt, even if it won't lead to sex. I turn her and push her onto the bed, refusing to look at her face as I kneel above her. Before she's settled I grab the material at her beautiful hips and pull it down her legs.

A single sight catches my eye and puts the dark part of me to rest. There's a bruise on her thigh, and as I pull her shorts the rest of the way off, I see a series of purple-greenish markings down her calves. I stop breathing. My sweet girl has been injured.

Badly.

Fury burns like heated coals under my skin. Who did this to her?

The whisperer gurgles and flies over us, excited. I can't stop to demand answers. With great effort I force myself not to stare at her bruises, or her breasts, or . . . well, anywhere.

I move off the bed and stand at the end. She stares hard at me as I unclasp my belt and unbutton my shorts. I'm trying very hard not to look at her body. I want to, desperately, but not like this. However, I'm more than happy to let her see all of me.

It doesn't happen. As soon as I'm nearly naked, her eyes shift and I'm quite proud to see the look of Neph nonchalance on her face. But I also know her well enough to notice the set of her jaw jutting out—a sign she's trying not to cry. And behind that glazed expression I can see her hurt, her fear.

I've hurt her. I'm *scaring* her. Does she think I'm going to do this, for real? If she thinks that, I will stab my own damn self with her sword. She has to know I would *never* force myself on her. Anna's opinion of me is the only one in the world that matters.

I have to get rid of the damn spirit so I can explain. Just another minute more.

All I have to do now is climb onto the bed with her—*breathe*—throw a sheet over us—*breathe*—and pretend. And then it will be over. I won't let anything happen. I swallow hard and yank the blanket down from underneath her. She scoots back and I put my hands on the bed. Then a knee. Anna's eyes are on my chest. She knows I'm coming for her, and she's breathing fast.

I am nearly on top of her when the demon spirit makes a disgusting sound, like something gurgling inside a zombie's throat. Anna flinches from it, then her eyes light up and she surprises the hell out of me.

"Do you have to be here?" she yells at it. "You're really distracting."

"Shut up," it hisses into our minds, diving forward. *"As if I want to be here with you boring Neph!"*

Bingo, baby.

"Then leave," I say in a lazy voice. "We're almost finished here. Anyway, I think you'd find room 108 far more interesting."

My heart is pounding. The whisperer goes still. Then moves up and down, pondering. *Please, let this work.*

"You won't tell?" it hisses.

"Tell what?" I snap, as if I'm eager to get back to work. "You did what you bloody came to do—you saw me find the girl and assure she's impure. Your job is done, and I can finish mine much better if you're not hovering."

For a horrible moment I imagine it will refuse, then it spins and disappears through the side wall into the hall. Just like that. I stare at that spot forever, because it's too bloody good to be true. When he doesn't come back, I fall to my face on the bed beside Anna, screaming into the mattress with relief and tension.

My man parts are crying.

I want Anna so bad. My girl is naked next to me. I didn't even get a proper glimpse. I want to beg her to let me climb atop her, just for a moment, if I swear not to let it happen, just to have our bare bodies touching. . . .

Anna scrambles under the covers away from me and

throws something soft over my bum.

Right. That's a no.

I look at her face as she stares at the wall in agony, and I can't take it any longer. I reach a hand over her waist and lay my head in her blanketed lap, breathing in her sweet scent. I have to erase any shred of doubt, fear, or distrust in her mind.

"I would have stopped, Anna. I swear," I babble with desperation. "I'd die before I took you against your will. Please tell me you believe me."

Her voice is filled with emotion when she says, "I believe you."

My head is suddenly too heavy to lift, though I know I should move away from her. Then I feel Anna's fingers tentatively push into my hair, moving through the strands so tenderly. I cannot move away.

"Get under the covers with me," Anna whispers. "We need to lie here for a little while in case it comes back."

Yes. I lift my head and the doubt is gone from her eyes. Only love and concern are there, and I feel myself melt.

Her head tilts and she touches my cheek. "There you are."

Here I am.

She pulls back the sheet and I move next to her, shielding myself with a pillow. We lay silent, side by side, and I'm trying damn hard not to think about our nakedness. About her waist and hips and thighs and legs . . .

I bolt upright. The bruises!

I take her arm and gently twist it to find fingertip bruises on the soft flesh underneath. The smoking coals beneath my skin reignite with a vengeance.

"Anna . . . ," I whisper in disbelief as I think about her being hit and kicked. Bright spots soar in my vision. "What. The bloody hell. Happened? Who did this to you?"

"Listen, Kai." It's her calming voice, but it's not working. "I'm all right now, okay?"

No. Not okay at all. Anyone who is capable of putting marks like this on Anna does not deserve to live. "*Who?*" I demand.

"The sons of Thamuz."

HolyMaryMotherofGod.

My mouth goes completely dry as I recall the things they did to Marna when she was so young—things that forced her to begin seeing evil whisperers. "What did they do?" I don't want to hear it, but I need to know. If they raped her and stole her innocence, her power . . . "So help me God—"

"Nothing!" she assures me, grabbing my arm. She sounds as if she means it, and I try to calm my breathing. "They tried to take me, but I fought. And . . . Kope showed up."

I'm sorry, what? "Kope?"

Her eyes dart about like she wants to run. "Yeah. Um. I figured it might be safe to call him for information. I didn't ask him to come. I didn't have any idea the sons of Thamuz were going to attack me. I was only planning to meet with the son of Shax to see if he was an ally. But I guess Kope was worried and came to make sure I was okay, and he showed up just in time. He went sort of crazy and beat the crap out of them."

I can see the worry on her face, that I might get jealous, but I'm not jealous of Kope anymore. I know there's nothing between them except friendship. However, my foolish pride makes me hate the fact that she had to ring another person for help while I had no clue what was happening. And I hate that Anna charges into these dangerous situations with no thought for her safety. She's still too trusting.

I rub my face hard as exhaustion hits me.

"I can't . . . I just . . . Anna, swear you'll never engage another Neph like that. You're bloody lucky Kope showed! God, what would I do? Look at you!" I move her hair aside and look at her back.

Her shoulder blade is swollen and purpled. I want to vomit, remembering how she'd yelped when I pushed her against the wall. "I'd no clue you were injured. I was too rough. . . ."

She takes my hand and angles herself so I can't see it. "I'm okay. I swear. You had to be rough. It was more convincing that way."

But I don't hear her. I'm too busy picturing the evil sons of the Duke of Murder manhandling her. "I'll kill them."

Anna shushes me and pulls me back down until we're lying close, facing each other.

"If it makes you feel any better," she says, "I zapped one of them pretty good."

"You did what?"

She points at the torch on the ground by the door. "It's a stun gun."

I chuckle at the thought of this, and Anna gives a small smile. We can't stay in this hotel room long, but for now, Anna is safe, and Kope nearly beat the sons of Thamuz to death. I let myself picture it, and I feel a bit better.

We dodged a bullet tonight, but we're not out of the dark

yet. What happened tonight was only a temporary fix on a major problem. Father and the others will come looking for Anna eventually, and when they do, the true darkness will show itself. For now, I will hold her close.

CHAPTER THIRTY

BLAKE AND THE TWINS

"Bright and early for the daily races, going nowhere, going nowhere . . .
I wanna drown my sorrow, no tomorrow, no tomorrow."
—*"Mad World" by Michael Andrews, featuring Gary Jules*

I don't want to leave Anna. Not when I know she's being sought by madmen, and they've already laid hands on her once. I will never rest when she's out of my sight. I trust that her father is working on a plan, but he's MIA and Anna's not sure where to turn next.

Too much has happened in the short time since she was in California. She tells me about her strange interactions with the son of Duke Shax, named Marek, and the daughter of Duke Jezebet, named Caterina. I don't trust them. We know Caterina is not on our side—she was the one who told the Dukes that Flynn was lying, which led to his death. Marek is a wild card.

Anna's mobile rings, and when she sees it's Marna, she begins trembling. I've no clue why the sight of her friend's name would cause her to go pale. But the way she looks up at me tells me something big is going on.

On the other end of the line, Marna is equally distraught. "Anna. She's still not back and she won't answer her phone. It's been more than a day, and I'm too scared to wait any longer. I'm going to her."

Who's she going on about? Ginger? I move closer, trying to figure out what's happening.

"Are there any Dukes in California?" Anna asks me. "Blake's dad?"

I shake my head. "All the Dukes should be back in their respective areas," I say. "What's going on?"

"Is that Kai?" Marna asks. "What's he doing there?"

"Yes, it's him," Anna tells her. She puts the phone to her shoulder and looks at me. "Can you call Blake and see if he answers? We think Ginger's with him."

What? That makes no sense. They'd never be so stupid.

I dial Blake and leave him a message telling him to ring me back straightaway.

"I'm going to meet you there," Anna tells Marna. "I think it's going to take more than just you to break the two of them apart."

Wait just a damn minute. They're going to Santa Barbara?

"I'm going," I say.

Anna doesn't argue. She hangs up with Marna and buys tickets, then gets her things together in a rush. Her lips are pursed and there's obvious sadness in her eyes. Whatever's going on, she doesn't want to talk about it, but I need to know.

"Did Gin go mad when she found out Blake's engaged?" I ask.

She stops and chews the inside of her lip for a second before standing to face me.

"She *was* upset about that, but it's not what sent her over the edge."

"So what did?" What on earth could possibly cause Gin to leave her sister and do something as reckless as shack up with another Neph?

"The twins had a . . . disagreement." Anna looks scared to death, and I'm starting to get bloody nervous.

"About what?" I ask.

She swallows. "Marna's pregnant." The words come out dry and brittle, and I cannot make sense of them. Those two simple words cannot possibly go together. Marna . . . no. NO. There's been a mistake.

"I sensed it," Anna whispers. "It's Jay's."

"Bloody *hell*." Each of her words slams into me like a bullet and I cannot stand. I fall back onto the bed and grab at my hair as if I might rip the words out of my mind. This cannot be happening. Marna. She's like a baby sister to me. God, no wonder Anna didn't want to tell me. We only have Marna for nine more months, and then she'll be . . . no. I shake my head. I can't fathom it. I cannot think about Marna in hell.

I raise my heavy eyes to Anna, and my heart sinks further. Her eyes are lowered. Devastated. I think of Jay, how Anna never told him what we were, or that her mother died in childbirth, as all mothers of Neph do. I imagine how she must've felt when she sensed the pregnancy, when she had to tell them.

354

Ginger's reaction would've been colossal. I can't bloody believe this is happening. It's madness.

"Come here," I say to her, holding out a hand. I pull her to my lap and she wraps her arms around me. "It's not your fault."

She lets out a sob. "It *is* my fault they got together. I didn't think they'd move so fast, and if I'd known she could get pregnant—"

"Sh, Anna. Those two always fancied each other, yeah? This whole thing is awful, but you can't stop the inevitable."

I hold her a moment longer before she wipes her eyes, pulling herself together. "We'd better go," she says, standing. "I'll tell you everything on the plane."

"Wait," I say. "How much does Jay know?"

"He knows everything," she says with downcast eyes.

Everything. That his best friend Anna, along with the girl he's fallen in love with, are the daughters of demons. That Marna will die in childbirth, because their child will also be a Nephilim. That the baby's soul will essentially rip Marna's soul from her body when it's born. That we're all fighting for our lives right now. What a thing for Jay to walk into. Poor sodding chap.

Blake and Ginger, two of the most careful Neph I know, have bloody well lost their minds. They're bunked up in the mansion while his psychotically envious fiancée rages outside the gate. News vans are there to catch it all. He's a local motocross celebrity whose fabulously rich father has just "died," and this is what they choose to do?

Yes, they've wanted each other for a bloody long time and

have always held back. Yes, Ginger's just found out she's losing the person she loves most in the world, but getting themselves killed is not the answer. Especially now that the prophecy is on the horizon. It's no longer about us as individuals. Each ally is important.

I am livid when we finally get inside the gate. I bang on Blake's front door, but they don't answer. I bang again. "Open up, idiot! This is bloody stupid!"

Finally they come to the door. They're clearly lost to their beasts—Blake is feeding off his fiancée's envy while Ginger gets her kicks off causing Blake to cheat. They're both half dressed, showing signs of a shag fest with wild hair and flushed skin. For a moment I am jealous they've been able to give in to their need for each other, and that jealousy makes me even angrier.

"It's time to go, Gin," Marna tells her.

Ginger gives her a malicious stare. "You're one to talk. I seem to recall that line didn't work on you." So, Ginger tried to warn Marna, to get her away from Jay. That makes this all the worse. "I'm quite fine where I am, thanks," Gin snaps.

"Like hell." I shove open the door and stride past them, the others following. I slam the door once we're all inside. I point at Blake. "Have whisperers seen you together?"

"Course not." He sounds far too blasé, and I want to beat some sense into him.

"You're bleedin' lucky!"

"Back off, brah." He gets in my face. "What, you're the only one who can be with your girl?"

I want to point out that I haven't even shagged my girl, but

I know this is about more than sex. It's about the danger of even being seen together, as we are now.

"The Dukes were at their summit when we were together," I remind him.

Anna tries to intervene and calm us, but Ginger moves in. "Why do you care?" she asks me. Her eyes are wet and hardened.

"Because we're this close." I lean toward her, enraged. "*This* close to fulfilling the prophecy, and the two of you are likely to get yourselves killed!"

"As if you care!" Ginger screams at me. "You only give a shite about yourself. You want everyone to be willing to sacrifice themselves so you can finally be with your precious Anna. Well, I'm not waiting around anymore. I'm taking what I want from this damned life while I can!" Her cheeks have gone red.

"It's about all of us!" I shout back.

"Oh, right!"

God, this is too like our fights as children, matched in temperament. I'm filled again with a sibling-like sentiment as I let myself feel the ache Ginger must be living with.

I take her by the shoulders. "I don't want you dead, Gin."

Her eyes fill with tears. My strong Ginger, who, like me, never cries. "I've nothing to live for now, don't you see? She'll be gone. My sister is dying! And Blake will be married off to that cow. I'd rather be dead."

Oh, Gin. I swallow hard and take her into my arms, where she breaks down and lets me hold her up. Marna, sobbing, comes forward, and I open the embrace to include her. I want to fix this for them. It's all so wrong. Why should mothers of Neph have to die? It's all shite. Nothing about the life of a Neph makes any sense.

Soon the twins are moving from my arms to embrace each other, their heads buried in each other's shoulders as they grieve. I rub their backs and swallow again. I know they need this moment, but I turn my head and look around, wondering how long it will take for the whisperers to find us. We can't stay here. We could ruin everything.

When the twins pull themselves together and wipe their eyes, we all sit together in the sitting room. It's an awkward, sad, guilty sort of silence.

And then my mobile rings and I stare at Father's name on the screen, feeling ill. I hold it out for the others to see and their eyes go wide.

"Hallo," I say.

"I assume you took care of the girl, then?"

"Of course, Father. She wasn't a virgin anyhow."

"Interesting." He pauses and I raise the phone to hide the deep breath I'm taking to calm my pulse. "The spirit I sent to oversee the operation has been sent back to the pit of hell, never to return to earth. Do you know why?"

My eyes meet Anna's worried ones. "No, Father."

"Because he admitted he did not stay to see your mission through to the end. He says the two of you persuaded him to leave."

"Bollocks!" I jump to my feet, my heart in my throat. "That disgusting wanker was distracting. It's hard enough to try and bang a Neph without a spirit interfering."

"A whisperer should hardly distract you from your task, son."

I go still, my mind racing. I must make him believe me. "You're right, Father. But the deed was done, and the whisperer left on his own. Obviously I couldn't force him."

"Hm. I think I'll pay the girl a visit myself. A lot's riding on her lack of purity."

Over my dead body will I let him near her. I clench my jaw and force polite words out. "Do what you must, Father, but I hate to see your valuable time wasted."

"Good of you to care," the bastard says before hanging up on me.

Will it never end? Will we never get a bloody break? I yell through my teeth and kick the coffee table, flipping it with a *crash*.

I feel Anna's tentative hand on my shoulder as I pant through the rage.

"Everything's going to be okay," she soothes. "We all need to get back to work. At this rate the prophecy's bound to go down soon, and we can't afford to lose anyone."

"What about you?" Marna asks her. "Where will you go?"

Anna looks at me. "I don't know."

"Well, I don't think you should be alone," I tell her. Not after that phone call.

"We're all gonna have to be alone if we want to convince them we're working," Blake says.

Screw that. I'm not concerned with pretending to work anymore. Father obviously doesn't trust me, and Anna's in immediate danger. The others should still pretend, but I need to take Anna with me, make a run for it. We are arguing about the best plan of action when the room suddenly darkens. Sunlight from the arched windows is shadowed by an enormous dark angel pushing through the window and walls, into the room, its wings outstretched wide enough to engulf the lot of us.

Shite! It's too late to run. I lean back hard into the chair as I take in the whole sight, its ramlike horns curling wickedly upward and its massive body like a humanesque beast. Then I nearly swallow my tongue as it advances on Anna.

A dreadful sense of powerlessness overcomes me and I want to throw myself between them and yell for Anna to take out the sword. And then she whispers a single word.

"Daddy?"

My eyes bug out. *Belial?* Holy shit! I've never seen a Duke outside of its body. Whisperers have nothing on him. And why has he left his body? Things must be getting dire.

"Thank God it's you," Anna says, talking fast. "So much is happening. Pharzuph is hounding me, and I don't know where to go."

"That's why I'm here." Belial's low rumble of a voice fills my mind, so he must be projecting it to all of us. We gather to listen.

Belial turns his huge celestial horned head to me expectantly.

"What do you suggest?" I ask him.

"You have only one safe option," he says. *"Get married."*

Wait . . . what . . . ? There's no fucking way he just said that. Everyone is staring back and forth between me and Anna, and

Anna is looking at her father as if he's spoken an alien language. She's shaking her head in disbelief.

"We can't," she says. "I have to stay a virgin. The sword—"

"No." Belial lowers himself so he's eye to eye with his daughter but projects his thoughts on me, as well. *"You have to stay pure of heart, Anna. What's more pure than committing yourselves in love?"*

"But . . ." Anna's head slowly swivels to mine. His words replay in my ears and the only ones I hear are *purity* and *marriage.*

"No." I stumble back. Those words are Anna, not me. They can never be me. "It won't work."

Belial is wrong. He's desperate and he hasn't thought this through. If I join myself with Anna, I will be one degree of separation from the Sword of Righteousness. It will sense me through her. It's smart.

"I'm sorry, Duke Belial. I can't marry."

I cannot even believe he'd think this was viable. Does he not remember how he'd wanted to keep me away from her? His reasons, the acts of my past, still live inside me. I can't let this mistake happen.

"Don't be stupid, Kai," Ginger says. "There's no time for this. If it can save you both, you need to do it."

No. They're all watching me like I'm being unreasonable, but they don't get it. I'm too ashamed to even look at Anna, but surely she'll understand. The stakes are too high to take this sort of chance.

"Duke Astaroth will be able to see the bond of marriage," I remind them.

"Well, he'll see the bond of love between you, which is just as bad," Gin says.

Has the entire world gone mad? A million pounds of pressure are suddenly stacked on my shoulders and I turn, shoving my hands into my hair, struggling to breathe.

Marrying Anna . . . being with her in all the ways we so desperately want . . .

Blake steps closer. "Dude, come on—"

"Don't pressure him," Anna says, hurt in her voice. "If he doesn't want to do it, he shouldn't have to."

What? She's got it all wrong.

"Anna . . ."

"It's okay," she says. "It was a bad idea."

Does she understand, then? Or is she being passive-aggressive? Am I the only one who sees the danger here?

"It's not a bad idea," Marna pipes in. "Really, Kai. Why the hell not?"

I don't want to argue with her. "Marna—"

"That's pants!" she shouts. "What's the problem?"

I turn to face her. "She can't tie herself to a bloke like me and expect to come out of it white as snow. It won't work!"

Marna's eyes soften as if she's finally getting it. But then she says, "She loves you. And you love her. You're not going to soil her soul, babe."

What if I do? "My past has to be taken into account."

"Your past is in the past," Anna says. "And it's not going to . . . rub off on me or something. You know it doesn't work like that."

Do I? Because I've always had the Midas touch, only the

things I touch don't turn to gold. They turn to ruin and brokenness and depression. It's one thing to dream of being with Anna, but to actually take that chance is too much. I feel the eyes of the room on me and realize I'm alone in my way of thinking.

In the next moment, Belial is in my face, his horned head large and fierce.

"Don't play games with me, boy. Do you love her or not?" he hisses.

One glance at the others in the room and their wonder makes it clear I'm the only one hearing this conversation.

"Yes, I love her." I press this thought at him silently.

"Then what is your fear?"

I swallow. *"That once she's been with me, she'll not be able to use the sword. Because of who I am, because of what I've done."*

"You have to let go of that fear. Let go of your past, and focus on your love. You are changed, and it's time to embrace your future. You're not that same self-serving boy I drove away from my daughter. Marry her and buy yourselves time to fulfill this prophecy. Otherwise Pharzuph will find her and learn the truth. This is what will keep her safe. Do you understand?"

He sounds so certain, but it feels impossible. A wedding? Anna deserves the whole nine yards, but that can't happen.

"With all respect, Duke Belial, we don't have time for a wedding."

"Leave the details to me."

"But—"

"If you love her," his voice rumbles in my ear, *"you will marry her. End of discussion."*

Everyone's eyes are still on me, suffocating me. "I need some time to myself," I mutter. I need air.

I turn and make a beeline for the back door, flinging it open and letting the sea breeze blast me with its warmth. I stand on the edge of Blake's deck, staring out at the magnitude of the Pacific Ocean, and allow myself to feel small.

Marry Anna.

Perhaps that is what Belial had in mind all along. For someone, hopefully Kope, to secretly marry Anna and keep her safe from my father. But Anna and Kope didn't fall in love, did they? No, it was me.

All my life I've been selfish. I don't trust the instinct inside me, shouting, *Yes, make her yours and finally be with her!* What if I only want this for selfish reasons? I press my thumbs into my eyes and think of Anna up there on the stage at the summit in New York so long ago. I remember the fear when I was so certain Duke Rahab would kill her. My only thought was that my knife would be through his head before his finger could reach the trigger.

I am capable of selflessness.

I close my eyes. Time to sort out the facts.

I'm the only man who Anna loves. And I'm the only man who loves her. Therefore, only *I* can do this for her. The fact that it will fill me with immeasurable joy does not make me selfish. It makes me a living, breathing man with something worth living for.

I'm tired of being ruled by fear.

I fill my chest with fresh air and turn to go back inside and face my future. Anna meets me at the door, and the sight of her is exhilarating. I take her hand and she twines her fingers between mine. I lead her down to Blake's theater room, my favorite place in this mansion.

We sit in the red velvet chairs and I turn to face her, still holding her hand. I'm nearly bursting with all I want to say. But Anna opens her mouth first.

"Look, I don't know what my dad said to you, but don't let him pressure you. You don't have to do this. I'll find a way to hide from Pharzuph."

Before I address what her father said to me, I need to make something clear. "You can't hide from him forever, Anna."

"Yes, but I don't want that to be our sole reason for getting married."

I look down at our joined hands. Fear may have prompted this decision, but is it the driving factor behind it? Would Belial give his blessing if we weren't in peril? Would I care?

"I'm telling him no," she says.

My eyes snap to her. I'm doused with loss. She tries to stand, but I grip her hands. "You don't want to get married?" Is she having doubts?

"Of course I want to, but you have to want it, too. And it has to be for the right reasons."

"I'd do anything for you—to keep you safe," I try to explain. "When I think of what those sons of Thamuz could've done—"

"Wrong reason," Anna whispers. "We can't do this."

She tries again to pull away, and I want to curse myself. I'm not explaining myself well. I'm better at talking in facts than feelings.

"Anna—"

"Let me go, Kai." Shite, now she's upset. I'm mucking it up.

"No, please," I beg. "God, I'm just not good at this, luv. Any of it. I know this is something you've always wanted."

She closes her eyes. "That was a long time ago. When I thought I was normal. I never wanted it to be like this."

I don't want it like this for her either, rushed and secretive. I want her dreams to all come true.

"That's what I tried to tell your father. We've no time to plan a fancy ceremony or to have a gown tailored—"

"Whoa, stop." She holds up a hand and gives me a strange look. "I don't need any of that fairy-tale stuff. It's the marriage that matters to me, not the wedding. As long as our hearts are in the right place, we could be in pajamas for all I care."

"But . . . I wanted to give you all that." I watch her pretty face, trying to figure out what can make this right. What does she want?

"Kai, please, tell me what you're thinking. We don't have much time, and we have to make a decision."

A decision? Does she think I haven't decided?

"I . . ."

She's watching me, searching my face for something. The only thing I can think to give her is so simple. So traditional. So *not me*. I slide down to one knee, still holding her hand, and look up at her. "My sweet, lovely Anna. I love you . . . and I want to marry you." Wait, I don't think I said that bit right. Shite, I was supposed to *ask* her, not *tell* her, as if it's all about me. "But only if you want to. Do you? I mean, will you?" *Spit it out!* "Marry me?"

She breaks into exultant laughter and falls to her knees

with me, grabbing my face and pressing her soft lips to mine. We kiss over and over, but still she hasn't responded.

"Does it always take this long for someone to answer? It's making me bloody nervous."

She pulls back and meets my eyes, filled with mirth. "Yes, Kai. I'll marry you."

Sweeter words have never been uttered. This time I kiss her, and I wrap my arms around her to keep from trembling. I've never felt happiness like this. When our mates burst through the door, cheering, all I can do is grin like an idiot and say, "So much for privacy."

Nothing, *nothing* can bother me at this moment, because I'm going to marry Anna Whitt. I'm going to love her and protect her and keep her safe any way that I can.

And it just so happens that the key to keeping her safe from my father is to shag her senseless.

I think I can handle that.

CHAPTER THIRTY-ONE

TILL DEATH

"My walls are falling and my white flag is high,
I've surrendered to the feeling inside."
—*"The Only One" by Hot Chelle Rae*

Everyone takes off and I'm left standing at Blake's, a bit shell-shocked, blinking into the bright sun. What do blokes do to prepare for weddings? I rack my brain, thinking about grooms in commercials. Tuxedos are out. I could get her a garter. . . .

Wait. Rings! Brilliant. And, where will we go afterward? We'll need a honeymoon suite somewhere. Look at me, already a pro at this husband business.

The first place that comes to mind is the one place Anna wanted to see that I didn't get to take her to—the place I've only seen alone when I was at the lowest point in my life. Seeing it with Anna at my side will, no doubt, be a different experience. It's time to set things right.

I do an internet search for Grand Canyon honeymoon destinations. Of course the best places have no vacancies tonight. I get on the phone with the owner of a set of luxury cabins.

"I'm so sorry, but we're all booked."

I put on my most polite English voice. "Yes, but I'm wondering if you can point me in the direction of anyone who might have a place. I know it's late notice. I'll literally pay *any* price they ask for one night. It's my wedding night, you see. Sort of an impromptu wedding because we're facing some rather worrisome issues." I clear my throat and shut my eyes.

"Oh, dear." The woman is quiet. "Well . . . there's our personal vacation cabin. . . ."

My eyes snap open. "I'd hate to put you out, miss."

"We don't usually rent it out, but you sound like a nice young man. I suppose one night would be okay."

I exhale a giant sigh and grin. "You are an angel. Thank you. I mean it. We'll take good care of it."

She sounds happy. "Let me make some calls and I'll give you the lock code."

I finish talking to the Grand Canyon angel, hoping her cabin is as beautiful as the ones posted online.

Next I scan through local jewelers on my mobile and head to the closest shop. As I browse at the counter, looking around for whisperers all the while, one thing becomes quickly apparent: I cannot buy Anna a diamond. They scream of matrimony. Every one of these sparklies would attract attention, even if she wore it on a different finger or hand. And the men's bands are quite obvious as well.

This could take a while. I call Marna to help with some other things I won't have time for.

"What can I do for you, darling?" she asks.

"I need clothes for tomorrow. I didn't pack enough and I'm running low on time. Can you manage?"

"Absolutely. Anything else?"

"Food, perhaps." I give her my sizes and get back to ring shopping.

In my search I happen upon a funky shop with artistic, handmade pieces. The prices are astronomical, but I don't care. In fact, I'm glad to spend a lot on something to commemorate this day.

I consult the almighty Google to learn of Anna's May birthstone, the emerald. Almost immediately my eye is drawn to a small ring with Celtic vines knotted around a circular emerald. The shop woman takes it out for me.

"What size do you need?" she asks.

Size? I haven't the slightest clue.

"Er, small?"

"This one is five and a quarter," she says. "It's a rather small size. It won't fit on my hand." She holds her hand out for me to see, and it's definitely larger than Anna's. I don't want to mess this up, but I haven't much choice. The look of it is perfect.

She shows me the men's rings next and I gravitate to the thick black tribal designs. I point to the most wicked-looking one, the design etched into silver just like Anna's.

"I'll take them both."

I scan the clear skies as I leave the shop with our rings. Our *wedding* rings.

I shake my head and drive for the airport.

Blake's plane is killer, roomier than Father's jet, with that new leather smell.

He welcomes me aboard with a grin and a salute.

"This is brilliant, mate."

He crosses his arms, peering around. "Yeah, being the son of Envy has its advantages."

"Bloody right," I say, setting down my bag.

"Well, we're all fueled up and ready to go when everyone gets here."

My insides dip with a fluttery, falling sensation and I grip the top of the seat I'm standing near. Blake laughs.

"You nervous, man? Don't puke on the upholstery."

"I won't," I mutter, forcing myself to straighten. I've no reason to be feeling strange.

Except perhaps for the fact that I'm going to be a *husband*. This wasn't exactly something I envisioned for myself. It was never in my nature to commit. Anna's shown me it's okay to hope for something more, to want something better. The things I was taught to think of as weaknesses I now recognize as strengths. I can't explain why I'm so jittery when everything feels so *right*. I just don't want to bung it up.

"So, what's the plan?" Blake asks. "You thought about where I should take you guys afterward?"

"Yeah." I tell him about the Grand Canyon. He fist-bumps me again before returning to the cockpit to ready the plane.

I sit at the open space in the back where I can rest my head in my hands and think for a minute. I want this to be perfect for Anna.

I've sat like that a long while, trying to get rid of these ridiculous nerves, when I hear feminine giggles coming up the jet steps. The twins burst through the doors, Marna chipper and Ginger looking exhausted. Behind them is Anna, and when I see her staring around the cabin in awe, I remember who I'm dealing with here. Anna is not your picky perfectionist. My girl finds beauty in the small things. Seeing her puts me at ease. I lean back and watch her, one hand behind my head.

She's changed into a white, summery halter dress that makes me want to drool. It also makes me wish I'd at least changed my clothes. Blond layers lay across her shoulders. Her dress is open at the back, revealing tanned, smooth skin in stark contrast against the white. The silky material hugs her, flowing down to her ankles. She is a sight.

I'm going to strip that dress from her body tonight. Along with everything underneath it.

Behind Anna, Marna holds up a bag, pointing to it. *I downloaded mood music!* she signs.

I raise my eyebrows and give her an unenthusiastic thumbs-up. I hope she's grown out of her love of boy bands.

Anna finally finds me, and her smile disappears as our eyes meet. My confidence returns, obliterating all traces of nerves. I'm going to take care of this girl in every possible way. Judging by how she nibbles her lip, she knows it.

I lift a hand to call her over. Moments later she's standing before me, the dress accentuating her waist.

"Hey," she says, a bit bashful.

"Hey, yourself. You're stunning. I feel like a slob."

She looks me over, taking me in. "You always look good." Her shy smile melts me.

I ignore Gin's gagging noises from where she's sitting nearby, and I wrap my hands around Anna's hips, leading her

372

toward me. She sits beside me, lifting her hair, fanning herself with a shaking hand.

I take that hand and place a soft kiss in her palm.

Don't be nervous, I sign to her with my other hand.

Her face still looks pinched with tension, so I pull her onto my lap and she lays her head on my shoulder.

"Are you sure about this?" Her whisper is warm against my neck.

"I am," I assure her. "Are you?"

"Yes."

Well, there you have it.

Blake ambles out of the cockpit and I circle a finger in the air as if to say, *Let's go.* He nods his agreement. The sooner we're in the air where the whisperers don't venture, the better.

We all take our seats, and fifteen minutes later we're lifting off smoothly. I'm rather impressed with Blake's flying skills. Once we've reached our altitude, Blake puts the plane on autopilot and joins us, as the girls freak out about it. It's quite humorous, and I can't help chuckling, relieved to have all my closest mates by my side.

When we stand, I'm racked with nerves again, and I hope it doesn't show.

"I didn't prepare vows or anything," Anna says. "I guess we're just winging it?"

Vows? Was I supposed to do that?

Blake shakes out a piece of paper and my worry subsides. He's printed out traditional vows, and he even got an official license to marry us, per Belial's suggestion. But leave it to Blake not to be serious.

He puffs out his chest and declares, "Dearly beloved!" like an old, Southern minister.

We all lose it. And shite, I don't realize how blazin' tense I am until we're all falling over with laughter.

"All right," Blake says when we finally calm down. He looks at me. "For real this time. Keep your eyes on Anna and repeat after me. You ready?"

I run my hands through my hair, frustrated by this persistent nervousness. Nothing has ever been this important to me. I've been thinking of this as Anna's special day, but as I exhale sharply and take her hands again, I realize I want this as much as she does. I lock eyes with Anna and prepare to vow my love and loyalty to her alone. My voice drops an octave as I fight back emotion.

"I, Kaidan, take you, Anna, to be my wedded wife. To have and to hold from this day forward, for better or worse, for richer or poorer, in sickness and in health." I struggle to get the next words out. ". . . till death do us part."

Anna's eyes drift closed, forcing tears to roll out. I quickly wipe them and whisper, "No tears, luv."

Her chin quavers but she nods. We grip hands tighter. Her voice is pure and angelic when she says her vows, and I let each word soak into my skin, through muscle and bone, into my very soul where I'll cherish them for eternity.

She beams up at me when she finishes, and my broad smile matches hers.

"Time for the rings," Blake says.

Anna's face falls. "Oh, I didn't—"

"Don't worry," I say, reaching into my pocket. I know she

is a reasonable girl, I hope too reasonable to expect diamonds, but I'm still anxious about her reaction. I open my palm to show her.

"I figured we'd have to wear these on our opposite hands after today," I explain when she says nothing. "And since it's our secret, I decided on your birthstone instead of a diamond. I had to guess your size."

She stares a moment longer before grinning up at me. "I love it." The awe in her voice makes me stand taller.

I hand her the men's band and we exchange rings, sliding them on to each other's fingers as a symbol of our love and commitment.

Blake claps a hand onto my shoulder. "Now for the good part. You may kiss your bride."

"'Bout time," I say, leaning forward to seal the most important moment of my life.

"No tongue!" Gin shouts.

"Yes tongue!" Marna counters.

Oh, for the love of—

Anna flings her arms about my neck and snogs me good to shut them up. Marna and Blake cheer and Ginger snorts. I drown them out and focus on Anna's lips.

We press our foreheads together, and her eyes sparkle with glee.

"Did we really just do that?" I ask.

She smiles and nods and bursts into excited giggles. I grab her around the waist and lift her up, kissing her again, fighting the instinct to take her straight into the loo for a bit of privacy.

"Should I be this turned on by a wedding?" I ask.

"You get turned on when the wind blows!" Ginger says with a laugh.

Right enough. Anna laughs and I grin at her.

We're all a bit mad at that moment, as if we've had loads to drink, though in fact we're sober as nuns. I suppose that's how rebellion feels—living with purpose—like each second is monumental and full. I soak it in, because I'm not fool enough to think it will last forever. But it's ours now, all ours.

CHAPTER THIRTY-TWO

FINALLY

"You trace my lines, stirring my soul,
Shoot sparks at the heart of the world and I watch it explode."
—*"Run" by Matt Nathanson*

The extravagant cabin is even better than I'd hoped. Anna certainly seems to agree. She's rushing about the rooms in hyper speed, sighing and touching and exclaiming about every detail. The bed looks as if it's been carved from an ancient tree, complete with overhanging branches and wood beams in the ceilings. Everything resembles autumn, with fabrics of red, brown, and yellow, and rustic wood furniture. I want to kiss Anna every time she flits past, but I can't bloody catch her. Finally I nab her in the ginormous bathroom, and our mouths meet.

When she tenses, I pull back. "What's wrong?"

She glances down. "I don't know what I'm doing."

Ah. She's already thinking ahead.

"Anna?" I ask.

"Hm?" She's gone shy.

"Have you ever felt as though you were fumbling around awkwardly when we're together?"

"Um . . . I guess not."

"Exactly. Some things come naturally, so don't overthink it. I'm going to take care of you."

She talks quietly, not looking me in the eye. "But I want to take care of you, too. You have to show me what to do."

My lovely Anna is too kind. She has no clue how anything she does this night will only further satisfy my growing need for her.

"I'm not as hard to please as you might imagine. I'll show you anything you want."

She swallows and nods.

"Also . . ." I clear my throat. "Two days ago when Father told me he was sending me to seek you out . . . I had a test done. Just in case anything were to happen with us—I just wanted to be sure."

Damn good thing, too, because after Marna, I'd be paranoid as hell tonight.

"Oh," Anna says. "To make sure you're really . . ."

"Sterile, yes. And I am."

"Thank you," she whispers. And she finally gets brave enough to look up at me. Her eyes widen and I feel a stirring in my belly. For so long I've held back with her. I will still have to hold back a bit, because she's not yet ready for it all. But there are things I can and will do tonight. Starting with seeing every bit of her skin. I glance over her mouth, at the freckle at the corner of her lips.

"Anna . . ."

"Hmm?" Her voice goes high. She clears her throat.

"Remember when I told you I wanted to introduce myself to every freckle on your body?"

She nods slowly.

"Well, it's time."

Her cheeks bloom with color. I close my eyes as a warm wave of pears and freesia permeates the air. "You smell so damn good."

Though this moment feels long overdue, I know neither of us was truly ready until this night. This is how it was meant to be for us.

I take her hand and lead her back into the main room. I want to put on music, but mine's a bit dark. I dig through the bag from Marna and stare down at the music player she sent.

"Marna downloaded mood music as a gift," I mutter. "I'm a bit frightened."

Anna giggles at my apprehension. I set up the dock and turn it on. Sure enough, the first song is twangy.

"Country music?" Since when does Marna listen to this?

"I love this song!" Anna says, and I groan. Of course she does, Georgia girl. And I suppose it's not *that* terrible. But still. Who knows what the rest of this playlist will bring.

"Maybe we should listen to my playlist instead." I reach for my device.

Anna gives her head a shake and takes a bold step toward me. "Come on, Kai . . . my freckles are getting impatient."

Bloody hell . . . did my little vixen just tell me to hurry up? I forget all about the playlist. I advance toward her, wondering if she has any clue what she's sparked in me.

My freckles are getting impatient. . . .

"Well, then," I say. "Let's not keep them waiting."

I'm standing in front of her now and her chest is rising and falling rapidly.

Take it easy, mate. I've waited too long to rush. I slip my hand under her hair and tilt her face up to mine. Her eyes close and I taste her lips. Softly at first, taking her bottom lip between mine and then seeking her tongue with a gentle swipe of my own. As our mouths tangle and play, I walk forward and she walks backward until we're stopped by the bed.

I need the dress off, now. I begin gathering it between my fingers, working it upward until the hem is in my hands. She lets me raise it over her head, and she's standing before me in her bra and silk underwear. Her eyes are still nervous, but she moves for my shirt and I raise my arms for her to pull it over my head.

I swish the hair from my eyes, then feel her hands on the buckle of my shorts. I take her hands away, saying, "Not yet." It's been so long that I don't want to test my self-control. Right now, I need to see all of her. I slowly reach behind and flick open the clasp of her white strapless bra. As it falls, she covers her chest.

"They're . . ." She bites her lip and looks down.

I place my hands over hers. "I assure you, they're *perfect*." I gently pry her hands away and look down at Anna, exposed before me.

My breath hitches like I'm a lad. I have to close my eyes and gather my wits before I can look at her again. Every curve, peak, and valley . . . I can't believe she's mine. All mine.

"Like I said," I grit out. "Just right. On the bed with you now."

She obeys and I know she'll do anything I say right now, because she trusts me, she wants me. It fills me with a masculine pride that makes me want to roar. I lie next to her on the bed and force her to stay on her back while I peruse every inch of her skin. Each time she attempts to touch me or pull me, or move closer, I stop her. It's driving her mad, and the delicious power rush makes me want to go even slower.

Shoulders, collarbones, breasts—she lets me kiss her and taste her and learn her—waist, belly button, hips, stomach, every inch of her as smooth and sweet as the next. She squirms and groans, grabbing sensually at my hair. When I get to her panty line, and go lower, down to her thighs, she lifts her hips and I firmly push them back down.

"Please," she whispers.

"Not yet."

I know what she needs, and I know I can make it even better by building that need within her, just as my own is building. I flip her to her stomach and start at the top of her body again, moving her hair aside so I can kiss her upper back. She gasps and cries out when I get to the base of her spine. I smile to myself, having found one of her zones. And when I get to her arse—the most perfect, round bit of flesh to ever exist—I nearly lose my head and rip the tiny piece of lace from her body. A low rumble emits from my chest.

Anna takes advantage, saying, "Take them off." I am too lost to drag this out a moment longer. I sit up and pull the knickers down her smooth legs. What's left before me is my sexy little Anna's backside, completely naked.

"My *God*," I whisper. She's more perfect than I imagined, and I imagined this a lot.

Anna turns over and I soak in the front image of her. . . . Heaven.

She reaches for my shorts, but I grasp her hand and gently bite her naughty finger.

"I'm not done yet."

She falls back with a moan as I make my way straight to her lower stomach again, this time with no barrier of fabric to block me. I kiss down her inner thigh, and Anna's breathing goes ragged. I kiss her again, right where she needs, and my sight shatters into a myriad of white shards.

Within seconds Anna cries out and I tighten my grip on her hips. She overwhelms my senses. Anna is the scratching of nails in my hair. She's the sound of high moans in my ears. The firm thighs against my unshaven cheeks. The sweet scent that surrounds us.

Her cries turn to tired breathing, and her grip on my hair relaxes. Only then do I relent and move up to place kisses on her flushed face and closed eyelids. I love knowing I've done this to her.

"You can nap, luv," I whisper.

She sags further into the bed, murmuring. Then her eyes pop open. She pushes to her elbows and glares as if I'd said something offensive. I have to laugh. Her hair has gone a bit poofy in the back, and she's a right gorgeous sight.

"It's your turn," she says.

Oh. I go still, wondering exactly what she has in mind. Inside, my body claps like a damn seal, but outside I'm suddenly too nervous to move. She leans forward and kisses under my ear. Ah, yes. That's nice. She kisses my neck and I reach for her hip, pulling her closer.

"My sweet little vixen."

She licks my earlobe, and a bolt of arousal forces me on top of her.

Anna is naked underneath me. All mine.

But she *tsks* and makes a little *uh-uh-uuh* sound, as if I've got it all wrong. She pushes me off her and continues pushing me until I'm on my back and she's beside me on her knees, looking down at my body as I did to hers. She bites her lip. Her hands are shaking as her fingers trail over my chest and down my abs. I want to tell her she doesn't have to do this, but she reaches for my belt, determined.

Oh, dear God. I could quite possibly make a terrible fool of myself right now. I grasp her hands and breathe out harshly. Her eyes fill with worry and I have to say something.

"Sorry . . . it's just that . . . it's been a while."

"It's okay," she whispers. It's as if she's relieved that I'm showing weakness, though I am not at all happy about it.

Once I've taken several breaths, I release her hands and she continues to undress me. I lift my hips for her and kick off the shorts.

"Um, *wow*," Anna murmurs. She stares so hard that I'm about to lose it. *Damn it, Rowe, be cool*, I chide myself as she takes her visual fill of me with an expression of awe and curiosity.

I close my eyes and swallow. I try to imagine non-sexy things, but it's difficult when she's hijacked all of my senses. I breathe, trying to regain control, but when Anna finally touches me, I have to wrap my hand over hers again.

"Just a sec," I say. She bites her lip, and I hope like hell she's not about to laugh at how my voice cracked.

"Kai . . ." Her voice beckons me to look at her. I lift my eyes. "It's just me."

This is Anna. This isn't work. She wants something genuine from me, not an act. I release her hand, and allow myself to feel her touch. To watch her face as she discovers me for the first time.

"Like this?" she whispers, sultriness underlying her voice.

She goes slow, and it's pure torture. Though I suppose it's only fair play after what I put her through.

I shut my eyes and flex every muscle. "Yes, luv. Bloody hell. Just like that."

Heaven.

I talk her into taking an outdoor shower, and I promise to keep an eye out for whisperers, but there are a few moments as we wash where hands wander and I get a bit distracted. It'd be safe to assume the wandering hands belong to yours truly, but I'm happy to announce Anna was the culprit. Can't keep the girl's hands off me.

Afterward I wrap her in an oversized towel and take her inside to feed her berries and cheese and crackers.

She falls over with laughter when I turn on Marna's music and belt out the chorus of "You Don't Know You're Beautiful."

"Oh my gosh!" she says through her laughter. "You sound just like them, and you know every single freaking word!"

"Bit hard to avoid that song, yeah?"

We laugh together and I happen to glance over and see the hilt, wrapped in its case by her bag. My smile falls and my pulse spikes.

I know Anna is ready, but that stupid fear rises up, clawing at me. I rip my eyes away from the sword and stand to stare out the window at the blackened night. If the Sword of Righteousness rejects Anna, it will be my fault.

"Hey," Anna says softly, coaxing my eyes across the room to her. She stands on the opposite side of the bed, still in her towel, as am I. "It'll be midnight soon. Our wedding day is almost over."

I want to tell her it's not too late to change her mind. That I'll understand if she wants to remain a virgin, but then she says in a seductive voice, "Come here," and I know her mind is set.

I slowly walk to my side of the bed, across from her, and put my hands on my head. Her hair is damp and her cheeks have pink spots. I feel so bloomin' lucky for this entire day—the best day of my life.

In the next moment, when I blink, Anna opens her towel and drops it to the floor. Her chest rises and falls faster as she watches me. Then she climbs onto the bed and crawls, like a prowling cat, toward me. My body stiffens, in shock.

By the time she makes her way to me, rising up onto her

knees, I am awake and alert.

"Are you scared?" she purrs. "Been too long? Out of practice?" Her head cocks to the side, a bad-girl grin on her face.

And then her words register.

Too scared to shag her? I can't even dignify that with a response. I can't even sputter. And then she gives me a purple-nurple, twisting my nipple.

"Oy!" I grab her wrist, the mad little cat. I should spank her arse for that.

Suddenly my towel is gone and my body is announcing just how much I've enjoyed her naughty act, complete with the ripping-off-of-the-towel finale. There's laughter in her eyes. Time for me to take control.

I swing an arm behind her legs and a hand behind her waist, and I have her on her back before she can blink. I'm pressed heavily on top of her, and from the satisfied smile on her face, this is exactly what she wants.

"You win," I say.

She doesn't gloat. She simply reaches up and cups my face, running her fingers down my cheek and jawline. I lower my forehead to hers, overcome.

"This is right, Kai. We love each other."

I close my eyes. Is our love enough to blot out my past? It's always there, in my mind, a foul and murky swampland. How can Anna not feel it when she's with me? She seems so certain this is right. And sword or no sword, this will at least keep her safe from Father for the time being.

"I'd do anything for you," I say.

"Just love me." She strokes my cheek again.

There's so much I've never had the nerve to tell her. So much I should have said before now. She watches me intently.

"I need you to know this is different for me," I manage. "I've never felt like this with someone." I take a shaking breath. "I don't just love you, Anna. I *adore* you."

She kisses me, her hands traveling over my arms and shoulders until they're at my face again and her eyes are on mine.

"Don't look away from me," I whisper. Her eyes will tell me if I'm hurting her.

She nods and whispers back, "Okay."

"If you need to stop—"

"Kai. I'm not fragile."

"Right." She's strong, I know that. I also know how to make her first time a *very* pleasant experience. I move my hips and nuzzle myself between her legs. She lets me. I watch her mouth open for a silent gasp of air when I circle my hips against her to make sure she's ready.

And because I still feel like I haven't said enough—because I need to prove just how momentous this is for me, I bash down the barriers I've kept up for eight years, unleashing my aura for Anna to see. I shiver as I bare myself, and I feel Anna holding me tighter. I want her to see my love, like I saw hers once upon a time.

"*Oh . . . ,*" she whispers. "It's beautiful."

I shake my head. Only one thing deserves that word. "*You're* beautiful."

She wraps her leg around me and I move my hips until I find her.

We arch, slowly, and Anna gasps. Her hands go around my

lower back, holding me tight.

I move slowly. So slow.

Oh, dear God. It is killing me to go slow.

Her eyes shut and I stop. She opens them and nods. "I'm okay."

I move again, slowly, gritting my teeth, watching her eyes. I move a bit more, ignoring my bastardly instincts not to be gentle. Her eyes flutter and a whimper escapes, but she quickly meets my eyes again and says, "Don't stop."

I fight for breath. Slow movements.

There. My hips are flush against hers and we're both breathing heavily. She lets out a breathy sound of joy and I grin at her. My wife.

I kiss her. She keeps one hand on my back and the other in my hair as the kiss deepens. My hips begin a slow circular motion, grinding gently against her. Anna breaks the kiss to catch her breath and let out a moaning, "Oh, my *gosh*, Kai."

Everything we've gone through has led to this moment.

For the first time in my life I make love, and my heart is full. And though I've been a man by society's standards for a while now, this is the first time I've felt like one. I am Anna's man. Her lover. Her husband. Her ally and friend.

Always.

CHAPTER THIRTY-THREE

CELEBRATION ABOVE

"The heart is a bloom, shoots up through the stony ground . . .
What you don't know you can feel it somehow."
—*"Beautiful Day" by U2*

I am immediately ready to go again when I wake in the middle of the night. I can't remember the last time I slept so well. I reach for Anna in the darkness and bolt upright in the bed. She's not there.

"Anna?"

It's too quiet in the cabin. I leap from the bed and sprint to the bathroom, but she's not in there, either. "Anna!" I wrench open the door to the outdoor shower—empty as well. I rush to the front door and realize I'm completely naked.

"Fuck!" I run back to the bedroom and flail through the clothing on the floor until I find a pair of shorts. My heart is banging in my throat. Did they take her while I slept?

I barrel through the front door barefooted and stare wildly around the darkened area. Forests. Road. No lights anywhere. I force myself to concentrate on my hearing, sending it out in a circle around me, slowly letting it extend outward, trying not to miss a single sound.

"Anna!" I call. I am fighting to breathe. *"Anna!"*

How could she disappear from under my nose? How could I let this happen?

I stop and stare toward the path that leads to the canyon. Yes. Footsteps. Maybe half a mile. The steps stop and it gets quiet. I take off running.

Jagged rocks and branches cut into my feet, but I can hardly feel their sting. My extended night vision is on high to make use of the tiny bit of moonlight. I still cannot sense anything up ahead. A minute later I think I hear a feminine giggle.

"Anna? Anna!" I race ahead faster now. Two seconds later I hear her call to me.

"Kai! It's all right. I'm at the canyon!"

Christ Almighty, I'm about to have a heart attack. I've never run so fast. She sounds okay, but I have to see her for myself. I burst through the trees into a sudden open space and halt at the sight of a massive spirit, bright white. I nearly fall back, but Anna rushes to me.

"It's okay," she says, wrapping her arms around my heaving chest. I hold her, never taking my eyes off the exquisite spirit. It's not Belial. It's not a demon at all. Nor is it a warrior angel.

As Anna tugs me forward, I feel stranger and stranger the closer I get to it. This spirit doesn't fill me with a sense of threat like the warrior angels from the summit. In fact, it's as if this spirit has purified all the dark feelings from my soul, and I'm left only with love and happiness within.

The spirit watches me closely as Anna brings me to stand before it, and I'm astonished by the overpowering sense of peace that blankets me. Anna squeezes my hand and stops short at the cliff's edge, never letting me go. She looks up at me. "Kaidan . . . this is my mother, Mariantha."

My face snaps back to the angel, who levitates over the empty space with a contented smile. I have no words. Just . . . wow. Anna's mother.

I lower my head and say, "It's an honor to meet you."

"It is I who am honored to meet the soul who loves my daughter more than any other."

I am too full. Her words, the emotion she's emitting, it all makes me want to inexplicably weep. I keep my head down and swallow.

"You have embraced life and the truth, Kaidan Rowe, and are now reaping the blessing."

Yes. I raise my eyes to her and nod, then swallow again, overly grateful. I'm feeling like a boy next door, all wholesome and shit—er—*stuff.* I drop my eyes again.

"I must go," Mariantha says. *"Guard your love, for it will lead you through the darkness."*

I nod again and stand there stunned beyond belief as she and Anna say their good-byes. Then her mother's spirit stretches its wide wings and flies away.

I search all around us, but nothing else is in sight. I take Anna's hand and we race back down the path, eager to get out of the open. But I don't feel any fear. The exalted feeling still swirls around inside me, making me want to laugh with unfathomable joy. Anna feels it, too, because a smile is on her lips as we run.

"What did she say to you?" I ask Anna when the cabin is in sight.

"That they're celebrating our marriage in heaven!" She laughs, and I shake my head at this astounding turn of events.

We burst through the cabin doors and I shut the door, locking it. Then I take Anna's face in both my hands and walk her over to the wall where I can hold her in place. I'm finally coming down from the adrenaline rush of fear.

"You scared me to death," I tell her. "Don't ever leave me like that again."

"I'm so sorry. You were sound asleep, and I saw her . . . I know it was dumb, but she was like . . ."

I think of her mother's bright, welcoming form. "A beacon?"

"Yes." She takes my wrists, rubbing them to soothe me.

"Were they really celebrating us? Up there?"

Her smile is luminous. "They really were."

Unbelievable. I try to imagine it, that the souls in heaven know us—not just Anna, but *me*, as well—and they're cheering for us. I want to ask why they would celebrate us but never give us the chance to be there with them, to join them in heaven, when we leave this place.

Anna breaks my desolate train of thought by crushing her lips to mine, and I react on instinct, pressing her back against the wall and dropping my hands to her body. I remember how

I felt when I awoke, before I knew she was gone, and that need returns with a vengeance.

"Let's not sleep tonight," Anna says.

Oh, woman, you're speaking my language. "I'm going to let you make all the rules in this marriage, Anna."

"Good boy."

I laugh and grasp her around the waist. She looks down and gasps.

"You're bleeding!"

I glance at the scrapes and cuts along my feet, ankles, and legs from where I ran in the darkness. Most of the blood is already dry.

"I'm fine. Nearly healed already." But she frowns, and I know she wants to nurse me. I kiss her pouting lips and tighten my hands around her waist.

When I lift her, she wraps her legs around me and I carry her to an oversized chair. I fall back onto it and give her bum a good slap, making her scream. "Hey!"

I hush her complaint with another kiss, and pull her hips down against mine until she lets her head fall back and sinks into my lap perfectly.

It's still our wedding night. She's all mine until the sun rises and it's time to release her back into the world. Until then, let the celebration continue.

CHAPTER THIRTY-FOUR

UNEXPECTED

"Miles away I can still feel you,
Lay your head down on my embrace."
—*"When You Can't Sleep at Night" by Of Mice & Men*

When I get off the plane in L.A., there are two messages waiting for me from a hospital in Atlanta. I nearly lose my mind until I hear the words "Richard Rowe. . . ." I hail a cab as I ring the number and get transferred to the doctor on duty.

"Kaidan Rowe?" asks the man solemnly.

"Yes. That's me." I climb into the cab and show the driver my address on my ID so he knows where to go.

"I'm terribly sorry to have to tell you this, son, but your father had a heart attack at home early this morning or possibly during the night. One of his employees found him and called nine-one-one, but it was too late at that point. I'm very sorry. Your father is gone."

What? Was this planned? I am gripping the phone and staring blankly at the city as it passes by the windows.

"Um . . ." I need to say something. "But, he was so . . . healthy."

Lame. My shock is real, but it's hard to fake grief.

"Yes, he did appear to be quite healthy. I know this must be difficult. We're doing a full autopsy to see for certain what the cause of death was."

I can tell them the cause—a demon leaving a body equals death of said body.

My eyes dart around the skies. I've no clue what Father looks like in spirit form. Or where his next duty station will be, if this is his changing of the guard. Nice of him to clue me in that this madness would be happening.

The doctor clears his throat. "Do you have family or anyone you can call for help? There's quite a bit you'll need to look into right away, son. It can be overwhelming. I'd recommend contacting his lawyer first, to see if he has a will with instructions, and an insurance policy."

"Oh, er, yes." I sniff loudly. "I'll do that. Thank you. Thank you for your help."

I hang up and glare out the window. Bloody hell. This is just what I need. I've no idea who Father's lawyer is or where to begin. I let my head fall back onto the seat as we weave in and out of traffic on the highway, slamming on the brakes and racing forward again, then coming to another dead stop. Damned L.A. traffic.

* * *

My apartment feels like an abandoned place where I don't belong. It's depressing without Anna. For the second day in a row, I open the freezer and stare at the meals she made for me. I don't want to eat them, because then they'll be gone and I won't be able to gaze at them like a bloody sap anymore.

I can imagine her indignant face if she finds out I'm not eating the food she prepared—her little fists on her hips, scolding me with that accent. Most likely naked. I grin at the imaginary Anna. Okay, I'll eat them. Eventually. One a week, perhaps.

We'll see.

I pace the kitchen and living room. I have practice tonight with the band, so that'll be good. I need distractions, to keep me busy. Hopefully Anna Malone won't be there.

I want the drama over with. I told everyone at work that my father died and I'd have to fly to Georgia for a few days. Thankfully that put them off from questioning my love life for the moment.

The lawyer rang me yesterday, saying he'd been instructed to contact me if anything ever happened to Father. His Atlanta estate is to be sold, Father's body is to be cremated, and the insurance policy will cash out. As Richard Rowe's only known family member and heir, I will be receiving the entire "sizable" payout. The lawyer used the word "sizable" several times.

Thing is, I won't get to keep all that. Father will need the fortune to live his next life in style. I'll get my cut, and then I'm on my own. Financially. But I'll always answer to him.

I wish I knew where he was. The only good thing is that it takes quite a while to find a new body. At least that's what I've heard. The Dukes are right picky. Father won't be able to sniff Anna out if he doesn't have a nose, so I don't have to worry about him going after her just yet.

Belial told Anna to go on to college like she'd planned, and pretend to work. He thinks staying on the run will look too suspicious for her. Now that she's not a virgin, Belial is hoping the Dukes will second-guess themselves.

I worry about Belial's assumptions, but he's known the other Dukes a bloody long time. I hope he knows their behaviors well enough not to put Anna's neck on the line.

I shut the freezer door and order out for Thai. I hate standing around waiting and worrying like a useless git. In two days I'll fly to Georgia to sign estate paperwork and retrieve Father's remains, which are going straight down a toilet at the dodgiest petrol station I can find. But at least I'll be in the east, on the go.

I slump onto my leather couch and grab a pad of paper and a pen, ready to scratch out some lyrics.

And then my mobile dings with a text.

It's a picture from Anna. That's strange. I open it and stare.

And stare some more.

Fucking hell, little Ann.

I ogle a picture of her tangled in a sheet, a knee up; her hip, thigh, and arse showing beautifully against a scrap of black fabric that hardly qualifies as knickers.

A low, long groan erupts from my throat.

She's too sexy. It hurts to look at it, but I can't stop. She's too bloody far away. Why, why, why? My hands shake as I type.

OH GOD.

I stare. I type. **What r u doing to me??**

I am gobsmacked. **I can't believe u took a pic.**

I stare. I cram my hand into my hair and pull. **CANNOT STOP STARING.**

Too much sexy. I can't even . . . **Just wait little vixen.**

I fall over on the couch. **F me. Ur so fn hot.**

I think I might die here, a lump of lust. **Ur in serious trouble when I see u again.**

I stare. **Serious. Trouble.** I curl into a ball of pain and die.

A moment later my mobile chirps in my dead hand. I open it with trepidation. Thankfully it's only words, and not more skin I'm not able to touch.

Baby steps for your nerdy girl, she writes.

The girl clearly underestimates the power of her bum and a seductively minimal pose.

Nerdy my arse, I type back. **All the cold showers in the world can't cure what u've done to me.**

Cruel wife.

Sorry, she says, but I can see her smiling in my mind.

U r not. Leave me alone. I'll b busy 4 a bit.

Cold showers . . . not again. I want to cry. But then a horrible thought occurs—I hope she doesn't think I'm truly angry. I quickly type out another message.

PS . . . ilu.

ilu2, she says.

I catch myself smiling and shake my head. *Sap.*

Then, as much as I hate to do it, I delete each message one by one. When I get to the photo, I take one last long stare, groan deeply, and delete it. Then I trudge heavily to the loo, all by my lonesome, where I might die again. Sexting is dangerous business. I don't recommend it.

CHAPTER THIRTY-FIVE

ONE-TRACK MIND

*"The only heaven I'll be sent to
Is when I'm alone with you."*
—*"Take Me to Church" by Hozier*

I'm at a bar with my bandmates at midnight, nursing a Jack and Coke and dodging pitiful looks from the blokes who think I'm broken up over Father's death.

Honestly, I've been a bit of a disaster ever since the picture text from Anna. It sparked a single-mindedness in me, worse than ever before, and I cannot cope. No amount of Dead Daddy talk will make this raging problem of mine go away.

I keep thinking about our wedding night. We had less than twelve hours together, and yet it's given me three days' worth of nonstop memories. It feels as if I'm living in a fog of Anna.

Shite, I think I'm obsessed with my wife. I want to hide her away and keep her all to myself, always. That's psychotic thinking, even by my low standards.

Oy, that damn picture.

My mobile buzzes in my pocket, sending my heart into race mode, as it always does these days. I dig it out and hold my breath when I see it's a text from Anna.

Book a flight to Va tmrw.

Right. I don't think Anna would send me a command like that jokingly. Not these days. Belial must've contacted her and said it's safe. So I grin, because if all is well with her, she will pay dearly, in equal measure, for the suffering she's inflicted with her sexiness.

With pleasure, I type. **U ok? It's been insane here.**

Here too, she says. **Lots to tell.**

Hm. I wonder what she's been up to. Hopefully no visits from unwanted Neph. My neck goes hot with irritation thinking about other Neph hunting her down.

She texts me with an address in Riner, Virginia, and I book my flight for the following morning. All joking aside, I hope she's all right.

And I hope she's naked.

The fog of Anna finally lifts when I open my eyes to find her on top of me in the passenger seat of a car in Virginia. I feel as if I've been hit with a sledgehammer of clarity as I realize what a single-minded dolt I'd been since I showed up this afternoon and found her lying at the poolside in a bikini.

Bum side up.

Yeah. I'm pretty sure I spent a good part of the day making everyone uncomfortable as I stalked Anna, trailing her through Patti's house. And it's just my luck the whole lot would be here to witness my temporary madness—Kope, Zania, Jay, the twins, Blake, and worst of all, Patti. They all know we're married, but that doesn't make it any less inappropriate.

I'm just glad my head is semi-clear when her father shows that afternoon—in the body of the famous rapper who'd been hospitalized days ago, no less. Big Rotty. As far as Duke blunders go, this one is fucking brilliant. If I weren't still so afraid of the bastard, I would've laughed my arse off. Then, before he leaves, he puts his hands on my shoulders and says, "You take care of my girl, you hear me?"

It's still strange to hear him say things like this. To have his approval.

And now, here we are at two in the morning, snuggling in the twin bed of Anna's dorm room, as if this day hasn't been one strange event after the next. Despite the madness of our lives, anyone who saw us on campus tonight probably thought we were your average college couple.

Funny thing, appearances.

Anna's news was unsettling. I can't handle thinking about how my father was here, in this room, just a short while ago. In his new, young, American body, no less. Apparently the "new" Pharzuph is an even grander piece of work than the old one. Anna says he wreaked havoc on campus after cornering her. I can't believe he found a new host body so quickly, never bothering to inform me, but I *can* believe he didn't waste any time sniffing out Anna. I'm immensely relieved we decided to get married when we did.

Anna snaps me from my dark musings as she runs a hand

teasingly up and down my forearm, which is flung across her waist. She's acting as the small spoon, nuzzled tightly in the crook of my torso and thighs. "I want you to dream big with me," she whispers.

Dreams . . . This is dangerous territory for me. I know I'm lucky to have this moment, and all the moments that led up to this one. To wish for a future? It feels like tempting fate. Nothing except this very second is guaranteed. But for Anna, dreams fuel her, give her hope. So I'll let her have her fun.

"Tell me *your* dreams for us, sweet Anna."

She snuggles closer to my chest. "It starts with us defeating the Dukes. We survive and they're gone." I peer around the dark room as she talks. "We can do whatever we want with our lives. I know you love music, so I figure you'll still work in the industry in some way. When I finish college, I want to be a social worker. I'd be able to gauge the danger kids are in better than a human would, since I can see their emotions. I'll be able to rescue children from bad situations."

I immediately think of Marissa's nieces, and how Anna would have probably tried to save them by now, with no fear for her own well-being.

"I can picture that," I whisper. I move the hair off Anna's shoulder and kiss her warm skin. If only more people had Anna's bravery. If only I had it.

"We could live wherever you wanted," she goes on. "Patti would probably follow us. After a few years of working, we could think about adopting. I know Patti would just die to babysit while we work."

Er . . . "Wow. Kids."

"Yeah," she says dreamily. "Like five or six."

"*Five or six?* You're a nutter!" I have to laugh at the thought of little Kaidans-in-training. "One boy. *Maybe* two boys, but even that's pushing it."

Shite, she's got me entertaining this ridiculous notion.

"We have to have girls, too!" Her voice is filled with happiness, but again the thought of Marissa's nieces flashes through my mind, and all the girls I've hurt. All the daughters and sisters and future mums I helped lead down paths they may or may not have been able to find their way back from.

"No girls," I say.

She turns to look at me, and the small space is suddenly stifling. I sit up.

"What's wrong?" Anna asks.

I rub my eyes to clear their faces from my vision.

"I can't even . . . Just the thought of having to care for a girl, watching all the bloody gits sniff around her with their red auras . . . it would kill me and I would deserve it, because I was the worst offender of all."

"Kai . . ." She touches my arm, and I feel like shit.

"No." I can't play along anymore. "I'm sorry, luv, but kids are not my dream. Especially girls."

"Okay." Her voice is soft and gentle. "Let's try to get a little sleep."

"I'm sorry," I say, hating that I've ruined the moment.

But Anna only lies back down and leads me to do the same. She pulls my arm around her waist, nudging me to spoon her from behind again, and I press my nose into her hair.

Why must I always be such a prick? It was harmless

make-believe. I should've just let her have her fun and kept my mouth shut.

"Are you angry with me?" I whisper.

She rolls over to face me, touching my cheek. "No, Kai." She tries to reassure me and kisses me before rolling back over. I pull her closer to my chest and listen to her breathing change as the minutes tick by, until it becomes slow and even.

I can't afford to dream like Anna does. *This* moment, and every moment I get to have with her, is my dream come true.

"You're my dream," I whisper to my sleeping angel. "My only dream."

CHAPTER THIRTY-SIX

HEARTWARMING

"Exit light.
Enter night."
—*"Enter Sandman" by Metallica*

The following morning we return to Patti's new home and say good-bye to all our Neph mates. It feels strange when they leave, and I realize that yesterday was the first time we've all been together and just let ourselves be semi-*normal*. We sat around a table and had a proper meal, like a real family. Marna and Ginger even had a row, of course, because what would a family holiday be without drama?

It was actually quite nice. Aside from the fighting bit.

I'm not ready to leave, but it's nearly time. The Dukes will all be returning to their stations now that their Switzerland gathering is over. I've got to take care of this estate business in Georgia and head back to L.A. I'm a bit peeved Father still hasn't bothered to contact me, but I suppose he's never been the most considerate soul.

Anna shows me to the upstairs shower and I resist the strong urge to pull her in with me. Not sure Patti would appreciate that. So I reluctantly let her go, and climb under the warm stream alone.

I'm halfway through washing my hair when I get a prickly sensation on my neck. I stand very still as bubbles rinse down my face and neck, and I push my hearing down the hall, down the stairs, down to the family room where I believe Patti, Jay, and Anna are likely sitting.

What I find is commotion—bangs and grunts, a moan. What the hell?

I spin and shut off the water, then rip the curtain so hard the damn rod comes off the wall and I'm tangled in loads of plastic and ruffles. I finally get the curtain off and jump from the tub. Nobody is saying anything, but it sounds like a definite fight down there. I bypass my boxers and grab my shorts, yanking them onto my soaking wet legs and diving for the door, slipping a bit on the tiles.

"Don't come down!" Anna yells, but to hell with that.

I run down the hall and fly down the steps, bursting into the family room just as Anna is racing out the back door. A quick survey of the room shows Jay standing there shell-shocked, and Patti on the floor, ashen, but alive. I run to the door and see Anna staring around the garden and trees, hilt in her hand. Nothing else is in sight.

Patti moans and I rush to her side where she's leaning against the couch.

"Oh, my God, dude," Jay is saying to himself. "*Oh, my God . . .*"

"Are you all right?" I ask Patti.

She nods weakly. "I—I think so." I look her over but see no signs of injury.

Anna comes back in and slides to Patti's side, gathering her into her arms. "Are you okay?"

"I don't know what happened," Patti says. Her eyes are clearer now. "I felt so sick and scared . . . and . . ." She trembles.

"Who was here?" I ask, trying not to sound as freaked as I am.

"It was so weird," Jay says. "You should have seen Anna! What is that thing?" He points to the hilt. "It was all lit up. She moved so fast. I've never seen anyone move like that!"

She actually *used* the hilt? I stare at Anna, who's pale, her lips in a stern line. Stray hairs are plastered to her sweating forehead. I take her face in my hands.

"What happened?"

"Three whisperers were on Jay. Two on Patti. One was trying to possess her." Patti covers her mouth and gags. I can't bloody blame her. "I killed four of them, but . . . one got away."

"One got away," I whisper. Anna and I stare at each other as it sinks in.

One got away. One who saw her with the sword. One is all it takes. It feels as if my innards are on a carnival ride, because this is it. This is the catalyst—the beginning of the end. Anna has started it, and she'll lead us into it, and *oh, God.*

I stand, grasping my hair roughly. I feel the same nervous energy course through me as when I had to watch Anna work on New Year's Eve, and when she entered the summit in New York the next day. That same bloody powerless feeling. I lean against the wall, my head spinning.

"Shite. Shite, Anna . . ." I'm not ready for this. It's too soon. *I'm not ready!* A yell forces its way upward and out of my mouth, and I punch the wall with all my strength. My fist goes through drywall.

I have to protect her. I can't let anyone hurt her. I know she's strong, and though we don't look at things the same way, or think things through the same, she is smarter than me in many ways. I know all of that, but I am still crazed with the need to hide her from the world.

I turn and lean against the wall, pressing the heels of my hands into my eyes.

I'm not ready. . . .

"Kai." Anna's voice is clear and calm.

I drop my hands. She has brushed the stray hairs from her face. I don't know how she can look so certain at this moment.

"I don't think they know you're here," she says to me. "That's to our advantage."

I nod, though it's hard to believe anyone's got the advantage here but the Dukes.

"You're not on the suspicion list," she goes on. "So you can stay 'in the know.' We'll go our separate ways and—"

"No," I interject to stop her. She's mad if she thinks I'm letting her out of my sight. "I stay with you."

If she refuses, I will follow her. I stare at her, daring her to argue. She sighs and looks aside, thinking.

"Okay. Let's get our stuff and get out of here."

Bloody right. Together.

We say our good-byes to Jay and Patti. Anna hugs her mum tight, and then we run. I drive Anna's car and she lies low in the backseat.

When an unknown number shows up on my mobile, I know it's Father straightaway. I'd been curious to hear from him before, but now? Not so much.

"Hallo," I answer.

"It's Pharzuph." I knew he was young and American now, but hearing his new voice is still fucking weird.

"Yes, sir."

"Are you in Atlanta?"

"Not yet." I glance at Anna, who's bloody adorable in a baseball cap, and for half a second I'm distracted. And then young, twatty Pharzuph speaks again.

"Meet me at our former home tonight at nine p.m. I'm flying in, and we have some things to discuss."

All I can think of is that I have Anna with me, and how fantastically horrible his timing is. "I'll see you at nine o'clock, sir," I say, like a good boy.

"Don't be late." He hangs up and my jaw locks with annoyance at his insolence. It's a good thing we've got a seven-hour drive ahead of us, because it's going to take at least that long to mentally prepare for this. I won't just be swallowing my pride; I'll be choking on it.

At eight thirty I'm back in my old room, and I feel no warm and fuzzy memories. In fact, I'm entirely creeped out to be back here, surrounded by the ghosts of my past.

I focus on the fact that Anna is parked up the street, and I've got knives in my pockets and boots—the blades have even been dipped in holy water. If demon legend is correct, holy water does more than repel demons—it's like a poison to them, like prayer in liquid form.

I push my hearing down to where I know Anna's parked, but I hear nothing. She is silent and unmoving. Good girl. Now I just hope she stays there. I hope she has no reason to come charging at the house, sword blazing.

Although, that would be a brilliant sight.

I pace the room. Perhaps I should go upstairs to wait, but this room feels like *my* territory. I'd prefer to meet here if he'll allow it. I flick on my old stereo system and smile as the high volume vibrates the floor under my feet.

Screaming lyrics. The whine of electric guitar chords. An unrelenting drum beat. Lovely.

A strand of my hearing remains on the front door, so I know when Father comes in. I'm on my third Nine Inch Nails song. My hands clench and stretch open. Clench and stretch. I stare at the door. When it swings wide, a tall blond bloke stands there with his face scrunched in disgust. We are matched in body thickness, but he might have an inch of height on me. He carries himself like a wanker.

Three grungy spirits fly next to him and over him, filling the room with half their wingspans spilling through the walls. I hope they don't venture around the premises during this visit.

"Shut this racket off!" he yells.

Yep. Wanker.

I flip the stereo off and he lets out an annoyed sigh.

"Good to see you, Father." I nearly trip over the word *Father.* He's got the large red badge, but he can't be older than twenty or twenty-one. "Excellent choice on your new host body."

"Yes, it was," he says, running a hand through his thin, silky-looking hair. He'll probably be balding by thirty. "You sign the estate paperwork tomorrow?"

Is that what this is about? "Yes, sir. In the morning."

He pulls a folded paper from his back pocket. "Here's my new account information. You'll receive your own funds from the life insurance and inheritance. Everything else needs to be transferred to me. If a penny is missing, I will know it."

"I understand." Git. He just wants to make sure he gets his money so he can start his new life ASAP. Could've just rung me, but I suppose he wanted to show off his pretty new body.

The spirits circle us, restless. Father ignores them.

"Good." He sniffs the air and glances at the king-sized bed with its black and gray silk bedding. I'm going to sell all of it. I don't want anything that's been in this house. "Smells like old lust in here. You were always a good worker."

I blink. Wow. A compliment. "Thank you, Father."

Then I remember Anna is listening. I hope he won't go into any details.

"Things aren't always what they appear, are they?" he asks. The whisperers hiss in anticipation as his voice takes on a silky edge.

I feel my eyes narrow. What's he going on about? Is he talking about my working? Shite, has he had someone watching me in L.A. that I don't know about?

I force myself to ask nonchalantly, "In what way?"

"Something's not right." He slowly walks the room, running a finger over my black dresser, which has gathered a light layer of dust since nobody's been here. He wipes the finger on his jeans and holds his hands behind his back, much like he used to in his old body, but it looks strange. His muscles are bulkier.

"I haven't been able to put my finger on it. . . ." As he talks, he looks at my framed posters of favorite bands, all autographed. He's acting as if what he's saying is no big deal, but it feels as if he's about to drop a bomb. Dread trickles down my spine. "Ever since that summit when the damned angels showed up, we've been watching the daughter of Belial."

Do not react.

Lie through your teeth.

I snort a derisive laugh. "Her? No offense, Father, but I don't see why an unremarkable Neph like the daughter of Belial would warrant such attention. I've worked with her. She's excellent at her job, but on a personal level she's rather . . . boring."

He turns to face me now, amused. "So you took no pleasure from your time with her?" Tricky bastard. Always with the games. His new grin is too wide. The whisperers turn their ugly, hazy heads to hear my response.

"Oh, I took my pleasure. I also got out of there as quickly as I could. She's got zero personality unless she's wasted." The whisperers hiss and make raspy, choking sounds of laughter.

Father chuckles low. "I know being with her was a chore, but it was necessary. She's somehow been able to fly under the radar. Now we know for sure that she's a threat."

"A threat?" I laugh, as if it's a ridiculous notion. He takes three quick steps toward me and points in my face, hair slanting across his forehead as he tilts his head almost comically. The spirits bob up and down in agitation.

"You think this is funny? You think I have time to joke around?"

I keep a straight face and force a respectful tone. "Of course not, but having spent a good bit of time with her, it seems preposterous. She cares about nothing except where she'll find her next drink."

His eyes narrow and his voice lowers. "Then she's fooled you as well. That boring Neph who you think's so benign was caught being affectionate with her human mother-figure this morning." He spits the words. "We sent five Legionnaires to get more information, and the girl took out four of the spirits! She's a mercenary of heaven."

He snarls the last sentence with venom and his whisperers move about the room faster, upset, making scratchy noises like dry, noiseless screams.

I school my face into concerned shock. "Wha—? How is that possible?"

He stands straighter and runs a hand through his hair again, as if trying to decide if he'll trust me with the next bit. Thankfully, he does, but his eyes flash red as he talks. "She's somehow able to wield a Sword of Righteousness. Only angels of light have been able to do that."

I force my eyes wide and shake my head. "But . . . why would an angelic weapon allow her to use it? I've watched her lead souls astray, and I nailed her myself. She's hardly angel material."

Those words feel especially acidic on my lips.

"I . . ." He shakes his head, looking almost frightened. "We don't know."

We have stumped the Dukes, for what it's worth. Now to attempt to lead them astray.

"Is it possible someone is trying to deceive all of you? Point you in the wrong direction? I mean, how do you know about the sword, and the spirits she supposedly killed?"

He ponders this, still appearing baffled. "One of them escaped."

"I hope that spirit isn't misleading you," I say. The trio of whisperers advance on me with claws and teeth bared. I wave a hand to ward them off.

"They're too stupid to come up with something like that." The whisperers reel back and glare at Father as if deciding whether or not to be offended. He gives a flick of his wrist and points to the door. They swoosh out and Father goes on. "Unless they're being led by someone. But I haven't seen a spirit that terrified since the Fall. We sent it down to Lord Lucifer for further questioning. He'll get the truth out of it."

I can't respond because my muscles are tensed against the shudder that Satan's name elicits.

"We've got Legionnaires on the hunt for both her and her father. Belial's been eluding us for a while now, so he's definitely up to something."

I nod. "I see you're keeping several whisperers with you to keep an eye out. That's good."

He puffs his chest out and *hmphs*. "I'm not going to let that girl get in a sneak attack. The other Dukes and I are staying armed and ready. We'll find her and hold an emergency summit to learn the truth and get rid of her once and for all. Angels be damned."

And that is when the truth will be made known. Please, let this work.

"What can I do to help?" I ask.

"Search for her. If you find her, she becomes your prisoner, and you'll notify me immediately. Do whatever is necessary to keep her with you and get her to the location we choose for the summit. And most important, disarm her. Under no circumstances should she be allowed access to the Sword of Righteousness."

"Of course. I'll begin immediately. I have a few ideas where she might be."

"Good." He steps closer and looks me dead in the eye. "It's in your best interest not to fail me in this endeavor. Do you understand?"

Another death threat. How original. Thing is, I'm no longer scared for myself. My only concern is Anna. For her sake, I won't punch old Pharzuph in his new face. Yet.

"I understand," I answer.

His eyes are bright; he's probably feeling the glorious weight of his power trip. "I'm going to Marissa's tonight, and I leave in the morning. My new duty station will be in New York City, so it's time for me to get settled there. Don't waste any time getting to work on your task."

"Yes, sir," I say absently, still stuck on one tiny detail. "But you're going to Marissa's, you say?" Doesn't she think he's dead?

He chuckles and flashes that obnoxiously wide grin again. "Marissa is a special human. She knows about our kind. She's expecting me, and can't wait to get her claws into my new skin."

His grin is still huge and I force a nod. Yeah, she's special all right. An especially evil bitch. "She must be an exceptional woman if you've been able to trust her in such a way."

Father pulls out his mobile and glances at it, then pockets it again. "Exceptional, yes. And I still expect you to be at her service if she calls on you, regardless of whether or not we live here."

Like hell I will. "Of course, Father. Enjoy your evening. I'll begin my search for the Neph straightaway."

"If you need to involve the son of Melchom to help you, then do that. He has a lot of resources at his disposal on the West Coast."

"Brilliant idea," I say.

He turns from me, pulling out his mobile again as he walks out. I stand there alone and listen to him ascending the stairs to the upper floor.

Another heartwarming conversation with Father has ended.

CHAPTER THIRTY-SEVEN

READY OR NOT

"If love's a fight, then I shall die,
With my heart on a trigger."
—*"Angel with a Shotgun" by The Cab*

The full weight of our situation doesn't hit me until I'm with Anna again that night. I stare at her brown eyes in the backseat of her car at Lookout Point, where we went after my meeting with Father. Trepidation is heavy on me.

Anna is strong, yes, but she is flesh and bone. She has a tender, sensitive heart. And our grand plan is to set her in front of all the Dukes and Legionnaires in order to play out this prophecy?

Can anyone else see what a bad idea this is? I have a hard time believing this is how it must go down. There has to be another way. She is *one* being with *one* sword. There are 666 of them. Granted, we have a handful of Neph allies, but the odds are stacked against us.

Perhaps Anna and her father and the others are okay with handing her over to the Dukes to be slaughtered, but I'm bloody well not. I have to make her see straight.

"We don't have to do this. You can stay hidden, like Zania." I could take Anna to the very same convent.

"I can't hide forever. And what would that mean for you? Your father will expect you to be working. Marissa will be calling you."

No. None of that matters. "I'll go into hiding with you."

"That's no way to live."

Isn't it? We'd be together. Her shoulders are set as she examines my face. I know she can't understand my selfishness, but damn it, I can't understand her self*less*ness either.

"Are you truly not afraid?" I ask. "At all?"

"Of course I am . . . but the chain of events has started, and we can't stop the prophecy now."

"We can try." We can slow it down. We don't have to rush straight into the burning fire. Why is she in such a rush to do this? I know the Dukes are evil and the whisperers are a bloody nuisance, but this prophecy could kill her. Could kill all of us. I can't be left on this earth without her. And I can't stand the thought of Anna suffering.

She shakes her head, and her eyes droop as if she feels sorry for me.

"I finally have you, Anna." I sound so pathetic.

She touches my hand. "And every second we've had together is a blessing I never thought we'd get."

She takes my shoulder, but I'm so tense I can hardly feel

her hands on me. Anna's hands move up my body and curve around the back of my neck. She holds me hard and kisses me.

This, I feel.

I kiss her back like her mouth offers sustenance. I pull her close and revel in the feel of her hands scratching through my hair. "God, Anna," I say against her mouth. I hold her so hard, hard enough to keep her here forever. Hard enough that nobody can take her from me.

I tear my mouth from hers and pant for air. "I can't lose you."

Her hands pull at me, and her voice is ragged with emotion. "Stop thinking that way. I can't fight them if you're not on board, Kai."

I look at her, and I fucking hate myself. Anna wants to save the world. Not for her own glory, but because she cares about the people who are terrorized by the demons. She cares about the Neph and our way of life. She cares about all the things that I don't. I can't give her what she needs from me right now—my support—and I hate myself for it.

I try to pull away, disgusted with myself, but she takes my face in her firm grasp and puts us nose to nose. "You haven't lost me, Kai. I'm right here with you. Hold me."

I pull her to my lap and bury my face in her neck. She's right here. In my arms. She knows I'm a selfish prick, but she's still here. I breathe and swallow and hold on tight.

I hold her as the stars light the night sky and the crickets send up their cacophony of mating calls. I hold her as the hours pass and our bodies wind down and weariness catches up with us.

All the while I keep an eye out for whisperers, and I scan with my hearing. It's eerily quiet.

Anna turns against my chest and reaches up to stroke my face. I close my eyes and feel her kind touch. I soak in her love.

"Kaidan, if anything happens to me—"

I jerk, and my eyes snap open, catching hers. "Don't! Don't you dare finish that sentence. Nothing is going to happen to you."

The pit of dread opens up inside of me. I don't want to talk about this, but she is persistent and unnervingly gentle.

"If we both, you know, end up down there . . . in hell. We can make it through together. We'll keep each other strong until it's time for our judgment."

I've never heard anyone talk about hell in this way. As if it's something that can be faced and endured. I swallow hard at Anna's vision. To think that even in complete darkness and despair, our souls can cling to each other and still feel this love. I want this dream of hers to be true. I want to cling to this one.

"I'll never leave your side," I tell her. "I swear it."

I hold her tight until she falls asleep. And at some point, I let myself drift away, as well.

"No more sex."

I blink several times at Anna as we stand outside the car the next morning. Have we been married long enough for her to say that?

"Just until after the summit," she rushes on.

The summit. The summit where we might die. And then we'll never have sex again anyway. What rubbish.

I am not ready for this conversation. I want to go back to last night.

"Kaidan . . ." She takes my hands in hers and tries to explain, but I am numb. "You have to pretend not to like me. It sucks, but it's the smartest plan. If we're both going to survive this, which I really think we can, and *will*, this is our best bet. You're better at hiding your feelings than I am, but at this point it doesn't matter if they think I have feelings for you. You can even say you made me fall for you to lure me in. Your father trusts you to find me and get me to the summit on your own. That's huge. He has to think you're in his pocket until the very last minute. We'll have freedom to communicate with each other and warn the others. Do you really want to jeopardize one of the only things we have going for us?"

I close my eyes.

Why must she be such a reasonable, positive little pixie?

I squeeze her hands.

"No, I don't," I say. "I'm sorry. I'll do whatever I have to do. Or *not* do."

I'm about to ask for one last shag when Anna says firmly, "From here on out, no kissing, no holding hands or touching until this is all over. No doing anything that could look suspicious."

Her eyebrows go up and I reluctantly nod, then let her hands slide from mine. I am secretly *not* in agreement, though I understand her caution. When did Anna become the cautious one when it comes to being caught?

This blows.

* * *

I take care of Father's death rubbish later in the morning—funeral home, Realtor, and lawyer. It's not hard to feign mourning, being as I've been sworn off sex. I sign loads of papers and nod, frowning, as people pat my back and shake my hand, and say they're sorry for my loss.

If only that arsehole were truly dead.

I take Father's urn and all the paperwork, and leave the lawyer's office, grumpy as ever.

The plan is to call Father and tell him I've captured Anna, but every time I think about it I want to be sick.

Anna is ready. Her father is ready. The other Neph are at the ready. I'm the only one who's not bloody ready. But I tell myself I'll keep playing along until it gets to be too real. Then I'll call it off and take us into hiding. I'll force her. I'm bigger than her.

It's after one in the afternoon when we get to my old house. Whisperers are still out searching for Anna, and I figure they won't bother looking there. I walk her down to my old room and she glares at the bed like it's a murder scene, probably imagining how it's been worked. I should have taken her upstairs to use the shower, but the other bathrooms have been emptied. I clear my throat and give her a towel.

She goes in the bathroom and I turn on the stereo. I sit on the edge of the bed and lean my forehead against my hands as the music fills my ears. I hope it will drown out all my thoughts of what's to come. Anna doesn't take very long in the bathroom. When the water shuts off I switch off my stereo and look at my dresser. A dark thrill snakes across my skin as I eye the second drawer.

I have to make this "capture" of Anna look believable, don't I?

I slide open the drawer and see the flash of silver in the corner—my high-grade handcuffs. I take them out and shut the door. I can hear Anna humming and I glance around for whisperers. How she can feel content enough to hum is beyond my understanding. Must be the angel blood. I sit back on the bed and turn the handcuffs over and over in my hands while Anna gets ready.

She opens the door and I slowly lift my eyes to her. She's fresh and natural with her summery clothes and wet hair. She stares at the handcuffs with apprehension as I turn them over. That's good. I want her to be scared.

"It's not too late to run," I say.

She stares a minute more, then whispers, "Yes, it is."

She stays exactly where she is when I stand and move toward her. I watch her chest rise and fall a bit faster as I stand before her and slide the bag from her arm. I watch her face and she says nothing as I click the cuffs first around one wrist, and then the other. Her breathing is quicker now, and she's right to be frightened. She's mine and I will do what I want with her. That includes throwing her arse into a car and disappearing into the boonies of West Virginia. I hear it's quite nice there.

I look down at her body and the severity of the metal holding her wrists together. The contrast is something beautiful.

"Damn."

"What?" she whispers.

"You look amazing in handcuffs. And you're officially my prisoner."

I'm blasted with the warm scent of pears and freesia and I know that if I wanted to, I could make Anna take back that "no sex" rule.

"We can't," she says, reading my mind. But her words are breathy and unconvincing.

We most definitely *can*. And the low pain in my abdomen begs me to.

She fumbles for words, trying not to look in my eyes. "Remember, you told your father you don't like me. You're not supposed to want me. The whisperers could find us any second. We can't lose our advantage."

Mm-hm.

"It's time to call him, Kai. Tell him you've found me. And then we'll call the others to let them know it's starting."

Wait. Call him? Now? I shake my head. "Not yet—"

"Yes. *Now*. Let's get it over with before we lose control and ruin everything." She sounds steely and passionate. And scared. But it kills me that it's not the Dukes she seems afraid of—her fear seems to be that we, *I*, am going to ruin our opportunity to take them by surprise.

Why did this have to happen so fast? We haven't had enough time.

My thoughts are punctured by the feel of Anna's hand on me. *Down there.*

Jackpot.

I look down, and she's pulling my mobile from my pocket, holding it out to me.

Damn. Major false alarm.

"That was brave," I tell her, but she doesn't smile. She

remains completely serious, and I don't like it one bit.

"It's time," she whispers.

No . . .

She is still holding out the phone and I feel dizzy as I take it. She goes up on her toes and kisses my cheek, staying there, so close. "I love you, Kai. Let's bring them down. You and me and the others, together. We'll use the element of surprise while we have it. *It's our time.*"

Her words ping through me, and her desperation, her optimism, seep into the cracks of my heart just enough to make me momentarily feel what she feels: hope. This is our chance. Our only chance. Eventually the Dukes will learn about each of us disloyal Neph, and we can spend our lives running in fear, but they will find us and pick us off one by one.

This, right now, is the best chance we possibly have to get rid of them and live a life here on earth without them. Anna's eyes plead with me to support her, and I want to. I do.

I nod and stare down at my phone, then pull up Father's new number. I think about nothing except that sliver of hope. My throat nearly collapses when I hear his new voice answer.

"Father . . ." Oh, God. What have I done? I look at Anna and she nods. I open my mouth and can hardly believe when the next words tumble out. "I've got her."

The second I say it, all of the hope abandons me.

"You're kidding me!" He whoops loudly and laughs like a damn hyena.

Oh, God. Oh, God.

"She's cuffed," I say stupidly, feeling like I have to say something.

426

"Did you find the sword?"

My heart is racing. "No, sir. I searched her belongings but found nothing."

"Shit. She must have hidden it somewhere. Doesn't matter. We'll get her to tell us."

He sounds so bloody carefree and sure of himself. There's no way in hell I'm handing Anna over. No way.

"Nice job, Kaidan," he says. "You accomplished what over five hundred prowling Legionnaires couldn't do last night." Yeah, yeah, blah, blah. Why is he being so bloody chatty? I need to get Anna out of here. "They searched damn near every bar, club, and hotel on the East Coast. Where the hell'd you find her?"

In the back of my car on Lover's Lane, you git.

My mind flips through things to say. "She had a group of mates in her old town who always partied at a lake house. I thought perhaps she'd fall back on them, and I was right."

Okay, then. Enough chitchat. I glance at the door, itching.

Father laughs again, like we're best mates sharing jokes. "Where are you now?"

"Our old house." Shite . . . I should have lied.

"Excellent. I'll call an emergency summit in Vegas and we can take care of her. It's our most secure location, and we're always looking for an excuse to visit Sin City, right?"

Weren't they *just* there? Awkward pause. Oh, right. I'm supposed to answer.

I force out a laugh and roll my eyes. Are we done here yet?

"All right," he says. "Meet me at the Atlanta airport in two hours."

What? I whip my face to Anna and her eyes are like saucers.

"Er, it's not necessary for you to fly down here, Father," I insist. "I'll book our flights and deliver her to the summit."

"Oh, it's definitely necessary. I want to be the one to escort her into the summit tonight. See you at the jet."

I will throat-punch him.

"We'll be there," I lie. I press End and check the screen to be sure we've disconnected. Right. Done. I turn to Anna. "We're not going."

"Kaidan!" She pumps her bound fists against her thigh in frustration.

How can she still want to do this? It's madness! I launch my vile phone at the bed and cram my fingers into my hair. "What have I done?"

I pace the room as Anna fumbles through her bag and starts texting people.

No, no, no. It's not happening. We can still run. She has to see reason.

"Anna—"

"Stop!" She advances on me with the most severe, stern look I've ever seen from her, and she yells in a strong voice. "No more. Get it out of your head, Kai! We are not running. This is happening whether you like it or not. It's time to get your game face on and get ready to kick some ass."

Holy . . . I honestly didn't think her capable of this kind of verbal badassery. Even in handcuffs she has taken control, walloped me, and forced my whiney inner child into a corner. I'm sorry I made her yell, but I think I needed to hear that. I needed to hear her say she's not going to put up with my fears anymore. Anna is the one who was chosen, and for good reason. My only job is to be at her side and trust her judgment, though it kills me.

I look down and nod. "You're right."

Ready or not, it's time.

CHAPTER THIRTY-EIGHT

ANNA'S VICE

"Trash the hotel,
Let's get drunk on the minibar."
—"Fancy" by Iggy Azalea

That was the bloody worst plane ride of my life. Fucking Pharzuph. I nearly handed Anna the hilt so she could strike his arse down when he felt her up from behind, supposedly looking for the sword, then tried to get me to shag the flight attendant. I'm really regretting not getting rid of him when we had the chance, but his disappearance would've thrown off the summit and sent everyone scrambling.

I still have my doubts about how this prophecy will play out, but I'm getting right chipper at the idea of watching his demise.

I walk beside Anna down a lavishly carpeted hall in Vegas's Venetian resort. I haven't taken my extended hearing off

Father, and I think for once Anna is actually listening as well. Her face is pinched and I've had to grab her elbow to keep her from bumping into fire hydrants and maid carts.

We stop in one of the hotel's many shops to buy Anna an outfit for tonight, per Father's orders. I'm certain he was expecting something nightclub worthy, like a cocktail dress. I can't wait to see his face when he gets a look at what she's chosen.

We've just turned onto our hall when Father knocks on a hotel room door two floors up.

I recognize Duke Astaroth's poncey English voice straightaway. "Brother Pharzuph. Didn't I just see you on the slopes in Switzerland?"

Father laughs. "Yes, well, this summit's going to be much more enjoyable. Let me in."

It's not completely unusual for Father to seek the Duke of Adultery's company, but usually it's to work, not talk. I don't like this at all.

"Do you have the sword?" Astaroth asks when they're in the room. They lower their voices and I strain to hear.

"No. She's hidden it. That's not why I'm here. I need a favor. It will only take a moment. I'm curious about a possible bond between two people, though there's probably nothing there. I've just got a nagging feeling and I want to rule it out."

Bile burns its way up my throat.

"Ah," Astaroth croons. "A possible conquest?"

Father responds to him in Russian, a language he knows I don't speak. I stop dead in my tracks.

This is about us. He's suspicious of a bond between me and

Anna. Astaroth will see it. The love. The marriage. All of it.

I think we both realize this at the same time, because we take off down the hall as quickly and quietly as we can manage.

One of us needs to drink. Now.

I burst through the doors of our suite, through the bedroom, down the steps, and straight to the mini-fridge. I can't ask Anna to drink. It's not right. But I'm not sure she's comfortable keeping an ear on Father and Astaroth. So I use a hand to sign, *One of us has to stay sober to listen.*

She immediately points to me, so I give her cinnamon liqueur. She downs it with barely a cringe, blowing out a stream of cinnamon air. Father and Astaroth are climbing on the elevator now, flirting with a random woman. I hope like hell they'll be distracted by her.

I hand Anna the orange liqueur and she frowns as she swallows. I wonder if she's feeling it yet. She looks . . . normal. She taps her wrist and I hold up three fingers, then make a zero. Thirty seconds. The Dukes are not distracted enough by the woman and are now heading down our hall.

I try to give her the amaretto next, but she shakes her head hard and reaches over me for the tequila. She throws it back with a smack, and for a split second I forget who we are and who's after us, because hot damn. I love when she is hard-core.

Then my stomach flips with remembrance and Anna holds out her hand, shaking it with impatience. I thrust the vodka into her hand and she downs it, smacking the carpet with a slight grimace. Yeah, that didn't go down as pleasantly as the tequila. She holds out her hand again, but she's already had four big shots.

Are you sure? I sign. It would be terrible for her to get too drunk, but she still looks okay. She nods fast and I hand her the rum, both impressed and frightened by her high tolerance. She drinks the last one like it's nothing.

Father and Astaroth are nearly at our door. They've stopped chatting and I can only hear their footsteps on the thick carpet.

Please let this work. Anna and I move to stand at the same time and she tips to the side before catching herself and sitting on the floor.

Then she giggles and my heart sinks to my feet.

Oh. *Shit.*

She stares over at the minibar and I slash a hand across my throat. *Cut off.* She frowns. She'd better not even think about having another! Damn it! She has to keep her wits about her when the Dukes get here.

I brush my hair back roughly with my fingers. So much for high tolerance.

The Dukes are right outside the door, silent. I look at Anna and put a finger to my lips. I don't want her to say a word. A knock fills the room. Anna stares back at me, kind of glossy, and I think I might've just ruined the entire operation. As I jump to my feet I realize that in this state she won't even be able to use the hilt that's hiding in her bag. I should have been the one to drink. I grind my teeth together, furious with myself, and pull the door open.

"Father. Duke Astaroth." I tilt my head as if I'm curious about their visit. "What can I do for you?"

Young dickhead flicks his hand to the side. "Let us in and close the door. Astaroth just wants to have a look at her."

I step aside and close the door when they pass, then I walk

to the sitting area behind them, straining my neck for a look at Anna. She's sitting in front of the mini-fridge just as I left her, looking like a lush.

She stares up at Astaroth, the Fabio of the Dukes, as he sneers down at her.

"This one's piss-drunk," says Astaroth. "I can't get a reading."

My heart gives a giant throb of reprieve, but the show is not over. He will be suspicious if I don't react somehow.

"A reading on what?" I ask. "A bond? You can't be serious." He ignores me.

Suddenly Anna stands, or tries to stand, and takes a stumbling set of side steps into the couch. She bursts into laughter, unable to fully stand, and I think I might die.

"You don't waste any time," Father says.

Ugh, no. Don't talk to her. Go away, go away.

"There's more!" Anna flings an arm behind her to point at the fridge. "I didn't drink it all. Want some?"

Shite, Anna, shut up!

"I'll pass," Father says. He's got an impish grin on his face. "But I think you should have another."

No, you giant knob, she should not. Damn, how long until this begins to burn off her? I feel like we've been standing here forever. Anna drops to the floor in front of the fridge, her shorts riding up her thighs and showing a sliver of bum crack. Father most definitely notices, making a lewd gesture, and I want to take him down.

Astaroth gets bored and leaves. I'm so itchy a hive of bees covers my skin. It is killing me to stand here. I move to the entertainment center, mere feet from where Anna crouches, and I lean against it, crossing my arms.

"They need more tequila in these minibar fridge thing-amajigs," Anna says. She sits up with a bottle in her hand and I nearly drop-kick it from her fingers.

Father looks at me with absolute mirth.

"I told you," I spit. "She's a lush. An idiot. I can't believe you'd think there was a bond between us."

Please, Anna, do not say anything. Stay quiet. Tear through the sweets in the fridge. Pass out. Do anything except drink or talk.

"Eh, you can't really blame me for wondering when you wouldn't even screw the stewardess today. You're usually all about cougars." Shite . . .

"Eww!" Anna squeals, stuffing her hands over her ears.

"See," I mutter. "Completely immature."

She twists open the bottle of gin, and I can't keep my mouth shut.

"You're trashed. You don't need any more."

"Oh, shaddup," she says. I dart forward, but she pulls the bottle to her chest and throws back a sip, wagging her other pointer finger in the air. Where are my handcuffs?

"No touchie the drinkie. That's bad, bad, bad. Why're you bein' so grumpy, anyways? We're in Vegas, baby!" She stands awkwardly, grabbing the fridge and laughing. She jumps and puts her arms up, splashing a bit of gin. I would probably be laughing my arse off if this were any other time. But now?

Not amused. Any moment it's going to begin wearing off. Any moment now would be brilliant. Until then, I must try to talk some sense into her. Father is watching with far too much interest.

"You are being obnoxious," I tell her. "It's bad enough I have to babysit. I'm not holding your bloody hair if you puke."

She laughs and saunters toward me, wobbly, poking my chest. "Isss funny to annoy you. You're, like, sooo hot when you get mad."

Father moves into our space, sandwiching Anna between us and putting his mouth to her ear. "I'd watch it, if I were you. He can get pretty rough when he's upset."

I'm about to get rough with him if he doesn't take his bleedin' hand off her waist. I have a sick, awful feeling that Father would not be above the idea of trying to punish her before the summit in his own wicked ways.

Anna spins and pushes off our chests, moving to the middle of the room and looking around, bleary-eyed. "Whurs the music?"

Father, who does not like being pushed away, is now staring at her with menace. He moves to her and grabs her arms, shaking her. "Where's the sword?"

"I ain't got no swooord, crazy ass," she says in a heavy drawl. She thinks he's being cheeky.

"Don't talk to him like that," I say, moving toward them. I couldn't care less that she's disrespected him, but I don't want her to make him angry.

Father chuckles without humor. "We'll see, little girl."

"Yeah, we will!" She smiles, then flops down on the couch and gets a goofy look. "What the heck are we even talkin' 'bout? I thought we were gonna dance."

She rolls off the couch and crawls toward the minibar. Father claps a hand on my shoulder and cocks his head toward

Anna. The stare he gives her is full of loathing. "Yeah, good luck with that. And be careful. I wouldn't put it past her to use your lust inclination as a distraction to escape. Don't let her get the upper hand, you know what I'm saying?" He winks wickedly and I nod. "Don't leave the room, and don't let her out of your sight."

"Yes, sir."

Just leave!

He puts his mouth too close to my ear and whispers. "She thinks she's cute. She thinks she can pull one over on you. Don't trust her. Don't even get near her, if you can help it." I give a tight nod.

Anna loudly cracks open a bottle of beer and I give her my harshest glare. She flicks the cap at me and I smack it away.

"Shame to waste such a fine body on her," he murmurs to me.

I grit my teeth.

Father pokes fun at the drunk girl a bit longer, amused by her cluelessness, and then he *finally* leaves. I flick him off with both hands when the door closes, bloody glad he's gone and that things didn't escalate further. We're unbelievably lucky. I lean back against the entertainment center and cross my arms. Now I just have to get Anna sobered up and . . .

Why is she staring at me like that?

She licks her lips and gives me the classic "come hither" look. But that would be bad. Very bad right now. I shake my head. My hearing is out the door, and Pharzuph whistles as he enters the elevator.

Anna sets down her beer and stands. She's still obviously

inebriated, but she's not falling over anymore. She's just sloe-eyed and sexy, and I have to keep shaking my head. But she's coming my way, and I feel the stirring. My head fills with fog, and my gut aches with a deep throb.

Anna presses her entire body to mine, and her hands are on my waist. My teeth clamp together. I grasp her shoulders and push her away as gently and quietly as I can, but she is unrelenting. I shake my head, feeling weakened by the emotion of the afternoon. Father is off the elevator now, walking, saying hello to people, flirting with strangers.

Anna's hands roam over my chest, and down. I grab her hands but she yanks them away and says, "Don't."

Uuuugh, little vixen, do not do this to me. Don't touch. Don't speak. Just . . . I cover her mouth.

"Shut up," I say in a low voice.

She goes still. Her eyes are on me, and they are sweltering, her lids dipping low. Come to think of it, I should probably cover her eyes, too. I should put her to bed and tuck her in tightly. All by herself. Fully clothed. Until she's ready to behave again.

Sounds of the casino ring out in my extended hearing.

"You look familiar," I hear Father say. *"Are you an actress?"*

A feminine giggle. *"Nope."*

"Come on, with a face like that . . ."

Anna gently peels my hand from her mouth. She kisses my palm, and it's so simple and sensual that I'm suddenly fighting for normal breath.

"I'll buy you a drink," Father says smoothly.

Anna kisses her way up my middle finger. I step back, but

she's still holding my hand, and she runs her tongue across my fingertip.

"Ah, damn it," I whisper, yanking my hand away. She's killing me. She's going to kill *us*.

"Please . . ." She pulls her hair tie out, releasing her blond hair about her shoulders, those eyes still melting into me, begging me. It is nearly too much.

My ears fill with laughter from Father and the woman downstairs. I have no idea if he's listening. He seems fully focused on his prey, but I don't trust him. He clearly warned me against Anna.

"I will tie you up again if you don't behave," I warn Anna.

Her eyes narrow wickedly. "Oh, you'd like that, wouldn't you?"

Anna Whitt just got sassy with me. And that is my breaking point.

The beast is alive, warnings be damned.

I grab her waist and turn her, pressing her back into the entertainment center so that I have leverage to press hard against her. The entire thing clatters madly. Her arms and hands are everywhere, clinging, digging, pulling. I kiss her hard, wanting to own all of her—every alcohol-laced breath of air that escapes her mouth—I want it all. We grope as we move to the couch.

Multiple footsteps are moving quickly down the hall.

I am on top of her, between her legs, realizing I should have ripped those shorts off before getting her this far. But I can't stop moving; her body feels so good against mine, her kisses and moans a delicacy.

"*Sounds like the daughter of Belial is drunk again,*" comes Blake's voice down the hall.

"*Shocker,*" snaps Ginger.

"We're about to have company," I say, devouring the soft skin at her neck. I push my hand up her shirt, feeling her silky skin, and let my thumb rub under her bra. She gasps and undulates beneath me.

Banging echoes through the room. "Oi!" Ginger shouts. "Open the damn door."

"I'm busy." I nip Anna's bottom lip. The other Neph can lay off.

"The more the merrier," Blake says.

I look at Anna and she shakes her head. Her eyes are still heavily lidded. "Just ignore them." She grabs the bottom of my shirt and pulls it up, forcing me up, and she kisses a path across my pecs. Oh, yes.

I smash her into the couch with another blazing kiss.

"Don't let that skank take advantage of you when you're bored, son of Pharzuph."

Anna tries to push her way up, shouting, "Who you callin' a skank, you—"

Oh, hell. I quickly cover her mouth and she struggles to get free. I wish they'd just bloody go away. Just one more time together before this godforsaken night begins. I can make it seem like an act of sheer lust. . . .

"Open up." Kopano's voice is like a solid thing that rolls into the room and stares at us. I reel back and jump to my feet. Anna is still lying there, as if waiting for me to come back and take care of her. I turn away and press my forehead against the entertainment center.

I cannot answer the door just yet. I give the others a guttural whisper. "Hold on a moment."

Once I calm down, I walk to the door and let them in. Their faces are disappointed and angry. One look at my eyes and Marna softens. Kope just nods and brushes past. Blake bumps my shoulder and I move aside.

I feel like an ass. This is too big, too important to mess around about. I trudge into the sitting area, where Anna has curled into a lounging position, and Ginger signs, *Are you mad? Or stupid?*

We have to use caution, Marna signs.

You could have gotten carried away and said something dumb, Blake adds.

I'm sorry, I sign.

"We're here to chaperone your guard duty and help out," Marna says out loud. I suppose it's time to play this game.

"Let's get it started," Blake says.

"I have to watch the wino," I deadpan.

"She can sit there and watch us," Blake says. "We won't let her go nowhere, ain't that right, Kope?"

"That's right," Kope says with complete seriousness.

Blake bounces on the balls of his feet, getting into his role. "Pre-party, then summit, then we're back in business."

"Fuckin' right," Gin says. She glares at Anna.

When I look over, Anna is holding an empty beer bottle. Bloody hell—she drank the rest of the one on the table! Damn it! She should be starting to sober up now!

"Someone put on some music!" Marna cheers.

"Ezzactly!" Anna says. "I been trying to say that."

I seem to recall Anna having a much higher tolerance a

441

year and a half ago when she'd worked on New Year's Eve, but then again, that's when her father had been training her up.

I pace my way up to the bedroom level overlooking the seating area, while the twins, Anna, and Blake begin to dance. Watching Anna dance isn't helping my frame of mind. Now that she's no longer falling down, she's carefree, lithe, and sexy.

I watch her like a hawk, so when she makes her way back over to the minibar, I'm ready. The others might not care if she has another, but I do. I march down there and take the bottle of chardonnay from her hand as she's tipping it back. A bit spills down her chin and she swallows.

"Hey! Give that—"

I press a hand over her mouth and look at her sternly. Her eyes blaze up at me. She is pushing *all* my buttons.

I turn her over to Marna because I don't know what to do with half-drunk sexy girls other than shag them, and Anna keeps touching me, making me want to do just that.

I hate watching everyone pretend they're living it up in Vegas while what we're really doing is sitting around waiting for this *thing* to happen, the moment that will define us. It's maddening.

I temporarily lose Father, then find him again at the high-stakes table with that same woman. Nothing seems out of the ordinary.

The twins take Anna into the bathroom to clean her up, and then I hear her getting sick. Kope and I look at each other. He shakes his head. I know. I shouldn't go in there. I can't show concern.

When she starts to cry, my heart shatters and I ignore

Kope's outstretched hand to stop me. I push past Blake and burst into the bathroom. The twins silently try to stop me as well, but I know what I'm doing. I'll be quiet. I have to comfort her.

Anna is on her knees under the running water, sitting back on her heels in the shower stall, soaking wet in her underwear. Her hands are on the tiles. She looks up at me with the saddest, reddest eyes. I quickly unbutton my dress shirt and throw it to the sink, followed by my undershirt. Then I open the stall door and crouch behind her, taking her in my arms. She sinks back into me, shaking. We sit there for the next twenty minutes with my arms around her while her bloodstream clears.

When she finally turns to look at me, her eyes are clear, and I nod.

I stand, dry my arms, and leave her to get ready.

I hate this night. It's hard to imagine that things will look up from here. I can only imagine all the ways they can get worse.

CHAPTER THIRTY-NINE

IT'S TIME

"We are the lions, free of the coliseums . . .
We're the beginning of the end."
—*"Young Volcanoes" by Fall Out Boy*

I knew things would get worse.

Whispered voices down the hall catch my attention, European accents. I hear the name Marek and I listen intently. It's a language I don't understand, but the man speaking sounds urgent. He slips into English at the end. *"Find it."*

Footsteps head down the hall, our direction. It's Marek, and I know what he's after. I run to my duffel bag and yank out Anna's bag from within, shoving it toward her.

"Here's your bag. Get ready." She stares at me like I've gone crazy. I sign, *Hide the hilt! The son of Shax is coming!*

She pales and opens the bag. We all watch, tense, as she pulls out a sack of wrapped sweets, looks around the room frantically, and then shoves the sack into the rubbish bin. The hilt has traveled the world, hidden in this fashion, with no notice, undetected by man-made machines. But something tells me the son of Theft will be harder to fool.

Moments later he's at the door, with a whisperer following him in. Marek is matter-of-fact, completely at ease. It's almost eerie the way Marek seems to know exactly what he's looking for—the bag of taffies. He fishes it from the bin and opens it, removing the hilt.

He turns to me. "She had it all along. Don't you know never to trust a pretty face?" His eyes scan me from top to bottom. I'm getting a sense from this guy that I can't place. It's nothing to do with the sensual way he takes me in. It's in the way his eyes seem to be trying to communicate something more. I am rigid from the fact that he's taking the Sword of Righteousness on his father's orders, but something in his gaze tells me not to fight it.

When Marek and the whisperer leave, Shax gives him instructions: *"Dispose of it. Bury it in the desert if you must."*

We've lost our solitary weapon, and it's almost time to leave for the summit. Panic flares in my chest, and then oddly subsides. From the look on Anna's face, she's got enough anxiety for the both of us.

It's not until an hour later, as Marek is checking us over at the door to the nightclub, that I figure out what's strange about him—he gives off no evil vibes, no malicious intent. I don't get the feeling from him that I get with the Dukes and sons of Thamuz and other likely suspects. Marek takes his time patting me down. When the metal detector blares at my boots, and he checks them over with care, I am not nervous. He wears a malevolent expression, but I am the king of masks, and his feels false.

Despite appearances, I have the feeling Marek is an ally. I think he knew how the hilt was hidden because Belial got ahold of him. When he glances up at me from where he's crouched at my feet, we share the smallest of inconspicuous grins. He knows there are compartments in the underside of my boots, but he doesn't open them. He merely stands and nods for me to move along. I don't linger. I want to tell Anna my suspicions, to ease her mind, but it's not safe. As we enter the club, I bloody hope I'm right about Marek. I hope the son of Theft has the hilt up his sleeve, ready to play.

I keep myself consistently buzzed with a constant stream of alcohol. I have to keep the bonds between me and Anna hidden from Astaroth. I wish I could stay sober, but I must remain on that cusp of fuzziness.

As promised, Father shows to walk Anna into the summit, ready to take full credit for her "capture." He looks her over with a sneer, and I know what he's thinking.

She looks the part—a badass mercenary in black leather with heeled boots, and bright blond hair flowing wildly. Her eyes are dark and her lips are red. She doesn't back down from his stare.

Father turns to me with an abrasive glare. "This isn't exactly what I had in mind when I said to get her different clothes."

I don't respond. He grabs her arm and yanks her toward the VIP room where the summit will take place. Anna turns her head to capture my gaze over her shoulder. She is afraid, but pushing forward. My brave girl. Anyone else, including me, would have tried to run from this fate.

I'm here, I tell her with my eyes. *I'm not going anywhere.*

Father struts into the darkened lounge, shooting a haughty look at the other Dukes, and shoves Anna away. "Go sit down until we're ready to deal with you."

I want to grab him by the thick neck and deal with *him* right now. I feel Marna scratch me gently on the back to calm me, and we all move forward, following Anna to the long black couches along the wall. Fake stars twinkle down on us from the black ceiling. Other Nephilim from around the world filter in and sit along the walls with us.

I search the room for exits. Aside from where we entered, there seems to be a door on the side wall that blends in with all the black. It has no exit sign. The club is underground, so that door could lead to a cellar or closet. I wish I could check for certain.

When Astaroth arrives, Marna inconspicuously leans forward and glances between me and Anna, checking to see if the bond will be visible to her father. She gives a satisfied nod to say we're okay, and I exhale. I'm more nervous than I've ever been, but it's different than the last summit. We still don't have a plan. We've no clue how to take down all of these Dukes and spirits. Anna keeps talking about having faith, how this battle is bigger than just her, bigger than any of us, but I just want her to live. And yes. I want the demons gone for good.

I haven't let myself imagine what life will be like without them, but as I watch the eleven of them mingling—all present except Belial—the lot of them unconcerned and unbothered by the hell they've put everyone through, I want them gone so badly it burns like acid in my blood. I want them to pay.

I sit very still, as do the other Neph. We learned early on not to fidget. Not to draw attention or show weakness or disrespect. Anna starts to nibble on her nail and I nudge her leg with mine. She drops her hand to her lap.

Moments later Duke Rahab fills the open spot in the center of the room. All attention is on him as he speaks in a French accent, malice lacing each word. "I never believed this summit would be called. But alas . . . the great prophecy is upon us." He motions to Father. I tense as Father strides straight to Anna, yanking her to her feet. My lungs constrict, watching him pull her to the middle of the room.

I slide to the edge of my seat.

"Her badge holds the white of innocence," Rahab spits. "First the angels intervened to keep her alive, and then her father goes missing when we attempt to question him. But once we take out his offspring, we will find Belial, and he will be dealt with."

"How can this be, Brother Rahab?" asks Blake's dad, Melchom. Blake stares at his father in his new, young body— he looks like a Chinese movie star, and he's modeled his hair to look just like Blake's. "The prophecy was a myth!"

Rahab grins wickedly. "We have reason to believe that eighteen years ago a guardian angel broke ranks and possessed her human to be with a Duke. Some of you might recall the angel Mariantha and her touching bond with Belial?"

"The traitor!" bellows Zania's father, Duke Sonellion. His

eyes burn red and he bashes a fist against the table. Other Dukes follow suit, shouting their disgust.

"I am not sold on this so-called prophecy," calls the smooth voice of Duke Alocer, Kope's father. "How do we know it's true? What proof do we have?"

The Dukes are so accustomed to being lied to from every angle that they break into an argument about the prophecy's validity. I'm quite pleased about this development, as watching them squabble among themselves makes me feel that our ranks of Neph are stronger. Plus, it gives me a chance to discreetly bend my knee up and reach down, prying my knife from the sole of my boot. And then, slowly, I grab the other, sliding them both into my pockets.

The only person in the whole room who subtly glances at me is Marek, from his station at the door. His cheeks tighten as if he's holding back a grin, and that seals my earlier wonderings. He's golden.

The Dukes are raising their voices now over confusion about the prophecy. Rahab's version completely leaves out the pivotal bit about the demons being given a chance at redemption—he thinks the prophecy is only about banishing them from earth, back to hell. Anna watches them intently, her forehead pinched.

The first true wave of terror hits me when I hear her speak. Her voice reaches above them all. "You're all being given a second chance at heaven!"

Rahab's hand flies back and he hits her so hard she falls to the floor. I am on my feet, but I'm not alone. Our entire row has stood.

"What are we waiting for?" Duke Thamuz yells. "Let's kill her!"

If he goes near her, he will be the first to see the edge of my knife this night. I watch him carefully for any sign that he'll pull a weapon. But he is shushed by the other Dukes who want to find out what Anna's talking about.

Now they're fighting over whether or not to let her talk and whether or not to believe her. They finally decide to let Anna state the prophecy in its entirety, and Jezebet, the Duke of Lies, confirms that Anna's telling the truth. But none of this is working. They're too thick to see this is a good thing for them. The Dukes hate hell, but they love earth. Here, they are gods. Why would they want to return to heaven, where everyone is equal? They want to kill Anna purely for suggesting it.

Father yanks Anna by the hair and grabs her, putting an arm around her throat. I move forward quickly, but Ginger grabs my back pocket to hold me in check. I push her hand away and stare at Anna—they're scaring her to death. I can't bloody stand here much longer.

Duke Thamuz is practically drooling, his eyes bright red. "Enough games. I want blood." I palm my knife in my pocket. If it's blood he wants, I'll give him his own.

I search the walls and ceiling desperately for that bright light, thinking now would be a brilliant time for the angels to show, but there are only demons and Neph.

Father chuckles and I seethe at how he holds Anna against himself, eyes bright with hunger for his prey. "We will savor her. I won't even have her first. She's my little gift to you, brothers. Just be careful not to kill her yet, because she needs to suffer in every possible way. Heaven is watching. Let's give them a show."

I can hardly breathe as the Dukes move toward her, their eyes glowing red—Mammon, Thamuz, and Sonellion—Dukes of Greed, Murder, and Hatred. My eyes dart across the walls. Where are the bloody angels???

Anna struggles against Father as he laughs, darkly, getting his kicks off her fear, feeding off the rabid look in the others' eyes. I can't take it.

"Father . . . ," I call.

"Not now!" He doesn't even turn.

Mammon, the bastard who killed his own son, Flynn, is mere feet away from Anna, and he's unbuckling his pants. I glance at Kope, his eyes severe, and he gives me a nod.

I zone in on Mammon as he licks his lips lewdly and reaches for Anna. Before I can blink again, my knife is out, opened, and flying directly toward its target. It imbeds deep in his eye, only the handle showing.

My God.

I hold my breath. He staggers back, then to the side as he tries to right himself, and ultimately falls to his knees. His spirit starts wrenching itself out before the body is dead, frantically fighting to release itself as if it's on fire. I pull out my second knife and snap it open. All eyes are on Mammon, in horror and confusion.

Father turns abruptly, dragging Anna sideways. His face is contorted, livid, and he sprays spittle when he snarls at me. *"What have you done?"*

"Just a bit of holy water on the blade," I tell him.

Mammon's body dies with a *thunk* on the floor, and his spirit writhes in midair, in agony.

"You," Father whispers. He advances on me, pulling Anna, and my stomach twists. I have publicly shamed him in the worst possible way, and if something doesn't happen soon, it could get very ugly. "I trusted you."

I nearly laugh. "No, you didn't."

Father gapes. Neph and Dukes alike gasp at my backtalk. I have to be careful here—I need to get Anna away from him, and I only have one knife left. He's pulled her body in front of his, practically crouching behind her.

"You filthy, weak idiot!" Father shouts. "You had more potential than all my past sons combined! How could you let yourself be charmed, like a dog, by a Neph girl? You're a failure."

You're a failure. Nothing I ever did was good enough.

"Kill him," Rahab demands.

Nobody moves.

Adrenaline beats through me as I stare around at the room, glad to have the attention off Anna. I weave the blade through my fingers, hoping they will forget about her and let her go while they're focused on me. I wait for them to advance, but they simply stare at me with red eyes, quickened breaths, and ferocious faces.

I've pissed off the lot of them. Except perhaps Jezebet, the one female Duke. She looks rather amused. And Alocer is stoic and unmoved, very much like Kopano, his son.

"Brother Pharzuph," Astaroth begins. I know what he is going to say, and I steel myself. "I'm afraid this is more dire than we thought. Your son and the traitor's daughter are quite . . . *in love*."

Hm. I like the sound of that. It's the worst possible kick in the balls I can give Father, who looks as if he might vomit. "You jest," he snarls.

"Not in the least," Astaroth says. "And they've acted on it. They're *married*."

The room erupts in loud gasps and sounds of outrage.

Our Nephilim revolt has begun.

The sons of Thamuz are next to disobey their father, although it's under the influence of Anna—she telepathically sends them the order, even as she's being gripped from behind by my father. She rarely uses her unique power of influence unless it's to stop an evil act such as this. Much to their own confusion, the sons of Thamuz put down their guns and won't shoot us.

The twins are next, refusing to move away from my side when Astaroth orders. The Dukes are seething at the audacity of the Nephilim not to obey them.

"Excuse me, Duke Rahab," calls Marek from the door he guards. "I apologize for the interruption, but I believe Duke Belial approaches."

Belial enters in his rapper body, sporting a pinstriped suit with a gorgeous Zania at his side, standing tall and strong. Her father, Sonellion, lets out a growl of outrage.

"Traitor! You were behind all of this! You stole my daughter!"

Belial laughs at this notion. Everyone knows Sonellion discarded his daughter. "We got a lot to talk about," Belial tells his fellow Dukes. "I know I'm not the only one in this room who knew after the Fall we'd been used like a bunch of fools. Lucifer's the one who did us wrong—"

"How dare you!" Rahab bellows.

Sonellion reaches for his gun, but Belial points a finger straight at me.

"You'd better rethink that, my man. You see my son-in-law over there? He got damn good aim with that knife, as y'all have seen."

I hold my shiny blade out for them to see. Eyes glow red all around me.

Belial challenges the other Dukes to consider returning to heaven, and they argue fiercely among themselves. I watch Father carefully, waiting for the moment I can extract Anna from his grip. He's loosening his hold as he joins the argument, and has got her only by the wrist now. I'm about to rush the center of the room to make my move when something incredible happens.

The Neph Marek brilliantly pulls something from under the back of his shirt and tosses it to Anna, who snatches it from the air. Father leaps away when he realizes what it is, and I run to Anna's side as the blade brilliantly bursts to life in her hands. She wields the sword, bathing the room in its celestial glow.

It's absolutely beautiful. And so is she. My warrior.

Screams and shouts erupt as the Dukes and whisperers knock into each other, clamoring to distance themselves from the Sword of Righteousness.

Belial, Marek, Blake, the twins, Zania, Kopano, and his

brothers all join me as we stand behind Anna. The Dukes slink back, looking as if they might piss themselves, and the spirits overhead hiss and stir.

I'm still expecting, *hoping*, the angels will come at any moment. How will Anna get rid of the demons on her own? The room holds more than a hundred Neph, but I'm certain not all of them will want to fight. Some are too old, or too young. Some of them are loyal to their fathers and will fight against us.

I bloody hate it that I cannot figure out a strategy. It's beyond me. Anxiousness is threatening to overtake me when something horrendous happens.

It's Patti. They bring her in through the hidden door I'd noticed. They captured poor Patti and dragged her here, to torture her in front of Anna.

I have witnessed my share of heartbreaking events, but none has affected me like this. When Anna sees her earthly mum, her wail is agonizing to my ears. Patti's love blooms out from her body when she hears Anna's voice, and then she's surrounded by an aura of peace. I've always admired this woman, from the day I met her, long before I knew she'd become my mother-in-law. She's the only woman who's ever loved me in a purely motherly way.

My eyes burn. She's been like a mum to me—to *all* of us.

Anna holds the sword in both hands, moving her weight from foot to foot. Tears stream down her face, and the twins are silently crying. I am dizzy with the horror of it all. I hold my knife, keeping my wrist loose.

Thamuz cuts Patti across the face, but Belial grabs my arm

before I can throw my knife. His eyes are pained as he shakes his head. How can he stand there and let this happen? I know it's some bloody test of faith for Anna, but this is wrong!

I could ignore Belial and kill Thamuz now. I can see Anna wants to leap forward, wants to run to her, but if she gets herself in the thick of the Dukes she will be overpowered, even if she manages to take out one or two before she goes down.

I understand all of this, but I hate it. Two seconds ago we were gaining an upper hand, and now it's like we're powerless all over again. They've got one of ours for leverage. One of our most beloved.

When Thamuz attacks Patti, stabbing her, I grasp Anna to hold her up. The shrieks from Anna and the twins are the sounds of night terrors. Everything in me feels heavy and hollow.

"Bastards," I say through gritted teeth.

Thamuz raises the knife again, but I cannot let it happen. This must stop now. Anna mirrors my thoughts: "Stop him, Kai."

With pleasure.

Thamuz is turned away from us, facing Patti with his arm raised, and I hurl my knife into the back of his thick neck. When his feral spirit heaves itself from its body and comes racing jaggedly toward us, Anna slashes him through. We watch as his spirit evaporates. Disappears. The Dukes back away—watching another from their ranks obliterated seems to stun them. I can see their minds working, though they make no move to fight.

Belial scoops up Patti and brings her to Anna. It's not

good. She's only human. She can't heal from this kind of injury on her own. Patti's eyes move to each of our faces in turn, to say her good-byes. When her eyes meet mine she tries to smile and I'm slammed with angry sorrow. Anna is crying, still clenching the hilt in her hands, and I hold her by the shoulder, wishing I could fix this.

"I'm not scared, honey," Patti says to Anna. "I'm ready." We watch, helpless, as she takes her last breath, and her spirit rises gracefully from her body, smaller than an angel, and without wings, but beautiful in its own way. Her guardian angel bows its head over her, gathering her close. It lifts her straight up and out of sight, taking her home. Anna grits her teeth, her face wet and her eyes filled with the shock of loss.

Pandemonium arises as Neph, fed up from years of abuse, stampede toward the Dukes. Other Neph, who're loyal to their fathers, try to shield them, and the fighting begins.

"Work to disarm them!" Belial shouts.

Belial is right. Several of the Dukes have guns. They have to be dealt with first. I stand in front of Anna with Belial at my side, blocking her from any stray bullets as our allies bear down on the Dukes with weapons.

Fighting back, rebelling, is far more exhilarating than I ever expected. The fear is still there, but when it blends with all the other feelings, the need for revenge, for freedom, it adds to the ripe recklessness within. I grasp this feeling, holding tight.

To the left, Duke Kobal tries to aim at Anna, leaning to the side. I instinctually lean as well, shielding her.

"Get Kobal!" I yell, and point at him.

Marna kicks him in the leg just before she's yanked back by the hair by the small but substantial Neph Caterina. Kobal jerks when he's kicked, shooting Duke Jezebet in the arm. She screams. Kobal aims again, but Kopano bursts through the crowd and takes him down. They wrestle on the ground. An enemy Neph runs past me, toward them, but I snatch him by the back of his shirt, spinning him and smashing my fist into his nose with a crunch. Then I shove him aside to deal with his bleeding and I shake out my hand. Blake dives for Kobal's arm, wrenching the gun away and cracking Kobal in the eye with the handle.

I want to dive into the fight, but I refuse to leave Anna unguarded. Belial looks at me and nods his approval. We are her last line of defense.

As spirits swoop down, trying to overpower Anna with their vile whispers, I cast furtive glances back to be sure she's okay. She is slashing the hell out of any who are stupid enough to get within arm's reach.

Our allies work together to take down Dukes and enemy Neph. Marek retrieves my knife from Thamuz's dead body and corners one of the enemy Neph. I can only assume we're rounding up the Dukes in order to fulfill the prophecy, but as the battle rages on I'm beginning to wonder when the hell that's ever going to happen.

In the middle of the fighting I see one of the sons of Thamuz crawling forward, grabbing for a small handgun that's been knocked to the ground.

I shout to one of Kopano's brothers, who's standing closest, and he rushes for the Neph, but it's too late. The son of

Thamuz has made it to his knees and shoots half a second before he's knocked down violently by Kope's brother. Zania cries out as Kopano curls in on himself, shot in the chest, and falls to the ground.

Oh, fuck.

"No!" Anna screams. She tries to run, but I grab her arm and yank her back behind me.

Zania is at Kopano's side, trying to stop the bleeding with her hands. From the corner of my eye I see someone rushing our other side and hear Belial yell. I turn just as Belial and Blake are grabbing Duke Sonellion's arms. He thrashes, pushing toward Anna, and Blake swipes his feet out from under him. Anna raises the sword and I get the hell out of the way. She stabs him straight through. His chest arches up, then there's a puff of smoke as his soul is extinguished.

Good riddance, Duke of Hate.

We look back over at Kopano, who's now surrounded by Zania, his brothers, and his father. He's so still. It makes something in my chest twist in agony.

"It's not his time!" Duke Alocer cries out. My eyes are glued to the scene as Alocer's spirit begins to rise from his skin, and his body slumps to the floor.

Anna gasps. "Oh, my gosh . . ."

Alocer, in spirit form, floats above Kope for a mysterious moment, and then sinks, disappearing into Kope's body. My mouth drops. My God . . . his father is possessing him. He's healing him. Saving him. Zania lets out a sob as Kopano's body lurches. When his chest rises and falls in a pattern of regular breathing, his body heaves to dispense the invasive spirit. Alocer pulls himself from Kope's form and looks down at his son. A few people cheer. Zania looks at his father's spirit with open gratitude. Kope blinks up at him.

I've always known Duke Alocer loved Kopano, but to see it burns my chest with longing. I seek out my father in the mass, and he is watching the interaction with loathing. He can make no move, though. Duke Jezebet, who turned out to be a longtime ally of Belial, stands behind him, pointing a knife at his back.

Zania kisses Kope's forehead, crying with joy, and I nod to myself, huffing out a breath of relief. Anna lets out a laugh. He's going to be okay.

Nearly all of the remaining Dukes and enemy Neph are disarmed and detained, but I'm not sure how long we can hold them. They are still struggling viciously and screaming their anger like savages.

"It's time," Anna says.

"Yes!" I shout over my shoulder.

Does she know what's to happen next? Does she sense that angels are coming?

And then her voice turns sweet and reverent in the air behind me. . . .

"Father . . . let your will be done."

She's . . . *praying*? That's not at all the tactic I was expecting, but each word sends a tingle down my spine. I'm not the only one who feels it. Others around us look up.

Through the fighting I see my father again. He's staring at Anna. For a moment I imagine that the look of shock on his face means something different, like perhaps he's having an epiphany, and I feel a lightness of hope. And then his eyes burn red and he opens his mouth with a war cry. All hope vanishes when I see the bloodlust in his eyes—his hatred of her and what she's trying to do. He backhands Jezebet, who drops the knife and grabs her bleeding nose. Father charges. I raise my arm to stop him, knife up.

Belial rushes from the side and tackles him with a forearm to the throat. His head slams against the floor. Father is large in his new body, but Belial is massive and holds him down while I crouch at his side.

He struggles against Belial, his face furious, and I shake my head. "It's too late, Father. This is your opportunity to make amends."

It would be stupid to harbor a grain of hope at this point. And yet, I am still disappointed in his response.

"I will not grovel at His feet!"

Belial shakes his head and mumbles, "You gonna be groveling in hell, brother."

Father tries to spit at him, but it ends up on his own chin. I look up at Anna, nodding for her to continue.

Her voice is clear. "I pray forgiveness, for the souls who once betrayed you and have reconciled. Return them to their rightful home, and let those spirits who still harbor hatred be returned to hell. . . ."

The dark room begins to glow, as if night-lights have been switched on. Whisperers circle and spin above us. Belial grins at me.

"It's working!" I say to Anna. "Keep going!"

Her eyes are closed and her face is luminescent. She stands

with her feet apart, the sword still blazing in her hands, and says the magic words: "Banish all the demons from earth!"

I'm racked with a sudden bout of dizzying vertigo, but when I look around I see I'm not alone. Everyone's eyes have gone round as they're staring at the floor. Blake's eyes lock with mine across the room. I skate my gaze to the twins, Kope, and Z.

What is happening? It feels like a bloody earthquake. Are we *all* going to be killed? Will we all be taken tonight?

The fear that threatens to rise up is suddenly snuffed out by a glorious warmth that envelops me and sends an absolute hush over the room.

Anna belts out the last of her prayer. "I ask with all my heart that the demon stains be washed from the souls of all Nephilim, both here on earth and those who came before us. Please allow us a chance at redemption!"

The ground cracks open with a shattering *boom*, throwing the room off balance. Anna stumbles and drops the sword. It rolls straight into the depths of the crack. I grab her and pull her aside as tables slide past and chairs fall over. I look toward the side door, not twenty feet away. We have to make it there.

The room stills again.

One by one, the souls of the Dukes are sucked from their bodies. One by one the dark souls are siphoned into the crack, returning to hell for good. I watch with more sadness than I want to admit as Father's soul lifts and his hand reaches for me before it goes lifeless. And then his soul is spiraling away. Down, down, down.

Gone.

Now angels appear from above, a whole slew of them lighting up the room, and I want to say, *Bit late, aren't you?* But then I have to smile, because we handled it without them—with Anna leading the way.

With the angels comes that warm feeling again. Belial closes his eyes and lifts his face. Something alive is in the room. Something I can't see, but I can feel. It's like the warm joy I get when I'm with Anna, and when I saw her mother, but even purer. Even stronger. It's all-encompassing.

It's a feeling of love.

"It is well," says a soothing whisper in my ear like the wind. My heart is beating too fast. I remember what I'd said that day at the Grand Canyon. *We can talk peace when You get rid of the demons.* Well, I'll be damned. I think I've just been humbled.

"Thank you," I whisper.

I look over at Anna, who's watching in awe as the few redeemed demons' stains are lifted from their badges, and their souls rise.

Belial and Anna look at each other.

"You did good, baby girl," he says. He grasps Anna tightly, and she all but disappears inside his large embrace. And then, like the others, his soul rises, leaving Big Rotty's body lying there. He smiles down on us, shining in the newness of his cleansed soul, white wings flapping. With a final grin, he shoots up and away.

The angels ascend, leaving us, and I stare at Anna. Her eyes are aglow with joy. She's alive. She made it. We both did. I pull her to me and hold her tight. She laughs in my arms.

And then something feels . . . strange. My entire torso is

463

heavy and overly hot, then there's a pull, like a vacuum is on my sternum. I watch in shock as dark red smoke leaves my body where my badge is, and wafts away.

What the . . . ?

I look at Anna as a fizzle of putrid yellow seeps from her badge, leaving it white as snow. She puts a hand over her chest, then looks at my badge and grins. I lift my eyes to the other Neph in the room, who are all staring around at each other's white badges. What does it mean?

There are roughly fifty Neph left alive in the room. All of our allies are miraculously accounted for, though some are worse for wear, with bloodied limbs and torn clothing. The room is strewn with bodies and debris. It's quiet, as if we're all too afraid to ask . . . is it over, then? Truly?

The floor abruptly shudders and tilts, knocking Anna into me, and a creak of metal cries out. This building is about to come down.

"We have to get out of here!" I yell.

Everyone in the room struggles to stand and run at once. Ginger falls, pulling at Marna, who twists her leg. I grab them both under the arms and pull them to their feet. Then Kope and I grab Zania, who falls next. I grasp Anna's hand and keep her by my side as we hurdle toppled chairs and clumsily wade over rubble. I press Anna through the door before me, exhaling a huge breath when we make it up those basement stairs and away from the building, into the dark night. We're all out, staring back at the shaking building as we run, helping to hold one another up.

We made it. I can't believe it bloody happened, but the

demons are gone and we made it. I squeeze Anna's hand and a laugh escapes me. Ginger flashes me an astonished smile and pulls Marna closer. Her other hand reaches for Blake's arm and he kisses her shoulder. I marvel at the firm warmth of Anna's hand in mine, and I keep staring down at her, black leather covered in dust. Her face is streaked with dried tears and dirt.

We don't stop moving until we get to our hotel, which feels solid and sound. Together, we stand staring out the glass window at Las Vegas, linked hand in hand. All around us people are running, terrified, and though we are dazed and overwhelmed and mourning those we've lost, we are no longer afraid.

We are free.

CHAPTER FORTY

GOOD

"I believe now, there's a reason why I'm here.
It's to try to do good, it's to try to do better."
—"Free Now" by Sleeping with Sirens

Six years later . . .

I'm sure everyone's curious about what it's like to be married to me. It's awesome, if I do say so myself. In many ways we're just like other couples. She gently scolds me for leaving dirty dishes all over the house, and I have to sit through cheesy chick flicks. But it's so much more than that.

Anna was there for me when I typed an anonymous letter to the FBI and Atlanta police department, detailing the work of Marissa, her location, and as many of her accomplices' names as I could remember. It was a risk, even anonymously, because if Marissa caught wind of the letter she could have easily tried to find me, to kill me.

I spent seven months worrying, listening out, watching for her goons, and not letting Anna out of my sight. And then the news hit, causing an international media blitz. It was the largest bust the world had ever seen. It shed light on sexual slavery around the world. Anna stood behind me squeezing my shoulders as we watched the news that night. Tears streamed down her face as Marissa was led away in handcuffs. Then Anna wrapped her arms around my neck and kissed my cheek, whispering, "I am so proud of you."

Six weeks later I held Anna as she cried against my chest when we lost Marna. Baby Anise was born healthy and thriving, but she would never know her mother.

"She's in heaven," Anna said, wiping her eyes. "An angel came down and took her."

I'd swallowed hard as I held Anna, both relieved and saddened. While some curses for our kind were lifted, others remained. We still feel the weight of our sinful Nephilim natures, but we're no longer condemned straight to hell when we die.

Like other couples, Anna and I are a sounding board for each other on work issues and other problems. As a social worker, Anna is still trying to save the world, but she's held back by the system of rules and regulations. I comfort her when she cries about frustrating cases of child abuse, when it becomes too much for her to bear.

As for my job, in Lascivious's fourth year of success, Raj went off the deep end and OD'd on a mix of drugs. An accidental death, but the band never came back after losing him. We went our separate ways, and I'm now working with Jay on the business end of the industry, making music and learning about producing. I do miss the rush of being onstage, but at least Anna doesn't have to deal with girls grabbing at me after events.

Though it was a complete turn-on when she once grabbed a girl's arm backstage, saying, "Excuse me, but that is *my* husband you're trying to grope, and I suggest you keep your hands to yourself." She'd said it with Southern charm, but I could see in her stance that my girl had been ready to throw down.

I rewarded her well that night for saving me from the groper.

And I suppose that's where we differ from other married couples.

We spend a lot of time in the buff. It's not really fair to compare, since we've been through so much together, seen so much in our lives. We don't have the same worries that other people do.

But what can I say? Life is good. Every time I see Anna's little arse wiggling as she washes dishes, or see her bending over the tub to scrub a corner, I become more and more glad she refuses to hire a maid. I know, I'm swine. I am a master of the sneak attack from behind. I prowl as she's stirring or baking or rinsing, and then I pounce. I'm all over her and she's screaming, "Kai—!" and trying to get back to doing whatever thing she's doing at that moment.

But I'm quite persuasive.

***

One year ago, as we lay together on the couch, she ran her fingers through that small patch of hair in the middle of my chest. A pang of old worry crept in.

"Do you suppose I should get rid of that?" I asked. "Shave it off or laser it or something?"

She'd looked at me with confusion. "What? This hair? Why? I like it."

She'd laid her head back on my arm, and I held her tighter. I am a lucky bastard.

That's why I tried not to blanch when she hesitantly brought up the idea of adopting from Malawi. She puts up with a lot of shit from me, so I fought back my initial instinct to run screaming at the idea of a tiny person invading our content little bubble. A lot would change.

No more walking about naked.

No more shagging Anna anywhere and everywhere I pleased.

No more playing the drums at night as loudly as I want.

No more blasting music with colorful language.

No more shagging Anna anywhere and everywhere—oh, wait. I said that. But it's worth repeating.

I'm still a selfish bastard who doesn't care to share, especially where Anna is concerned. But I long ago learned that she doesn't belong to me. She allows me to hold her heart, but she's not fulfilled if she isn't sharing her love and kindness with as many people as possible.

I know she misses Patti like mad. I do as well, so I can't imagine how it is for her. I know Anna is craving a family, and the more she talks about it, the more I start to vaguely see her vision as something . . . nice.

You can teach him drums and music, and dress him in tiny rocker clothes, and show him how to skateboard, and . . .

Then she mentions a set of brothers, instead of just one child, and I think she's trying to kill me. She claps her hands, and her face is so filled with joy that I throw my hands up and sigh. Why the hell not? Let's do it.

And that's how we ended up here in Malawi at the orphanage owned by Kope and Zania. They're looking well. I suppose if caring for loads of children hasn't aged them terribly, Anna and I can handle just two.

I'm far more nervous than I care to admit, so I hold Anna's hand tightly. She smiles up at me when Kope goes to get them. Her eyes are already damp with emotion, and I think to myself that these two boys are the luckiest lads in the world to be getting Anna as a mum.

Kope comes back in with a toddler and a baby, one on each hip, and they're bloody cute as can be. A burst of excitement I hadn't planned to feel flares through me, followed by even more nervousness.

These are my boys. My *sons*.

My God, I can't believe this is happening.

Anna goes to the baby, who takes to her straightaway, and I've never seen my woman smile so big. She is radiant. The baby flaps his arms, making bubbling sounds and grabbing her hair.

"Hi, Onani," she says to him, laughing.

I can't help but smile. I look down now at the older boy,

Mandala, and he's clearly going to be a tougher sell. He looks a bit untrusting, and I can understand that feeling. But I've come prepared. I squat next to him and pull out a toy car, a red hot rod. I hold it out, not getting too close. He takes a tentative step toward me.

"It's yours, mate," I say, stretching my arm closer to him. "I brought it just for you."

I keep my arm extended until he slowly walks forward and takes it from me. He stares at my eyes, as if expecting me to take it back or yell. I nod and smile. I crouch and urge him to roll it on the ground. I even make some awesome engine sound effects and he suddenly looks up at me and smiles.

I have to swallow back a bout of mounting emotion. I want this boy to trust me. I want him to never fear me. I want to do right by him.

It's funny how even yesterday I was still feeling wary, though I'd never tell Anna that. She was so thrilled, and I felt like a gobshite for not being excited. I couldn't see how I'd have room in my heart to care for two children, two strangers, the way they would need me to. I'd hoped, over time, I'd get the hang of it, but it turns out some things truly do come naturally.

Like loving a child. My heart expands and makes room for them without any effort from my mind. And once they're in, they're there to stay. They're mine to care for. Mine to provide for and support.

We remain at the orphanage for hours, getting to know the boys' personalities, and letting them become accustomed to us. I can already imagine them at our home just outside of L.A.

We have a small yard. There is a park down the street. I can see them there. I can see *me* there with them.

The room opens and other children filter in to look us over with curiosity. They all seem to be fascinated with Anna's bright hair, and drawn to her lovely smile. Can't blame them.

The children are easy to entertain. They mostly just want attention, so I give it to them, and find that they make me laugh.

"Kai," I hear Anna say. "I think someone wants to meet you."

I look up to where I sense that I'm being watched. A little girl, maybe four years old, stands next to the door, staring so hard at my face that I go still. Her aura is powerful—much fuller than most children's. Her negative emotions run deep, and I wonder what she's been through. Orange excitement zaps like tiny lightning bolts through the gray cloudiness as she watches me. But the strangest part is the top of her aura. It goes fuzzy, then pink, like cotton candy.

She's staring straight at me . . . and feeling love? I think she must be confused, but that stare of hers is potent, and I can't look away.

"Hi there," I say to her. "What's your name?"

She points at me and says, *"Bambo."*

I look up at Zania, whose forehead scrunches. Both she and Kope crouch on either side of the girl, but she pays them no attention. Her eyes are on me.

"Her name is Alile," Zania tells me. *Ah–LEE–leh.* "It means 'she weeps.' "

"Alile," Kopano says to the girl. *"Zikuyenda bwanji?"*

"She speaks Chichewa," Zania whispers. Anna scoots closer to me.

Alile's guardian angel dips low to whisper, and the darkness in her aura lightens. It is highly unusual for most adults, much less a child, to be this open to the spirit. The girl walks toward me and I hold my breath, curious and a bit nervous.

I remain very still as she reaches out to touch my face with dry, dusty hands. Her face is close to mine, and it's like she can't get deep enough into my eyes. She keeps a small, cool hand on my cheek and climbs confidently into my lap, sitting. She speaks clearly up at me again. *"Bambo."*

Something is happening here. I don't know what, but it's making me dizzy with anxiousness. I can't look away from Alile, but in my peripheral vision I see Kope and Zania staring at each other.

"What does *Bambo* mean?" Anna whispers.

Kopano clears his throat. Pauses. "It's a word for father."

Holy mother . . .

If I wasn't sitting down already I might pass out. Father? But why on earth . . . ? I look down at the delicate girl, who is now patting at my shirt, checking me over.

Zania begins to sign. *She came to us from another orphanage that shut down because of sexual abuse.*

My gut sours and tightens. I look at Anna, whose face is horrified. My teeth grind as I think about this poor little girl. She is so small. She's been a victim of heinous acts in a world I'm all too familiar with. It's no wonder her aura is so dark. I want to find and kill whoever touched her.

Kopano speaks to Alile in Chichewa, and Zania interprets.

"He tells her Kaidan is his friend and wants to know why she calls him Father."

I hold my breath as Alile leans against me with complete comfort and familiarity, her head turned toward Kopano as she answers him. Again Kope clears his throat.

"She says, 'In my dream, he was my father.'"

I can't breathe. I . . .

This girl dreamed of me. It *had* to be an angel, or else she has a very special gift that few are given and few are privy to. My eyes dart to Anna and she seems to be holding her breath, eyes wide with wonder. This is huge. This cannot be brushed aside or laughed off or ignored.

I try to imagine leaving this orphanage with Onani and Mandala, leaving this little girl behind. A fierce, urgent, possessive urge rises up in me like a windstorm and I wrap my arms around her. I will not leave her. I will never let anyone hurt her again.

She's my daughter. A gift. A blessing. Something I never thought I wanted, but now I'd fight anyone who tried to take her from me. My heart stretches wide to let her in, and I am full with the rightness of it. Alile snuggles closer, as if her home is right there in my lap. When the burn begins behind my eyes and the moisture builds, I'm too overcome to bother stopping it.

The tears are hot on my cheeks, and I wipe them away. I don't feel weak. In fact, I've never felt stronger. Anna takes my hand and I hold tight to her. Onani and Mandala play at our feet, the baby patting Alile's bare foot.

My wife. My sons. My daughter.

I will do right by them. I swear it. I am my father's son, but he does not live in me. This, right here, is who I choose to be. I imagine the Maker, Belial, Patti, Mariantha, and all the angels smiling down on me, saying, "It is good."

And I have to agree. It's damn good.

DUKE NAMES AND JOB DESCRIPTIONS INDEX

Duke Name: *Focus:* Job Description:
Neph Children (those mentioned in story)

Pharzuph (Far-zuf): *Lust*: craving for carnal pleasures of the body; sexual desire outside of marriage: Kaidan (Ky-den)

Rahab (Rā-hab): *Pride*: excessive belief in one's own abilities; vanity; the sin from which others arise

Melchom (Mel-kom): *Envy*: desire for others' traits, status, abilities, or situations; jealousy; coveting: Blake

Mammon: *Greed*: desire for earthly material gain; avarice; selfish ambition: Flynn (deceased)

Alocer (Al-ō-sehr): *Wrath*: spurning love, opting for destruction; quickness to anger; unforgiving nature: Kopano (Kō-pah-nō)

Kobal (Kō-bal): *Gluttony*: consumption of more than one's body needs or requires. *Sloth*: avoidance of physical or spiritual work; laziness; apathy: Gerlinda (deceased)

Astaroth: *Adultery*: breaking marriage vows; cheating on one's spouse: Ginger and Marna

Jezebet: *Lies*: being dishonest or deceptive: Caterina

Thamuz (Thā-muz): *Murder*: taking the life of another person: Andre and Ramón

Shax: *Theft*: stealing: Marek

Belial (Beh-leel): *Substance Abuse*: physical addictions, primarily drugs and alcohol: Anna

Sonellion: *Hatred*: promoting prejudices; ill will toward others; hostility: Zania

GLOSSARY

aura: Each person's emotions are given off in tiny particles around their torso region. Positive emotions are colorful, usually pastel. Negative emotions are shades of gray. Nephilim often refer to auras as one's "colors." Nephilim and Dukes can hide their auras.

badge: All Dukes and Nephilim have badges in the center of their sternums, signifying their sins. A badge is a supernatural starburst of color that represents the dark stain within the being's soul. Only other demons and angels can see these badges, and they do not convey onto pictures or film.

demons: Angels who fell from heaven and now possess a dark stain on their souls. Most demons, including their leader,

Lucifer, are confined to hell, but 666 are allowed to roam the earth in order to tempt humans. They are not allowed to kill humans, or force them into action. Demons can go anywhere, but they tend to avoid churches and places where people are praying.

Dukes: The demon bosses on earth. Of the 666 earthly demons, only the twelve Dukes are allowed to possess human bodies and masquerade as humans. Each Duke has a specialty sin. They rise to high positions in order to have influence over higher-up humans and the societies they live in. Over time, the Dukes change bodies and duty stations. When this happens, it is called the changing of the guard.

guardian angels: Each human on earth is given a guardian angel to watch over them throughout their life and whisper positive thoughts. When given permission from above, a guardian angel can interfere in events, unbeknownst to the human charges.

Legionnaires: Lucifer's legion of demon spirits on earth. Of the 666 earthly demons, 654 are the legion of spirits who roam and whisper to unsuspecting humans, urging them to sin. Each Legionnaire is assigned to one of the Dukes and reports to him or her regularly (also known as whisperers).

Nephilim/Neph: Child of an angel (usually a demon, since angels of light are forbidden) and a human. Mothers of Nephilim cannot survive the childbirth. Nephilim are bred to further the demonic cause of influencing humans negatively. They can see auras in color, and their five senses are heightened.

summit: A demon meeting. These can be regional or global, in different locations. Summits are usually for the demons only, but Nephilim are occasionally invited when a Neph is to be brought forward and punished.

Sword of Righteousness: A heavenly relic that can only be used by angels or Nephilim who are pure of heart. The sword can sense the heart of its beholder and if its user is in danger. The Sword of Righteousness was used in the war of the heavens and is the only known weapon that can extinguish a demon soul or send the soul back to hell.

whisperers: See Legionnaires.

Acknowledgments

This is the book I swore I'd never write. Funny how that happens. And funny how it happened at just the right time. I wrote this book when our family was in the midst of a major move, and it was a tough transition. Kaidan got me through it. Having him in my head was the best distraction imaginable. So thank you to all the Sweet trilogy readers who begged for this. And thank you to my agent, Jill Corcoran; my editor, Alyson Day; my marketing/publicity peeps, Jenna Lisanti, Abbe Goldberg, and Stephanie Hoover; my copy editor, Jon Howard; and the team at HarperTeen for allowing this to happen. Also a big thanks to the cover artist, Tom Forget, for stepping up to do one last Sweet creation—my fave yet!

It's no fun chasing dreams alone. To my family and friends, as always, I can't thank you enough for your constant support during this wild ride. With you guys at my side, I feel like I can do anything.

Gigundo thanks to my beta readers: Nyrae Dawn, Nicola Dorrington, Morgan Shamy, Chanelle Gray, Hannah McBride, and Jolene Perry!!

I want to thank my talented graphic artist friend, Jennifer Munswami, for all of her gorgeous Kaidan teaser images for this book! *drools*

With a bursting heart of gratefulness, I thank my readers, my "Sweeties." You guys make me cry with joy and pinch myself every day. From your help with Kaidan's playlist to your excitement at trying to get your names in the book, you make everything worthwhile. I wish I could meet and hug each one of you.

1 Corinthians 13:13. Love, love, love.

Read a teaser from
Wendy Higgins's new duology,
The Great Hunt

Chapter

1

A late summer breeze blew warm over the deep and wide Lanach Creek. Moonlight caught the shock of Wyneth's red-orange curls as she let her fiancé, Breckon, lay her back on the end of the dock. She could scarcely see his face in the dark of night as he hovered gently above her, but she knew every angle and plane by heart.

Another breeze crested down the creek from the nearby sea, but the couple's combined heat warded them against it.

"I don't want you to leave," Wyneth whispered.

"If it were up to me, I'd stay right here with you. But I

have a duty." He leaned down and kissed her gently at first, then deeper. Wyneth bent her knee, letting the silken layers of her dress fall back to expose her leg. Breckon's hand cupped behind her knee, sliding up farther than she'd ever allowed him to touch before.

"Just think," Breckon said, his breaths coming faster, "in three months, I'll be back from the sea and we'll finally marry."

Wyneth moaned, not wanting his hands to stop moving. "I wish it were now."

She pulled his face to hers again, feeling brazen and greedy for his soft lips. She hated when he left for the sea; it always filled her with a pang of worry and longing. Wyneth urged Breckon closer.

A rustle sounded from the nearby dark woods. They stilled, listening.

The noise came again like a crackle of dead leaves and brush. Definite movement.

In a rush, they sat up, Wyneth pulling her skirts down. Breckon readied his hand over the dagger at his waist.

All was quiet except the muddle of water bugs, frogs, and the splashing of tiny waves at the shore.

"Do you think someone's spying?" Wyneth whispered. She imagined her young cousin Prince Donubhan and his gang of trouble seekers, but the queen would have his hide if he sneaked out after dark.

"No." Breckon shook his head, a lock of hair falling across his worried brow. "It's most likely a deer." But to Wyneth's ear, he didn't sound so sure.

He relaxed and gave Wyneth a smile, but the mood had been broken by thoughts of anyone witnessing their intimate time together. It was impossible to find privacy within the castle walls with the royal family, servants, and naval guards running about. The private docks at night had been their only hope without leaving royal lands.

"Perhaps we should go back," she said halfheartedly as Breckon leaned in to place a trail of warm kisses down her neck to her collarbone. "We can fetch Harrison and wake Aerity and sneak down to the wine cellars again."

Breckon chuckled. "The only matchmaking I'm interested in tonight is you and I."

"But that noise—"

"You worry too much. We're safe and alone out here, I assure you. I'd never put your safety or reputation at risk."

Or his own. As the youngest naval captain, Breckon Gillfin's actions were under constant scrutiny. Gossipmongers said he'd risen the ranks quickly because of his long engagement to the king's niece, but anyone who'd seen Breckon in action knew that wasn't the case. King Charles Lochson did not play favorites. Breckon was brave, loyal, and driven.

These were all reasons her family accepted Breckon's courtship and offer of marriage when Wyneth was only sixteen. He'd waited patiently these two years since, working hard all the while, and after this next short stint at sea their long wait would at last be over. And if Wyneth had her wish, her cousin Princess Aerity would finally fall in love with Breckon's cousin Harrison, and all would be right in the world.

Another abrasive rustle from the trees caused them to break away again. This time they both stood. Something or someone was surely out there. Breckon scanned the trees with a scowl.

In the darkness, a large shadow moved within the mossy trees as they swayed. Wyneth grabbed Breckon's arm, and he stared intently into the trees. His dagger, which she hadn't seen him unsheathe, glinted in the moonlight.

"Who's there?" Breckon called. "Show yourself!"

The trees stilled. Even the bugs and frogs stopped their chatter. It was too quiet. Wyneth's heartbeat quickened.

"What if it's the great beast?" she asked, a tremor in her voice.

Breckon shot her a rueful smile and rubbed her hand, which was likely cutting off the circulation in his bicep. "You know the great beast is only a tale among the commoners to impose a curfew on their youth. Besides, the royal lands are protected by the stone wall and the seas. It's probably a buck. Wish I had my bow . . ."

His voice trailed off as they stared into the dark woods.

Rumors of a great beast had arisen through the waterlands of Lochlanach over the summer. Four watermen villagers had been killed, all at night, leaving behind only scraps of bodies. Tale or not, the royal maids who did their shopping beyond the royal wall said they'd never seen such fear among the people.

Just as Breckon was about to sheathe his dagger, a deep snort rumbled from the trees.

"Oh, my lands!" Wyneth was frozen. "What was that?"

Breckon had tensed and lowered his voice. "Wild boar, perhaps?"

Wyneth had never heard of wild boars on royal lands. Only deer and small creatures.

"Stay here," Breckon ordered. "I'm going to scare it off."

"No!" She grabbed for his hand and he kissed her forehead, gently prying himself away.

Before he could take two steps from her, the dark shadow in the trees resolved itself into a brown mass on the sandy walkway. They both stared, not daring to move.

It was taller than any man, standing on its hind legs. Wyneth gasped and questioned her own sanity as she stared in disbelief. Its body was massive, the size of a bear, with wiry hair like nothing she'd ever seen. Its face was as ugly as a boar's. Tusks curled up around a dripping snout, sharp teeth shining. Its beady eyes eerily caught the moon's reflection. Everything about its stance and posture screamed feral. Deadly. Impossible.

The length of the dock separated them from the thing, but it was not far enough for her. Not nearly far enough.

Wyneth couldn't breathe. Her jaw hung open, poised for a scream, but not a sound escaped. She'd never known such crippling fear. Even Breckon made no move except the heaving of his chest from jagged breaths.

The great beast was not a carefully devised tale. It was real.

"Stay behind me," Breckon whispered without moving. "If anything happens, swim for your life across the creek. Do you understand?"

For a moment Wyneth could not respond. Then her voice broke as she frantically whispered, "I can't leave you! Come with me. We'll swim together." She wanted to reach for his hand, but she was stiff with terror and feared giving the beast reason to attack. Perhaps if they stayed very still and quiet it would go away.

When Breckon turned his head to her, insistence in his eyes, that small movement was all it took. The great beast let out a roar, forcing a startled scream from Wyneth. Breckon bit out a curse. The thing charged down the long dock, its steps shockingly quiet, for Wyneth had expected the thunder of hooves, not large paws. But then she felt its heaviness shake the wood beneath her feet with each landing.

"*Go!*" Breckon yelled.

At the same time, she grabbed for his arm and screamed, "*Jump!*"

But Breckon had no plans to run from the beast. He grasped Wyneth's waist and pushed her backward with all his might. She felt herself flying through the air off the dock, all breath leaving her lungs as her body submerged with a crash into the cool water. All sound muted. Disbelief struck her once again.

This could not be happening. It couldn't. It wasn't real.

But when her wet face hit the air and she gasped for breath, it took only a moment for her to turn toward the growling sounds and see the monster reach Breckon, towering over him.

Skies above! "Breck!"

"Swim!" He angled himself to avoid the beast's mouth. "Get help!" Breckon launched his strong shoulder into the beast's abdomen and they began to grapple, sounds of grunting and snorting carrying over the water.

Finally Wyneth snapped from her fear-induced stupor and the instinct of flight kicked in. She couldn't fight this thing with Breckon, but she could do what he'd commanded: get help. She turned and swam with all her might. She kicked and her arms sliced through the water as if the beast were right behind her. Indeed, she expected to hear the splash of the thing following at any moment, but it never came. Wyneth hardly heard her fiancé's strangled screams as he fought for his life on the dock behind her.

Breckon was an excellent sailor and soldier. A fearless fighter. He had his knife. The beast was only an animal—no match for her betrothed.

He'll be okay, Wyneth reassured herself with each quick stroke through the water.

After swimming nearly a hundred yards, her body was numb when she reached the dock on the other side of the creek. She pulled herself up, panting for air and cursing her wet, heavy garments. Her eyes scanned the water, but it moved at the same calm, slow speed as always. Then she allowed her eyes to seek out the dock beyond.

The great beast was nowhere in sight, and hope rose in her chest.

The dock was covered in patches of dark moisture that glinted in the moonlight against the dry wood—a sickening trail of it. All hope vanished as she comprehended what lay at the edge of the wooden planks. In the very place she'd been kissed only moments before, were the remains of her life's great love.

Chapter
2

Paxton Seabolt sat on a wooden stool with his elbows on the beaten plank bar, sipping his ale and listening to the chatter of two excitable lasses at a table behind him. He felt their eyes on his back, but he wasn't in the mood for flirtations. Didn't they know one of their own watermen had been killed two nights before by the great beast?

The man had worked with his father for years, hauling in oysters and clams. Paxton recalled his husky laugh, which always seemed too deep for his gaunt face and thin body.

Other men and women from the village of Cape

Creek spilled into the dim pub straight from work, bringing marshy smells of salt water, morose faces whispering rumored details.

"It killed six others in water towns during the summer months, you know. . . ."

"Old man Pearl said he saw it with his own eyes . . . said it was a giant creature like nothing he'd ever seen before."

Paxton would doubt that statement if old man Pearl wasn't as sound and respectable as they come.

As a couple of older women bustled in, Paxton caught sight of the notice that'd been nailed to the door the day prior—an official order from the royal army to stay indoors when the sun went down. A night curfew. Apparently the beast was nocturnal.

"Did you hear?" asked one of the women to the people in the pub. "They're sayin' royal lands were attacked by the beast last night!"

"Impossible," said the barkeep. "It's fortified. Nothing can get past that wall or the navy."

"I don't know how the thing got in, but it killed one of their officers."

The barkeep grabbed a rag and scrubbed a wet spot. "Well, if that's true, perhaps they'll finally do something about it."

"Aye," Paxton agreed gruffly. "Perhaps they'll finally believe us filthy commoners."

The barkeep glanced at Paxton's nearly empty glass and filled him another without asking. "How fared the hunting today, Pax?"

Paxton shrugged, frustrated he hadn't seen any deer that day. "Only a rabbit."

"Your mother will surely make something nice with it." He set the ale in front of Paxton, then wiped his hands on his dirtied apron.

Just as Paxton lifted the full glass to his lips, someone jostled too close and bumped his arm, spilling ale down his chin and the front of his tunic. He glared at the grinning face of his younger brother, Tiern.

"Oy, got a little something there, Pax." Tiern pointed at his older brother's dripping chin. The girls behind them laughed, and Tiern rewarded them with a smile.

"Don't make me snap you, clumsy twig." Paxton wiped his chin with the back of his wrist, but Tiern was unperturbed by his dark mood. The younger Seabolt brother appeared as put together as always, with his brown hair tied back neatly, in contrast to Paxton's wavy strands hanging messily around his face.

"Everyone's right shaken up about this monster, aye?"

Tiern pulled out a wobbly stool, scraping the hard dirt floor, and sat.

The barkeep peered down at Tiern's boyish face. "What're you having today?"

"Just water for him," Paxton said. When Tiern frowned, he continued. "We don't need you getting silly off one ale."

"I don't get silly."

The barkeep chuckled and poured water from a jug. "Aye, you do. You start hugging everyone and telling them all the things you love about them."

Tiern pulled a face and took his water, muttering, "It's no crime to be friendly." He abruptly set down his water. "Oh! Did you hear about Mrs. Mallory?" His face was uncharacteristically serious.

Paxton's ears perked. "Is she in labor?"

"Already?" asked the barkeep.

"Aye, she is, and it's too early. Mum was running to their cottage to help when I left."

Paxton's stomach soured. The barkeep shook his head and looked away. It was never a surprise when pregnancies failed, yet each time felt like a blow to the village. The birthrates in Lochlanach were at an all-time low—only four children under the age of five in their entire village. It was said to be that way through all the lands of Eurona, having declined drastically in the past hundred years, though nobody could say why. Many blamed the Lashed Ones, as if it were some sort of magical curse. Paxton knew the truth, but he could not voice his theory without being seen as a Lashed sympathizer.

At that moment the oak door to the pub flew open with a bang and Mallory's husband ran in, his face ashen and his eyes red. People made a quick path for him as he moved to the bar, peering around frantically as if lost.

"Mr. Sandbar," the barkeep said. "What do you need?"

"I . . . alcohol. To stave off infection." He looked about wildly, shoulders stooping. "There were two. Twins . . . boys. Both gone." The entire bar gasped as a wave of sorrow passed through the room. Mr. Sandbar lifted a shaking hand to his disheveled hair. "Mallory's bleeding too much."

"Okay, man. Stay calm for her." The barkeep filled a cup with clear liquid and thrust it forward.

"I can't pay you right now. I—"

"Don't worry about that. I know you're good for it."

Before Mr. Sandbar could take the cup the door opened again and everyone went still. In the doorway stood Mr. Riverton, an ordinary-looking man in his early thirties. But to the village he wasn't ordinary at all—he was their one and only registered Lashed. He rarely came out except to pick up a bottle of mead from the bar now and again. Paxton felt himself go tense all over as his fellow villagers glared at the man. Mr. Riverton hadn't fared well in the last few years, but Lashed never did. They seemed to age faster than normal people, dying decades sooner than they should. It didn't help that most couldn't find jobs and had to support themselves on the land or starve.

Paxton had caught his own mother sneaking food to Mr. Riverton's lean-to porch early one morning, but he'd never told her he saw.

Mallory's husband began breathing fast and ragged as he took in the sight of the Lashed man.

Mr. Riverton looked about at the staring faces, landing on Mr. Sandbar's. "S-sorry, I was only picking up something to go . . . I'll just . . ." His hand fumbled for the door handle to exit, but Mr. Sandbar flew across the room in a rage, brandishing a knife from his pocket that he shoved to the Lashed man's throat, pressing him against the wall. Everyone crushed forward to see. Paxton and Tiern leaped from their stools, pushing through the crowd.

"What did you do to her?" Mr. Sandbar shouted.

Mr. Riverton kept his hands up, his eyes closed. "I didn't do anything. I swear!"

"I saw you look at her two days ago. You stared at her

stomach! What did you do?"

"I was glad to see how well she was progressing—that's all!"

"Lies!" Mr. Sandbar pressed forward, piercing the Lashed man's throat, causing a trickle of blood to flow. "You're a filthy murderer! Just like your hero, Rocato!"

Mr. Riverton's panicked eyes shot open. "Rocato was a madman! I'm nothing like him—"

"More lies!" Mr. Sandbar's shout came out a sob as tears began to seep from his angry eyes. "You took my boys, just by looking at her!"

"Mr. Sandbar!" Paxton shouted. He grabbed the mourning man by the shoulder. "He can't hurt her with his eyes. You know this. He has to touch with his hands to work magic, and I'm certain he's never gotten that close. Am I right?"

Paxton looked at Mr. Riverton, who whispered hoarsely, "I never touched her."